Laurell K. Hamilton is the bestselling author of the acclaimed Anita
Blake, Vampire Hunter, Novels. She lives near St Louis with her
husband, her daughter, two dogs and an ever-fluctuating number of
on.org.

![London Borough of Hounslow coat of arms] **London Borough of Hounslow**

Hounslow Library Services

Hounslow Library
CentreSpace
Treaty Centre
TW3 1ES
0845 456 2800   P10-L-2106

This item should be returned or renewed by the latest date
shown. If it is not required by another reader, you may
renew it in person or by telephone (twice only). Please
quote your library card number. A charge will be made for
items returned or renewed after the date due.

06/10 AA

| | | | |
|---|---|---|---|
| 22 JUL 2010 | 1 t6 | 0794 | |
| 14 AUG 2010 | | | |
| | | | |
| | | | |
| | | | |
| | | | |
| | | | |
| | | | |
| | | | |

C0000 002 519 7

D1344870

s

s since

Anita

*Booklist*

erizing

*iction*

savvy,

ampire

*Anita Blake, Vampire Hunter, Novels*

# LAURELL K. HAMILTON

# AND

# STRANGE CANDY

An Anita Blake,
Vampire Hunter, Novel

headline

This omnibus edition copyright © 2007 Laurell K. Hamilton

MICAH
First published in the United States in 2006 by
The Berkley Publishing Group, Penguin Group (USA) Inc.
Copyright © 2006 Laurell K. Hamilton

STRANGE CANDY
First published in the United States in 2006 by
The Berkley Publishing Group, Penguin Group (USA) Inc.
Copyright © 2006 Laurell K. Hamilton

For a listing of copyright details for previously published stories see page 384

The right of Laurell K. Hamilton to be identified as the Author of
the Work has been asserted by her in accordance with the
Copyright, Designs and Patents Act 1988.

First published in Great Britain by Orbit, an imprint of Little, Brown Book Group in 2007

First published in this edition in 2010 by
HEADLINE PUBLISHING GROUP

1

Apart from any use permitted under UK copyright law,
this publication may only be reproduced, stored, or transmitted, in any form,
or by any means, with prior permission in writing of the publishers or,
in the case of reprographic production, in accordance with the terms
of licences issued by the Copyright Licensing Agency.

All characters in this publication are fictitious and any resemblance
to real persons, living or dead, is purely coincidental.

Cataloguing in Publication Data is available from the British Library

ISBN 978 0 7553 5544 0

Typeset in Monotype Fournier by Ellipsis Books Limited, Glasgow

Printed and bound in Great Britain by
Clays Ltd St Ives plc

Headline's policy is to use papers that are natural, renewable and
recyclable products and made from wood grown in sustainable forests.
The logging and manufacturing processes are expected to conform to
the environmental regulations of the country of origin.

HEADLINE PUBLISHING GROUP
An Hachette UK Company
338 Euston Road
London NW1 3BH

www.headline.co.uk
www.hachette.co.uk

| HOUNSLOW LIBRARIES | |
| --- | --- |
| HOU | |
| C0000 002 519 770 | |
| Askews | 18-Jun-2010 |
| AF HORROR | £7.99 |
| | |

*My idea of love is not everyone's ideal.*
*Some have broken under the strain of it.*
*This one's for Jon, who sees love*
*not as a burden, but as a gift.*

## ACKNOWLEDGMENTS

To all the people that help keep my life running smoothly: Darla Cook, Sherry Ganey, Lauretta Allen, Mary Schuermann, and Richard Nichols (no relation to the character).

To my writing group: Tom Drennan, Debbie Millitello, Rett MacPherson, Marella Sands, Sharon Shinn and Mark Sumner. *Nill illigitamus carborundum.*

# I

IT WAS HALF past dawn when the phone rang. It shattered the first dream of the night into a thousand pieces so that I couldn't even remember what the dream had been about. I woke gasping and confused, asleep just long enough to feel worse but not rested.

Nathaniel groaned beside me, mumbling, 'What time is it?'

Micah's voice came from the other side of the bed, his voice low and growling, thick with sleep. 'Early.'

I tried to sit up, sandwiched between the two of them where I always slept, but I was trapped. Trapped in the sheets, one arm tangled in Nathaniel's hair. He usually braided it for bed, but last night we'd all gotten in late, even by our standards, and we'd just fallen into bed as soon as we could manage it.

'I'm trapped,' I said, trying to extract my hand from his hair without hurting him or tangling worse. His hair was thick and fell to his ankles; there was lots of it to tangle.

'Let the machine pick up,' Micah said. He'd raised up on his elbows enough to see the clock. 'We've had less than an hour of sleep.' His hair was a mass of tousled curls around his face and shoulders. His face was dim in the darkness of the blackout curtains.

I finally got my hand free of Nathaniel's warm, vanilla-scented hair. I lay on my side, propped on my elbow, waiting for the machine to kick in and let us know whether it was the police for me or the Furry Coalition hotline for Micah. Nathaniel, as a stripper, didn't get emergency calls much. Just as well; I wasn't sure I wanted to know what a stripper emergency call would be. The only ideas I could come up with were either silly or nefarious. Ten rings, and the machine finally kicked on. Micah spoke over the sound of his own voice on the machine's message. 'Who set the machine on the second phone line to ten rings?'

'Me,' Nathaniel said. 'It seemed like a better idea when I did it.'

We'd put in the second phone line because Micah was the main help for a hotline that new wereanimals could call and get advice or a rescue. You know, *I'm at a bar and I'm about to lose control, come get me before I turn furry in public.* It wasn't technically illegal to be a wereanimal, but new ones sometimes lost control and ate someone before they came to their senses. They'd probably be shot to death by the local police before they could be charged with murder. If the police had silver bullets. If not . . . it could get very, very bad.

Micah understood the problems of the furred, because he was the local Nimir-Raj, their leopard king.

There was a moment of breathing on the message, too fast, frantic. The sound made me sit up in bed, letting the sheets pool into my lap. 'Anita, Anita, this is Larry. You there?' He sounded scared.

Nathaniel got the receiver before I did, but he said, 'Hey, Larry, she's here.' He handed me the receiver, his face worried.

Larry Kirkland – fellow federal marshal, animator, and vampire executioner – didn't panic that easily anymore. He'd grown, or aged, since he'd started working with me.

'Larry, what's wrong?'

'Anita, thank God.' His voice held more relief than I ever wanted to hear in anyone's voice. It meant he expected me to do something important for him. Something that would take some awful pressure or problem off their hands.

'What's wrong, Larry?' I asked, and I couldn't keep the worry out of my own voice.

He swallowed hard enough for me to hear it. 'I'm okay, but Tammy isn't.'

I clutched the receiver. His wife was Detective Tammy Reynolds, member of the Regional Preternatural Investigation Squad. My first thought was that she'd been hurt in the line of duty. 'What happened to Tammy?'

Micah leaned in against me. Nathaniel had gone very quiet beside me. We'd all been at their wedding. Hell, I'd been at the altar on Larry's side.

'The baby. Anita, she's in labor.'

It should have made me feel better, but it didn't, not by much. 'She's only five months pregnant, Larry.'

'I know, I know. They're trying to get the labor stopped, but they don't know . . .' He didn't finish the sentence.

Tammy and Larry had been dating for a while when Tammy ended up pregnant. They'd married when she was four months pregnant. Now the baby that had made them both change all their plans might never be born. Or at least not survive. Shit.

'Larry, I'm . . . Jesus, Larry, I'm so sorry. Tell me what I can do to help.' I couldn't think of anything, but whatever he asked, I'd do it. He was my friend, and there was such anguish in his voice. He'd never mastered that empty cop voice.

'I'm due on an eight A.M. flight to raise a witness for the FBI.'

'The federal witness who died before he could testify,' I said.

'Yeah,' Larry said. 'They need the animator that brings him back to be one of us who's also a federal marshal. Me being a federal marshal was one of the reasons the judge agreed to allow the zombie's testimony.'

'I remember,' I said, but I wasn't happy. I wouldn't turn him down or chicken out, not with Tammy in the hospital, but I hated to fly. No, I was afraid to fly. Dammit.

'I know how much you hate to fly,' he said.

That made me smile, that he was trying to make me feel better when his life was about to break apart. 'It's okay, Larry. I'll see if the flight has some empty seats. If not I'll get a later flight, but I'll go.'

'All my files on the case are at Animators, Inc. I'd stopped by the office to get them and load up the briefcase when Tammy called. I think my briefcase is just sitting on the floor in our office. I got all the files in it. The agent in charge is . . .' And he hesitated. 'I can't remember. Oh, hell, Anita, I can't remember.' He was panicking again.

'It's okay, Larry. I'll find it. I'll call the Feds and tell them there's been a change of cast.'

'Bert's going to be pissed,' Larry said. 'Your rates are almost four times what mine are for a zombie raising.'

'We can't change the price in midcontract,' I said.

'No –' and he almost laughed – 'but Bert is going to be pissed that we didn't try.'

I laughed, because he was right. Bert had been our boss, but he'd been reduced to business manager because all the animators at Animators, Inc. had gotten together and staged a palace coup. We'd offered him business manager or nothing. He'd taken it when he realized his income wouldn't be affected.

'I'll get the files from the office. I'll get a flight. I'll be there. You just take care of yourself and Tammy.'

'Thanks, Anita. I don't know what I . . . I've got to go – the doctor's here.' And he was gone.

I handed the phone to Nathaniel, who placed it gently in the cradle.

'How bad is it?' Micah said.

I shrugged. 'I don't know. I don't think Larry knows, not really.' I started to crawl out of the covers and the nest of warmth that their bodies made.

'Where are you going?' Micah asked.

'I've got a plane to schedule and files to find.'

'Are you thinking of going out of town on a plane by yourself?' Micah asked. He was sitting up, knees tucked to his chest, arms encircling them.

I looked back at him from the foot of the bed. 'Yeah.'

'When will you be back?'

'Tomorrow, or the day after.'

'Then you need to book at least two seats on the plane.'

It took me a moment to understand what he meant. I raised the dead and was a legal vampire executioner. That's what the police knew for certain. I was a federal marshal because all the vamp executioners who could pass the firearms test had been grandfathered in so that the executioners could both have more powers and be better regulated. Or that was the idea. But I was also the human servant of Jean-Claude, the master vampire of St Louis. Through ties to Jean-Claude I'd inherited some abilities. One of those abilities was the *ardeur*. It was as if sex were food, and if I didn't eat enough I got sick.

That wasn't so bad, but I could also hurt anyone that I was metaphysically tied to. Not just hurt, but potentially drain them of life. Or the *ardeur* could simply choose someone at random to feed from. Which meant the *ardeur* raised and chose a victim. I didn't always have a lot of choice in who it chose. Ick.

So I fed from my boyfriends and a few friends. You couldn't feed off the same person all the time, because you could accidentally love him to death. Jean-Claude held the *ardeur* and had had to feed it for centuries, but my version was a little different from his, or maybe I just wasn't as good at controlling it yet. I was working on it, but my control wasn't perfect, and it would be a bad thing to lose control on an airplane full of strangers. Or in a van full of federal agents.

'What am I going to do?' I asked. 'I cannot take my boyfriend on a federal case.'

'You aren't going as a federal marshal, not really,' Micah said. 'It's your skills as an animator that they want, so say that I'm your assistant. They won't know any different.'

'Why do you get to go?' Nathaniel asked. He lay back on the pillows, the sheets just barely covering his nakedness.

'Because she fed on you last,' Micah said. He moved enough to touch Nathaniel's shoulder. 'I can feed her more often than you can without passing out or getting sick.'

'Because you're the Nimir-Raj and I'm just a regular wereleopard.' There was a moment of sullenness in his voice, and then he sighed. 'I don't mean to be a problem, but I've never stayed here with both of you gone.'

Micah and I looked at each other and had one of those moments. We'd all been living together for about six months. But he and Nathaniel had both moved in at the same time. I'd never dated either of them alone, not really. I mean I'd gone out with them individually, and sex wasn't always a group activity, but the sleeping arrangements were.

Micah and I both had a certain need for personal time, alone time, but Nathaniel didn't. He didn't much like being alone.

'Do you want to stay at Jean-Claude's place while we're gone?' I asked.

'Will he want me there without you?' Nathaniel asked.

I knew what he meant, but . . . 'Jean-Claude likes you.'

'He won't mind,' Micah said, 'and Asher won't mind at all.'

There was something about the way he said that last that made me look at him. Asher was Jean-Claude's second in command. They'd been friends, enemies, lovers, enemies, and shared a woman that they both loved for a few decades of happiness in centuries of unhappiness.

'Why'd you say it like that?' I asked.

'Asher likes men more than Jean-Claude does,' Micah said.

I frowned at him. 'Are you saying that he made a pass at you or Nathaniel?'

Micah laughed. 'No, in fact, Asher is always very, very careful around us. Considering that we've both been naked in a bed with Asher, Jean-Claude, and you more than once, I'd say that Asher's been a perfect gentleman.'

'So why the comment about Asher liking men more than Jean-Claude?' I asked.

'It's the way Asher watches Nathaniel when you aren't looking.'

I looked at the other man in my bed. He appeared utterly at home half-naked in my sheets. 'Does Asher bother you?'

He shook his head. 'No.'

'Have you noticed him looking at you the way Micah just said?'

'Yes,' Nathaniel said, face still peaceful.

'And that doesn't bother you?'

He smiled. 'I'm a stripper, Anita. I get a lot of people looking at me like that.'

'But you don't sleep naked in a bed with them.'

'I don't sleep naked in a bed with Asher either. He takes blood from me so he can fuck you. It may be sensual, but it's not about sex; it's about blood.'

I frowned, trying to think my way through the tangle that had become my love life. 'But Micah's implying that Asher sees you as more than food.'

'I'm not implying,' Micah said. 'I'm stating that if Asher didn't think you and Jean-Claude would be pissed, he'd have already asked Nathaniel to be more than friends.'

I stared from one to the other of them. 'He would?'

They both nodded in unison, as if they'd practiced.

'And you both knew this?'

They nodded again.

'Why didn't you tell me?'

'Because you, or I, were always there to protect Nathaniel,' Micah said. 'Now we won't be.'

I sighed.

'I'll be okay,' Nathaniel said. 'If I'm really that worried about my virtue, I'll bunk in with Jason.' He smiled even wider.

'What's so funny?' I asked. I sounded angry, because I had totally missed the whole Asher-liking-Nathaniel thing. Sometimes I felt slow, and sometimes I felt totally unprepared for dealing with the men in my life.

'The look on your face, so worried, so surprised.' He bounced up off the bed, leaving the sheet behind him. He crawled toward me, naked and beautiful. I was at the end of the bed and had nowhere to go. But he came at me so fast that I tried to back up and ended up falling off the bed. I sat naked on the floor, trying to decide if I had any dignity left to save.

Nathaniel leaned over the bed and grinned at me. 'If I tell you that was really cute, will you be mad at me?'

'Yes,' I said, but I was fighting not to smile.

He leaned his upper body off the bed, toward me. 'Then I won't say it,' he said. 'I love you, Anita.' He leaned down, but if we were going to kiss I'd have to come to my knees and meet him halfway.

I moved into the kiss he was offering and whispered against his lips, 'I love you, too.'

'Tell me what city we're flying to,' Micah said from the bed, 'and I'll see about flights.'

I broke the kiss enough to mumble, 'Philadelphia.'

Nathaniel leaned in to me again, one hand holding on to the bedpost to keep him in place. The muscles of his arm flexed effortlessly as he used the other hand to smooth hair away from my face. 'I'll miss you.'

'I'll miss you, too,' I said, and I realized that I meant it. But one 'assistant' I might be able to explain to the FBI, not two. Two and they'd begin to wonder who they were and exactly what they were assisting me with. Or that's what I told myself. Staring into the startling lavender of Nathaniel's eyes, I wondered if I cared what the FBI thought of me enough to leave him behind. Almost not. Almost.

# 2

WE PICKED UP Larry's files on the way to the airport. Micah drove so I could find a phone number to call and let everyone in Philly know that there'd been a change of cast. The business card read, *Special Agent Chester Fox*.

He answered on the second ring. 'Fox.' Not even a hello. What was it about police work that made you have bad phone manners?

'This is Federal Marshal Anita Blake. You're expecting Marshal Kirkland this morning?'

'He's not coming,' Fox guessed.

'No, but I am.'

'What happened to Kirkland?'

'His wife is in the hospital.' I wondered how much I owed him on the phone. I decided not much.

'I hope she's going to be all right.' His voice had lost some of its edge. He sounded almost friendly. It made me think better of him.

'She probably will, but they're not sure about the baby.'

Silence for a moment. I'd probably over-shared. That girlness again. Harder to be terse.

'I didn't know. I'm sorry that Marshal Kirkland couldn't make it and even sorrier for the reason. I hope things work out for them.'

'Me, too. So I'm filling in.'

'I know who you are, Marshal Blake.' He was back to not sounding entirely happy. 'Your reputation precedes you.' That last was definitely not happy.

'Are we going to have a problem here, Agent Fox?'

'Special Agent Fox,' he said.

'Fine, are we going to have a problem here, Special Agent Fox?'

'Are you aware that you have the highest kill count of any legal vampire executioner in this country?'

'Yeah, actually, I am aware of that.'

'You're coming here to raise the dead, Marshal, not execute anyone. Is that clear?'

Now I was getting pissed. 'I don't kill people for the hell of it, Special Agent Fox.'

'That's not what I've heard.' His voice was quiet.

'Don't believe all the rumors you hear, Fox.'

'If I believed them all, I wouldn't let you step foot in my city, Blake.'

Micah touched my leg, just to be comforting, while he drove one-handed. We were already on 70, which meant we'd be at the airport in moments.

'You know, Fox, if you're this unhappy with me, we can turn around and not come. Raise your own damn zombie.'

'We?'

'I'm bringing an assistant,' I said, voice angry.

'And exactly what does he assist you with?' And his voice was full of that tone, that tone that men have been using against women for centuries. That tone that manages to imply we're sluts without ever saying so.

'I'm going to be very clear here, Special Agent Fox.' My voice held that calm, cold anger that I used in place of screaming. Micah's hand tightened on my thigh. 'Your attitude makes me think we won't be able to work together. That you've listened to so many rumors that you wouldn't know truth if it bit you on the ass.'

He started to say something, but I cut him off.

'Think very carefully about the next thing you say, Special Agent Fox, because depending on what it is, I may or may not be seeing you in Philly today, or ever.'

'Are you saying if I don't play nice, you won't play at all?' His voice was as cold as mine had been.

'Nice, hell. Fox, I'd just take professional at this point. What has got your panties in a twist about me?'

He sighed over the phone. 'I researched the federal marshals who are also animators. It's a short list.'

'Yeah,' I said, 'it is.'

'Kirkland comes in, does the job, leaves. Every time you get involved in a case, it all seems to go to hell.'

I took a deep breath and counted to twenty. Ten didn't do it. 'Go back through and look at the kind of cases that I get called in on, Fox. No one calls me in unless things have already gone south. It's not cause and effect.'

'You have worked some rough shit. I'll grant that, Marshal Blake.' He sighed again. 'But you've got a reputation for killing first and asking questions later. As for rumors, you're right – they don't paint a very flattering picture of you.'

'You might bear in mind, Fox, that any man you've heard dirty stories about me from didn't get to fuck me.'

'You're sure of that.'

'Absolutely.'

'So you're saying that it's sour grapes, because he didn't get the prize.'

'So we are talking about someone specific. Who?'

He was quiet for a second or two. 'You worked a serial killer case in New Mexico about two years ago. Do you remember it?'

'Anyone who worked that case will remember it, Agent Fox. Special Agent Fox. Some things you don't forget.'

'Did you date anyone while you were out there?'

The question puzzled me. 'You mean in New Mexico?'

'Yes.'

'No, why?'

'There was a cop named Ramirez.'

'I remember Detective Ramirez. He asked me out, I said no, and he didn't trash me.'

'How can you be sure of that?'

'Because he was a good guy, and good guys don't trash you just because you turned them down.'

Micah was idling in front of one of the parking garages on Pear Tree Lane. We'd turned off of 70, and I hadn't really noticed. 'Are we parking?' he asked. What Micah was asking was, Are we going to Philadelphia?

'Did any of the agents on scene ask you out?' His voice was serious and not hostile now.

'Not that I remember.'

'Did you have a problem with anyone while you were there?'

'Lots of people.'

'You admit it.'

'Fox, I am female, I clean up well, have a badge and a gun, raise the dead for a living, and slay vampires. A lot of people have issues with some of the above. Hell, a lieutenant in New Mexico quoted the Bible at me.'

'What quote?'

'"Thou shalt not suffer a witch to live."'

'He did not.' He sounded shocked, something you don't hear much from the FBI.

'Yeah, he did.'

'What did you do?'

'I planted a big kiss right on his mouth.'

He made a startled sound that could have been a laugh. 'You really did?'

'It bothered him a hell of a lot more than hitting him would have, and it didn't get me dragged out in cuffs. But I'm betting the other cops who saw me do it gave him hell.'

Fox was laughing now.

There were cars behind us, honking. 'Anita, are we going?' Micah asked.

'My assistant wants to know if we're going to Philly today. Are we?'

Fox's voice still held that edge of laughter. 'Yeah, come on down.'

I said to Micah, 'We're going to Philly.'

Fox said, 'Marshal Blake, I am going to do what I never do, and if you tell anyone I did, I'll deny it.'

'What are you going to do?'

Micah pressed the big red button on the little stand-up ticket machine. He waited for our parking ticket to pop out. I'd told him to do valet. When you drag your ass in at zero-dark-thirty, valet was worth it.

'I apologize,' Fox said. 'I listened to someone who was there in New Mexico. His version of your run-in with the lieutenant was different from yours.'

'What did he say?'

We were in the dimness of the parking garage now.

'He said you hit on a married man and got pissy when he said no.'

'If you'd ever met Lieutenant Marks, you'd know that wasn't true.'

'Not cute enough?'

I hesitated. 'I guess physically he wasn't that bad, but looks aren't everything. Personality, good manners, sanity – all nice things to have.'

Micah had pulled around the little glass building.

The attendant was coming toward us. We were moments away from needing to get out of the car. 'If we're going to make the flight, I gotta go.'

'Why'd you turn down Detective Ramirez?' he asked.

I wasn't sure it was any of his business, but I answered. 'I was dating someone back home. I didn't think it was fair to any of us to complicate things.'

'Someone said you were all over him at the last crime scene.'

I knew what he was referring to. 'We hugged each other, Agent Fox, because after seeing what was in that house I think we both needed to touch something warm and alive. I let one man hold my hand and all the other men think I'm fucking him. God, there are times when I really hate being the only woman around this kind of shit.'

I was out of the car. Micah was getting our bags from the back.

'Now that's not fair, Marshal. If I'd hugged Ramirez or let him hold my hand, there'd be rumors, too.'

It stopped me for a second, and then I laughed. 'Well, damn, I guess you're right.'

Micah had traded the key for a little ticket stub. He popped the handles on the carry-on bags so they'd roll. I took one of them but let him take my briefcase, since I was still on the phone. The little bus was waiting for us and a few more passengers.

'I look forward to meeting you, Marshal Blake. Time I stopped listening to secondhand stories.'

'Thanks, I guess.'

'See you on the ground.' And he was gone.

I folded the phone shut and was already going up the bus steps before the attendant tried to take my bag. It was the skirt outfit and the heels. I always had more offers to help with luggage when I was dressed like a girl.

Micah came up behind me, mostly ignored, though he was dressed up, too. We'd chosen his most conservative suit, but there's only so much you can do with a black Italian-cut designer suit. It looked like what it was: expensive.

No one would mistake him for a Fed of any kind. We'd pulled his thick, curly hair back in a tight French braid, which almost gave the illusion of short hair. He'd put on a white shirt with the suit and a conservative tie.

We settled into the back row of seats. He'd kept his sunglasses on even in the darkened parking garage, because behind those dark glasses was a pair of leopard eyes. A very bad man had forced him into animal form long enough, and often enough, that he couldn't return completely to human form. His eyes were yellow-green, chartreuse, and not human. They were beautiful in the tan of his skin, but they tended to freak people out, hence the glasses.

I wondered how the FBI would take the eyes. Did I care? No. Things had worked out with Special Agent Fox, or seemed to be working out. But someone who had been in New Mexico was trashing me. Who? Why? Did I care? Yeah, actually, I did.

# 3

I HATE TO fly. I'm phobic of it, and we'll leave it at that. I didn't bleed Micah, but I left little half-moon nail impressions in his hand, though I didn't realize it until after we'd landed and were getting our bags from overhead. Then I asked him, 'Why didn't you tell me I was hurting you?'

'I didn't mind.'

I frowned at him, wishing I could see his eyes, though truthfully they probably wouldn't have told me anything.

Micah had never been a cop, but he had been at the mercy of a crazy person for a few years. He'd learned to keep his thoughts off his face, so that his old leader didn't beat those thoughts off for him. It meant that he had one of the most peaceful, empty faces I'd ever met. A patient, waiting sort of face like saints and angels should have but never seem to.

Micah didn't like pain, not the way Nathaniel did. So he should have said something about the nails digging into his skin. It bugged me that he hadn't.

We got trapped in the aisle of the plane, because everyone else had stood up and grabbed their bags, too. We had time for me to lean in against his back and ask, 'Why didn't you say something?'

He leaned back, smiling down at me. 'Truthfully?'

I nodded.

'It was sort of nice to be the brave one for a change.'

I frowned at him. 'What's that supposed to mean?'

He turned enough so he could lay a kiss, gently, on my lips. 'It means that you are the bravest person I've ever met, and sometimes, just sometimes, that's hard on the men in your life.'

I didn't kiss him back. For the first time ever with him, I did not respond to his touch. I was too busy frowning and trying to decide if I should be insulted.

'What, I'm too brave to be a girl? What kind of macho bull-shit—' He kissed me. Not a little kiss, but as if he'd melt into me through my mouth. His hands slid up over the leather of my jacket. He pressed himself against me, so that every inch of him was pressed against every inch of me. He kissed me long enough and held me close enough that I felt when his body began to be happy to be there.

He drew back, leaving me breathless and gasping. I swallowed hard and managed a breathy, 'No fair.'

'I don't want to fight, Anita.'

'No fair,' I said again.

He laughed, that wonderful, irritating masculine sound that said just how delighted he was with the effect he could have on me. His lips were bright with the red of my lipstick. Which probably meant I looked like I was wearing clown makeup now.

I tried to scowl at him but couldn't quite manage it. It was hard to scowl when I was fighting off a stupid grin. You cannot be angry and grin at the same time. Dammit.

The line was moving. Micah started pushing his carry-on ahead of him. I liked to pull mine behind me, but he liked to push. He had the briefcase, too. He'd pointed out that as the assistant he should be carrying more. I might have argued, but he'd kissed me, and I could-n't think fast enough to argue.

Micah had had about the same effect on me from the first moment I'd met him. It had been lust at almost first sight or maybe first touch. I was still a little embarrassed about that. It wasn't like me to fall for someone so quickly, or so hard. I'd really expected it to burn out or for us to have some huge fight and end it, but six months and counting. Six months and no breakup. It was a record for me. I'd dated Jean-Claude for a couple of years, but it had been off again, on again. Most of my relationships were. Micah was the only one who had ever come into my life and managed to stay.

Part of how he managed it was that every time he touched me I just fell to pieces. Or that's what it felt like. It felt weak, and very girlie, and I didn't like it.

The flight attendant hoped I'd had a pleasant flight. She was smiling just a little too hard. How much lipstick was I wearing and on how much of my face?

The only saving grace was we could hit a bathroom and get cleaned up before we met the FBI. They could pass through security with their badges, but these days even the Feds didn't like to abuse their privileges around airport security.

I was wearing my gun in its shoulder holster but I'd been certified to carry on an airplane. Federal marshal or no, you had to go through special training these days to carry on a plane. Sigh.

I got some looks and a few giggles as I hit the main part of the airport. I sooo needed a mirror.

Micah turned, fighting not to grin. 'I made a mess of your lipstick. Sorry.'

'You're not sorry,' I said.

'No,' he said, 'I'm not.'

'How bad is it?'

He let go of the carry-on handle and used his thumb to wipe across my chin. His thumb came away crimson.

'Jesus, Micah.'

'If you'd been wearing base, I wouldn't have done it.' He lifted his thumb to his mouth and licked it, pushing way more of the thumb into his mouth than he needed to. I watched the movement sort of fascinated. 'I love the taste of your lipstick.'

I shook my head and looked away from him. 'Stop teasing me.'

'Why?'

'Because I can't work if you keep making me moon over you.'

He laughed, that warm masculine sound again.

I took hold of my carry-on and strode past him. 'It's not like you to tease me this much.'

He caught up with me. 'No, it's usually Nathaniel, or Jean-Claude, or Asher. I behave myself unless you're mad at me.'

I thought about that and it made me slow. That and the three-inch heels. 'Are you jealous of them?'

'Not jealous in the way you mean. But, Anita, this is the first time that you and I have ever been on our own. Just you, just me, no one else.'

That stopped me, literally, so that the man behind us cursed and had to go around abruptly. I turned and looked at Micah. 'We've been alone before. We've gone out just the two of us.'

'But never for more than a few hours. We've never been overnight, just us.'

I thought about it because it seemed like in six months we should have managed at least one night with only the two of us. I thought, and thought, until my puzzler was sore, but he was right. We had never been overnight, just us.

'Well, damn,' I said.

He smiled at me, his lips still bright with my lipstick. 'There's a bathroom right over there.'

We pulled the suitcases over against the wall and I left Micah in a small line of men who were also watching bags and purses. Some of them had children in tow.

There was a line in the bathroom, of course, but once I made it clear I wasn't jumping the line but repairing makeup, no one got mad. In fact, a few of them speculated, good-naturedly, on what I'd been doing to get my lipstick smeared that badly.

I did look like I was wearing clown makeup. I got my little bag of makeup, which Micah had made sure I took in with me, out of the briefcase. I'd have probably forgotten it. I had very gentle eye makeup remover that worked on anything, including lipstick. I got the mess cleaned off, then reapplied lip liner and lipstick.

The lipstick was very, very red. It made my skin seem almost translucent in its paleness. My hair gleamed black in the lights, matching the deep, solid brown of my eyes. I'd added a little eye shadow and mascara at home, and called the makeup done. I rarely wore base.

Micah was right, without the base the makeup wasn't ruined, but . . . but. I was still pissed about it. Still wanted to be angry. Wanted to be angry, not was still angry. Why did I want to hold on to the anger? Why did it make me mad that he had the ability to drown my anger with the touch of his body? Why did that bug me so much?

Because it was me. I had a real talent for picking my love life apart until I broke it. I had promised myself, not that long ago, that I'd stop picking at things. That if my life worked, I'd just enjoy it. It sounded so simple, but it wasn't. Why is it that the simplest plans are sometimes the hardest to do?

I took a deep breath and paused at the full-length mirror on the way out. I would have worn black but Bert always thought that that gave the wrong impression. Too funereal, he'd say. My silk shell was the red of the lipstick, but Bert had already complained months ago: no more black and red – too aggressive. So I was in charcoal gray with a thin pattern of black and darker gray through it. The jacket hit me at the waist to meet up with the matching skirt.

The skirt was pleated, forming a nice swing around my upper thighs when I moved. I'd tested it at home, but now I tested it again, just in case. Nope, not a glimpse of the top of my stockings. I didn't own any panty hose anymore. I'd finally been won over to the truth that a comfortable garter belt, hard to find but worth the search, with a pair of nice hose was actually more comfortable than panty hose. You just had to make sure that no one caught a glimpse of them when you moved, unless you were on a date. Men reacted really oddly if they knew you were wearing stockings and a garter belt.

If I'd known that Agent Fox had already been prejudiced against me, I might have worn a pantsuit. Too late now. Why was it a crime for a woman to look good?

Would I get fewer rumors if I dressed down? Maybe. Of course, if I wore jeans and a T-shirt I got complaints that I was too casual and needed to look more professional. Sometimes you just can't win for losing.

I was delaying. Dammit. I did not want to go back out to Micah. Why? Because he was right, this was the first time we'd ever been alone together for this long.

Why did that thought tighten my chest and make my pulse speed like something alive in my throat?

I was scared. Scared of what? Scared of Micah? Sort of. But more scared of myself, I think. Scared that without Nathaniel, or Jean-Claude, or Asher, or someone to balance things, Micah and I wouldn't work. That without everyone interfering, there wouldn't be a relationship. That there would be too much time, too much truth, and it would all fall apart. I didn't want it to fall apart. I didn't want Micah to go away. And the moment you care that much, a man has you. He owns a little piece of your soul, and he can beat you to death with it.

Don't believe me? Then you've never been in love and had it go to hell. Lucky you.

I took a deep calming breath and let it out slow. I used some of the breathing exercises I'd been studying. I was trying to learn to meditate. So far I was good at the breathing part, but I just couldn't still my mind, not without it filling with ugly thoughts, ugly images. Too much violence inside my head. Too much violence in my life. Micah was one of my refuges. His arms, his body, his smile. His quiet acceptance of me, violence and all. Now I was back to being scared. Shit.

I took another deep breath and walked out of the bathroom. I couldn't hide in there all day; the Feds were waiting. Besides, you can't hide from yourself. Can't hide from your own head going ugly. Unfortunately.

Micah smiled when he saw me. That smile that was just for me. That smile that seemed to loosen something tight and hard and bitter inside me. When he smiled at me like that, I could breathe better. So stupid, so stupid, to let anyone mean that much to you.

Something must have shown on my face because the smile dimmed around the edges. He held his hand out to me.

I went to him but didn't take his hand because I knew the moment I did I wouldn't be able to think as clearly.

He let his hand fall. 'What's wrong?' The smile was gone, and it was my fault. But I'd learned to talk about my paranoias. Otherwise they grew.

I stepped closer and dropped my voice as much as the murmurous noise of the airport would allow. 'I'm scared.'

He moved closer to me, lowering his head. 'Of what?'

'Being alone with you.'

He smiled and started to reach for me. I didn't step away. I let his hands touch my arms. He held me and searched my face as if looking for a clue. I don't think he found one. He drew me into a hug and said, 'Honey, if I'd dreamed that you'd be spooked about being alone with me, I wouldn't have said it.'

I clung to him, my cheek pressed into his shoulder. 'It would have still been true.'

'Yes, but if I hadn't pointed it out, you probably wouldn't have thought about it.' He held me close. 'We'd have had our time away and it would never have occurred to you that it was the first time. I'm sorry.'

I wrapped my hands tighter around the solidness of him. 'I'm sorry, Micah. Sorry I'm such a mess.'

He drew me away enough so he could gaze into my face. 'You are not a mess.'

I gave him a look.

He laughed and said, 'Maybe a little messy, but not a mess.' His voice had gone all gentle. I loved his voice like that, loved that I was the only one his voice went soft for. So why couldn't I just enjoy him, us? Hell if I knew.

'The Feds are waiting for us,' I said.

It was his turn to give me a look. Even with the dark glasses, I knew the look.

'I'll be okay,' I said. I gave him a smile that almost worked. 'I promise to try to enjoy the parts of this trip that are enjoyable. I promise to try to not get in my own way, or weird myself out about us being . . . just us.' I shrugged when I said the last.

He touched the side of my face. 'When will you stop panicking about being in love?'

I shrugged again. 'Never, soon, I don't know.'

'I'm not going anywhere, Anita. I like it right here, beside you.'

'Why?' I asked.

'Why what?'

'Why do you love me?'

He looked startled. 'You mean that, don't you?'

I realized I did. I had one of those *aha* moments. I didn't think I was very lovable, so why did he love me? Why did anyone love me?

I touched his lips with my fingers. 'Don't answer now. We don't have time for deep therapy. Business now. We'll work on my neuroses later.'

He started to say something but I shook my head.

'Let's go meet Special Agent Fox.' When I took my hand away from his lips, he just nodded. One of the reasons we worked as a couple was that Micah knew when to let it go, whatever the 'it' of the moment happened to be.

This was one of those times when I truly didn't know why he put up with me. Why anyone put up with me. I didn't want to ruin this. I didn't want to pick at Micah and me until we unraveled. I wanted to leave it alone and enjoy it. I just didn't know how to do that.

We got our bags settled, and off we went. We had FBI to meet and a zombie to raise. Raising the dead was easy; love was hard.

# 4

WE MET THE Feds at the baggage return area, as arranged. How did we know who the FBI agents were in the crowd of people, most of the men dressed in suits?

They looked like agents. I don't know what it is about FBI training but Feds always just seem to look like what they are. All flavors of cops tend to look like cops, but only FBI looks like FBI and not plain cops. Don't know what they do to them down in Quantico, but whatever it is, it sticks.

Special Agent Chester Fox, agent in charge, was very Native American. The short hair, the suit, the perfect fitting-in couldn't hide the fact that he was so very not like the rest of them. I understood now some of his pissiness on the phone. He was the first Native American agent that I'd ever found involved in a case that had nothing to do with Native Americans. If you happened to be Native American, you could usually look forward to a career of dealing with cases that called for your ethnicity but not necessarily your talents. Cases involving Native American issues were also not usually career makers, though they could be career breakers. Another interesting thing about the FBI and its dealing with Native Americans was that if you looked Indian enough, they would assign you even if the case involved a totally different tribe, with a totally different language and customs. You're Indian, right? Aren't all Indians the same?

No. But then the American government – whatever branch – has never really grasped the concept of tribal identity.

The agent with him, I knew. Agent Franklin was tall, slender with skin dark enough to actually be black. His hair was cut shorter and closer to his head than the last time I'd seen him in New Mexico, but his hands were still graceful and nervous. He smoothed those poet's hands down his overcoat. He caught me looking and stopped that nervous dance. He offered me a hand just as if he hadn't called me a slut to his partner.

I took his hand. No hard feelings here. I even smiled though I knew it didn't reach my eyes. Franklin didn't even try to look pleased to see me. He wasn't rude, but he didn't pretend he was happy either.

'Agent Franklin, I'm surprised to see you here.'

He took back his hand. 'Didn't your friend Bradford tell you I'd been reassigned?' He said *friend* like he meant more, and the rest was bitter. Not obvious bitter, but it had that feel to it. Nothing he said was rude enough to start a fight, but it was close.

Special Agent Bradley Bradford was head of the FBI's Special Research section, which dealt with preternatural serial killers, or crimes involving the preternatural.

There'd been a lot of controversy about splitting those crimes out of the Investigative Support unit, the one that usually handled serial killers. At short acquaintance, Franklin had made his feelings clear on the situation. He'd been against it.

Since Bradford was his boss at the time, that had been a problem. Apparently, Franklin had been reassigned, a nonvoluntary reassignment. Not good for a career in the FBI. I was taking fallout for a political squabble that I'd had nothing to do with. Great, just great.

I started to introduce Micah, but Fox beat me to it. 'Callahan, Micah Callahan.' Fox was already offering his hand and smiling, way more broadly than he'd smiled for me. How did an FBI agent know Micah? 'You look good.'

Micah smiled not quite as broadly, like he wasn't as happy to see Agent Fox. What the hell was going on?

'Fox, I . . .' Micah tried again. 'The last time you saw me, I was still in the hospital. I must have looked like shit, so I guess anything's an improvement.' I could hear the uncertainty in his voice, though I doubted anyone else could. You had to know him really well to hear that note in his voice.

'Someone who came that close to dying is allowed to look like shit,' Fox said.

I knew then that this probably had something to do with the attack that had made Micah a wereleopard. All I knew about it for certain was that it had been violent. Once someone uses the words *violent* and *attack*, you don't press for details. I'd figured he'd tell me more when he was ready.

Micah turned to me. His face was having trouble deciding what to do, and I was betting he was glad that the glasses hid his eyes. 'Special Agent Fox was one of the agents who questioned me after my attack.'

I hadn't known that his mauling had gotten federal attention. I couldn't think why it would have but I couldn't ask that here and now because it would be admitting too much ignorance. Also, I wasn't sure how much Micah wanted to share in the airport with people walking around us.

I covered. I can do blank pleasant cop face with the best of them. I did it now. 'What are the odds that he'd be the agent in charge of this case?' I said, smiling, as if I knew exactly what we were talking about. I'd give Micah a chance to explain later, when we didn't have an audience.

'I didn't know that you were an animator,' Fox said, still talking to Micah.

'I'm not.' And Micah left it at that.

Fox waited for him to add more, but Micah smiled and didn't. Fox would have let it go, but Franklin didn't. Some people just can't leave well enough alone.

'Are you a vampire executioner?' Franklin asked.

Micah shook his head.

'You're not a federal marshal.' And Franklin said it like he was positive.

'No. I'm not.'

'Let it go, Franklin,' Fox said.

'She's brought a civilian along on a federal case.'

'We'll talk about this in the car,' Fox said, and the look he gave Franklin stopped the taller man in midsentence.

Fox asked me, 'Do we need to wait for more bags?'

'No,' I said. 'We're going back home tomorrow, right?'

'That's the plan,' he said, but his face was not happy, as if the whole thing with Franklin was still bothering him.

'Then we're ready to go.'

He actually smiled. 'A woman who packs light – that's rare.'

'Sexist,' I said.

He gave me a nod. 'Sorry, you're right. I apologize.'

I smiled and shook my head. 'No sweat.'

He led the way out the doors, and there were two cars waiting. One had two other agents with it, and the other was empty and waiting for us.

Fox spoke over his shoulder at us. 'With the new regulations, even the FBI doesn't get to leave cars parked unattended.'

'Glad to hear the new rules apply to everyone,' I said, more for something to say than because I cared. I wanted to look at Micah and was afraid to. Afraid if I gave him too much attention, he'd fall apart or feel like he had to explain in front of them. Of course, by not looking at him, he might think I was mad about him not sharing details. But . . . oh, hell.

We were pretending he was just my assistant. Holding his hand or giving him a kiss might expose that lie. Or give Franklin even more reason to think I was sleeping around. I hadn't thought about what it might mean to introduce Micah as my assistant. I guess I hadn't really thought it through at all. In my own defense, I hadn't had time to come up with a good explanation for why I needed to bring my boyfriend along. *Assistant* had seemed like a good idea at the time.

I did the only thing I could think of to reassure him and keep the assistant thing going: I patted him on the shoulder. It wasn't much, but he rewarded me with a smile, as if he'd known the mental gymnastics I was going through. Maybe he did.

Fox drove. Franklin rode shotgun. Micah, the briefcase, and I rode in the backseat. The other car followed us as we pulled away.

'We'll drop you at the motel,' Fox began.

Micah interrupted him. 'Actually, I booked us into the Four Seasons.'

'Jesus,' Franklin said.

'The FBI won't pick up the tab for the Four Seasons,' Fox said.

'We wouldn't expect it,' Micah said.

I sat there wondering why Micah had changed hotels, then realized that Fox had said *motel*. Oh. Micah wanted a nicer place for our first night alone together. Logical — so why did it make my stomach tight? What was he expecting of our first night alone?

'Are you really going to let her bring a civilian into our case?'

Fox looked at Franklin. Even from the backseat it didn't look friendly. 'I suggest, strongly, that you let this go, Agent Franklin.'

'Jesus, what is it about her?' Franklin said. 'She blinks those big brown eyes and everyone just looks the other way while she breaks a dozen rules and bends the very law we're sworn to uphold.' He turned around in the seat as far as the seat belt would let him. 'How do you do it?'

Fox said, 'Franklin,' and the word was a warning.

'No, Fox, it's all right. If we don't get this settled, Agent Franklin and I won't be able to work together, will we, Agent Franklin?' My voice wasn't friendly when I said all that. 'You want to know how I do it?'

'Yeah,' Franklin said, 'I do.'

'I know how you think I do it. You think I fuck everyone. But I've never met Fox, so that can't be it. So now you're scrambling, trying to figure it out.'

He scowled at me.

'When you thought it was just sex, just a woman sleeping her way through her career, you were sort of okay with it, but now, now you just don't get it.'

'No,' he said, 'I don't. Fox is the most by-the-book agent I've ever worked with, and he's letting you cart around a civilian. That's not like him.'

'I know the civilian,' Fox said. 'That makes a difference.'

'He was a victim of a violent crime. So what? You knew him how long ago?'

'Nine years,' Fox said in a soft voice, his dark eyes on the traffic, hands careful on the wheel.

'You don't know what kind of person he is now. Nine years is a long time. He must have been a teenager then.'

'He was eighteen,' Fox's careful voice said.

'You don't know him now. He could be a bad guy for all you know.'

Fox glanced in the rearview mirror. 'You a bad guy, Micah?'

'No, sir,' Micah said.

'That's it?' Franklin said, and he looked like he was going to work himself into hysterics or a stroke. 'You ask if he's a bad guy, and he says no, and that's good enough?'

'I saw what he survived; you didn't. He answered my questions when his voice was only a hoarse rasp because the killer had clawed out his throat. I worked for Investigative Support for five years and what was done to him is still one of the worst things I've ever seen.' He had to slam on the brakes to keep from hitting the sudden line of traffic in front of us. We all got very well acquainted with our seat belts, and then he continued. 'He doesn't have to prove anything to you, Franklin, and he's already proven anything he ever needed to prove to me. You are going to lay off him and Marshal Blake.'

'But don't you even want to know why he's here? What she

brought him for? It's an ongoing case. He could be a reporter for all you know.'

Fox let out a long, loud breath. 'I'll let them answer this question once, just once, and then you let it go, Franklin. Let it go before I start having more sympathy with why Bradford had you reassigned.'

That stopped Franklin for a second or two. The traffic started creeping forward. We seemed to be caught in rush-hour traffic. I thought at first that the threat would make him give it up but Franklin was made of sterner stuff than that.

'If he's not an animator or a vampire executioner, then what does he assist you with, Marshal Blake?' He almost managed to keep the sarcasm out of the 'Marshal Blake.'

I was tired of Franklin, and I'm not that good at lying. I'd had less than two hours of sleep and had to fly on a plane. So I told the truth, the absolute truth.

'When you need to have sex three, four times a day, it's just more convenient to bring your lover with you, don't you think, Agent Franklin?' I gave him wide, innocent eyes.

He gave me a sour look. Fox laughed.

'Very funny,' Franklin said, but he settled back in his seat and he left us alone. The truth may not set you free, but used carefully, it can confuse the hell out of your enemies.

# 5

THE HOTEL WAS nice. Very nice. Too nice. There were people in uniforms all over the place. Not police – hotel employees. They sprang forward to get doors. To try to help with luggage. Micah actually let a bellman take our bags. I protested that we could carry them. He'd smiled and said to just enjoy it. I hadn't enjoyed it. I had leaned against the mirrored wall of the elevator and tried not to get angry.

Why was I angry? The hotel had surprised me, badly. I'd come expecting a clean-but-nothing-special room. Now we were going up in a glass and gilt elevator with a guy in white gloves pressing the buttons, explaining how the security on our little key cards worked.

My stomach was a tight knot. I had crossed my arms under my breasts, and even to me, I looked angry in the shiny mirrors.

Micah leaned beside me but didn't try to touch me. 'What's wrong?' he asked, voice mild.

'I didn't expect this kind of . . . place.'

'You're mad because I booked us into a nice hotel with a nice room?'

Put that way, it sounded stupid. 'No, I mean . . .' I closed my eyes and leaned my head back against the glass. 'Yes,' I finally said, voice soft.

'Why?' he asked.

The elevator doors opened and the bellman smiled and stood so he held the doors open but left us plenty of room to move past him. If he'd figured out we were fighting, it didn't show.

Micah waved me in front of him. I pushed away from the elevator wall and went. The hallway was what I'd expected from the rest of the hotel; all dark, expensive wallpaper with curved candlelike lights at just the right intervals, so it was both well-lit and strangely intimate. There were real paintings on the wall, not copies. No big-name artists but real art. I'd never been in a hotel so expensive.

I ended up in front with Micah close behind and the bellman bringing up the rear. I realized halfway down the dark, thick carpeting that I didn't know what room I was looking for. I looked back at the bellman and said, 'Since I don't know where I'm going, should I be in front?'

He smiled, as if I'd said something clever. He walked faster without seeming to hurry. He took the lead and we followed him. Which made more sense to me.

Micah walked beside me. He still had the briefcase over one shoulder. He didn't try to hold my hand; he just put his hand down where I could grab it if I wanted to. We walked like that for a few steps. His hand waiting for mine, my arms crossed.

Why was I mad? Because he'd surprised me with a really nice hotel room. What a bastard. He hadn't done anything wrong, except make me even more nervous about what he expected from me on this trip. That wasn't his bad, it was mine. My issue, not his. He was behaving like a normal civilized human being. I was being churlish and ungrateful. Dammit.

I unwound my arms. They were actually stiff with anger and holding so tight. Shit. I took his hand without looking at him. He wrapped his fingers around mine and just that little bit of touch made my stomach feel better. It would be all right. I was living with him, for God's sake. He was already my lover. This wouldn't change anything. The tight feeling in my chest didn't get better, but it was the best I could do.

The hotel room had a living room. A real living room with a couch, a marble-topped coffee table, a comfy chair with its own reading lamp, and a table in front of the far picture window that was big enough to seat four. And there were enough chairs to do that. All the wood was real and polished to a high shine. The upholstery matched but not exactly, so that it looked like a room that had grown together piece by piece instead of being bought all at once. The bathroom was full of marble-and-gleaming everything. The tub was smaller than the one we had at home, let alone Jean-Claude's tub at his club, the Circus of the Damned, but other than that, it was a pretty good bathroom. Better than any I'd ever seen in a hotel before.

The bellman was gone when I wandered out of the bathroom. Micah was putting his wallet back in that little pocket that good suit jackets have for wallets, if your wallet is long enough and slender enough not to break the line of the suit. The wallet had been a gift from me, at Jean-Claude's suggestion.

'Whose credit card did you put this on?' I asked.

'Mine,' he said.

I shook my head. 'How much are you blowing on this room?'

He shrugged and smiled, reaching for the bag with the clothes in it. 'It's not polite to ask how much a gift cost, Anita.'

I frowned at him as he moved past me to a pair of huge French doors on the far wall. 'I guess I didn't think of this as a gift.'

He pushed one side of the doors inward and moved through it, talking over his shoulder. 'I was hoping you'd like the room.'

I trailed behind him but stopped in the doorway. The bedroom had two dressers, an entertainment center, two bedside tables with full-size lamps, and a king-size bed. The bed was piled high with pillows, and everything was white and gilt and tastefully elegant. And way too bridal suite for me.

Micah had the suiter in the lid of the carry-on unrolled. He unhooked the hangers from the loops and turned to the large closet.

'This place is bigger than my first apartment,' I said. I was still leaning against the folded door, not quite in the room. As if, by keeping one foot in the other room, I'd be safer.

Micah still had his sunglasses on as he unpacked us. He hung up the other suits we'd bought so they wouldn't wrinkle. Then he turned to me. He looked at me, shaking his head. 'You should see the look on your face.'

'What?' I asked, and even to me it sounded grumpy.

'I'm not going to make you do anything you don't want to do, Anita.' He sounded less than pleased. Micah seldom got upset about anything, and almost never with me. I liked that about him.

'I'm sorry this is weirding me out.'

'Do you have any idea why it's bothering you this much?' He took off the glasses and his face looked finished, with his eyes showing. The kitty-cat eyes had bothered me a little at first, but now they were just Micah's eyes. They were an amazing mix of yellow and green. If he wore green, they looked almost perfectly green. If he wore yellow – well, you get the idea.

He smiled, and it was the smile he used only at the house. Only for me and Nathaniel, or maybe just for me. At that moment, it was just for me.

'Now, that is a much better look.'

'What?' I said again, but couldn't keep the smile off my face or out of my voice. Hard to be sullen when you're staring at someone's eyes and thinking how beautiful they are.

He walked toward me, and just that – him walking across the room toward me – sped my pulse, made my breath catch in my throat. I wanted to run to him, to press our bodies together, to lose the clothes and what was left of my inhibitions. But I didn't run to him because I was afraid to. Afraid of how much I wanted him, of how much he meant to me. That scared me, a lot.

He stopped in front of me, not touching me, just looking at me. He was the only man in my life who didn't have to look down to meet my eyes. In my heels, I was actually a little taller.

'God, your face! Hopeful, eager, and afraid, all there on your face.' He laid his hand against my cheek. He was so warm, so warm. I curved my face into his hand and let him hold me.

'So warm,' I whispered.

'I'd have had flowers waiting, but since Jean-Claude sends you roses every week, there didn't seem to be a reason for me to send you flowers.'

I drew back from him, searching his face. It was peaceful, the way it could be when he was hiding his feelings. 'Are you mad about the flowers?'

He shook his head. 'That'd be silly, Anita. I knew I wasn't the top of your dating food chain when I hit town.'

'So why bring up the flowers?' I asked.

He let out a long breath. 'I didn't think it bothered me, but maybe it does. A dozen white roses every week, with a red rose added since you started having sex with Jean-Claude. And now there are two more red roses in the bouquet; one for Asher and one for Richard. So it's like the flowers are from all three of them.'

'Richard wouldn't see it that way,' I said.

'No, but he's still one of your lovers, and you still get something every week that reminds you of him.' He frowned, shook his head. 'This room is my flowers to you, Anita. Why won't you let me give it to you?'

'The flowers are a lot less expensive than this room,' I said.

He frowned harder and it wasn't a look I'd seen much on his face. 'Is it money that makes the difference for you, Anita? I draw a decent salary from chairing the Furry Coalition.'

'You've earned the salary, Micah. You average, what, sixty hours a week?'

'I'm not saying I don't deserve the money, Anita. I'm just asking why you won't take this from me, when you take gifts from Jean-Claude?'

'I didn't like the flowers at first either. You got to town just after I'd given up fighting about it with him.'

He smiled then, but it wasn't a really happy smile. More rueful. 'We're going home tomorrow, Anita. I don't have time for you to get used to the idea.' He sighed. 'I was looking forward to spending some time, just us, and you aren't happy about it. I think my feelings are hurt.'

'I don't want to hurt your feelings, Micah.' I really didn't. I touched his arm, but he stepped out of reach and went back to unpacking. The tight feeling in my stomach returned, but for a different reason.

Micah never fought with me. He never pushed about our relationship. Up until that moment, I'd have thought he was happy. But this didn't feel happy. Was that my fault because I wasn't enjoying the room? Or was this a talk that had been coming, and I just hadn't known it?

'You know,' he said from the bed, 'you are the only woman I know who wouldn't be asking me questions about how I met Agent Fox.'

The change of topic was too fast for me. 'What? I mean, do you want me to ask?'

He stopped with the toiletries kit in his hands, as if he had to think about his answer and moving would have interfered with the thinking. 'Maybe not, but I want you to want to ask. Does that make any sense?'

I swallowed past my rapidly speeding pulse. This felt like the beginnings of a fight. I didn't want to fight, but without Nathaniel or someone else to help me talk my way out of it, I wasn't sure I knew how to derail it. 'I'm not sure I understand, Micah. You don't want me to ask, but you want me to want to ask.' I shook my head. 'I don't understand.'

'How can you, when even I don't understand it?' He looked angry for a moment, and then his face smoothed out to its usual handsome, pleasant neutrality. It had only been in the last month that I'd realized how much pain and confusion he hid behind that face. 'I want you to care enough about me to be curious, Anita.'

'I do care,' I said, but I kept myself pressed against the open

French door. My hands were behind my back, fingers clutching the door like it was an anchor to keep me from getting swept away in the emotional turmoil.

I puzzled for a way out of the fight that was coming and finally had an idea. 'I thought you'd tell me when you were ready. You've never asked me about my scars.' There. That was a valid point.

He smiled, and it was his old smile, the one I'd almost broken him of. The smile was sad, wistful, self-loathing, and had nothing to do with anything pleasant. It was a smile only because his lips went up instead of down.

'I guess I haven't asked about the scars. I figured you'd tell me if you wanted me to know.' He had all the clothes put away, only the toiletries case still waiting on the bed. 'I promised Nathaniel I'd order food when we got here,' he said.

Again the conversational switch was too fast for me. 'Are we changing the topic?'

He nodded. 'You scored a point.' He said, 'You didn't like the room, and it hurt my feelings. Then you didn't seem to care about meeting Fox and hearing more details about my attack. I thought, if she cared, she'd want to know more.'

'So we're not going to fight?'

'You're right, Anita, I've never asked how you got any of your scars. I've never asked you, just like you've never asked me. I can't get angry with you for something I've done myself.'

The tightness in my chest eased a little. 'You'd be amazed by the number of people who would still fight about it.'

He smiled, still not happy, but a little better. 'But I would really like it if you'd try to enjoy the room and not act like I've lured you here for nefarious purposes.'

I took a deep breath and let it out, then nodded. 'It's a beautiful room, Micah.'

He smiled, and this time it reached his kitty-cat eyes. 'Just like that, you'll try.'

I nodded. 'If it means that much to you, yes.'

He took a deep breath, as if his own chest had been a little tight. 'I'll put the toiletries up, then look at the room service menu.'

'Nathaniel was pretty put out that he didn't get to make us a real breakfast,' I said, still clinging to the door.

'I remember when a bagel was breakfast,' Micah said.

'Hell,' I said, 'I remember when coffee was breakfast.'

'I don't,' he said. 'I've been a lycanthrope too long. We have to eat regularly to help control our beasts.'

'One hunger feeds the other,' I said.

'I'll order food. You look at the file.'

'I looked at it on the plane.'

'Do you remember anything you read?'

I thought about it, then shook my head. 'No. I'd hoped it would help take my mind off of the whole being hundreds of feet above the ground situation, but I guess it didn't really help.'

'I noticed just how unhelpful it was.' He raised his hand up. There were still dim marks of my nails. Considering how fast he healed, that meant I'd actually hurt him.

'Jesus, Micah, I'm sorry.'

He shook his head. 'I'm not complaining. Like I said on the plane, it was interesting to see you so . . . so shaken.'

'You being there helped,' I said in a small voice.

'Glad to hear that I spilled blood for a good cause.'

'Did I really bleed you?'

He nodded. 'It's healed, but yeah, you did. You still aren't quite used to being more than human strong.'

'I'll read the file because I need to before tonight, but if you want to tell me about how you became a wereleopard, you can. Honestly, once you told me it was an attack, I treated you like any survivor. You don't question survivors about the trauma; you let them come to you.'

He walked toward the doors, and for a moment I thought he'd

walk by without touching me. Which would have been bad. He gave me a quick kiss and a smile, then moved past me to put the toiletries kit in the bathroom.

I stood there for a moment, leaning against the door. We were doing the exact thing I'd feared we'd do alone together. We were raking emotional shit. I sighed and moved into the living room. The briefcase was waiting beside the couch. I got the file out and took it to the four-seater table by the big picture window. The main road was just outside, but it wound around a sidewalk that wound around a large fountain. It somehow made it seem less of a road and more of a view.

I could hear Micah puttering in the bathroom. He had to be putting out the toothbrushes, deodorant, etc. . . . I would have stopped unpacking once the good clothes were hung up. Both Micah and Nathaniel were neater and more domestically organized than I was. So was Jean-Claude I guess. I wasn't sure about Asher. But I was definitely the slob of the group.

I opened the file and started to read. There wasn't much there. The deceased's name had been Emmett Leroy Rose. He'd had a double degree from the University of Pennsylvania in accounting and prelaw. He'd gotten his law degree at the University of Pittsburgh School of Law. He'd died of a heart attack at the age of fifty-three, while in federal custody waiting to testify at an important trial. He'd been dead less than three months. It listed his race as African American, which wasn't important to me. His religion was listed as Protestant, and that information I did need. There were a few religious persuasions that could interfere with zombie raising. Vaudan – voodoo – was the big one. It could be tricky to raise someone who messed with some of the same magic that I would be using. Wiccan could also make things difficult, and so could some of the more mystically oriented faiths. Straight Christian of whatever flavor wasn't a problem. And psychic abilities could mess with a zombie and make it either hard to raise or hard to control once you raised it. If there was anything less than normal human about Emmett Leroy Rose, it wasn't in the file.

In fact, there were some important things missing from the file. Like what had he been arrested for – what illegal activity did they catch him at that was bad enough to get him in federal custody awaiting his testimony? And exactly what did an important trial mean? Was it mob business? Was it government business? Was it something else I couldn't even think of? Who did Mr Rose have dirt on, and what had the Feds had on him that made him willing to shovel it? Did I need to know any of the above to raise him from the grave? No. But I wasn't used to going into this blind. If they'd sent me this file, I'd have told them no dice without more info. Yeah, they'd have replied it was a need-to-know basis, and I'd have said if they wanted me to raise the zombie, I needed to know. Larry had just taken the crumbs they gave him and not complained.

I wondered how Tammy was doing. Did I call and ask? Later, I decided. I'd try to get some more info out of Fox first. Truthfully, I'd had about as much emotional angst as I could deal with for a little bit. If the news was bad it would wait, and I wouldn't know what to say anyway. I said a quick prayer that Tammy and the baby would be all right. That was the most concrete thing I could do.

I called the number I had for Fox. No emotional problems, just business. What a relief.

'You have everything in the file that you need to raise Rose from the dead, Marshal Blake,' Fox said.

I'd figured he'd say that, but . . . 'Just tell me this. Fox, how hot was Emmett Leroy Rose?'

'What do you mean, "hot"?' he asked, but his tone said he knew.

'How important a witness was he?'

'He died of natural causes, Blake. He wasn't murdered. There wasn't a contract out on him. We just caught him doing something bad. So bad, he didn't want to go to jail over it. So he gave us more important people. Or was going to.'

'Did he have a bad heart?'

'No, if he had, we'd have had a court reporter in to take down his testimony, just in case. We found out later that his father had died of an unexpected heart attack at almost the same age.'

'You see, Fox, if you'd known that, you might have gotten his testimony down sooner, right?'

He was quiet a second, then said, 'Maybe.'

'Is anything you haven't included in this file going to bite me on the ass later? Like a father who died of a sudden heart attack.'

He made a sound that might have been a laugh. 'It's a good point, Marshal Blake, but no, there's nothing we left out that will impact you or your work.'

'Have you ever seen someone raise the dead, Special Agent Fox?'

He was quiet again. Then, 'Yes.' Just that one word.

I waited for him to say more, but he didn't. 'So you're happy with the information I've got.'

'Yes,' he said again, and there was a tone that said this conversation was about over. 'Why do I think that if I'd called you in first instead of Kirkland, you'd have been a much bigger pain in the ass?'

That made me laugh. 'Oh, yes,' I said. 'I'm a much bigger pain in the ass than Larry.'

'How's his wife doing?'

'I'm going to call them when I get off the phone with you.'

'Give him my best.' He hung up.

I sighed and hung up my end. Then I went for my cell phone in the front of the briefcase. I turned it on, and there was a message. I pushed buttons until the phone gave up the message. Larry's voice: 'Anita, it's Larry. They've got the labor stopped. They're going to keep her overnight, just to be safe, but it looks good. Thanks for taking the run to Philadelphia. Thanks for everything.' Then he laughed. 'How do you like the file? Real informative, isn't it?' He laughed again, then hung up.

I sat down on the couch sort of suddenly. I don't think I'd realized how worried I was until it was all right. I didn't even like Tammy much, but Larry was my friend and it would have broken his heart.

Micah was standing in front of me. I looked up. 'Tammy and the baby are going to be fine. He must have called while we were in the air.'

Micah smiled and touched my face. 'You're pale. You were really worried about it, weren't you?'

I nodded.

'Were you hiding it from me or didn't you know either?'

I gave him a smile that was a bit too wry to be happy. 'Stop knowing me so well, dammit.'

'Better than you know yourself, sometimes,' he said softly. And that was a little too close to the truth.

# 6

ROOM SERVICE CAME with a knock and a polite voice. Micah got to the door before I did, but he didn't just open it. Some people in my life I've had to teach caution to, but Micah had come with it as part of the standard boyfriend package.

He checked the peephole, then looked at me. 'Room service.' But he didn't open the door. I watched him take a very deep breath, scenting the air. 'Smells like room service.'

My hand eased back from the gun under my arm. I hadn't even realized my hand was on it until that moment. His scenting at the door had made me think, just for a second, that something was wrong, not that he was simply scenting the air because it smelled good.

He put his sunglasses on before he opened the door. I made sure my jacket was covering the gun. Didn't want to weird anyone out, and definitely didn't want to give the staff a reason to talk. Hiding how far outside normal we were was standard practice. People tend to get nervous around guns and shapeshifters. Go figure.

The guy smiled and asked where we'd like the tray set up. We let him put a cloth on the table by the window.

It seemed to take a long time for him to get everything ready. He placed water glasses, real napkins, even a rose in a vase in the center of the table. I'd never seen anything this elaborate from room service.

Finally, he was done. Micah signed for the food, and the guy left with a *Have a nice day* that actually sounded sincere.

Micah shut the door behind him, putting all the locks in place. I approved. Locks don't help you if you don't use them.

I was trying to decide whether to frown. 'I like the caution – you know I do.'

'But,' he said, setting the sunglasses on the coffee table.

'But I thought I should compliment you before I complain about something else.'

His smile slipped a little. 'What now?'

'There's a salad here with grilled chicken on it and a butterflied chicken breast grilled with veggies. The salad better not be mine.'

He grinned then, and it was that sudden grin that gave me a glimpse of what he might have looked like at fifteen.

'You get the chicken breast.'

I frowned. 'I would have preferred steak.'

He nodded. 'Yes, but if you eat that heavy then sometimes the food doesn't sit well if the sex is too, um, vigorous.'

I tried not to smile and failed. 'And is the sex going to be, um, vigorous?'

'I hope so,' he said.

'And you got the salad, because . . .'

'I'll be doing most of the work,' he said.

'Now, that's just not true,' I said.

He wrapped his arms around me, and his being the same height made the eye contact very serious, very intimate.

'Who does the most work depends on who is doing what.' His voice was low and deep. His face leaned closer as he said, 'I know exactly what I want to do to you and with you, and it means that I will be doing' – and his mouth was just above mine – 'most of the work.'

I thought he'd kiss me, but he didn't. He drew back and left me breathless and a little shaky. When I could talk without sounding as wobbly as I felt, I asked, 'How do you do that?'

'Do what?' he asked as he sat down on his side of the table, spreading his napkin in his lap.

I gave him a look.

He laughed. 'I am your Nimir-Raj, Anita. You are my Nimir-Ra, my leopard queen. The moment we met, my beast and that part of you that calls and is called to the wereleopards were drawn to each other. You know that.'

I blushed, because the memory of just how much we'd been drawn together from the moment we'd met always made me a little embarrassed. All right, more than a little.

Micah was the first man I'd ever had sex with within hours of meeting him. The only thing that had kept it from being a one-night stand was the fact that he stuck around, but I hadn't known he would when it first happened. Micah had been the first person I fed the *ardeur* off of, the first warm body that I slaked that awful thirst on. Was that the bond? Was that the foundation of it?

'You're frowning,' he said.

'Thinking too hard,' I said.

'And not about anything pleasant, from the look on your face.'

I shrugged, which made the jacket rub on the gun. I took the jacket off and draped it across the back of the chair. Now the shoulder holster was bare and aggressive against the crimson shirt. My arms were exposed, which showed off most of my scars.

'You're angry,' he said. 'Why?'

I actually hung my head, because he was right. 'Don't ask, okay? Just let my grumpy mood go, and I'll try to let it go, too.'

He looked at me for a moment, then gave a small nod. But his face was back to being careful. His neutral, pleasant *I'm managing her moods* face. I hated that face because it meant I was being difficult, but I didn't know how to stop being difficult. I was tripping over issues I'd thought I'd worked out months ago. What the hell was the matter with me?

We ate in silence, but it wasn't companionable silence. It was strained, at least in my own head.

'Okay,' Micah said, and his voice made me jump.

'What?' I asked, and my voice sounded strident, somewhere between breathy and a yell.

'I have no idea why you are this' — he made a waffling motion with his hand — 'but we'll play it your way. How did you get the scars on your left arm?'

I looked down at my arm as if it had suddenly appeared there. I stared at the mound of scar tissue at the inside of the elbow, the cross-shaped burn scar just below it, the knife cut, and the newer bite marks between the two. Those bites were still sort of pink, not white and shiny like the rest. Okay, the burn wasn't white, darker actually, but . . . 'Which one?' I asked, looking up at him.

He smiled then. 'The cross-shaped burn scar.'

I shrugged. 'I got captured by some Renfields — humans with a few bites — who belonged to a master vampire. The Renfields chained me up as a sort of snack for when their master rose for the night, but while we were waiting they decided to have some fun. The fun was heating up a cross-shaped branding iron and marking me.'

'You tell the story like it doesn't mean anything to you.'

I shrugged again. 'It doesn't. Not really. I mean it was scary and horrible, and hurt like hell. I try not to think about it. If I dwell too much on the things that could go wrong or have gone wrong in the past, I have trouble doing my job.'

He looked at me, and he was angry. I didn't know why. 'How would you feel if I told my story the same way?'

'Tell your story any way you want, or don't tell it, Micah. I'm not the one forcing us to play true confessions.'

'Fine,' he said. 'I was eighteen, almost nineteen. It was the fall I went away to college. My cousin Richie had just gotten back from basic. We both came home so we could go hunting with our dads one last time. You know, one last boys' weekend out.' His voice held anger, and I finally realized that he wasn't angry at me.

'At the last minute, Dad couldn't come with us. Some hunters had gone missing, and Dad thought one of his patrols had found them.'

'Your dad was a cop?'

He nodded. 'County sheriff. The body they found turned out to be a homeless guy who got lost in the woods and died of exposure. Some animals got to him, but they hadn't killed him.'

His face had gone distant with remembering. I'd had a lot of people tell me awful truths, and he told it like most of them did, no hysterics. No anything, really. No effect, as the therapists and the profilers would say. He looked empty as he told his story. Not matter-of-fact the way I told my story, but empty, as if part of him wasn't really there. The only thing that showed the strain was that thread of anger in his voice.

'We were all armed, and Uncle Steve and Dad had taught Richie and me how to use a gun. I could shoot before I could ride a bike.' He set his silverware down on the table, and his fingers found the salt shaker. It was real glass, smooth and elegant for a salt shaker. He turned it around and around in his fingers, giving it all his eye contact.

'We knew it might be the last time the four of us got to hunt together, you know? College for me, the army for Richie – it was all changing. Dad was really upset that he didn't get to come, and so was I. Uncle Steve offered to wait, but Dad told him to go ahead. We wouldn't all get our deer in one day. He was going to drive up and join us the next day.'

He paused again, this time for so long that I thought he'd stopped for good. I gave him the silence to decide. Stop, or go; tell or not.

His voice when it came was emptier; no anger now, but the soft beginnings of something worse. 'We'd gotten a doe. We always got two buck tags and two doe tags, so between the four of us, we could shoot what we found.' He frowned, then looked at me. 'You don't know what a deer tag is, do you?'

'The deer tag tells you what you can shoot, buck or doe. You don't get a choice some years, because some years there are more does than bucks, so they give out more doe tags. Though usually it's buck that's more plentiful.'

He looked surprised. 'You've been deer hunting.'

I nodded. 'My dad used to take me.'

He smiled. 'Beth, my sister, thought it was barbaric. We were killing Bambi. My brother, Jeremiah – Jerry – didn't like killing things. Dad didn't hold it against him, but it meant that Dad and I were closer than him and Jerry, you know?'

I nodded. 'I know.' And just like that he'd told me more about his family than I'd ever known. I hadn't even known he'd had siblings.

He kept his eyes on my face now. He stared right at me as he said the next part, stared so hard that even under normal circumstances it would have been difficult to hold his gaze. Now, like this, it was like lifting some great weight just to meet the demand in his eyes. I did it, but it was hard work.

'We had a doe. We'd field dressed it and put it on a pole. Richie and I were carrying it. Uncle Steve was a little ahead of us. He was carrying Richie's gun and his. I had my rifle on a strap across my back. Dad always told me that if it was my gun, I needed to hold on to it. I had to control it at all times. Funny. I don't think Dad really liked guns.'

His face started to break, not badly, but around the edges. All the emotions that he was trying not to have chased around the borders of his face. If you didn't know what you were looking at, you might not have understood it, but I'd had too many people tell me too many awful things not to see it.

'It was a beautiful day. The sun was warm, the sky was blue, the aspens were like gold. The wind was gusty that day. It kept blowing the leaves around in showers of gold. It was like standing inside a snow globe except instead of snow, it was golden, yellow leaves. God, it was beautiful. And that was when it came for us. It moved so fast, just a dark blur. It hit Uncle Steve and he just went down, never got back up.' His eyes were a little wide, his pulse jumping enough in his throat that I could see it. But other than that his face was neutral. Control – such tight control.

'Richie and I dropped the deer, but Richie didn't have a gun. I got my rifle almost to my shoulder when it hit Richie. He went down screaming, but he drew his knife. He tried to fight back. I saw the knife sparkling in the sunlight.'

He stopped again, and this time the pause was so long that I said, 'You can stop, if you want to.'

'Is it too horrible for you?'

I frowned and shook my head. 'No, if you want to tell it, I'll listen.'

'I made a big deal out of this, not you. My own fault.' He said that last word with more feeling than it needed. *Fault*. I could taste the survivor's guilt on the air.

I wanted to go around the table and touch him but was afraid to. I wasn't sure he wanted to be touched while he told the story. Later, but not now.

'You know how time can freeze in the middle of a fight?'

I nodded, wasn't sure he saw it, and said, 'Yes.'

'I remember the face, its face, when it looked up at me from Richie's body. You've seen us in half-man form. The face is leopard, but not. Not human, but not animal either. I remember thinking, *I should know what this is*. But all I could think was *Monster. It's a monster.*'

He licked his lips and drew a breath that shook when he let it out. 'I had the rifle to my shoulder. I fired. I hit it. I hit it two or three times before it got me. It ripped me with its claws, and it wasn't a sharp pain. It was like being hit with a baseball bat – hard, thick. You know you're hurt, but it doesn't feel like you'd imagine claws would feel – do you know what I mean?'

I nodded. 'Yeah, actually, I know exactly what you mean.'

He looked at me, then down at my arm. 'You do know what I mean, exactly what I mean, don't you?'

'More than most,' I said, voice soft and as matter-of-fact as I could make it. He had so much emotion that I gave him none back. It was the best I could do.

He smiled at me. Again it was that sad, wistful, self-deprecating smile. 'The rifle was gone. I don't remember losing it, but my arms wouldn't work anymore. I lay there on the ground, with that thing above me, and I wasn't afraid anymore. Nothing hurt, nothing scared me. It was almost peaceful. After that it's only snatches. I remember voices, being on a stretcher. I remember being put in a helicopter. I woke up in the hospital with Agent Fox on one side and my dad on the other.'

I realized then what had sparked the trip down memory lane. 'Seeing Fox today brought it back.' Some days I'm just slow.

He nodded. 'It scared me to see him, Anita. I know that sounds stupid, but it did.'

'It doesn't sound stupid, and it didn't show. I mean, even I didn't pick up on it.'

'I wasn't afraid in the front of my head, Anita. I was afraid in the back of my head. And then you didn't like the room, and—'

I went to him then. I wrapped my arms around him, pressed his face against my chest. He hugged me back, tight, so tight, as if he were holding on to the last solid thing in the universe.

'I love the room. I love you. I'm sorry I was shitty.'

He spoke with his face still buried against my body, so his words were muffled. 'I didn't survive the attack, Anita. The wereleopard that attacked us ate as much of my uncle and Richie as it could hold, and left. Some hunters found us, and they were both doctors. I was dead, Anita. No heartbeat, no pulse. The doctors got my heart started again, got me breathing again. They patched me up as best they could, and they got me to a clearing so a chopper could get me to a hospital. No one expected me to live.'

I stroked his hair, still slick and tight in the braid. 'But you did,' I whispered.

He nodded, rubbing his head against the silk shirt and my breasts underneath. Not sexual, but comforting.

'The wereleopard was a serial killer. He hit only hunters, and only after they'd killed an animal. The FBI put out a warning to hunters after we were attacked. Fox said they put it together as a serial case only a few hours before we were attacked. The first attack had been on a reservation where he was assigned.'

'He solved it,' I said.

'He caught the . . . monster. He was there when they killed it.'

He kept saying *it* and *monster*. You didn't hear that often from shapeshifters – not about other shifters. 'I died, was brought back, survived, and healed. Healed so fast. Incredibly fast. Then a month later I was the monster.' His voice was so sad when he said it, so unutterably sad.

'You're not a monster,' I said.

He drew away enough to look up at me. 'But a lot of us are, Anita. I joined Merle's pard, and he was a good leader, but Chimera came and took us over, and Chimera was crazy and cruel.'

Chimera had been the leader I'd killed to save Micah and his people, and a lot of other people. Chimera had been the only panwere that I'd ever heard of, someone who could turn into a variety of animals. Before I'd seen him I'd have said it was impossible, but I'd seen him, and had to destroy him. He'd been real and powerful, and a very creative sexual sadist.

I held his face in my hands. 'You are a good person, Micah. You are not a monster.'

'I used you when we first met, Anita. I saw you as a way to save my leopards. To rescue us all.'

'I know,' I said. 'We talked about it. You asked me what I would have done to save Nathaniel and all the leopards from Chimera. I agreed that I would have done anything, or at least what you did to get me involved. I couldn't fault you on it.'

'From the moment you touched me, the plan changed. You changed it. You changed everything. You never looked at me like I was a monster. You were never afraid of me, not in any way.'

'You make it sound like someone else was afraid of you.'

He sighed again. 'I had a high school sweetheart. We weren't exactly engaged, but we had an understanding that once we got our college degrees, we'd marry.'

'Sounds good,' I said.

He shook his head. 'We waited for sex, a year of waiting. We both wanted to be out of high school first, be eighteen. Her older sister had gotten pregnant in high school, and it had wrecked her life, so Becky was careful. I was okay with that. I planned to spend the rest of my life with her, so what was a year or more?'

He spilled me down into his lap so I was sitting across his legs, very ladylike, thank you. 'What happened?' I asked, because he seemed to want me to.

'What made her finally break up completely with me was me being a monster. She couldn't love an animal.'

I couldn't keep the shock off my face. 'Jesus, Micah, that's—'

He nodded. 'It was rough, but me being a shapeshifter was the last straw, not the first one.'

I frowned a little. 'What was the first straw?'

He looked down, and I realized he was embarrassed.

'What?' I asked.

'I was too big.'

I opened my mouth and closed it. 'You mean you were too well endowed for her?'

He nodded.

I looked at him and tried to decide what to say. Nothing good came to mind. 'She didn't like having sex with you?'

'No.'

'But – but you're, like, amazing in bed. You're—'

'But you weren't a virgin, and I wasn't eighteen and a virgin, too.'

'Oh,' I said, and thought about it. Micah was very well endowed. Not just long but wide, which I'd discovered could be a harder problem to deal with than length. There were positions you could do or modify for length. Width you just had to adjust to. I thought about having all that shoved inside for the first time, maybe without enough foreplay. 'I guess I can see the problem.'

'I hurt her. I didn't mean to, but I did. I got better at it. More foreplay, more – just better.'

'There is a learning curve,' I said.

He rested his forehead on my shoulder. 'But Becky never really enjoyed me inside her. We had sex, but I always had to be so careful of her or she said it hurt.'

'You know women have different sizes of vaginas, just like there are different sizes of penises. Maybe she was small inside, and you are *not* small.'

He looked up at me, his cheek resting on my bare arm. 'You think so?'

'I do.'

He smiled. 'You don't have a problem with me, any of me.'

I smiled back. 'No, and she was just one person. One negative doesn't make it a problem.'

'It wasn't just one vote, Anita.'

I raised my eyebrows. 'What do you mean?'

'I've had dates in college where everything was fine until they saw me, all of me. Then they picked up their clothes and said no way.'

I gave him a look. 'You're serious.'

He nodded.

Another man, I might have accused of bragging, but Micah wasn't bragging. I had a thought. It was almost insightful. 'Becky said you hurt her because you were so big, and then you had girls in college who wouldn't even try it. That must have really messed with you.'

'It was either a really big plus or a really big minus with women. But most of them, even the ones who said yes, didn't want a standard diet. I was like a novelty.' His voice held unhappiness the way it had held anger earlier. 'Becky made me feel like a monster for wanting to hurt her, for wanting to be inside her, for wanting sex so badly I'd hurt her. Most of the women I dated made me feel the same way, or like I should have had a dial on my hip and a battery case, like I was some sort of toy they'd bought in a sex store. Just wind me up.'

I looked at him again.

'Trust me, Anita, there are just as many bastards out there who are girls as bastards who are guys. Except when a girl treats you like a sex object, it's supposed to be all right because you're a guy and you only want sex anyway, right?'

'The old double standard,' I said.

He nodded and patted me. 'Until you.'

I thought about it for a second. 'Wait a minute. How did you know I wouldn't have a problem with your, um, size?'

'You know how wereanimals are always walking around naked, unless you make us put on clothes?'

I smiled. 'Not all of you guys are comfortable nudists, but most, yeah.'

'First, I'd seen Richard nude, and I knew he had been your lover. He isn't small either.' I fought not to blush again. 'Second, you'd seen me nude and you hadn't reacted badly.'

'So you saw an ex-lover and he was well endowed. And I hadn't told you to be careful where you point that. It might go off.'

He smiled. 'Something like that.'

'How did you know that I hadn't broken up with Richard because he was too much man for me to handle?'

'I asked.'

I must have looked as surprised as I felt.

He laughed. 'I didn't ask Richard. I asked around and found out he thought you were too bloodthirsty, and he didn't like the police work. None of that bothered me.'

'So you took a chance,' I said.

He nodded. 'And from the moment we made love, I knew I would do anything, anything, to be in your life.'

'You said that. It was one of the first things you ever said to me after we'd had sex. That you were my Nimir-Raj, and I was your Nimir-Ra, and you would do anything, be anything I needed, to be in my life.'

'I meant it.'

'I know you did.' I traced my finger down the side of his face. 'Admittedly, it took me a while to realize that you really did mean it. That you would do anything, be anything I needed. What if I'd asked awful things of you, Micah? What would you have done?'

'You wouldn't ask awful things of anyone.'

'But you barely knew me then.'

'I just had a feeling.'

I searched his expression, trying to see where that certainty had come from. His face was back to being peaceful but not empty. This was his peaceful *I'm happy* face.

'I would never have been able to trust a stranger like that.'

'We were never strangers, Anita. From the moment we touched, we weren't strangers. Our bodies knew each other.'

I gave him the hard look, but he just laughed. 'Tell me I'm wrong. Tell me that isn't how you felt, too.'

I opened my mouth, closed it, and finally said, 'So what? Not love at first sight, but love at first fuck?'

His face went all serious on me. 'Don't make fun of it, Anita.'

I had to look down then, sitting chastely on his thighs, and I had to look away. 'I did feel it, that draw to your body, from the first time we touched. It's just . . . I was raised believing that sex was bad, dirty. The fact that you got through all my defenses so quickly still sort of embarrasses me.'

He put his arms around me and scooted me higher up his lap, so I could feel that he was happy to have me there. Just feeling how hard he was, pressed against my thigh, made me catch my breath.

'Never be embarrassed about how your body reacts, Anita. It's a gift.' He slid his arm under my legs and stood up with me in his arms.

'I can walk,' I said.

'I want to carry you.'

I opened my mouth to tell him to put me down but didn't. 'Where are you carrying me to?'

'To the bed,' he said.

I tried not to smile, but it was a losing battle.

'Why?' Though I was pretty sure I knew why.

'So we can have sex, lots and lots of sex, and when we've had as much sex as we can stand, you can drop your shields and feed the *ardeur* now, early, so it doesn't try to rise while we're surrounded by FBI agents.' He started carrying me toward the bed again. He carried me easily, smoothly, even though there probably wasn't twenty pounds' difference in our weight.

I said the only thing I could think of. 'You do know how to sweet-talk a girl.'

He grinned at me. 'Well, I could have said that I plan on fucking you until you're unconscious, but then you'd just think I was bragging.'

'I've never passed out during sex,' I said.

'There's got to be a first time,' he said. And we were at the foot of the bed now.

'Talk is cheap,' I said.

He threw me on the bed. Threw me suddenly and far enough that I did that squeaky girlish scream when I bounced on the bed. My pulse was in my throat suddenly. He had his tie undone and was working on the buttons of his shirt. 'Bet I'll be naked first.'

'No fair,' I said. 'I've got the shoulder holster to get off.'

He was pushing the silk suspenders off his shoulders and pulling his shirt out of his pants. 'Then you better hurry.'

I hurried.

# 7

MICAH LAY BACK on the bed while I was still struggling out of my clothes. Seeing him naked against the pillows and the gold and white of the bedspread made me stop and stare. And, no, I didn't only stare at his groin. How could I stare at just one thing when all of him was lying there?

He didn't look that muscular clothed. You had to see him at least mostly naked to appreciate the fine play of muscle in his arms, chest, stomach, legs. Clothed, he looked delicate, especially for a man. Nude, he looked strong and somehow more . . . more something that clothes stole from him. His tan was dark against the cream of the bedspread, making his body stand out like it had been drawn there. His shoulders were wide, his waist and hips narrow. He was built like a swimmer, but it was his natural shape, not from any particular sport that he did.

I missed the spill of his hair around his face, but he'd left it in its braid, and I didn't tell him to take it down. Sometimes it was good not to have all that hair flying loose. It could get in the way.

I let my gaze settle last on the swell of him, so hard, so long. Long enough that he could touch his own belly button without using his hands. Thick enough that I couldn't get finger and thumb completely around him when he was at his thickest. I came back up to his face and met those eyes, the delicate curve of his face.

'You are so beautiful,' I said.

He smiled. 'Shouldn't that be my line?'

I pulled at the garter belt. 'You want me to leave this and the hose on, or take them off?'

'Can you get the underwear off without the garter coming off?' he asked.

I put my thumbs under the edge of the lace panties and slipped them off. Jean-Claude had broken me of wearing the panties on the inside. He said that was only for looks. For real, you put the panties on last, so they can come off first. I didn't say that out loud, because I wasn't sure Micah really wanted to be reminded right now that I was having sex with other men. He shared well and didn't seem to mind, but talking about another lover in the midst of sex just seemed bad form.

I stood there for a moment in nothing but the garter belt, the hose, and the heels. I stood there until his eyes filled with that darkness that men's eyes fill with in the moment they realize you won't say no. There is something of possession in that look, something that says *mine*. I can't explain it, but I've seen enough to know that all men do it, at least part of the time. Do women have a look that's similar? Maybe. Did I? Without a mirror I might never know.

He crawled across the bed to me and said, 'Come here.' His hand wrapped around my wrist, pulling me against the bed, but I had to climb up on it, had to let him help pull me onto it.

He led me until we crawled to the head of the bed. He pulled me onto all those pillows. So many pillows, so high, that I was propped up against them. I was almost sitting up. Almost.

I expected Micah to lie down with me, but he didn't.

He knelt and said, 'Bend your knees.'

I wasn't exactly sure what he had in mind, but I bent my knees firmly together, curling my legs, heels and all, against the front of my body. It felt very posed, but the smile on his face made it worth it. The smile said that I'd done exactly what he wanted me to do. He laid his hands on the top of the hose and ran them down that silky length until his hands curled around my ankles. He spread my legs with his hands on my ankles, spread me wide. He put my feet in the high heels to either side, knees bent. Apparently my legs weren't quite wide enough, because he spread them just a little wider.

He leaned back from me on his knees and just looked down at me. 'Wow,' he said, and his voice came out in a hoarse growl. An innocent word, said in a tone that made it anything but innocent.

'God, what a view.' And his voice was still that low, growling bass, as if it should have hurt to talk. He trailed his hands down my thighs until he ran out of hose and traced fingertips along my bare thighs. He slid his hands under my buttocks, cupping my ass. He lay down with his hands still cupped under my body. He propped himself up on his elbows and stared up the length of my body at me.

My voice was breathy. 'That's why you kept the braid in.'

'Yes,' he whispered, and began to lower his face down toward me, the way you'd move in slowly for a kiss. He hesitated. 'The angle's not quite right.' He lifted me up, as if he could hold me forever in his hands like an offering to himself. My feet came off the bed with his lifting. I was left with the choice of either holding my own legs up with my hands or putting my feet around Micah. If I hadn't been wearing high heels I wouldn't have worried about it, but the heels were not meant to stab into someone's back. Nathaniel might have enjoyed it, but Micah wouldn't.

He licked between my legs and the sensation stole my thoughts, my words, and my good intentions. I put my legs around his body. The shoes ended up resting on his lower back, the toes on the swell of his buttocks, the tip of the heels pressed into his back.

I waited for him to protest, but he didn't. He slid his face between my thighs, plunged his mouth into me, against me, over me. He kissed between my legs as if it were my mouth. Exploring with lips, tongue, and, lightly, teeth. He kissed me as if I could kiss him back, and the sensation of it made me move my hips against him, so that it became like a kiss. A kiss of his mouth between my legs, my hips rolling up to his mouth, my thighs pressing against his face, my heels digging into his back.

I felt a spasm pass up his body, shivering up his back, his shoulders, to his hands, making his fingers tighten around my ass.

He raised up enough to talk, his mouth shining. His voice was breathy, strained. 'I can't decide if the heels feel amazing, or just hurt. Can we lose them?'

I scraped one shoe off on the bedspread and used that foot to push the other shoe off. I put my feet back on his back, feeling the warmth and swell of him through the hose. 'All you had to do was ask.' My voice was breathless and lower than normal. It's called a bedroom voice for a reason.

He smiled at me and lowered his face slowly downward. He kept his gaze on my face as he slid between my thighs. Those chartreuse eyes rolled up to me as he licked between my legs, so that it gave the illusion that his face ended with the green-gold of his eyes.

'God, Micah, I love your eyes like that.'

He growled, and the sound of it vibrated across my skin. It made me cry out, head back, eyes closed. The growl turned to a purr as he drew the most intimate part of me deeper into his mouth. That purring growl sang across my skin, vibrating, building. He drew as much of me into his mouth as he could and sucked as hard and fast as he could.

That heavy, delicious warmth began to build between my legs. Micah drew that warmth, that weight of pleasure with his mouth, drawing it out and out, more and more, building it with every movement of his lips, every caress of his tongue, until with one last flick of his tongue he brought me. That weight burst over me in a rush of warm pleasure that pulsed through me, over me, again and again as if as long as Micah sucked, the pleasure would never stop. I was left gasping, eyes fluttered shut, boneless, helpless. I was wrecked, ruined, drowned in the pleasure of it. I felt the bed move, felt Micah over me. I tried to open my eyes, but the best I could do was flutter them enough to see light and shadows.

'Anita,' he said, voice soft, 'are you all right?'

I tried to say yes, but no sound came out. I could think it, but that was as far as I got.

'Anita, say something. Blink if you can hear me.'

I managed to blink, but even when my eyes fluttered open, I still couldn't focus. The world was blurred colors. I put up a thumb to let him know I was okay, because talking was still too hard.

He leaned close enough that I could see his face clearly. 'Now I'm going to fuck you,' he said.

I managed to whisper, 'Yes, please, yes.'

# 8

HE PUT HIS hands under my thighs and pulled me off the mound of pillows. Pulled me so that my lower body was flat to the bed, but my upper body was still a little propped up. He put a finger inside of me, just a finger, but the sensation of it writhed me across the bed, made me cry out.

'So wet, but so tight. You're always so tight after I do you by mouth.'

He was kneeling between my legs, his body so hard, so ripe, so ready. I said the only thing I was thinking.

'Fuck me, Micah, fuck me.'

'You're tight, Anita, really tight.'

I raised up on my elbows. 'But wet. I'm so wet. You've made me so wet.'

He licked his lips and swallowed. I could see his pulse jumping in his throat. 'I don't want to hurt you.'

'If it hurts, I'll say so.'

He looked down at me, and his face didn't look lustful now; it looked nervous, uncertain. I knew he wanted to try to shove himself inside me, but he was afraid to. How many women had hurt him? How many had told him he was a freak, a monster, simply because he was so very male? I sat up enough to wrap my hand around the hard length of him. Just holding it in my hand threw my head back, made me cry out. I stared at him, knowing my eyes were wild, squeezing my hand around him until his head went back, his eyes rolled into his head.

I slid my hand up over him, caressing the soft, luscious head. I leaned back on my elbows, looking at him. 'Fuck me, Micah. Fuck me before I stop having little spasms inside me. You made me so wet, so tight, my body is still having little mini orgasms. I want you inside me while my body is still spasming.'

He bent over and kissed me, his mouth still wet from me, still tasting like meat and that fresh taste, almost like rain. People can make fish jokes, but not every woman tastes the same.

He drew back from the kiss, kept himself propped up on his arms. But his body was already pushing against me.

Feeling the weight of him against me made me fall back against the bed. He kept his body above mine so I could see every inch of him as he began to try to push his way inside me.

I was wet enough, but he was so wide, so very wide, that he had to ease his way in, and even easing had a level of force to it. He had to force his way in. If I'd released the *ardeur*, I would have been more open, more ready for him. The *ardeur* alone without much foreplay could make my body ready, eager, and more open. But we both wanted me tight, both wanted to feel him fight his way inside me.

The tip vanished inside me, with so much left still. Watching him push inch by inch inside me made me cry out, made my body rise up, so that my hands went around my own thighs. So that I held my legs up and made my body a little ball. So I could see, and feel, all of it.

Halfway through his eyes closed, and he stopped moving, head down. His voice came strained. 'So wet. God, so tight. You keep gripping me with your body. It's like the farther in I push, the more you spasm. Just me pushing inside you, causing small orgasms.'

'Yes,' I said, and my voice was breathy, it was eager. 'Yes, the sensation of you inside me, when I'm this tight, this wet. It's amazing. Oh, God, Micah, don't stop, don't stop.'

He raised his face up then and met my eyes. He searched my face as if he thought I was lying to him.

'You're serious?'

'Yes, God, yes.'

'You're wet enough, but we've never tried this when you were this tight, Anita.' Eagerness fought in his eyes with worry. 'I can push in faster, but I don't want to hurt you.'

I stared into his face and said what I was thinking. 'I don't know whose ghost you're fighting right now, but it's not me. Whoever you thought you hurt, it wasn't me. Fuck me, fuck me, fuck me the way we both want you to.'

I watched him decide with our faces inches apart, our bodies already wedded to each other. I watched him decide. His hips moved forward, shoved himself inside me. I'd told him to stop being careful. He took me at my word.

He shoved himself inside me, fought to push his hardness inside me, as far and as fast as he could. I was too tight and he was too wide for speed, but whereas before when he felt resistance he'd hesitated, now he shoved harder. My body resisted, and his body crashed through. He shoved all that hard, wide meat inside me. He forced his way in, while my body was still trying to figure out if it was a good thing or a bad thing.

On one hand it felt amazing, so hard, so long, so wide, and all inside me. God, it felt good. It flung me back against the bed, tore screams of pleasure from my mouth. It made me writhe around him, wriggling and struggling, caught between orgasm and my body telling me that maybe we shouldn't be doing this. About the time I thought, *Too much, too wide, slow down*, and actually drew breath to say it, the orgasm stopped being spasms and was suddenly full-blown. It caught me off guard as a lot of intercourse orgasms did. It turned almost-pain to unbelievable pleasure. It made me throw my body around him, over him, fling my upper body against the pillows, over and over again like a puppet whose strings had been cut. I writhed and screamed, and fought, and danced under him. And he shoved himself as far inside me as he could, hitting the end of me when there was still some of him yet to go.

He drew himself out of me, and it rubbed, because orgasm was tightening me around him, trying to hold on to all of him as he pulled back out. He began to shove himself inside again as far and hard as the tightness would let him. He fought his way in and out, while I writhed and screamed. I had to hold on to something. My hands found his shoulders, his arms, and drew blood down them. Too much pleasure, too many sensations, as if all that pleasure spilled out of me in the blood that ran down his body.

His voice came gasping. 'Feed the *ardeur* soon, Anita, please. God, soon. I'm not going to last much longer.' I'd forgotten what we were doing. I'd forgotten about the *ardeur*. I'd forgotten everything but the sex. It took only a thought, and the *ardeur* was suddenly there. But I was too far gone in orgasm, pleasure, our bodies. Always before, the *ardeur* had felt like more, like its own presence, but now it was only another part of the sex. It was like an extra layer of heat added to a bonfire that was already burning down the room.

It tore sounds from my throat, raked my nails down Micah's back, and only then did I realize he was on top of me, not above me, but pressed on top of me in a more standard missionary position. I hadn't remembered when he changed position.

The *ardeur* had opened me to him, and he was finally able to shove himself in and out of me, not fighting my body now but sliding in and out. He came to the end of me before his thrust was finished, but there was no more of me, nowhere else for him to go. He raised up on his arms for a moment so I could gaze down my body at the meat of him going inside me, over and over and over, and the orgasm was almost, almost, almost. I could feel his body changing rhythm, feel that he was close. The *ardeur* couldn't feed off of Micah until he orgasmed. He was too dominant, too controlled; only orgasm let his shields down enough to be food for me.

He cried out above me, his hips doing one last thrust that brought me screaming off the bed, bowing my back, closing my eyes. I screamed for him a long time after he had finished, and he lay on top of me, trying to relearn how to breathe. I screamed and writhed underneath him, still caught in the aftershocks of what we'd done.

When he could move, he pulled out of me, and that made me writhe again, but almost as soon as he was out the ache began. That the endorphins had begun to fade that fast meant I'd be sore later. But it was the kind of sore I didn't mind. The kind of sore that would be like a keepsake, that I could take out and look at and remember what we'd done. I'd remember the pleasure of it with every ache between my legs.

Micah lay oddly, half on his stomach, half on his side. The arm that was toward me was bleeding. He'd have his own aches and pains to remember this by. He moved, propping himself up on his elbows, and I saw his back.

I gasped and said, 'Jesus, Micah, I'm sorry.'

He winced. 'The nails don't usually hurt this soon after great sex.'

I nodded. 'When the endorphins go quick, you know you're hurt.' His back looked like he'd been attacked by something with more claws than I had.

'Are you hurting?' he asked.

'A little ache.'

He gave me serious eyes. 'When I drew out, there was blood. Not much, but some.'

'We've had color before,' I said.

'Yeah, but that's usually near your period. This isn't.' His face was serious again. That shadow of old memories, old girlfriends in his eyes.

'How does your back feel?' I asked.

He grinned for me. 'It hurts.'

'Do you regret it?'

He shook his head. 'God, no, it was a-fucking-mazing.'

'Ask me how I feel,' I said.

'Did I hurt you?'

'I ache already, which means a little.' I touched his face before he could look away. 'Now ask me if I regret it.'

He gave me that sad, mixed smile of his. 'Do you regret it?'

'God, no,' I said. 'You were a-fucking-mazing.'

He smiled then, and it was a real smile. I watched the ghosts fade from his eyes until there was nothing but warm pleasure left.

'I love you,' he said. 'I love you so much.'

'And I love you.'

He looked down at the bedspread, which was a little worse for wear. 'I better get up off this before we get more blood on it.' He got to his feet, steadying himself on the edge of the bed as if his legs weren't quite working yet. I couldn't have walked if a fire alarm had gone off, so I sympathized.

There were spots of blood here and there, almost outlining the upper part of his body. There was also a spot of crimson where his lower body had been pressed to the bedspread. White had been a bad choice for it. I pushed myself up enough to look down at my own body. There was blood between my legs and a little on the bedspread below my body. 'Think the maid will call the cops?' I asked.

He started a shaky walk toward the door. I think he was headed for the bathroom. 'Not if we tip her enough.' He caught the door as if he'd have fallen without it.

'Careful,' I said.

He leaned against the door for a moment, then looked at me. 'You make everything all right for me, Anita. You make me feel like a human being instead of a monster.'

'And you love all of me, Micah, every last hard-boiled, ruthless bit of me. You make it okay that sometimes I am the monster. You know what I do, and you still love me.'

'You're not a monster, Anita –' he grinned at me – 'but you are ruthless. But then I like that in a girl.' He went toward the bathroom still a little shaky but moving better. I settled back on the bed and waited for my knees and thighs to work enough to walk. I might as well get comfortable; it was going to be a while before I could move.

# 9

PHILLY WAS A pretty city, what little I'd seen of it. The visit so far had consisted of the airport and the hotel room and some amazing sex. We could have been anywhere. The cemetery reminded me that the city was in one of the thirteen original colonies. It was old, that cemetery. It breathed its age and the age of its dead. Breathed it along my skin the moment we stepped out of Fox's car. Once, a cemetery this old would have been peaceful for me. Too old to have ghosts, maybe a few shivery spots if you walked directly over a grave, but mostly the dead here would be inert, earth to earth, dust to dust, and all that. But now the dead called to me, even through my shielding.

Theoretically, no one could raise the long dead without a human sacrifice. I probably held the record for oldest without one, but even two-hundred-plus years dead should have been beyond me. So why, lately, did the long dead whisper power across my skin?

I shivered, but it wasn't from the early November cold. In fact, I was too warm in the leather jacket. Micah was suddenly at my side. He helped me slip the jacket off, whispering, 'Are you all right?'

I nodded. I was all right, better than all right. Standing there in the power-kissed darkness was intoxicating. It was as if my skin were drinking magic from the very air. Which, with necromancy, wasn't possible.

Micah asked Fox if we could put the jacket back in the car. I didn't wait to hear what Fox said; I was already walking out into the dark. I absently trailed my fingers along the weathered tops of the tombstones as I walked between them.

Old cemeteries are crowded things. The ground was smooth and rough, but there was no longer much to differentiate ground from grave, so that I walked one step on the ground, then on the second step walked over a grave. You know the old saying *Someone walked over my grave?* This was like the reverse of that. I didn't feel bad, or shaky, or scared. With every grave I walked over, I felt better, steadier, more confident. I took a little energy from every body I passed over, no matter how old. I could have drunk in the power of the dead underneath me and done . . . Done what?

The thought stopped me literally in my tracks. What I hadn't realized was that Franklin was following me, close. I hadn't even known he was there.

He ran into me, or nearly. He had to grab my arms to keep from smacking into the back of me. It startled both of us. He apologized before I'd finished turning around.

'I'm sorry, I didn't know you were . . . stopping.' He sounded breathless and way more upset than he should have been.

I was left staring up at him, wondering why he was nervous. Then I saw what he was doing with his hands. He was running them up and down the sleeves of his trench coat, as if he'd touched something and was trying to wipe it off. He wasn't being insulting. I doubt he even realized he was doing it. I might have done the same thing if I'd touched someone else's magic unexpectedly. It was like walking through metaphysical cobwebs; you had to brush it off. He had felt at least some of the power I was getting off the graves.

I might have asked Franklin why he'd been hiding that he was psychic, but Fox and Micah came up to us, and somehow I didn't think Franklin would want me being that insightful in front of them. Had he told the FBI that he was talented? I was betting not. It had been a plus in only the last two, three years tops. Before that they looked at it as a psychological disorder. You didn't get to be a federal agent with a psychological disorder.

It did explain why he had a serious dislike of me. If he was hiding what he was, he wouldn't want to be around someone who complemented his talents, whatever they might be. No, if you were hiding, you didn't want to be around people who were out of the broom closet, as it were.

'Is there a problem?' Fox asked.

Franklin said, 'No, no problem,' a little too fast.

I just shook my head, still looking up at the taller man.

I don't think Fox believed us, but he let it go. We weren't talking, so he was out of options. He gave us both a look, then said, 'Then if there's no problem, everyone is waiting for us.'

I nodded again, then thought to ask, 'Is Rose's grave the newest one in this cemetery?'

Fox thought about it, then nodded. 'Yes, why?'

I smiled at him and knew that it was a dreamy smile, as if I were listening to music he couldn't hear. 'Just wanted to know what I was looking for, that's all.'

'I can take you to the grave, Marshal. You don't need to look for it.'

I wanted to look for it. I wanted to walk the cemetery a tombstone at a time and find it myself.

Micah answered for me. 'That would be good, Fox. Lead the way.'

I looked at him and fought to make it friendly

He gave me a look in return that was a warning. In the dark, with all the trees around, I doubted anyone else could have seen his expression as clearly as I did. But we both had better-than-normal night vision, though I doubted mine could compare to his kitty-cat eyes. Those eyes were bare for all to see now. Too dark for his black-lensed sunglasses, but you'd be surprised how many people wouldn't notice the strangeness of his eyes. Even in full light, a lot of people wouldn't see his eyes for what they were. People see what they want to see, unless forced to see the truth.

I looked full into his eyes and read the warning there, the worry. Was I really all right? the look asked.

The truth was yes and no. I felt great, but it was the kind of great that could go south fast and hard. One minute fine, the next moment the power could do something unfortunate.

I took a deep breath and tried to center and ground, the way I'd been taught, but that was a skill I'd learned from a psychic and witch. Her talents ran to prophecy and empathy so finely tuned it was almost telepathy. She didn't raise the dead. She didn't truly understand my talent.

Drawing myself into the center of my body was great – I felt steadier, more myself and less power-fuzzed – but the moment I tried to ground all that power into the earth, to bleed some of it off, it turned. Turned so that it didn't go deep but out and away. My power chased through the ground so that I sensed the graves, all the graves, like I was the center of a great wheel. The graves were the points along the spokes, and I knew them all. I didn't drop my shields that I hid behind to keep the dead from bothering me. The shields were just not there.

I'd known that my power was growing, but I hadn't truly understood what that might mean until right this second. I knew the dead in every grave here. I knew which still had a remnant of energy. What graves would have shivery spots if you walked over them, the last gasp of what had once been a ghost. Most of the graves were quiet, only bones and rags and dust. I'd been able to stand in a cemetery and do this for years. But what had changed was: one, I hadn't done it on purpose, and two, every grave I touched was a little more energetic for my power having breathed over it. That was new.

'Stop it, Blake.' Franklin's voice was tight with anxiety.

I looked at him. 'Stop what?' I asked, but my voice was lazy with power.

'Don't toy with him, Anita,' Micah said.

'I'm missing something,' Fox said.

I nodded. 'Yeah, you are.' I could have let Franklin's cat out of the bag, but I didn't. I knew what it felt like to be different and to want nothing, absolutely nothing, as much as simply to be normal. I'd given up on that a long time ago. It wasn't possible for me and never had been. Maybe it wouldn't be possible for Franklin either, but that wasn't my call. I did the only thing I could for him. I lied.

'When Franklin and I bumped into each other, he caught an edge of my power. It happens sometimes when my shields are down.' That was a lie. It happened only if your abilities were similar to mine in some way, or you were so strongly psychic in some other way that you would sense any strong psychic gift used near you. Either Franklin had abilities with the dead like mediumship, being able to talk with the recently departed. Or he was powerful in some other way. Naw. If he'd been that gifted, he wouldn't have been able to hide it. I was betting that somewhere in his background was a family member who could talk to spirits. Someone he probably hated or was embarrassed about. You dislike most in others what you hate in yourself.

Fox said, 'Is that right, Franklin? You bumped into the marshal.'

Franklin nodded. 'Yes.' One word, no emotion to it, but the relief in his eyes was too raw. He turned away from Fox, from me, to hide those relieved eyes. He knew I knew, and he knew I'd lied for him. He owed me. I hoped he understood that.

Fox looked from one of us to the other, as if he suspected we were lying, or at least hiding something. He looked at Micah and got a shrug. Fox shook his head and said, 'Fine.' He looked at us a heart-beat longer, then shook his head, as if he'd decided to let it go. 'We're going to be the last to arrive at graveside, Marshal Blake. I don't want to leave the federal judge and the lawyers waiting too long in the middle of a cemetery, so I'll lead the way. I think it will be faster that way.'

I couldn't argue the faster part. 'Then lead the way, Special Agent Fox.'

He gave me one more hard look. It was a good look, as those kinds of looks go. But if he thought I was going to break down and fess up because of a hard look, he was wrong. I gave him a pleasant, even eager face, but nothing helpful.

He sighed and settled his shoulders, as if his shoulder holster chafed. He started off through the cemetery. Franklin fell into line behind him without a backward glance.

Micah and I followed them. Micah had us drop back enough to whisper, 'You're having trouble controlling your power tonight, aren't you?'

I nodded. 'Yeah, I am.'

'Why?' he asked.

I shrugged. 'I'm not sure.'

'Then should you be raising the dead?'

'I think it will be one of the easier raisings I've ever done. There's so much power.'

He grabbed my arm. 'Do you even know that you're touching every tombstone as you walk by it?'

I stood there with his hand on my arm and stared at him. 'I'm what?'

'You're caressing the tops of the tombstones like you'd stroke a hand through flowers in a field.'

I looked at the worry in his face and knew that he wasn't lying, but . . . 'Was I?'

'Yes,' he said, and his grip on my arm was suddenly almost painful.

'You're hurting me,' I said.

'Does it help?'

I frowned at him, then realized what he meant. The small pain had pushed back the power. I could think about something other than the dead. My first clear thought was fear. 'I don't know what's wrong tonight. I really don't. I knew I was gaining abilities from the vampires, but I didn't think it would bleed over to the zombie stuff. I mean, that's my magic, not Jean-Claude's, not Richard's. Mine. Whatever happens metaphysically, it doesn't usually mess with my basic talent.'

'Should you cancel tonight?' he asked.

I licked my lips, tasting the fresh lipstick I'd put on after we'd made love. I shook my head, moving into the circle of his arms. I hugged him. 'If this is a new power level, then one night won't make a difference.' I held him, breathing in the warm solidity of him.

'There's always a learning curve to new abilities, Anita,' he whispered into my hair. 'Even if that ability is only a stronger version of something else. Do we really want the learning curve to be on the FBI's dime?'

He had a point, a good one, but . . . 'I'll be able to raise this zombie, Micah.'

'But what else will you raise?' he asked.

I drew back enough to see his face. 'How did you understand that?'

'Isn't that what you're afraid of? Not that you can't raise the dead, but that you'll raise more than you were paid for?'

I nodded. 'Yeah.' I shivered and drew away so I could rub my arms. 'That's exactly it.'

'The protective circle is usually to keep things out,' he said. 'Right?'

I nodded again.

'Tonight, I think maybe it will be to keep you in.'

'So I don't spread over more of the graves,' I said.

'Yes,' he said.

'They should have chickens waiting for me to slaughter. I know Larry would have told them to bring the livestock.'

Fox yelled, 'Marshal, Callahan, are you coming?'

'We'll be there in a minute,' Micah called. He leaned into me, hands on my arms. 'Do you really think chicken blood will keep this contained?'

'Not their blood, but their lives, yes,' I said.

'I'm not sure adding fresh death to your magic tonight is a good idea.'

'What choice do I have, Micah? I can make a small cut in my arm or hand and use the blood, but I'm not sure what my blood touching the graveyard will do tonight. So much power tonight, it's intoxicating.'

'Then use my blood,' he said.

I looked at him. 'You've never shared blood for a zombie raising.'

'No, but I let Jean-Claude take blood from me. How much different can it be?'

There were many answers to that, but I settled for 'A lot different. I can't cloud your mind to make it not hurt.'

'It's a little cut, Anita. I'm okay with it.'

I sighed and hugged him again. A lot of men will date you, and some will sleep with you, and a few are content to play second fiddle to your job, but how many will literally open a vein for you? Not many.

I gave him a quick kiss. 'Let's go raise Mr Rose from the dead.'

He picked up the bag with all the zombie-raising paraphernalia in it. He'd carry it. After all, he was the assistant. He needed to look useful. We finished the walk to the grave hand in hand. Maybe it wasn't professional, but I didn't care anymore. Besides, once I cut his arm open with the machete, no one would complain that he wasn't assisting me enough. No, they'd think he was more than earning his paycheck. The fact that he didn't get paid to be my assistant would be our little secret.

# 10

ONE OF THE THINGS in the gym bag that Micah was holding was a machete longer than my forearm. Even with a badge I might have had trouble getting it on the plane, except for the magical artifact law. Magical practitioners who earned their living from their magical talent could not be denied access to their magical tools. They were to be treated the same way as crosses, or Stars Of David. The machete had had to go through checked baggage until the Supreme Court put through the exclusion act. Made it all so much more convenient for me.

We were introduced to everyone. I gave a special nod to the court reporter, the only other woman there. I spent a lot of time being the only woman everywhere I went. I'd begun to like having other women around. It made me feel less like a freak. The only girl in the all-boys club had begun to get a little lonely of late.

The lawyers on one side were unhappy with me from the moment they saw me. How relieved they must have been when Rose died quietly of natural causes before he could testify. Now here I was, about to bring him back from the dead so he could testify after all. What's the world coming to when even the dead can testify in federal court?

Arthur Salvia was the head lawyer on the side that wasn't happy to see me. His name sounded vaguely familiar, as if he'd been in the news for something, but I couldn't place it. 'Your honor, I must protest again. Mr Rose died before he could testify in court. The testimony of a dead man is not admissible.'

'I get to say what is admissible, Mr Salvia. You'll get your chance to cross-examine the witness.' He frowned and turned to me. 'That is correct, Ms Blake? The zombie will be able to be cross-examined?'

I nodded, realized he might not have the night vision to see it, and said, 'Yes, your honor. The zombie will be able to answer questions and respond to cross-examination.'

He nodded too, then said, 'There, Mr Salvia. You will get your chance to cross-examine Mr Rose.'

'Mr Rose is dead, your honor. I renew my objections to this entire proceeding—'

The judge held up his hand. 'Heard and noted, Mr Salvia, but save the rest of your objections for the appeal.'

Salvia settled back. He was not happy.

Micah leaned in very close to my ear and whispered, 'He smells like fear.'

The lawyer for the accused was allowed to be nervous, but fear? That seemed a bit strong. Was he afraid of the graveyard and the whole zombie thing, or was it something else?

There was a wire mesh cage over to one side with a chicken in it. The bird clucked softly to itself, making the sleepy noises chickens make when they're settling down for the night. The chicken wasn't afraid. It didn't know it had been brought to play blood sacrifice. Larry would have needed it. I didn't. I'd discovered that I could use a little bit of my own blood to represent the sacrifice needed to raise the dead by accident. Or necessity, after Marianne, the woman who was helping me learn to control my metaphysical abilities, had gotten grief from her coven.

She hadn't been Wiccan when I first started going to her. She'd just been psychic. Then she got religion, and suddenly she was asking if I could raise the dead without killing an animal. Something about her coven speculating that she, as my teacher, would take on some of my bad karma from doing death magic. So I tried. I could do it. The zombie wasn't always as well put together, or as smart, but it still talked and could answer questions. Good enough for govern-ment work, as they say. But constantly having cuts all over my left hand and arm got old. I refused to cut my gun hand. It hurt, and I was beginning to run out of fresh places to cut. I decided that since I ate meat anyway, it wasn't so different from slaughtering a few animals to do my job. But the whole experience had taught me that I could, if I had to, raise the newly dead without killing an animal. Very recently, I'd discovered that I didn't need *any* blood to raise a zombie sometimes.

I guess I should have known I could, because I'd accidentally raised the dead when I was younger. A beloved dog that crawled out of the grave to follow me home; a college prof that committed suicide and came to my dorm room one night.

That should have told me that the blood wasn't absolutely necessary, but I'd been taught zombie-raising by a man who needed the blood, needed the sacrifice, needed the herbal salve, and all of it. I'd done it the way I'd been taught, until recently.

I was saving the lives of a lot of livestock, but it wasn't doing my nerves any good.

The judge asked in a voice that managed to be both friendly and condescending, 'Could you explain what you're about to do so we'll understand what's happening and for Elaine – Ms Beck – to get it into the court record?' He motioned at the dark-haired woman at her little folding stool and table.

His request stopped me. In all the years I'd been raising the dead, no one had ever asked me to explain. Most people treated me like a dirty little secret. Something you may need to do, but you don't want to know the details. Like sausage making. People love eating sausage, but they don't want to know too many details about how it's made.

I closed my mouth, then managed to say, 'Fine.' Of course, since I'd never explained before, I wasn't sure how to explain at all. How do you explain magic to people who don't do magic? How do you explain psychic gifts to people who have none? Hell if I knew, but I tried.

'First we'll do a circle of protection,' I said.

Salvia asked, 'I have a question for Marshal Blake.'

'She's not a witness, Mr Salvia,' the judge said.

'Without her abilities, this testimony would be impossible to retrieve. Is that not true, your honor?'

The judge seemed to think about that for a second or two. 'Yes, but all I've asked of the marshal is that she explain the mechanics of what she is about to do. That isn't witness testimony.'

'No, but she is an expert witness, the same as any other forensic expert.'

'I'm not certain that an animator is a forensic expert, Mr Salvia.'

'But she is an expert on raising the dead, correct?'

Again the judge thought about it. He saw the trap that his little request for an explanation for the court record had gotten us into. If I had information for the court record, then my information was suddenly open to questioning by the attorneys. Shit.

'I will concede that Marshal Blake is an expert on raising the dead.'

Laban, the head attorney for the other side, said, 'I think we'll all agree to that. What is the defense's point?'

'If she's an expert witness, then I should be able to question her.'

'But she's not giving testimony,' the judge said. 'She's explaining what she's doing so we'll be able to follow along.'

'How is that different from collecting any other evidence?' Salvia said. 'If she were any other expert, I would be allowed to question her methodology.'

I had to give it to him, he was making a point. A point that could keep us here for hours.

'Your honor,' I said, 'may I ask Mr Salvia a question?'

The judge gave me his long, considering look, then nodded. 'I'll allow it.'

I looked at the lawyer. He wasn't that much taller than me, but he stood straight for every inch of it. So did I, but his stance was more aggressive, as if he were squaring himself for an attack. I guess in a way he was.

I'd testified in court a few times when a lawyer got clever and tried to win an appeal on a zombie who had said this will is real, not this one. I'd even been called into court for an insurance company that decided to appeal the zombie's testimony on the grounds that the dead were not competent to give testimony. I'd stopped getting dragged into court to defend myself after I'd offered to bring the zombie into court to give open court testimony. The offer was accepted. And that was back in the days when my zombies actually looked more like the shambling dead than a person.

We'd all made the papers, and the media had made much of the fact that the mean ol' company had traumatized the family a second time. In fact, it had been the beginning of a countersuit for mental distress. The insurance company would eventually pay more in the second suit than in the original life insurance claim. Everyone learned their lesson, and I got to stay in the cemetery and out of the courtroom. But I'd spent weeks being drilled with the argument that I was not a true forensic expert. Salvia was about to hear me spit that argument back at him.

'Mr Salvia, would you say that most evidence is open to interpretation depending on which expert you get to interpret that evidence?'

He considered that for a moment. Most lawyers won't answer questions fast, especially not in court. They want to think it through first. 'I would agree with that statement.'

'If I was here to collect DNA or some other physical evidence, my actions might be open to scrutiny, because my method of collection could impact how reliable my evidence was, correct?'

Micah gave me a look. I shrugged at him. I could talk lawyer-speak up to a point, in a good cause. Getting us out of here before five A.M. was a good cause.

Salvia finally answered a cautious 'I would agree. Which is why I need to question your methods, so I can understand them well enough to represent my client.'

'But, Mr Salvia, what I'm about to do is not open to interpretation of any kind.'

He turned to the judge. 'Your honor, she is refusing to explain her methods. If I don't understand what the marshal is doing, then how will I be able to adequately defend my client?'

'Marshal Blake,' the judge said, 'I'm sorry that I opened this issue with my request for information, but I can see the defense's point.'

'For most experts, I would see his point, too, your honor, but may I make one more point before you rule on whether the defense gets to question my every move?'

'I won't allow him to question your every move, Marshal,' he said with a smile that even by moonlight seemed self-satisfied. Or maybe I was just watching the entire night go up in questions, and that was making me grumpy. I'd never had to raise the dead while being questioned by hostile lawyers. It didn't sound like a fun evening. 'But I will allow you to make your point.'

'If I raise Emmett Rose from the dead tonight, you'll be here to see it, right?'

'Are you speaking to me, Marshal Blake?' asked the defense lawyer.

'Yes, Mr Salvia, I am speaking to you.' I fought to keep the impatience out of my voice.

'Could you repeat the question?' he asked.

I repeated it, then added, 'If I fail to raise Emmett Rose from the dead tonight, you'll be here to see that, too, right?'

I could see him frown even in the cooler darkness under the trees. 'Yes.' But he said it slowly, as if he didn't see the trap but suspected that there was one.

'I will either raise the zombie from this grave, or I will not. Correct, Mr Salvia?'

'Your honor, what is Marshal Blake trying to get at?' Salvia asked.

'Do you concede that my raising Emmett Rose from the dead is either a yes or no question? Either he pops out of the grave, or he does not.'

'Yes, yes, I concede that, but I still don't see—'

'Would you say that the zombie rising from the grave is open to interpretation?' I asked.

Salvia opened his mouth, closed it. 'I'm not sure I understand the question.'

The judge said, 'Marshal Blake has made her point. Either the zombie will rise from the grave, or it won't. We will all be here to see the zombie either rise, or not rise. It isn't open to interpretation, Mr Salvia. Either she will do what she's being paid for, or she won't. It either works or it does not.'

'But the ritual she chooses to raise the dead could affect the ability of Mr Rose to give intelligent testimony.'

The judge asked me, 'Is that true? Marshal, could your choice of rituals affect the zombie?'

'Not the ritual. No, your honor. But the ability of the animator.' The moment that last bit left my mouth, I flinched. I should have stopped with 'No, your honor.' Dammit.

'Explain the last part of that statement,' the judge said.

See, I'd said too much. Given them something to question and be confused by. I knew better than that.

'The greater the degree of power the animator has, and sometimes the more practice he or she has at raising the dead, the better their zombies are.'

'Better how?' he asked.

'More alive. The greater the power used, the more alive the zombie will appear. You'll also get more of their personality, more of what they were like in life.'

Again, I'd overexplained. What was the matter with me tonight? The moment I thought it, I knew, or thought I knew. The dead were whispering to me. Not in voices – the true dead have no voices – but in power. It should have taken energy from me to raise a zombie.

They shouldn't have been offering power up to me, like some sort of gift. Power over the dead comes with a price, always. Nothing's free with the dead.

Micah touched my arm. It startled me. I looked at him, and he said softly, 'Are you all right?'

I nodded.

'The judge is talking to you.'

I turned back to the judge and apologized. 'I'm sorry, your honor. Could you repeat what you just said?'

He frowned at me but said, 'You seemed distracted just then, Marshal Blake.'

'I'm sorry, your honor. I'm just thinking about the job ahead.'

'Well, we'd like you to concentrate a little harder on this part of the proceedings before you rush ahead of us.'

I sighed, swallowed a half dozen witty and unhelpful things, and settled for, 'Fine, what did you say that I missed?'

Micah touched my arm again, as if my tone might have been a little less than polite. He was right. I was getting angry. That old tension in my shoulders and along my arms was settling in.

'What I said, Marshal, was I was under the impression that only a blood sacrifice would give you that much life in a zombie.'

I thought better of the judge. He'd done some research, but not enough. 'There's always blood involved in raising the dead, your honor.'

'We understand that the FBI was requested to supply you with poultry,' he said.

Any normal human being would have said, *Is that what the chicken is for?* Court time is not the same as real time; it's sort of like football time. What should take five minutes will take thirty.

'Yes, that is why the chicken was requested.' See, I could talk the long way 'round the mountain, too. If a question has a simple yes or no answer, then give that. Beyond yes or no questions, explain things. Don't add, don't embellish, but be thorough. Because you're going to have to talk one way or the other. I preferred to give complete answers in the beginning rather than have my explanations be made longer on cross-examination.

'How does the chicken help you with this protective circle?' he asked.

'You normally behead the chicken and use its blood, its life energy, to help put up a protective circle around the grave.'

'Your honor,' Salvia again, 'why does Marshal Blake need a protective circle?'

Laban, our friendly neighborhood prosecutor, said, 'Is my esteemed colleague going to question every step of the ritual?'

'I think I have the right on behalf of my clients to ask why she needs a protective circle. One of my objections to this entire procedure was the worry that something else could animate the corpse, and what is raised will be merely Mr Rose's shell but with something else inside it. Some wandering spirit could—'

'Mr Salvia,' Laban said, 'your fanciful worries did not convince the judge to grant your motion. Why bring it up again?'

Truthfully, one of the reasons we put up protective circles was to keep wandering spirits, as Salvia put it, from animating the corpse. Though I'm not sure spirits were what I'd worry about. There were other things, nastier things, that loved getting hold of a corpse.

They'd use it for walking-around clothes until someone made them leave it, or until they'd so damaged it that the body no longer functioned well enough to be useful. I did not say this out loud. To my knowledge, no animator had volunteered this part of the reason for the protective circle. It would open too many legal problems when we were still striving to have animation be accepted as standard practice for court cases. The circle also helped raise power, and that was the main reason for it. The whole corpse-being-highjacked thing was so rare that I actually didn't know anyone who had ever had it happen to one of their zombies. It was one of those stories that always seems to happen to the friend of your uncle's cousin, who no one actually ever met. I wasn't going to help Salvia keep us here all night.

'Mr Laban is right,' the judge said. 'There is nothing in the literature about zombies being taken over by alien energy.' His voice held distaste, as if Salvia had actually proposed some sort of alien possession theory.

For all I knew, he had. I guess if the prosecution's star witness can be raised from the dead to testify, then the defense is allowed to look for unusual help, too. Aliens seemed a little far-fetched, but hey, I raise the dead for a living and slay vampires. I really couldn't throw stones.

'Marshal Blake, once you have your protective circle, how much more ritual will you need?' I think the judge was tired of the delays, too. Good – me getting impatient didn't help much. But the judge getting impatient – that could be very helpful.

I thought about it and was glad he'd phrased the question the way he had. How much ritual would I need? A very different question from, *What comes next in animating the dead?* Once the circle was up, I deviated so far from normal animating ritual that it was like comparing apples to watermelons.

'Not much more, your honor.'

'Can you be more exact?' he asked.

'I'll call Emmett Rose from the grave. Once he's above ground, then I'll put blood on or in his mouth, and he'll be able to answer questions very soon after that.'

'Did you say you put blood on the zombie's mouth?' Salvia again.

'Yes.'

'You're going to have the zombie suck on the chicken?' This from one of the agents who had been waiting with the judge.

We all looked at him, and he had the grace to look embarrassed. 'Sorry.'

'Not suck on the chicken, no. But I'll spread the blood across the mouth.'

'Mr Rose was a good Christian. Isn't painting him up with chicken blood a violation of his religious freedom?' Salvia said.

The judge said, 'As much as I appreciate your concern over Mr Rose's religious freedom, Mr Salvia, I have to point out that he isn't your client, and that the dead have no rights to violate.'

Of course, I had to add my two cents' worth. I just couldn't help myself. 'Besides, Mr Salvia, are you implying that you can't be a good Christian if you sacrifice a few chickens and raise a few zombies?' The anger was creeping from my shoulders and into my voice. Micah started rubbing his hand up and down my arm, as if to remind me that he was there, and my temper was, too. But his touch did help make me think. I guess sometimes I needed an 'assistant' for more than sex and blood. Sometimes I just needed a keeper.

I got a few startled looks. Salvia wasn't the only one who'd assumed I wasn't Christian. I don't know why it still hurts my feelings, but it does. The judge said, 'You may answer Marshal Blake's question.' I was definitely not the only one sick of Salvia's bitching.

'I didn't mean to imply anything about your own religious beliefs, Marshal Blake. I apologize for assuming that you weren't Christian.'

'Don't worry about it, Salvia. Lots of people assume all sorts of shit about me.'

Micah whispered, 'Anita.' One word, but enough.

I could have used the dead as an excuse, and it might even have been true, but the real reason was I've never held my temper well. I'm better sometimes, worse others, but it never takes long for me to get tired of assholes.

Salvia was pissing me off, and the judge with his *Please explain the unexplainable, Marshal Blake* wasn't far behind in the pissing-me-off department.

'Sorry about that, your honor, but can we cut to the chase here?'

'I'm not sure what you mean by cutting to the chase, Marshal Blake.'

'Emmett Rose is the recently dead. I mean he hasn't hit one year dead. It's an easy job, your honor. A little blood, a little power, and voilà, a zombie. He'll be able to answer questions. He'll be able to be cross-examined. He'll do everything you want him to be able to do. Having experienced Mr Salvia's questioning technique, I think the cross-examination may last a long damned time. So in the interest of all of us not spending the entire bloody night in the cemetery, can I please get on with it?'

Franklin made a noise low in his throat. Fox was shaking his head. I knew I was fucking it up but I couldn't seem to stop. I wanted out of this cemetery. I wanted away from the graves and their promise of power. I needed my circle of protection up now, not an hour from now. My head would stop echoing with half-heard whispers like words from a distant room. Or a radio station turned down low. I could almost hear the voices, almost hear the dead. I shouldn't have been able to do that. They weren't ghosts. The quiet dead are just that, quiet.

'I will remind you, Marshal, that this is still a court of law. I can hold you in contempt.'

Micah turned me to him and drew me into a hug. His breath was warm against my face. 'Anita, what's wrong?'

I felt movement at my back a moment before Fox asked quietly, 'Are you all right, Blake?'

I leaned into Micah. His arms held me, tight and almost fierce, as if he would press me out the other side of his body. He whispered against my face, 'What is wrong, Anita? What is it?'

I grabbed on to him and pressed as much of him against me as I could, so that we were plastered against each other, as close as we could get with clothes on. I buried my face against the side of his neck, drawing in the warm, sweet scent of his skin. Soap, the slight sweetness of his cologne, and underneath that the scent of his skin. The scent of Micah. And underneath that, that faint, neck-ruffling scent of leopard. The moment I smelled it, I felt better. That musky, almost-sharp scent of leopard helped chase back the almost-voices of the dead.

'Do you want me to hold you in contempt, Marshal Blake?' The judge's voice dragged me back from Micah's skin, pulled me away from falling into the warmth and life of him.

I barely turned my head to look at the judge, but it felt like some huge physical wrenching. The moment I couldn't bury my face in Micah's skin, the voices were back. The dead were trying to talk to me. They shouldn't have been doing that. Ghosts would sometimes do that if they couldn't find a medium to speak with, but once you were in a grave, you weren't supposed to be this lively.

I looked at the judge and tried to explain what was happening without giving Salvia more ammunition to delay things. 'Your honor—' And I had to clear my throat to make my voice reach him only a few yards away. I tried again, pressing Micah's body against mine. Even with everything that was going wrong, I could feel his body beginning to respond to my nearness. We had that effect on each other. It didn't bring on the *ardeur* or distract me. Feeling his body respond helped me think, helped me feel alive.

'Your honor, I need my protective circle up sooner rather than later.'

'Why?'

'This is another tactic to rush these proceedings,' Salvia said.

'As you're trying to delay them?' Laban said. Never good when the lawyers start sniping at each other.

'Enough,' the judge said, and then he looked at me. 'Marshal Blake, why is it so important that you get your protective circle up?'

'The dead feel my power, your honor. They are, even now, trying to . . .' I sought a word that wouldn't be too much. If I said, *talk*, they might ask what the dead were saying, and it wasn't like that.

Micah answered for me. 'The circle isn't to protect the zombie, your honor. In this case it's to protect Anita, Marshal Blake. She let her psychic shields down when we entered the cemetery, and she's being overwhelmed by the dead.'

Fox said, 'Shit,' as if he understood more about that whole shielding thing than most people did.

'Was that wise, Marshal Blake, to let down your protection so early?'

I answered, 'This is a very old cemetery, your honor. Since I replaced Marshal Kirkland at the last minute, I didn't realize how old. There is a remote chance in a place this old that there might be problems that would affect the raising. It's standard practice to drop shields and let my power search the cemetery when I'm this unfamiliar with the area.' What I was saying was half-true. I was not going to admit that my shields had been ripped away by my own growing abilities.

'Search for what?' the judge asked.

'Sometimes very old cemeteries, especially those that haven't been used in a while, like this one, can become unconsecrated. It's like they need to be reblessed before they qualify as consecrated ground again.'

'And that would affect the zombie how?'

Micah's arms relaxed minutely, so that we were still holding each other but not pressed so fiercely against each other. He was right — we were going to be here awhile. I relaxed into his arms.

'Well, it could mean there were ghouls in the cemetery, and they're attracted to the freshly dead. They would have burrowed into the new grave and eaten Mr Rose by now. There might, or might not, have been left enough of him for him to be able to talk to you.'

'Ghouls, really?' He started to ask something else, but I think it was only curiosity and not the case, because he shook his head and frowned. 'Did you sense any ghouls?'

'No, your honor.' The fact that I'd actually dropped shields more by accident than design would be our little secret. I'd told the truth about the ghouls, but they hadn't been why my power danced out over the graves.

'All very interesting, Marshal,' Salvia said, 'but your shields being down doesn't change that you are trying to rush these proceedings.'

I turned in Micah's arms enough to give Salvia the look he deserved. He must have had bad night vision, because he didn't flinch. Franklin did, and it wasn't even directed at him.

'And what do you hope to gain by delaying things, Salvia?' I asked. 'What difference does it make to your clients whether Rose rises now or two hours from now? It's still going to happen tonight.'

Micah leaned his face against my ear and spoke just barely above a breath. I don't think he wanted to risk anyone else hearing. 'His fear spiked. He is delaying for a reason.'

I turned and breathed against his ear, 'What could he hope to gain by an hour delay?'

Micah nuzzled my ear and whispered, 'I don't know.'

'Are we interrupting the two of you?' Laban this time.

One of the agents muttered, 'Get a room.'

Great, we were going to piss everyone off. If I'd been working with police that I knew, I might have told them that the shapeshifter with me knew Salvia was lying and delaying with purpose, but over-sharing with the police – any flavor – isn't always wise. Besides, Fox had no reason to believe us, and even if he did, what good would it do us? Maybe Salvia didn't like cemeteries or zombies. A lot of people didn't. Maybe he was only delaying the moment when the walking dead rose from the grave. Maybe.

'Your honor,' I said, turning only enough to give them my face but keeping most of me in Micah's arms. The warmth and pulse of him helped me think. The whispers of the dead couldn't push past the life of him. He had become my shield. 'Your honor, I would love it if you would stop the arguing and let me raise Mr Rose from the dead. But if that isn't possible, can I at least put up the circle of protection? Mr Salvia will still be able to question me, but I will not have to cling to Mr Callahan quite so tightly.'

Micah whispered, 'Aww.'

It made me smile, which probably didn't help convince the judge I was serious, but it made me feel better.

'What does a protective circle have to do with why you are clinging to Mr Callahan?' the judge asked.

'It's hard to explain.'

'No one here is too terribly stupid, Marshal. Try us.' Maybe the judge was also getting impatient with everybody.

'The dead are crowding me. Burying myself against my assistant helps remind me of the living.'

'But you are alive, Marshal. Isn't that enough?'

'Apparently not, your honor.'

'I have no objection to you putting up your circle of protection, Marshal.'

'I object,' Salvia said.

'On what grounds?' the judge asked.

'It is only another ploy to rush these proceedings.'

The judge sighed loud enough for all of us to hear it. 'Mr Salvia, I think these proceedings have been delayed enough tonight. We are all past worrying about them being rushed.' He looked at the watch on his wrist, one of those timepieces with glowing hands. 'It is now after three in the morning. If we do not hurry this along, dawn will get here before the marshal gets to do her job. And we will have all wasted our night for nothing.' The judge looked at me. 'Raise your circle, Marshal.'

The bag was on the ground where Micah had dropped it when he grabbed for me. I let loose of him enough to kneel by it. The moment I wasn't pressed against him, that breathing, whispering presence was stronger. I was gaining strength from the dead, but they were also gaining something from me. I didn't understand entirely what that something was, but we needed to stop it. The circle would do that.

The only thing we needed for the circle was the machete. I pulled it out, and the moment the blade bared in the moonlight, people gasped. I guess it was a big blade, but I liked big blades.

I laid the machete on top of the gym bag and shrugged out of the suit jacket. Micah took it from me without being asked. He'd never actually helped me at a zombie raising. I realized that when I'd told the lawyers and agents what was about to happen, I'd been telling him, too. Funny, he was such a big piece of my everyday life that I had forgotten that this other big piece was something he'd never seen. Did I take Micah for granted? I hoped not.

Removing the suit jacket had left my shoulder holster and gun very naked. With normal clients I might have kept the jacket on, because guns spooked people, but the clients were the FBI – they were okay around guns. Besides, the jacket was new and I didn't want to get blood on it. I should have been cold in the autumn night, but the air was too full of magic. Since I was dealing with the dead the magic should have been cool, but tonight it was warm. Warm the way almost all other magic is warm.

Salvia said, 'Do you need a gun to raise the dead?'

I guess even when working for the FBI there are still civilians to placate. I gave Salvia a look and couldn't quite make it friendly. 'I'm a federal marshal and a vampire executioner, Mr Salvia. I don't go anywhere unarmed.'

I picked up the machete in my right hand and was holding out my other arm when Micah grabbed my right wrist.

I looked at him. 'What are you doing?' I asked, and I couldn't keep the unhappy tone out of my voice. Keeping it from being hostile was hard enough.

He leaned in, speaking low. 'Didn't we already discuss this, Anita? You're using my blood for the circle, right?'

I blinked at him. It actually took me a few seconds to understand what he meant. The fact that it took any time at all to see his logic meant that there was something going on with the dead in the ground that shouldn't have been happening. My power easing through the cemetery had done something to the graves. If I put my blood on the ground, what more would that do? But there was something in me, or at least in my magic, that wanted that deeper connection. My magic, for lack of a better word, wanted to pour my blood along the ground and bring the dead to some kind of half-life. Would it make them ghosts? Would they be zombies? Ghouls? What the hell was happening with my power lately? No answers, because there was no one living to ask. Vampires had made it standard policy to kill necromancers. Raise a zombie if you want to, talk to a few ghosts, but necromancers of legend could control all undead. Even the vamps. They feared us. But standing there with Micah's hand on my wrist, I felt the energy from the graves almost visible in the air. That energy was wanting the blood, wanting what would happen next.

Franklin's voice came strangled from the dark. 'Don't do it, Blake.'

I looked at him. He was rubbing his arms, as if he felt that press of power. Fox was looking at him, too. I hadn't outed Franklin, but if he wasn't careful tonight, he was going to do it himself.

'I won't do it,' I said.

Franklin's eyes were too wide. The last time I'd seen him had been over the bloody remains of a serial killer's victim. Did the newly dead talk to him? Was he able to see souls, too? Maybe it wasn't me he hadn't liked in New Mexico. Maybe it was his own untrained gifts.

I turned back to Micah. 'Your turn.'

I saw the tension in Micah's shoulders ease. He released my wrist, and I let the machete point at the ground. He smiled. 'Which arm do you want?'

I smiled and shook my head. 'You're right-handed, so left. Always better to use the nondominant hand for it.'

I looked back at Fox. 'If you could hold the jackets for Micah?'

Fox took them from him without a word. A very cooperative man, especially for FBI. They tended to argue, or at least question more. Micah took off his own suit jacket and laid it on top of the growing pile in Fox's arms.

Micah's shirt had French cuffs, which meant he had to undo a cuff link before he could roll up his left sleeve. He put the cuff link in his pants pocket.

'What are you doing, Marshal Blake?' the judge asked.

'I'm going to use Mr Callahan's blood to walk the circle.'

'Use his blood?' This was from Beck, the court reporter, and her voice was several octaves higher than when she'd said hello.

The judge looked at her as if she'd done something unforgivable. She apologized to him, but her fingers never stopped typing on her little machine. I think she'd actually taken down her own surprised comment.

I wondered if the dirty look from the judge got recorded, or if only out-loud sounds counted.

'My understanding is that if you were going to use the chicken, you would behead it,' the judge said in his deep courtroom voice.

'That's right.'

'I assume you aren't going to behead Mr Callahan.' He made it sort of light, almost joking, but I think that his prejudice was showing. I mean, if you'll raise the dead, what other evil are you capable of? Maybe even human sacrifice?

I didn't take it personally. He'd been polite about it; maybe I was just being overly sensitive. 'I'll make a small cut on his arm, smear the blade with the blood, and walk the circle. I may have him walk beside me, so I can renew the blood from the wound as we move around the circle, but that's all.'

The judge smiled. 'I thought we should be clear, Marshal.'

'Clear is good, your honor.' I left it at that. The nights when I would have gotten insulted because people hinted that all animators did human sacrifice were past. People were afraid of what I did. It made them believe the worst. The price of doing business was that people thought you did awful, immoral things.

I'd cut other people before, used their blood to help me or combine with mine, but I'd never held their hand while I did it. I stood on

Micah's left side and interlaced the fingers of our left hands together so that our palms touched. I stretched his arm out and laid the blade's edge against the smooth, untouched skin of his arm.

The underside of my left arm looked like Dr Frankenstein had been at me. Micah's was smooth and perfect, untouched. I didn't want to change that.

'I'll heal,' he said softly. 'It's not silver.'

He was right, but . . . I simply did not want to hurt him.

'Is there a problem, Marshal?' the judge asked.

'No,' I said, 'no problem.'

'Then can we move things along? It's not getting any warmer out here.'

I turned to look at him. He was huddled in his long coat. I glanced down at my own bare arms, not even a goose bump in sight. I gazed up at Micah, in his shirtsleeves. Being a shapeshifter, he wasn't really a good judge of how cold it was, or how warm. I took a moment to glance at everybody. Most of them were buttoned up, some with hands in pockets like the judge. There were only three people who had their coats open, and, even as I watched, Fox began to shrug out of his own trench coat. The other two people were Salvia and Franklin. Franklin I'd expected, but not Salvia. If he was that sensitive, it could explain his fear. Nothing like a little psychic ability to make you not want to be around a major ritual. I might raise the dead on a regular basis, but magically it's a big deal to breathe life into the dead. Even temporarily.

'Marshal Blake,' the judge said, 'I'll ask one more time. Is there a problem?'

I settled my gaze back on him. 'You want to open a vein for me, Judge?'

He looked startled. 'No, no, I do not.'

'Then don't rush me when I've got someone else's arm under my blade.'

Fox and Franklin both made noises. Fox seemed to be turning a laugh into a cough. Franklin was shaking his head, but not like he was unhappy with me.

The court reporter's fingers never faltered. She recorded his impatience and my angry answer. She, apparently, was going to record everything. I wondered if she'd tried to record the cough and the inarticulate noise from the agents. I should probably watch what I said, but I doubted I would. I mean, I could try, but watching what I said was usually a losing battle. Maybe I'd feel more polite after the power circle went up. Maybe.

Micah touched my face with his free hand, made me look at him. He gave me that peaceful smile. 'Just do it, Anita.'

I laid the blade edge against that smooth skin and whispered, 'If it were done when 'tis done, 'twere well it were done quickly . . .'

'Are you quoting *Macbeth*?'

'Yes.' And I cut him.

# 11

THE BLOOD LOOKED black in the moonlight. Micah was utterly silent as his blood eased from the cut, and I moved the blade so that it could catch the heavy drip of his blood. So calm. Calm about this as he was calm about nearly everything, as if nothing could move him from the center of himself. As I learned more of what his life had been like, I knew that this still-water calm had been hard won. My calmness was the calmness of metal, but he was water. He was the still forest pool. Throw a stone in, and once the ripples fade, it's as it was. Throw a stone at metal and it leaves a dent. There were nights when I felt like I was covered in dings and dents. Holding Micah's hand, with his blood welling onto the cool gleam of my blade, I could feel the echo of that watery calm.

The autumn night was suddenly scented with the sweet, metallic perfume of fresh blood. Once that smell had meant work: raising the dead or a crime scene. But thanks to my ties to Jean-Claude and Richard and the wereleopards, the scent of blood meant oh-so-much more.

Then I looked up from the blood and met Micah's eyes, those pale leopard eyes, and realized that I didn't need to look all the way to St Louis for why the blood smelled good.

His pulse began to beat against my palm like a second heartbeat. That heartbeat pushed the blood out of him faster than it should have, as if my power, or our power, called it. The cut wasn't that deep, but the blood poured over our hands in a hot wash.

'Oh, my God!' The only female voice, so that was the court reporter. Men cursed, and someone else was making sounds like he might lose his dinner. If this bothered them, then they'd never make it through the zombie part.

I let go of Micah's hand, and the moment I did, the blood flow slowed. Slowed to what it should have been. Something about our combined energies had made it flow faster, hotter. He watched me back away from him with the dripping machete. I started walking the circle, dripping his blood along the way, with my gaze still tied to his. There were no dead whispering in my head now. The night was too alive for that. I walked the circle suddenly painfully aware of how much I'd been missing in that nightscape. I could feel the wind against my skin in a way that I hadn't a second ago. There were so many scents, it was like being blind, and suddenly being given sight. Smell was something we humans didn't really use at all, not like this.

I knew there was something small and furry in the tree over the grave. Before I'd smelled only that dry autumnal scent of leaves. Now I could smell different leaves, different scents of the individual trees. I didn't know what each scent was, but I could suddenly pick out dozens of different trees, bushes. Even the ground underfoot was a wealth of scent. This wasn't even a good night for scent, too cool, but we could hunt. We could—

'Anita,' Micah said, his voice abrupt and startling.

It made me stumble and brought me back to myself. It was almost like waking from a dream. It had only been recently that everyone realized that some of my new abilities, though they came through vampire marks, made me more like a lycanthrope than a vamp. A new lycanthrope didn't always have the control you might want in public.

I was almost back to Micah. I'd nearly walked the complete circle, as if my body had gone on without me while my mind tried to cope with a thousand different kinds of sensory input. Moments like this gave me an entirely new sympathy with dogs that were nose-deaf. It wasn't that the ears didn't work but that the nose was working so much more that nothing mattered but the scent. The scent you were tracking. What was it, where was it, could we catch it, could we eat it?

'Anita?' Micah made it a question, as if he knew what I'd been sensing. Of course, it was his sense of smell I'd been borrowing. He did know.

My heart was in my throat, my pulse singing with that rush of adrenaline. I looked down at the ground and found I was only a few blood drops away from completing the circle.

But I hadn't concentrated at all. I'd walked circles with just naked steel and my will. Was the blood enough with me on automatic pilot? There was really only one way to find out. I let the blood drip from the machete and took those last few steps. I took my last step, but it was that last drop of Micah's blood that held power like the hot breath of some great beast. That power slid over me, over him, and out into the night, as that last drop of blood fell.

It had that feel that sometimes happens in emergencies where everything slows down, and the world becomes hard edge, like everything is carved of crystal. Painfully real, and full of sharp edges.

I realized in that crystalline moment that I had never used the blood of a shapeshifter to do a power circle, and the only time I'd used the blood of a vampire, the magic had gone horribly wrong. But that vampire had died to complete the circle, and Micah was alive. Not a sacrifice, only blood, but magically there wasn't as much difference between the two as we'd all like to believe. Cut yourself and it is a small death.

It was as if the power circle were a glass and power was poured into it, held in that small space. When I'd accidentally killed a vamp, the power had just been necromancy. This was warmer – it was like drowning in bathwater. So warm, hot, alive. The air was alive with power. It crawled over my skin, burned over me, so that I cried out.

Micah's cry echoed mine.

I turned through the heavy air and watched him collapse to his knees. He'd never been inside a completed power circle. Of course, I'd never been inside a circle when this kind of power went up. It was like some hybrid between the coldness of the grave and the heat of the lycanthrope. That's what had been wrong from the moment I'd hit the cemetery. That's why the dead had seemed more active than they should have been. Yes, my necromancy was getting stronger, but it was my tie to Micah that had made the dead whisper across my skin, Micah's nearness that had made the dead seem more 'alive' than they had ever been.

Now we were drowning in that living power. The air inside the circle was growing heavier, thicker, more solid, as if soon it wouldn't be air at all but something plastic and unbreathable. I had to fight to inhale, as if the air were crushing me. I fell to my knees on top of the grave and suddenly knew what to do with all that power.

I plunged my hands into the soft, turned earth, and I called Emmett Leroy Rose from the grave. I tried to shout his name, but the air was too thick. I whispered his name, the way you whisper a lover's name in the dark. But it was enough, that whisper of name.

The ground shivered underneath me like the hide of a horse when a fly lands on it. I felt Emmett below me. Felt his rotting body in its coffin, inside the metal of its burial vault. Trapped underneath more than six feet of earth, and none of it mattered. I called him, and he came.

He came to me like a swimmer rising up, up through deep, black water. He reached for me. I plunged my hands into that shifting dirt. Always before I had stood on the grave but never in it. I had never laid my bare skin into the grave while the ground was doing things that ground was never meant to do.

I knew I was touching earth, but it didn't feel like dirt. It felt warmer, more like very thick liquid, and yet that wasn't it either. It was as if the earth under my hands had become part liquid and part air, so that my hands reached impossibly down and through that solid-seeming earth until fingers brushed mine. I grabbed at those fingers the way you'd grab at a drowning victim.

Hands grasped mine with that same desperate strength, as if they'd thought they were lost and my touch was the only solid thing in a liquid world.

I pulled my hands out of that sucking, liquid, airy earth, but something pushed as I pulled. Some power, some magic, something pushed as I pulled the zombie from the grave.

The zombie spilled upward out of the grave in a shuddering burst of dirt and energy. Some zombies crawl out, but some, most of mine lately, are just suddenly standing on the grave. This one was standing, his fingers still intertwined with mine. There was no pulse to his skin, no beat of life, but when he stared down at me, there was something in his dark eyes, something more than there should have been.

There was intelligence and a force of personality that shouldn't have been there until I put blood on his mouth. The dead do not speak without help from the living, one way or the other.

He was tall and broad, his skin the color of good, sweet chocolate. He smiled down at me in a way that no zombie should have done without first tasting blood.

I stared down at my hands still grasping his and realized that my hands had been covered in Micah's blood when I plunged them into the dirt. Had that done it? Had that been enough?

Voices were speaking, gasping, exclaiming, but it was all distant and less real than the dead man who held my hands. I knew he'd be very alive, because there'd been so much power. But even to me, the only thing he lacked was a pulse. Even by my standards it was good work.

'Emmett Leroy Rose, can you speak?' I asked.

Salvia interrupted me. 'Marshal, this is highly irregular. We were not ready for you to raise Mr Rose from the grave.'

'We were ready,' Laban said, 'because the rest of us want to go home before dawn.'

Rose's head turned slowly toward Salvia's voice, and his first words were 'Arthur, is that you?'

Salvia's protests stopped in midsyllable. His eyes were wide enough to flash their whites. 'Should it be able to do that? Should it recognize people?'

'Yes,' I said, 'sometimes they can.'

Rose dropped my hands, and I let him. He moved toward Salvia's side of the circle. 'Why, Arthur? Why did you order Jimmy to put the boy's body in my car?'

'I don't know what this thing's talking about. I didn't do anything. He was a pedophile. None of us knew it.' But Salvia's words were a little too fast. I knew now why he'd been trying to delay the zombie-raising. Guilt.

Rose stepped forward, a little slow, a little uncertain, as if he looked more alive than he felt. 'Me, a pedophile? You bastard. You knew that George's son was a fucking child molester. You knew, and you helped cover for him. You helped get him his kiddies, until he got too rough and killed that last one.'

'You've done something to his mind, Marshal. He's babbling.'

'No, Mr Salvia, the dead don't lie. They tell the absolute truth as they know it.'

Micah came to stand beside me, holding his wounded arm up and pressing on it. He seemed as fascinated with the walking dead man as the rest of them. He might never have seen a zombie before, but then he wasn't really seeing one now, not the kind most people call from the grave anyway.

Rose had come to the edge of the circle. 'The moment you had Jimmy put the boy in my car, I was dead, Arthur. You might as well have put a bullet in me.' He tried to take another step toward Salvia. The circle held, but I felt him push against it. That shouldn't have been possible. No matter how good the zombie, the circle should have been sacrosanct, inviolate. Something was wrong.

I called out, 'Fox, your report said he died of natural causes.'

Fox came to stand a little closer to the circle but not closer to Rose, as if he found the dead man a little unnerving. 'He did. Heart attack. Not poison, or anything like that. A heart attack.'

'You swear it,' I said.

'I swear,' he said.

'Why put Georgie's last victim in my car, Arthur?' Rose continued. 'What the fuck did I ever do to you? I had a wife and kids, and you took me away from them the moment that body went in my car.'

'Oh, shit,' I whispered.

'What's wrong?' Micah asked.

'He blames Salvia for his death. Not the pedophile that hurt the kid.' My stomach clenched tight, and I started to pray, *Please don't let this go bad*.

Fox said, 'You'd think he'd blame the guy who put the body in his car.'

'He blames Salvia because that's who ordered it done,' I said.

'You're scared,' Micah said softly. 'Why?'

I spoke to Fox, trying to keep my voice low and not attract the zombie's attention. 'A murdered zombie always does one thing first and foremost: it kills its murderer. Until its murderer is dead, no one can control it. Not even me.'

Fox gave me wide eyes on the other side of the circle. Franklin had moved well back from the circle, from the zombie, from me. Fox whispered, 'Rose wasn't murdered. He died of a heart attack.'

'I'm not sure he sees it that way,' I whispered back.

Rose screamed, 'Why, Arthur!' And he tried to walk out of the circle. It gave, gave like a piece of plastic stretched tight by a pushing hand.

I yelled, 'Emmett Leroy Rose, I command you to stay.' But the moment I had to yell anything, I knew we were in trouble.

Rose kept trying to move forward, and the circle was no longer a wall. It was folding outward – I could feel it. I threw my will and power not into the zombie but into the circle. I yelled, 'NO!' and threw that *no*, that refusal, into the circle. It helped. It was as if the circle took a breath that it had needed. But I'd never tried to do anything like this before. I didn't know how long it would hold the dead man.

The dead man turned to me and said, 'Let me out.'

'I can't,' I said.

'He killed me.'

'No, he didn't. If he'd really killed you, you'd be outside this circle right now. If you were the righteously murdered, nothing I could do would hold you.'

'Righteously murdered.' And he gave a laugh so bitter that it hurt to hear it. 'Righteous. No, not righteous. I took money I knew was dirty. I told myself that as long as I didn't do any of the illegal stuff, it was okay. But it wasn't. It wasn't okay.' He glanced back toward the circle, but then his eyes were all for Salvia. 'I may not have been a righteous man, but I did not know what Georgie was doing to those kids. I swear to God, I didn't know. And you had the body put in my car. Did you see the boy before Jimmy moved him, Arthur? Did you see what Georgie had done to him? He ripped him open. Ripped him open!'

And he hit the circle, hit it with his hands like he was trying to reach through it, and it gave. I felt it begin to tear like paper.

I screamed, 'No! This circle is mine! Within the limits of this circle of power I command. *I* command, not you, and I say no, no, Emmett Leroy Rose, you shall not pass this circle.'

Rose staggered back from the circle. 'Let me out!'

I screamed, 'No! Fox, get Salvia out of here!' Then something hit me in the arm. Hit me so hard that it spun me around. I fell to all fours. I couldn't feel my arm, but I was bleeding. I had a second to think, *Oh, I've been shot*, before Micah moved past me, standing in front of me. Standing between me and where the shot had come from. He was pointing. I heard the second bullet hit the gravestone behind me, a sharp ping of sound.

Salvia was screaming, 'Don't shoot her! Don't shoot her, you idiot. The zombie is up – don't shoot her now. It won't do any good.'

I crawled around the tombstone, putting it between me and the shooter. My arm worked enough to help me scramble across the ground. The feeling was even returning to it, which was good, because that meant I wasn't hurt too badly.

The downside was that I was hurt, and now my body knew it. The bullet had only grazed me, but whatever grazed me had been of a big enough caliber that I could see things in my arm that were never meant to be visible to the naked eye. I hate seeing my own muscle and ligaments. It means the shit has hit the fan, and I'm standing downwind.

Gunshots were sounding, this time going away from us and out into the night. The FBI were returning fire. Good for them. I used my left hand to get my right one moving, so I could get my gun out. I wasn't as good left-handed, but it was better than nothing.

I yelled, 'Micah!' With bullets flying, I wanted him with me.

But it wasn't Micah who loomed over me. Rose bent his large dark shape over me, reaching for me. I ordered him, 'Don't.'

'Let me out,' he said.

'No,' I said. I fired into him, though I knew better than anyone there that bullets wouldn't do a damn thing.

He was a zombie; they didn't feel pain. He grabbed me and lifted me off the ground as I fired point-blank into his chest. His body rocked with the impact, but that was all.

Claws blossomed through his throat a moment before I realized Micah was on the zombie's back, only his hands in half-clawed form, like only the really powerful shapeshifters could do. But you can't kill the dead.

Rose smashed me down with everything that his more-than-human body had in it. I hit the gravestone. The inside of my head was suddenly filled with white starbursts, then the starbursts were crimson, and the inside of my head spilled to velvet dark, and that was all she wrote. The velvet dark, and nothing.

# 12

I WOKE STARING up at a white ceiling. Micah was standing by the bedside, smiling down at me. Bedside? My left arm was taped down to a little board and there were needles and tubes going into it. My right arm was bandaged like a mummy. Someone had left a florist shop in one corner near the window, complete with those silly character Mylar balloons.

'How long?' I asked, and my voice sounded funny. My throat felt like sandpaper.

'Forty-eight hours.' He found one of those cups with the little bendy straws and brought it to me. The water tasted stale and metallic in a none-too-tasty sort of way, but my throat felt better.

The door opened, and a doctor, a nurse, and Nathaniel came through the door. The doctor and nurse I'd expected. I reached for Nathaniel and found that my right arm actually did work.

He gave me that wonderful smile, but it didn't reach his eyes. They looked haunted, and I knew that I'd put that particular look there. Me, getting hurt.

The doctor's name was Nelson, and the nurse was Debbie. Nurse Debbie, like she didn't have a last name, but I didn't protest. If it didn't bother her, I guess it didn't bother me.

Dr Nelson was short and roundish, with most of his dark hair receding around a face that looked too young for either the hairline or the weight. 'It's good to see you awake, Marshal.' And he laughed, as if that amused him. 'Sorry, but every time I say it, I keep thinking of *Gunsmoke*, my dad's favorite show.'

'Glad I could be amusing,' I said, and I had to clear my throat again.

Micah gave me some more water, and Nathaniel moved up on the other side of him. He touched the side of my face, and even the brush of his fingertips made me feel better.

Nurse Debbie's eyes flicked to the two men, and then her face had that pleasant professional look again.

'First, you're going to be fine,' Nelson said. He had the nurse hold my arm up while he began to cut away the bandages.

'Good to hear it,' I said in a voice that was beginning to sound more like me.

'Second, I have no idea why. You took a very large caliber rifle round to your right arm. There should be muscle damage, but there isn't.' He slid the bandages off, handing them to the nurse to dispose of. He took my hand in his and raised my arm so I could see it. There was a slick, pink scar on the side of my arm, about an inch and a half wide at its widest. 'It's been only forty-eight hours, Marshal. Care to explain how you're healing this fast?'

I gave him nice blank eyes.

He sighed and lowered my arm to the bed. He got out one of those little flashlights and began to shine it in my eyes. 'Any pain?'

'No,' I said.

He made me follow his fingers back and forth; he even made me look up and down. 'Your head connected with a marble tombstone, so the FBI tells me. Our tests showed you had a concussion. Initially we thought your skull was cracked, and you were bleeding in places inside your head where you don't want to be bleeding.' His eyes were very serious as he studied my face. 'We ran a second set of tests before scheduling you for surgery, and what do you think, Marshal? No internal bleeding. Gone. We thought we'd read the first test wrong, but I've got the pictures to show what we saw that first night. There was a crack in your skull, and you were bleeding, but later that morning, it had stopped. In fact, the second set of tests shows the fracture healing. Healing like your arm is healing.' His serious expression intensified. 'You know, the only person I've ever seen heal damage like this was a lycanthrope.'

'Really,' I said, giving him my best blank face.

'Really,' he said, and looked at Micah. He had his sunglasses back on over his kitty-cat eyes, but something about the way Nelson looked at him said the doctor had probably seen Micah without the glasses. 'We had to type you for surgery. There are certain things we look at it in a blood test, just routine these days. Guess what we found?'

'No idea,' I said.

'Weird fucking shit,' he said.

I laughed. 'Should I be worried? I mean, are doctors supposed to say "weird fucking shit" to their patients?'

He shrugged, laughed, but it was too late to go back to the nice roly-poly doctor disguise. There was a very sharp mind in there, and someone who only did good bedside manner because he was supposed to.

Nurse Debbie moved, almost uneasily, beside him.

'You're not a lycanthrope, but you're a carrier, which is impossible. A person either has lycanthropy, or she doesn't. You're actually carrying around four different kinds. Wolf, leopard, lion, and one we can't even identify, all of which is impossible. You can't catch more than one kind of lycanthropy, because once you've got one, it makes you immune to the others.' He looked at me as if the look would be enough and I'd crack and confess.

I just blinked at him. I'd suspected the leopard and wolf, but the only time I'd been touched by a werelion had resulted in tiny wounds. They had been from Micah's old leader, Chimera, in lion-man form. He'd bled me, but it was unusual to catch feline-based lycanthropy from such small damage. Lucky fucking me.

'Did you hear me, Marshal? You're carrying four different kinds of lycanthropy.' He kept giving me his hard-as-nails look.

I kept blinking at him. If he thought his threatening doctor face was enough to get me talking, then he hadn't seen anything truly scary in his life. I just looked at him.

'Why do I think this isn't news to you?'

I shrugged, the tubes and needles pulling on my left arm. That hurt worse than anything else. 'I got attacked by some shapeshifters a few years back, but lucky me, I didn't catch anything.'

'Don't you get it, Blake? I'm telling you that you did catch it. It's floating around in your veins right now. But you aren't a lycanthrope, are you?'

I shook my head. 'No.'

'Why aren't you?'

I shrugged again. 'Honestly, Doc, I don't know.'

'Well, if we could figure out how to put this into other people and not make them shifters, we could make people pretty much indestructible.'

'I'd tell you how it works if I knew.'

He stared down at me with that hard look again. 'Why don't I believe that?'

I smiled. 'If I could tell you something that would help millions of people, I would. But I think I'm sort of a metaphysical miracle, Doc.'

'I read the papers. I watch the news,' he said. 'I know you're the human servant of the St Louis Master of the City. Is that what makes this kind of healing possible?'

'I honestly don't know, Doc. Not for certain.'

'Does being a vampire's human servant help you heal like this?'

'It helps me be harder to hurt,' I said.

'And the lycanthropy?'

'That I can't answer, Doc.'

'Can't, or won't?'

'Can't,' I said.

He made an impatient sound. 'Fine. You're fit, well enough to go home. I'll get the paperwork started.' He moved toward the door. He turned with his hand on the door. 'If you ever figure out how the healing works, I'd love to know.'

'If it's something that can be duplicated, I'll share,' I said.

He left shaking his head.

I looked at the nurse, and she wouldn't meet my eyes.

'I need to take out the IVs.' Debbie hesitated, then said, 'A little privacy, maybe?' She said it like she wasn't certain. Why was she so nervous?

Micah and Nathaniel glanced at me. I shrugged again. Nathaniel smiled at me, and the smile had a touch of mischief in it. Micah shook his head, smiling as well, and they left.

Debbie was as gentle as she could be. It actually hurt more for the tape to come off than the needle. When she had my arm free of all the paraphernalia, she said in an almost embarrassed voice, 'Which one of them is your boyfriend?'

'You mean, Micah and Nathaniel?'

'Yes,' she said.

'Both of them are.'

She gave me a look. 'Mr Callahan told you to say that, didn't he? They've been incorrigible, teasing all of us.'

'Teasing all of you?' I made it a question.

'Saying that you lived with both of them, then trying to make us guess which of them is your boyfriend.' She actually blushed. 'There's a betting pool, so whichever of us was here when you first woke had to ask.'

'A betting pool for what?'

'Which one is your boyfriend. Some people even bet that they both were. Some even said neither.' She looked almost painfully embarrassed. 'I have to ask. I'm sorry.'

'I live with both of them,' I said.

She gave me that look again, like she didn't believe me.

'Honest, cross my heart and hope to – well, you know.'

She shook her head. 'And what is Mr Graison's job?'

I had to smile. 'He s a stripper.'

She put her hands on her hips and almost stamped her foot at me. 'It can't all be true.'

The door opened behind her. It was my men and Special Agent Fox. The nurse threw them both a look, then hurried out.

'What have you been telling the nurses while I've been lying here?'

'The nurses were just trying to be friendly at first,' Micah said, 'but when we answered their questions truthfully, they didn't believe us.'

'No one lives with two men,' Nathaniel said, mimicking someone's voice that I didn't remember hearing. 'And federal marshals don't live with strippers.'

'Once we knew you were going to be all right, Nathaniel teased them a little,' Micah said.

Fox laughed. 'A little.'

I held my left hand out to Nathaniel, and he took it with a smile. 'You mad?' he asked.

'No. It was the crack about federal marshals not living with strippers, wasn't it?' I said.

He shrugged. 'Maybe.'

'The nursing staff seemed more interested in your boyfriends than in you,' Fox said.

'Well,' I said, 'it's hard to compete when the guys are this cute.'

Micah came around and took my other hand. He ran his finger over the new scar. 'You've finally got one on your right arm.'

I sighed. 'My only unscarred arm. Damn.'

Fox said, 'I come all the way down here to tell you what you missed, and I don't think you give a damn.'

I smiled at Fox. 'Truthfully, I'm just glad to be alive. When I hit that marble, I knew I was hurt.'

His face went very serious. 'Yeah, you were hurt. We all

thought . . .' He waved it away. 'It doesn't matter what we thought. When you went down, the zombie attacked Salvia. We couldn't stop him. Not to mention he had a shooter in the cemetery.'

'I remember Salvia saying something about not shooting me now. That the zombie was up and it wouldn't help anything.'

'He wasn't delaying to be irritating. He was delaying to give the new hit man time to get to the cemetery. The idea was that with you dead or badly injured, they'd have more time to think of a plan C.'

'Plan C? What happened to plan A and B?'

Micah began to rub his thumb over my knuckles in small circles. Nathaniel pressed my hand against his chest. Whatever I was about to hear, I wasn't going to like it.

Fox told me, 'After you and Micah went to a different hotel, a salesman checked into the room that we'd reserved for Marshal Kirkland. The salesman was shot in his room. Then the killer put a "Do Not Disturb" sign on the door and probably took a plane to a different country. A very clean, very professional hit. Micah wanting a romantic weekend may have saved your lives.'

Micah kept stroking my hand, and Nathaniel kept holding on, as if there was more to come.

'Salvia must have gotten the shock of his life when he got word that Marshal Anita Blake was coming to raise the zombie. He scrambled around and hired a not-so-clean, not-so-professional hit.'

'But it almost worked,' Micah said.

'I finally remembered where I knew Salvia's name from,' I said. 'He's a lawyer for some old-fashioned mob, real hard-core Italian.'

Fox nodded.

'If I understood what Salvia and Rose were arguing about, then Georgie is the son of the head of that family. He's a pedophile, and Salvia and others had helped cover it up.'

'Jesus, Mary, and Joseph, Fox, didn't you think the son's family would try to stop the testimony?'

'Old-fashioned mob does not attack federal officers. It's bad for business,' Fox said.

'Old-fashioned is the operative phrase here, Fox. If what's left of the Italian mob found out one of their own had hidden a violent pedophile, even his own son, the Feds would be the least of Georgie boy's family's worries. The other mobsters would clean house on their own long before subpoenas and trial dates caught up with them.'

'In retrospect, you're right,' he said.

'In retrospect, you could have gotten Anita killed,' Micah said.

Fox took in a lot of air and let it out slow. 'You're right, Micah. I almost fucked up your life again.'

I frowned at them both. 'What are you guys talking about now?'

'When Micah was in a bed like you are now, I told him that I had wanted to put out an alert two days before he and his uncle and cousin went hunting. I wanted to put out an alert to keep the hunters out of the woods, but I wasn't the agent in charge. Hell, I was just the Indian who got lucky, because some of the first kills were on Indian land. I was outvoted, and I liked my career more than I liked the idea of saving lives. I told Micah that I owed him for that.' Fox looked at all of us. 'And now I owe him again, because we should have taken more precautions for your safety.'

I looked at him. 'I didn't think the FBI was allowed to admit they were wrong.'

He smiled, but not like he was entirely happy. 'If you tell anyone, I'll deny it.'

I raised Micah's hand to my lips and kissed him. It took some of the anger out of his face. I kissed Nathaniel's hand too, and held them close. 'I'm just glad to be alive, Agent Fox.'

He nodded. 'I'm glad, too.' Then he headed for the door.

When the door closed behind him, Micah let out a breath I hadn't realized he'd been holding. 'Every time I see that man, something bad happens in my life.'

I tugged on his hand so he'd look at me. 'What happened to the zombie?'

He gave a frown that showed even around the sunglasses. 'I know Salvia tried to kill you, but you ask first about the zombie?'

'Salvia's dead,' I said.

He nodded. 'I thought you were unconscious by then.'

'I was, but once I wasn't there to help with the zombie, it tore him apart, right?'

'Yes,' he said.

'He deserved to die,' Nathaniel said, and there was a look in his face, so fierce, so pitiless, that it almost scared me. I'd seen a lot of looks on his face, but never one so cold.

'They shot the zombie, they cut at him, but he tore Salvia up.'

'Did they get the shooter?'

'They got him,' Micah said. 'He's dead, too.'

'Did they get Rose's testimony?' I asked.

He lowered his glasses enough to give me the full force of his chartreuse eyes. The look was eloquent. Nathaniel laughed.

Micah looked from one to the other of us, then finally back at me. 'Do you seriously think that with you dying, Salvia dead, and an assassin gunned down, they were going to question the zombie?'

'Well, why not? They had to wait for the ambulance, right?'

Micah shook his head. Nathaniel laughed again and leaned over to plant a kiss on my forehead. He looked at Micah. 'If she'd been there and awake, she'd have questioned the zombie,' he said.

'Fine, if they didn't question Rose, what happened to him? Without me they couldn't put him back in the grave.'

'Larry flew up.'

Nathaniel pointed to the huge bunch of Mylar balloons. 'Those are from Larry and Tammy.'

I realized then what the death of the salesman would have meant for Larry. It wouldn't have been some salesman in the wrong place at the wrong time; it would have been Marshal Larry Kirkland dead.

'He was really upset, Anita. He blamed himself.'

'Not his fault.' I squeezed Micah's hand. 'Though thanks for the romantic hotel room. Who knew it would be a lifesaver?'

'Let's get you dressed,' he said, 'and go home.'

Nathaniel kissed my hand and started finding my clothes, wherever the nurses had hidden them. Micah went for the door to see if Dr Nelson needed any help getting me signed out. He stopped in the doorway and said, 'You scared the hell out of me. Don't do it again.'

'I'll do my best,' I said.

He leaned his forehead against the door edge for a moment, then he looked at me. 'I love you.'

I had a lump in my throat that hadn't been there a second before. 'I love you, too.'

Nathaniel was suddenly airborne. I had a second to make that little-girl *eep* sound, and then he landed around me on all fours, perfectly. 'Does anything hurt?'

'No,' I said, breathless and laughing.

'Good,' he said, and he lay down on top of me, pressing his body against me hard enough that I had to either spread my legs for him or risk bruising tender bits on both of us. He lay above the sheets, both of us fully clothed, but he was suddenly above me, and the look in his eyes was more intimate than nakedness could have made it. Because what was in his eyes was emotion too real for lust, too real for anything but a very different four-letter word.

He kissed me. He kissed me as if my mouth were air, food, and water, and he'd been dying without the taste of it. That's when Nurse Debbie and the other members of her betting pool came in. They screamed like freshmen at their first frat party. And I'd thought nurses were jaded.

# STRANGE CANDY

*This one is for all those editors who took a chance on me when I was an unknown. To everyone who bought my stories when putting my name on the front of their magazine, or in their anthology, didn't guarantee them more sales. Thanks for taking a chance on me.*

# ACKNOWLEDGMENTS

To my husband, Jonathon, who knew me first through my stories, and now knows me better than anyone. He loves me still – the dark and light of me. To Darla and her husband, Jack, who were two of the four people who used to show up at my signings, when no one knew who I was. To Andrew, best man at our wedding, and the fourth of that long-ago four that kept me company at all those empty signings. You guys can truly say you knew me when, and the fact that you all still know me now is even better.

This one is also for the other readers who first discovered me not through the Anita Blake series, or the Meredith Gentry series, but through my short stories. Thanks also to all those fans who have asked over the years when am I going to do the sequel to *Nightseer*. Here, at least, are stories set in the same world – not the same characters, sorry about that, but the world and the magic system are here. I hope you enjoy seeing other parts of Keleios's world.

Thanks to Richard Nichols, who for the first time helped edit. Also, as I write this, he is turning thirty. Happy Birthday, Richard. Mark and Sarah Sumner, who were my next-door neighbors when many of these stories were written. Good neighbors, good friends. Rett MacPherson, one of the bravest women I know. Marella Sands, I look forward to your new world finding its footing and its fans. Deborah Millitello, who was there, almost from the beginning, and saw most of these stories in some rough form or another. Thanks for the encouragement. There were days when your support kept me from giving up. Sharon Shinn, for gripe sessions and an understanding ear. Tom Drennan, a quiet, comforting presence at all the meetings of the Alternate Historians. To Jannie Lee Simner, who had the audacity to move all the way to Arizona a few years back and abandon us all. Congrats on all your books. N. L. Drew, who also got to see some of these stories in rougher form. Robert K. Sheaf, who was with us early, and now is with us no longer. Are you writing stories up in Heaven, Bob? For you, and your so-firm faith, God bless. For my faith, blessed be.

# CONTENTS

# INTRODUCTION

Welcome to the parts of my imagination that don't get much play at book length. Some people see short stories as a way to further their book career. The last story, 'The Girl Who Was Infatuated with Death,' was commissioned by my publisher for a collection of pieces with other of their supernatural writers. So I guess that one was designed to further my reading audience and those of the other writers with me in the anthology. But as for the rest of the stories, these are ideas I was compelled to write by nothing but my sometime peculiar imagination and a desire to play. Short stories for me are like vacations. You know, those trips you take to new places to do things you don't normally get to do in your work-a-day life. These stories, with a few exceptions, are worlds where most of you have never been with me. Several of these are set in the same world as my first book, *Nightseer*. So for those of you who keep writing in, or asking at signings, when will I finish that series, here are at least a few more pieces of that world – though with different characters and countries. I thought once I would write only heroic fantasy like a mix of Tolkien and Robert E. Howard. But the bottom fell out of the heroic fantasy market and I was left scrambling to find a vision that the publishers would buy. I had a few stories that were different, set in modern day with fantastic elements. One was the first Anita Blake short story, 'Those Who Seek Forgiveness.' Another was 'The Edge of the Sea' – which is still an idea that intrigues me. You have also my only completed science fiction story, 'Here Be Dragons.' You also get the only story I've ever written in Anita's world that has none of the main characters in it, 'Selling Houses.'

I have dozens of other short story ideas, and most of them are very unlike Anita and Merry's adventures. My unwritten short ideas are vacations of the mind. The last thing you want to do on vacation is your normal job. So how does a girl get to a point where normal is vampire hunting, fairie princesses and private detectives, and some of the most erotic relationships on paper? Just lucky, I guess.

# THOSE WHO SEEK FORGIVENESS

*This is the first time Anita ever walked onto paper for me. The cemetery in this story is based on the cemetery where my mother is buried. It was a place I knew very well, because my grandmother, who raised me, took me often. I guess it was inevitable that I would write about the dead; my childhood was haunted by death. Not real ghosts, but the ghosts of memory and loss. Anita raises the dead in this story, which was all I had planned on her doing. The idea of her being a legal vampire executioner actually didn't hit my radar until quite late in trying to write the first book. Originally this story represented what I thought Anita would do: raise zombies. How different things would have been if I'd stuck to my original plan. No Jean-Claude, no Richard, not much of anybody except Anita. What a bleak world it would have been, with just Anita and me in it.*

'DEATH IS A very serious matter, Mrs Fiske. People who go through it are never the same.'

The woman leaned forward, cradling her face in her hands. Her slim shoulders shook quietly for a few minutes. I passed another box of tissues her way. She groped for them blindly and then looked up. 'I know you can't bring him back, exactly.'

She wiped at two tears, which escaped and rolled down flawless cheekbones. The purse she clutched so tightly was reptile, at least two hundred dollars. Her accessories – lapel pin, high heels, hat, and gloves – were all black as her purse. Her suit was gray. Neither color suited her, but they emphasized her pale skin and hollow eyes. She was the sort of woman that made me feel too short, too dark, and gave me the strange desire to lose ten more pounds. If she hadn't been so genuinely grief-stricken, I could have disliked her.

'I have to talk to Arthur. That's my husband . . . was my husband.' She took a deep breath and tried again. 'Arthur died suddenly. A massive coronary.' She blew delicately into a tissue. 'His family did have a history of heart disease, but he always took such good care of himself.' She finished with a watery hiccup. 'I want to say goodbye to him, Miss Blake.'

I smiled reassuringly. 'We all have things left unsaid when death comes suddenly. But it isn't always best to raise the dead and say it.'

Her blue eyes stared intently through a film of tears. I was going to discourage her as I discourage every one of my clients, but this one would do it. There was a certain set to the eyes that said *serious*.

'There are certain limitations to the process.' My boss didn't allow us to show slides or pictures or give graphic descriptions, but we were supposed to tell the truth. One good picture of a decaying zombie would have sent most of my clients screaming.

'Limitations?'

'Yes, we can bring him back. You came to us promptly. That helps. He's been buried only three days. But as a zombie your husband will only have limited use of his body and mind. And as the days go by, that will grow worse, not better.'

She stood up very straight, tears drying on her face. 'I was hoping you could bring him back as a vampire.'

I kept my face carefully blank. 'Vampires are illegal, Mrs Fiske.'

'A friend told me that . . . you could get that done here.' She finished in a rush, searching my face.

I smiled my best professional smile. 'We do not do vampires. And even if we did, you can't make an ordinary corpse into a vampire.'

'Ordinary?'

Very few people who came to us had even a remote idea of how rare vampires were, or why. 'The deceased would have to have been bitten by a werewolf, vampire, or other supernatural creature, while alive. Being buried in unconsecrated ground would help. Your husband, Arthur, was never bitten by a vampire while alive, was he?'

'No,' she half laughed, 'he was bitten by my Yorkshire terrier once.'

I smiled, encouraging her turn of spirits. 'That won't quite do it. Your husband can come back as a zombie or not at all.'

'I'll take it,' she said quietly, all serious and very still.

'I will warn you that most families find it advisable to lay the zombie to rest after a time.'

'Why?'

Why? I saw the happy family embracing their lost loved one. I saw the family sick, horrified, bringing the decaying corpse to be put down. The smiling relative reduced to a shambling horror.

'What exactly do you want Arthur to do when he arises?'

She looked down and shredded another tissue. 'I want to say goodbye to him.'

'Yes, Mrs Fiske, but what do you want him to do?'

She was silent for several minutes. I decided to prompt her. 'For instance, a woman came in wanting her husband raised so he could take out life insurance. I told her most insurance companies won't insure the walking dead.' She grinned at that. 'And that is what Arthur will come back as – the walking dead.'

Her smile faltered, and tears came again. 'I want Arthur to forgive me.' She hid her face in her hands and sobbed. 'I had an affair for several months. He found out, had a heart attack, and died.' She seemed to gain strength from the words, and the tears slowed. 'You see that I have to talk to him one last time. I have to tell him I love him, only him. I want Arthur to forgive me. Can he do that as a . . . zombie?'

'I've found that the dead are very forgiving of the living, when they die of natural causes. Your husband will have ample brain-power to speak. He will be himself at first. As the days progress, he will lose memory. He will begin to decay, first mentally, then phys-ically.'

'Decay?'

'Yes, slowly, but after all, he is dead.'

The relatives didn't really believe that a fresh zombie wasn't alive. Knowing intellectually that someone smiling and talking is the walk-ing dead is one thing. Emotionally, it is very different. But they believed as time passed and as he or she began to look like a walking corpse.

'It's temporary then?'

'Not exactly.' I came from behind the desk and sat next to her. 'He could stay a zombie possibly forever. But his physical and mental state would deteriorate until he was not much better than an automa-ton in tattered flesh.'

'Tattered . . . flesh,' she whispered.

I touched her hand. 'I know it's a hard choice, but that is the reality.' *Tattered flesh* didn't really touch the white sheen of bone through rotting flesh, but it was a term our boss allowed.

She gripped my hand and smiled. 'Thank you for telling me the truth. I still want to bring Arthur back. Even if it's just long enough to say a few words.'

So she was going to do it, as I had known she would. 'So you don't want him for weeks, or days, only long enough to talk.'

'I think so.'

'I don't mean to rush you, Mrs Fiske, but I need to know before we set up an appointment. You see, it takes more time and energy to raise and then lay to rest, one right after another.' If she laid and raised quickly enough, Mrs Fiske might be able to remember Arthur at his best.

'Oh, of course. If possible I would like to talk for several hours.'

'Then it's best if you take him home for at least the evening. We can schedule putting him back for tomorrow night.' I would push for a quick laying to rest. I didn't think Mrs Fiske could take watching her husband rot before her eyes.

'That sounds good.' She took a deep breath. I knew what she was going to say. She looked so brave and resolute. 'I want to be there when you bring him back.'

'Your presence is required, Mrs Fiske. You see, a zombie has no real will of its own. Your husband should be able to think on his own at first, but as time wears on, the zombie finds it very difficult to decide things. The person, or persons, who raised it will have control over it.'

'You and I?'

'Yes.'

She paled even more, her grip tightening.

'Mrs Fiske?' I got her a glass of water. 'Sip it slowly.' When she seemed better, I asked, 'Are you sure you're up to this tonight?'

'Is there anything I need to bring?'

'A suit of your husband's clothes would be nice. Maybe a favorite object, hat, trophy, to help him orient himself. The rest I'll supply.' I hesitated, because some of the color had crept into her face, but she needed to be prepared. 'There will be blood at the ceremony.'

'Blood.' Her voice was a breathy whisper.

'Chicken, I'll bring it. There will also be some ointment to spread over our faces and hands. It glows faintly and smells fairly strange, but not unpleasant.' Her next question would be the usual.

'What do we do with the blood?'

I gave the usual answer. 'We sprinkle some on the grave and some on us.'

She swallowed very carefully, looking slightly gray.

'You can back out now but not later. Once you've paid your deposit, it can't be refunded. And once the ceremony begins, to break the circle is very dangerous.'

She looked down, thinking. I liked that. Most who agreed right away were afraid later. The brave ones took time to answer. 'Yes.' She sounded very convinced. 'To make peace with Arthur, I can do it.'

'Good for you. How is tonight?'

'About midnight,' she added hopefully.

I smiled. Everyone thought midnight was the perfect time for raising the dead. All that was required was darkness. Some people did put a great deal of stock in certain phases of the moon, but I had never found it necessary. 'No, how about nine o'clock?'

'Nine?'

'If that will be all right. I have two other appointments tonight, and nine was left open.'

She smiled. 'That will be fine.' Her hand shook as she signed the check for half the fee, the other half to be delivered after the raising.

We shook hands, and she said, 'Call me Carla.'

'I'm Anita.'

'I'll see you at nine tonight at Wellington Cemetery.'

I continued for her, 'Between two large trees and across from the only hill.'

'Yes, thank you.' She flashed a watery smile and was gone.

I buzzed our receptionist area. 'Mary, I'm booked up for this week and won't be seeing any more clients, until at least next Tuesday.'

'I'll see to it, Anita.'

I leaned back in my chair and soaked up the silence. Three animations a night was my limit. Tonight they were all routine, or almost. I was bringing back my first research scientist. His three colleagues couldn't figure out his notes, and their deadline, or rather grant, was running close. So dear Dr Richard Norris was coming back from the dead to help them out. They were scheduled for midnight.

At three this next morning I would meet the widowed Mrs Stiener. She wanted her husband to clear up some nasty details with his will.

Being an animator meant very little nightlife, no pun intended. Afternoons were spent interviewing clients and evenings raising the dead. Though we few were very popular at a certain kind of party – the sort where the host likes to brag about how many celebrities he knows, or worse yet, the kind who simply want to stare. I don't like being on display and refuse to go to parties unless forced. Our boss likes to keep us in the public eye to dispel rumors that we are witches or hobgoblins.

It's pretty pitiful at parties. All the animators huddled, talking shop like a bunch of doctors. But doctors don't get called *witch, monster, zombie queen.* Very few people remember to call us animators. For most, we are a dark joke. 'This is Anita. She makes zombies, and I don't mean the drink.' Then there would be laughter all around, and I would smile politely and know I'd be going home early.

Tonight there was no party to worry over, just work. Work was power, magic, a strange dark impulse to raise more than what you were paid for. Tonight would be cloudless, moonlit, and starred; I could feel it. We were different, drawn to the night, unafraid of death and its many forms, because we had a sympathy for it.

Tonight I would raise the dead.

Wellington Cemetery was new. All the tombstones were nearly the same size, square or rectangle, and set off into the night in near-perfect rows. Young trees and perfectly clipped evergreen shrubs lined the gravel driveway. The moon rode strong and high, bathing the scene clearly, if mysteriously, in silver and black. A handful of huge trees dotted the grounds. They looked out of place among all this newness. As Carla had said, only two of them grew close together.

The drive spilled into the open and encircled the hill. The mound of grass-covered earth was obviously man-made, so round, short, and domed. Three other drives centered on it. A short way down the west drive stood two large trees. As my car crunched over gravel, I could see someone dressed in white. A flare of orange was a match, and the reddish pinpoint of a cigarette sprang to life.

I stopped the car, blocking the drive, but few people on honest business visit cemeteries at night. Carla had beaten me here, very unusual. Most clients want to spend as little time as possible near the grave after dark. I walked over to her before unloading equipment.

There was a litter of burned-out cigarettes like stubby white bugs about her feet. She must have been here in the dark for hours waiting to raise a zombie. She either was punishing herself or enjoyed the idea. There was no way of knowing which.

Her dress, shoes, even hose, were white. Earrings of silver flashed in the moonlight as she turned to me. She was leaning against one of the trees, and its black trunk emphasized her whiteness. She only turned her head as I came up to her.

Her eyes looked silver-gray in the light. I couldn't decipher the look on her face. It wasn't grief.

'It's a beautiful night, isn't it?'

I agreed that it was. 'Carla, are you all right?'

She stared at me terribly calm. 'I'm feeling much better than I did this afternoon.'

'I'm very glad to hear that. Did you remember to bring his clothes and a memento?'

She motioned to a dark bundle by the tree.

'Good, I'll unload the car.' She didn't offer to help, which was not unusual. Most of the time it was fear that prevented it. I realized my Omega was the only car in sight.

I called softly, but sound carries on summer nights. 'How did you get here? I don't see a car.'

'I hired a cab, it's waiting at the gate.'

A cab. I would love to have seen the driver's face when he dropped her off at the cemetery gates. The three black chickens clucked from their cage in the backseat. They didn't have to be black, but it was the only color I could get for tonight. I was beginning to think our poultry supplier had a sense of humor.

Arthur Fiske was only recently dead, so from the box in the trunk I took only a jar of homemade ointment and a machete. The ointment was pale off-white with flecks of greenish light in it. The glowing flecks were graveyard mold. You wouldn't find it in this cemetery. It only grew in graveyards that had stood for at least a hundred years. The ointment also contained the obligatory spider webs and other noisome things, plus herbs and spices to hide the smell and aid the magic. If it was magic.

I smeared the tombstone with it and called Carla over. 'It's your turn now, Carla.' She stubbed out her cigarette and came to stand before me. I smeared her face and hands and told her, 'You stand just behind the tombstone throughout the raising.'

She took her place without a word while I placed ointment on myself. The pine scent of rosemary for memory, cinnamon and cloves for preservation, sage for wisdom, and lemon thyme to bind it all together seemed to soak through the skin itself.

I picked the largest chicken and tucked it under my arm. Carla stood where I had left her, staring down at the grave. There was an art to beheading a chicken with only two hands.

I stood at the foot of the grave to kill the chicken. Its first artery blood splashed onto the grave. It splattered over the fading chrysanthemums, roses, and carnations. A spire of white gladioli turned dark. I walked a circle sprinkling blood as I went, tracing a circle of steel with a bloody machete. Carla shut her eyes as the blood rained upon her.

I smeared blood on myself and placed the still-twitching body upon the flower mound. Then I stood once again at the foot of the grave. We were cut off now inside the blood circle, alone with the night, and our thoughts. Carla's eyes flashed white at me as I began the chant.

'Hear me, Arthur Fiske. I call you from the grave. By blood, magic, and steel, I call you. Arise, Arthur, come to us, come to me, Arthur Fiske.' Carla joined me as she was supposed to. 'Come to us, Arthur, come to us, Arthur. Arthur, arise.' We called his name in ever-rising voices.

The flowers shuddered. The mound heaved upward, and the chicken slid to the side. A hand clawed free, ghostly pale. A second hand and Carla's voice failed her. She began moving round the gravestone to kneel to the left of the heaving mound. There was such wonder, even awe, in her face, as I called Arthur Fiske from the grave.

The arms were free. The top of a dark-haired head was in sight, but the top was almost all there was. The mortician had done his best, but Arthur's had been a closed-casket funeral.

The right side of his face was gone, blasted away. Clean white bone shone at jaw and skull, and silver bits of wire where the bone had been strung together. It still wasn't a face. The nose was empty holes, bare and white. The skin was shredded and snipped short to look neater. The left eye rolled wildly in the bare socket. I could see the tongue moving between the broken teeth. Arthur Fiske struggled from the grave.

I tried to remain calm. It could be a mistake. 'Is that Arthur?'

Her hoarse whisper came to me. 'Yes.'

'That is not a heart attack.'

'No.' Her voice was calm now, incredibly normal. 'No, I shot him at close range.'

'You killed him, and had me bring him back.'

Arthur was having some trouble freeing his legs, and I ran to Carla. I tried to help her to her feet but she wouldn't move.

'Get up, get up, damn it, he'll kill you!'

Her next words were very quiet. 'If that's what he wants.'

'God help me, a suicide.'

I forced her to look at me instead of the thing in the grave. 'Carla, a murdered zombie always kills his murderer first, always. No forgiveness, that is a rule. I can't control him until after he has killed you. You have to run, now.'

She saw me, understood, I think, but said, 'This is the only way to be free of guilt. If he forgives me, I'll be free.'

'You'll be dead!'

Arthur freed himself and was sitting on the crushed, earth-strewn flowers. It would take him a little while to organize, but not too long.

'Carla, he will kill you. There will be no forgiveness.' Her eyes had wandered back to the zombie, and I slapped her twice, very hard. 'Carla, you will die out here, and for what? Arthur is dead, really dead. You don't want to die.'

Arthur slid off the flowers and stood uncertainly. His eye rolling around in its socket finally spotted us. Though he didn't have much to show expression with, I could see joy on his shattered face. There was a twitch of a smile as he shambled toward us, and I began dragging her away. She didn't fight me, but she was a dead, awkward weight. It is very hard to drag someone away if they don't want to go.

I let her sink back to the ground. I looked at the clumsy but determined zombie and decided to try. I stood in front of him, blocking him from Carla. I called upon whatever power I possessed and talked to him. 'Arthur Fiske, hear me, listen only to me.'

He stopped moving and stared down at me. It was working, against all the rules, it was working.

It was Carla who spoiled it. Her voice saying, 'Arthur, Arthur, forgive me.'

He was distracted and tried to move toward her voice. I stopped him with a hand on his chest. 'Arthur, I command you, do not move. I who raised you command you.'

She called one more time. That was all he needed. He flung me away absentmindedly. My head hit the tombstone. It wasn't much of a blow, no blood like on television, but it took everything out of me for a minute. I lay in the flowers, and it seemed very important to hear myself breathe.

Arthur reached down for her, slowly. His face twitched, and his tongue made small sounds that might have been, 'Carla.'

The clumsy hands stroked her hair. He half fell, half knelt by her. She drew back at that, afraid.

I started crawling over the flowers toward them. She was not going to commit suicide with my help.

The hands stroked her face, and she backed away, just a few inches. The thing crawled after her. She backpedaled faster, but he came on surprisingly quick. He pinned her under his body, and she started screaming.

I half-crawled, half-fell across the zombie's back.

The hands crept up her body, touching her shoulders.

Her eyes rolled back to me. 'Help me!'

I tried. I tugged at him, trying to pull him off her. Zombies do not have supernatural strength, no matter what the media would like you to think, but Arthur had been a large, muscular man. If he could have felt pain, I might have pulled him off, but there was no real way to distract him.

'Anita, please!'

The hands settled on her neck and squeezed.

I found the machete where it had dropped to the ground. It was sharp, and did damage, but he couldn't feel it. I chopped at his head and back. He ignored me. Even decapitated, he would keep coming. His hands were the problem. I knelt and sighted at his lower arm. I didn't dare try it any closer to her face. The blade flashed silver. I brought it down with all the strength in my back and arms, but it took five blows to break the bone.

The separated hand kept squeezing as if it were still attached. I threw the machete down and began prying one finger at a time from her neck. It was time consuming. Carla stopped struggling. I screamed my rage and helplessness at him and kept prying up the fingers. The strong hands squeezed until there was a cracking sound. Not a sharp pencil break like a leg or an arm, but a crackling as the bones crushed together. Arthur seemed satisfied. He stood up from the body. All expression left him. He was empty, waiting for a command.

I fell back into the flowers, not sure whether to cry, or scream, or just run. I just sat there and shook. But I had to do something about the zombie. I couldn't just leave him to wander around.

I tried to tell him to stay, but my voice wouldn't come. His eye followed me as I stumbled to the car. I came back with a handful of salt. In the other hand I scooped the fresh grave dirt. Arthur watched me without expression. I stood at the outer edge of the circle. 'I give you back to the earth from which you came.'

I threw the dirt upon him. He turned to face me.

'With salt I bind you to your grave.' The salt sounded like sleet on his suit. I made the sign of a cross with the machete. 'With steel I give you back.'

I realized that I had begun the ceremony without getting another chicken. I bent and retrieved the dead one and slit it open. I drew still-warm and bloody entrails free. They glistened in the moonlight. 'With flesh and blood I command you, Arthur, return to your grave and walk no more.'

He lay down upon the grave. It was as if he had lain in quicksand. It just swallowed him up. With a last shifting of flowers, the grave was as before, almost.

I threw the gutted chicken to the ground and knelt beside the woman's body. Her neck flopped at an angle just slightly wrong.

I got up and shut the trunk of my car. The sound seemed to echo, too loud. Wind seemed to roar in the tall trees. The leaves rustled and whispered. The trees all looked like flat black shadows, nothing had any depth to it. All noises were too loud. The world had become a one-dimensional cardboard thing. I was in shock. It would keep me numb and safe for a little while. Would I dream about Carla tonight? Would I try to save her again and again? I hoped not.

Somewhere up above, nighthawks flitted. Their cries came thin and eerie, echoing loud. I looked at the body by the grave. The whiteness of it stained now with dirt. So much for the other half of my fee.

I got in the car, smearing blood over the steering wheel and key. There were phone calls to make; to my boss, to the police, and to cancel the rest of my appointments. I would be raising no more dead tonight. There was a taxi to send away. I wondered how much the meter had run up.

My thoughts ran in dull, frightened circles. I began to shake, hands trembling. Tears came hot and violent. I sobbed and screamed in the privacy of my car. When I could breathe without choking, and my hand was steady, I put the car in gear. I would definitely be seeing Carla tonight and Arthur. What's one more nightmare?

I left Carla there alone, with Arthur's forgiveness, one leg lost in the flowers of his grave.

# A LUST OF CUPIDS

*I feel like we need a depth chamber between this and the preceding story. We're moving from almost as dark as I get as a writer, to almost as light as I get. I got a lot of nice rejection slips on this story. Editors loved it, but not enough to buy it. One editor at one of the top-paying magazines at the time actually told me the truth: that since they published only one piece of fiction in each issue, I wasn't a big enough name to help their magazine sales. But she adored the story. When I became a big enough name to make a difference, I did not send the story back to her for another chance. One, I was too busy with novels to think about it. Two, I'm petty. It's the same story; the only thing that changed was that now I was a name. I rarely give second chances.*

I WAS WALKING along Market Street on my lunch hour, wishing I hadn't worn high heels today, or a skirt. Pantyhose were no protection at all against the icy winter air. I was minding my own business when I saw them. They floated by the streetlight at the corner like gigantic moths attracted to the cold electric light. Half a dozen small naked children with cotton-candy wings and curly ringlets, mostly blond. They were also carefully neuter, smooth as a Barbie doll.

Cupids. Shit. That was all I needed. I looked for a door, a shop, anything that I could take refuge in. The brick building stretched smooth and doorless. There was a small shop across the street, but I'd never make it, too open, no cover. I began to walk sideways, back down the street. One hand on the wall to make sure I didn't trip. If I could just make the far corner, maybe I could run for it.

But it was too late; they had spotted me. One of the chubby pink things strung his tiny golden bow and began to sift through his quiver for an arrow. His shiny little eyes never left me. I wasn't close enough to see his eyes, but I knew what color they were. All Cupids have sky-blue eyes, like Easter eggs, or baby blankets.

I didn't wait to see what color of arrow it chose, I turned and ran. My high heels seemed to echo the narrow street. They'd find me. Damn it!

I made it around the corner and found every building as blank and smooth as the Cupids themselves. I had just walked down this street. There should have been doors, shops, people. I had heard that Cupids could cloud your mind, but I had never believed, until now.

I darted a look behind me. Nothing. I wasn't sure if that was a good sign, or a bad one. They either had given up, or were so sure of me that they didn't need to hurry. Or, they were right above me and I just couldn't see them, like the doors that should have been here. I wanted to scream and rant and stomp my feet, but that wouldn't help. Think, Rachel, think.

If I couldn't see the doors, maybe I could feel them. Cupids wouldn't follow me inside. I had walked this street a hundred times, surely I could remember where one door was, any door.

My hands slid over cold, blank bricks. If there was something there, I couldn't feel it. The Cupids flew around the corner. There were six of them, hovering, soft pastel wings fluttering like lazy butterflies. The look in their eyes wasn't soft, it was cold.

I flattened myself against the wall and screamed, 'Leave me alone, you overweight cherubs!'

They glanced at each other; maybe I had offended them. I hoped so. A Cupid with soft pink wings drew an arrow from behind his back. The rest of them hovered like chubby vultures.

A man yelled, 'In here!'

I glanced to my right and found a door open and a man motioning to me. 'Run for it,' he said.

I ran for it. I was almost to the door when my heel broke and sent me sprawling on the sidewalk. Something whirred over my head and thunked into the door. The white arrow vibrated in the door. White, the color of true love. Shit!

A hand grabbed my arm and pulled me inside. I scrambled inside the shop on hands and knees, no time to be ladylike. A tall, broad-shouldered man closed the door and asked, 'Are you all right?'

I nodded, still sitting on the floor, staring at the arrow. It was already beginning to evaporate. In a few minutes it would be gone. No danger of us mere mortals getting hold of one of the arrows of love. Once fired they just didn't last.

'What did I do to deserve white?' I asked, not really expecting an answer.

'Are you over thirty?' the man asked.

I thought that was a rather rude question from a stranger, but he had saved me. 'Why do you ask?'

'Because once you're over thirty the little things get pesky. I'm thirty-five and never been married. Something in a Cupid just can't stand that.'

I smiled. 'Thirty-three, never married, never want to be.'

He offered me a hand up. I took it. His hand was big like him and nearly swallowed my hand to the wrist. His eyes were perfect brown like polished chestnut. Curly brown hair was cut short and had never seen the inside of a styling salon.

I couldn't stand straight with only one heel so I took the shoes off. 'It was lucky I wore heels today.'

'Damn straight. How many of 'em are after you?'

'Six.'

He gave a low whistle. 'They want you bad.'

I nodded. He was right. One Cupid was standard, maybe even two; they didn't seem to like to be alone much. But a lust of Cupids was a damn posse. All for little ol' me. Had I offended someone? I had an awful thought, an uncharitable thought. Had my mother paid them off, slipped one of the little winged horrors some sweets? Cupids didn't need money, but they loved candies and desserts. It was frowned upon, but everyone knew it happened. Corrupt Cupids with a sweet tooth.

'I'm Tom Hagan,' the man said.

'Rachel Carrdigan.' We shook hands again and his hand was warm and callused. There was something oddly appealing about his square face. If I hadn't known better, I'd have wondered if a pink arrow had gotten me. Pink for infatuation.

'Were you out to lunch?' he asked.

'Yes.'

He smiled. 'Well, it isn't much, but I'll split mine with you. Cupids don't have much patience. They'll wander off if you can hide long enough.'

'You sound like an expert.'

'Hey, I'm two years older than you. They've been after me longer.'

I laughed. 'All right, if you're sure it's not trouble.'

'It isn't like the shop is busy today.'

I glanced around the warm interior of the shop for the first time. Hand-carved wood was everywhere. Small furniture, shelves, animals. All the folksy wooden things the tourists bought in droves, but it was winter now and the tourists were gone. I always wondered how some of the shops made it through the off-season. One of the good things about being a lawyer, crime was always in season.

Tom brought a rocking chair he'd made himself to sit beside his own chair. He gave me a lap-size linen napkin to spread over my business skirt and shared a huge roast beef sandwich and apple pie. The pie was delicious and I said so.

'Made it myself.' He seemed embarrassed but pleased. Since I couldn't boil soup without burning it, I was impressed.

I called my office and said I'd be later without explaining the reason. We spent a very pleasant time drinking fresh coffee and talking about small things. Nothing major or earth shattering, but comfortable.

Tom glanced at the clock. 'I hate to say it, but it's probably safe for you to leave.'

'My God, it's two. I had no idea it was that late.' I smiled. 'Maybe I'll be needing a wooden shelf or two for my condo, soon.'

He grinned and, I swear, blushed. 'I'd like that.'

There was a little click down in my solar plexus, pleasure. Who needed Cupids? I limped in my high heels, one heel on, one heel off, but it was better than going barefoot on freezing cobblestones.

Tom let me out the back door, just in case. We both looked up and down the alley. Nothing, empty, home free. 'Thanks for everything, Tom.' I shook his hand and felt that warm tingle as our skin met. Probably nothing would come of it, but it was nice anyway.

I turned just before I rounded the corner and waved. He waved back, smiling, then his face changed and he was running for me. 'Behind you!'

I whirled. The Cupids were flying in at my back. I flung myself onto the ground. A white arrow buried itself into the cobblestones near my head. Tom was running toward me, shouting.

A white arrow took him through the chest. He staggered back, eyes wide and surprised. He stumbled back a few steps, then fell backward onto the cobblestones. I screamed, 'Tom!' I heard the whir of wings above me. I turned, slowly, and stared into shining blue eyes. A small feminine mouth smiled at me. The little gold bow pulled back, a white arrow pointing at me.

A second Cupid with slightly paler hair and baby-blue wings floated off to the left, bow trained on me. I wasn't getting away this time.

'Get it over with, you ugly little harpies,' I yelled. I threw my shoe at them, the one with the broken heel. The Cupid dodged effortlessly. How could something that chubby be so graceful? I saw the arrow leave the bow, then felt a sharp pain in my chest, over my heart. Then nothing but darkness.


Tom and I woke in the alley and did the only thing we were able to do, fall in love. It was a nice wedding as weddings go. Our mothers sat in the front rows beaming at us. Both of them admitted to having bribed the Cupids, but it had all worked out for the best, they said, smiling smugly.

We smiled back; what else could we do? Arrows of true love had hit both of us. We were in love, married, happy, vengeful.

My mother is a widow. Tom's mother is divorced. All we need now is a corrupt Cupid, with a sweet tooth.

# THE EDGE OF THE SEA

*This is another story that I wrote when I lived in California for a few years. It's the only time in my life that I've lived near the water. I've almost drowned four times. At one point I had my dive certificate. I thought it would help me overcome my phobias. Then I had a diving accident, and now I'm claustrophobic on top of being afraid of water. Oh, well. This is a very sensual story, and was the first peek of that side of me as a writer. But it is a melancholy story. The idea of it — that fear and longing that the ocean fills me with — will be visited at more length in an upcoming Anita book. Some of the characters introduced in* Danse Macabre *will be helping me explore some of the themes of this story in more loving, and even more frightening, detail.*

ADRIA WOKE TO the sound of the sea. She lay under the cool wash of sheets, wondering what had woken her. Moonlight spilled through the white curtains. The rushing hush of the sea poured underneath the balcony. It filled the bedroom with an intimate whispering noise. What had woken her? There was a sense of urgency, as if she had forgotten something.

She sat up, brushing strands of dark hair away from her face. She called out, not really expecting an answer, 'Rachel?'

The only sound was ocean, a purring roar along the sand.

Adria slipped on a pair of jeans that lay rumpled by the bed. Her nightshirt flapped almost to her knees, a man's extra large. She padded barefoot over scattered fitness magazines and clothes. The living room stretched perfectly neat, like a magazine cover, where no one lived. Rachel's neat and tidy hand was visible everywhere.

Adria's hand brushed the music box on the end table. It sang a few forlorn notes. The music boxes were Rachel's hobby. She called them her vice.

Adria walked across the thick white carpet to the short hall. It led to the bathroom and Rachel's bedroom. The door stood ajar, moonlight spilling into the black hallway. Adria froze, pulse thudding against her throat. The urgency she had woken with turned to fear. They had shared the house for almost two years. In all that time Rachel had never left her door open. She had a habit of listening to music as she fell asleep. The sound would leak through the house if the door were open.

No sound. The rushing sea seemed muted in the hall. Adria

paused, almost touching the door. 'Rachel?' Silence. 'Rachel, can you hear me?'

Adria touched the door; it swung inward. The bed was rumpled, pale sheets turned to silver by the moonlight. Rachel's clothes lay neatly folded on the back of the room's only chair. Even her shoes were toes out, heels touching, just waiting to be put on again.

The drapes flapped in the wind, cord slapping the screen. Adria jumped then laughed, but the laughter sounded wrong. So quiet. She walked to the window. There was always a chance Rachel had gone outside, though that was more something Adria would do than Rachel.

The beach was a narrow whiteness, heavy and pale under the moon. The ocean rolled gray and silver, white foam riding the waves, as it whisper-roared, eating away at the shore. Rocks gleamed dull black as the surf swirled and blew white spray up into the air. During the day Adria had jogged every inch of the beach but moonlight made it an alien place.

Adria heard something, a moan, a muffled cry. She wasn't sure if it was the sound of pleasure or pain. Adria smiled to herself. If she went out there and Rachel had a boyfriend on the beach . . . Adria turned back to the room. No, there were no other clothes. If Rachel had undressed, so would he.

Rachel had only brought two men home in as many years. Both times, she had given Adria advance warning. Rachel was not a casual person in her surroundings or her relationships.

Adria checked the open bathroom, but she knew, could feel, how empty the house was now. She was alone, alone with the sea. And Rachel was out there somewhere. Adria began listening to her own heartbeat. It was impossibly loud. Something was very wrong.

She slipped on a pair of deck shoes and opened the sliding glass door that led down to the beach. She left it open behind her; a vague thought that she wanted someone to know where she had gone.

The night air was cool; she shivered in the thin shirt. She debated on going back and getting a sweatshirt, but no, she needed to find Rachel.

Rachel's footprints started at the bottom of the steps. They led down near the surf, where the sand was firm, wet, and easier to walk in. Water swirled shockingly cold around Adria's ankles. The water was crumpling the edges of the tracks, sweeping them away. Adria began to jog, hoping to trace the prints before the sea took them. She fell into a familiar easy stride, arms pumping, breath deep and even. It felt good. Her fear faded in the face of something so ordinary.

The only sounds were the rush of waves and the slap of her feet as she ran. Moonlight gleamed along the shore, showing everything in stark shadows and silver light. The footprints ended at the rocks. Adria touched a cold boulder and began to clamber over them. She slipped on a strand of seaweed and fell hard on one knee. The sharp pain forced her to lean against the damp rock and wait for the knee to move again. She could see over the rocks now, to the beach beyond. They were there.

Rachel's long blond hair was spilled out across the sand. He lay on top of her, his nude body made up of muscle, pale flesh, and shadows.

Adria felt foolish, surprised, and relieved. She meant to turn away, to leave them to their privacy, but something stopped her. A wave curled up the beach and tugged Rachel's hand up and down, loose, limp, unresisting. Adria watched for a few minutes, embarrassment swallowed up by fear. Rachel never moved, not a hand, not her head, not her leg. There was a limp quality to her as the man rode her that was more terrifying than any struggle.

The man buried his face in the sand, baring Rachel's face to the sky. The face was totally slack, nothing.

Adria couldn't breathe for a moment, couldn't think. She screamed, 'Rachel!'

The man looked up, startled. Adria had an impression of dark eyes, impossibly large, a sculpted face. *Beautiful* was the word that flashed in her mind. She scrambled down the rocks, not sure what she would do if he didn't run. Had to try. She was screaming as she came. Someone would hear; someone had to hear.

He stood, and there was a tension to him. Adria stopped, panting, and stared at him across the sand, across Rachel's body. She had seen a wolf once, while hiking in the mountains. It had turned startled eyes to her. There had been nothing human in its eyes. There was nothing human now.

A light flashed on at the nearest house. He jumped, startled, and ran, not up the shore, but toward the sea. He ran into the surf, and it cut him across the waist and he dived between the waves, clean and neat, vanished. She watched his head surface and then his arms as he stroked for deeper water.

Then he dived, and what splashed after him was the curving lines of a tail, like a whale, or a dolphin. He vanished under the waves.

Adria stood there for a heartbeat. She couldn't have seen it. Could she? Adria glanced back at Rachel. She lay unmoving, horribly still.

Adria knelt in the wet sand. Her shaking hands couldn't find a pulse. She pressed her ear to the chest and held her own breath. Adria had expected to hear a heartbeat. Even though she had thought death, she wasn't prepared for silence. She pressed her cheek against Rachel's slack mouth, nothing, no breath. 'Oh, God, oh God.'

A man's voice called from the house where the light had flashed on. 'Is everyone all right down there?'

Adria couldn't answer for a minute, couldn't think, then she yelled, 'Get an ambulance, and get the police. It's an emergency! Hurry!'

'I'll call, don't worry.' He rushed back inside.

Tears threatened hot and close. 'No!' She tilted Rachel's head back, pinched off the nostrils, and began breathing for her. The chest rose and fell, four breaths, four rises. Adria stopped. 'Breathe, Rachel, breathe.'

Surf rushed in and tugged at her body. 'Damn it, Rachel, damn it!'

Adria breathed and then cupped her hands over the chest and pumped, counting, 'One one thousand, two one thousand, three one thousand.' She crawled back to Rachel's head and breathed. Then pumped the chest. 'Rachel, breathe, damn it, breathe. Oh, God! Help me!' Tears choked her, trying to steal her own breath away. She couldn't cry yet. Not yet!

A man was there in his pajamas and bathrobe. He knelt in the wet sand. 'I called the ambulance and the cops.'

Adria looked at him. She couldn't think what to say. 'Help me.'

'I'll pump the heart, if you breathe.'

She really looked at him for the first time, younger than she had thought. She nodded and breathed three quick breaths. He pumped the heart, like he knew what he was doing.

'Rachel, please, please.' Breathing, breathing until she felt light-headed. She looked at the man as he worked to start Rachel's heart. His eyes held hopelessness. Adria shook her head, tears tracing like fire down her cheeks.

'Don't worry,' he said, 'I won't give up until you do.'

'Then we won't give up.'

They were still trying to breathe life into Rachel when the ambulance came. Adria sat in the rising surf, watching as they worked on Rachel. They punched needles into her arm, set up an IV of some clear liquid. They did what Adria and the man had done, but nothing worked.

Adria noticed the world looked flat, one-dimensional. There was no depth to anything. And all the noises seemed distant, dreamlike. She stared at her own hand and couldn't figure out what was wrong. Why had everything changed?

They strapped Rachel to a gurney and began to carry her up the steps to the road. The police came in a flash of red and blue lights, a kaleidoscope against the darkness. There were men asking questions, but Adria couldn't concentrate on it, she couldn't hear them. Someone had thrown a jacket over her shoulders; it was too big and sleeves flapped in the wind as she followed the gurney to the ambulance.

A tall man with a gold shield clipped to his coat stopped her, putting a hand on her shoulder. 'We'll need to ask you a few questions.'

She nodded. 'I understand, but later.' She looked up at him. 'I have to go to the hospital, for Rachel.'

'I understand. Just tell us where he went. You are our only witness.'

She nodded, 'He swam out to sea.'

The detective frowned. 'Are you sure?'

'He swam out to sea.'

'Thank you.'

A second detective pushed close and looked ready to ask other questions, but there must have been something in her face that stopped him. 'We'll talk to you tomorrow then, miss.'

She nodded and crawled into the ambulance. Adria made herself as small as possible riding in the corner, not crying anymore. Everything seemed so distant, unreal, dreamlike. The world wasn't meant to be flat, like cardboard.

The sirens blared to life, and they were out on the highway in a spill of gravel and brakes. She looked up at the paramedic as he checked Rachel one more time. He met Adria's eyes once and then wouldn't look at her again. Wasn't it a bad sign when they wouldn't look at you?

'She's a doctor.'

He glanced at Adria. 'What?'

'Dr Rachel Corbin, that's her name.' It seemed important that he know she was a doctor. Adria wasn't sure why, but if anything made Rachel who she was, it was that. She was a doctor.

He whispered, 'Oh, God.' And shouted something through the window to the driver.

Rachel's hospital was the nearest one, so very close. They would take Rachel to Rachel's hospital, Rachel's emergency room.

\*　　\*　　\*

The police drove Adria back home as dawn was easing through the clouds. She stood in her own living room, looking out the sliding glass door. The sea was an immense blue, rolling out and out until it touched the sky.

The sun was rising and Rachel wasn't rushing out to her car. Adria would still be in bed. The vague roar of Rachel's car was one of the sounds of morning. But not today.

The doctors had given her something to take. They said she was in shock. She hadn't taken the pills yet, and if this was shock, it didn't feel so bad. It didn't feel like anything. Adria felt distant, light, as if a strong wind would blow her away, shatter her into slivers of glass. She knew Rachel was dead, but it was a distant knowing, as if all of last night had happened to someone else.

If she walked into the other room, Rachel's things would be there waiting. But Rachel would never come for them. Adria tried to make last night a lie as she stared out at the sea. So bright and blue, so inviting.

The dark-haired detective said, 'Ms Reynolds, do you feel up to answering questions now? I wouldn't ask, but you are our only witness, and the sooner we start, the sooner we can catch him.'

She answered without turning around, staring out the window. 'Yes, I understand.'

'Tell me what happened last night; take your time.'

Adria took a deep breath and let it out. Her voice belonged to someone else. She listened to some other person tell about waking up and going out to look for Rachel. The voice that was hers and not hers told everything, even glimpses of something impossible.

The second detective had gold-framed glasses that didn't quite hide his eyes. 'Excuse me, Ms Reynolds. Would you repeat that, please?'

'Repeat what?'

'The part starting, *I watched him swim out to sea, and then he dived, flashing a length of tail, like a whale or a dolphin*. Is that what you meant to say, Ms Reynolds?'

Adria thought about that for a minute, cheek pressed against the cool glass. 'I didn't mean to mention it to you, no. It's what I thought I saw.' She shook her head, forehead against glass. 'I don't know.'

'Ms Reynolds.' His voice was condescending, humor the poor hysterical witness. 'You're saying the perpetrator was a mermaid?'

She turned to stare at him, a small flash of anger making her feel more like herself. 'Not a mermaid — a merman, a triton. A male equivalent.'

His face showed what he thought of that theory.

'I don't know, detective. I don't know if I saw it, or dreamed it, or hallucinated. I'd just found my best friend murdered, brutalized. I don't know. Is there anything else? I'm very tired.' She wanted his condescension, his pity, out of her house, out of their house.

The dark-haired detective stood. Adria thought he frowned at his partner. 'Ms Reynolds, you had a very traumatic experience last night. There's nothing wrong with seeing things under that kind of stress.'

'I suppose not.' She hesitated and asked, 'Do other murder witnesses see monsters?'

He folded his notebook up and put it in his coat pocket. 'In a manner of speaking, yes, they do.'

She turned away from his eyes, kind, sad eyes that had seen too much until Rachel's death was just one more, among too many.

'We'll want you to come down and talk to a sketch artist when you're ready. I don't mean to rush you. I know how hard this is on you.'

She started to accuse him of not understanding, but his eyes wouldn't let her. They had seen more death than Adria would ever see, if she was lucky.

'Get some rest, Ms Reynolds. Use those pills the doctor gave you. That's what they're for.'

Adria turned back to the window.

'Let's go, Frank. We've got all we need for a while.' The detective with the gold-framed glasses seemed ready to argue, but he followed his partner.

'We'll leave a patrol car outside for a day or two. Don't be alarmed.'

'I'm not.' The thought that the killer might come back to hurt her didn't seem real or possible, not in the broad light of day.

The door shut, and she was alone. She took a long, hot shower and two of the pills the doctor had given her. Adria tracked water across the carpet. Rachel wouldn't care. She would never fix her famous apple omelets for them late at night. No more popcorn and sad movies. No more anything.

Adria choked back a sob. If she started crying, she felt as if she would split into pieces and fall down a long black hole. She collapsed on the unmade bed, hair wet, wrapped in towels. A deep, dreamless sleep pulled her under.

She woke to late-day sunlight. She had slept nearly twelve hours. The first thought was, *Rachel is dead*. The knowledge was a leaden emptiness. It was as if a great hole had opened up inside her. And the hole was full of pain, and rage and helplessness.

Rachel was the third victim of what the newspapers were now calling 'The Beach Rapist.' The only thing the victims had in common was where they had been killed, at the edge of the sea. Two victims hadn't been newsworthy. Three seemed to be the magic number. There was a serial killer loose.

What had Rachel been doing out on the beach? Why Rachel? Adria needed answers, but there was no one to ask.

She checked her watch, not for time, but for what day it was. It seemed like it had taken weeks for Rachel to die, the hospital. Days at least, but her watch said it was Sunday. Only hours had passed. Only hours and Rachel was gone, just like that.

Adria dressed and tried to comb the tangles from her hair, but it didn't seem to matter all that much. The numbness shredded, falling away. Tears choked at the back of her throat. She took another little pill, just one. She didn't want to sleep, but she wanted the pain to go away. Had she really told the detective the murderer was a triton? Had she really seen a tail? Adria closed her eyes and saw it, flashing in the moonlight, wet and slick, and attached to the man. Could she have made it up, to make the brutality more understandable? Like a child, saying a monster did it, instead of Daddy.

Adria shook her head. It didn't help to call the man a triton. It raised more questions. Why would she hallucinate the man was a merman?

Co-workers from the health club came in the next few hours, to cry, offer comfort, and be comforted. Adria didn't want any of them, didn't want to grieve in a group. It cheapened it to share memories and sob on each other's shoulders. None of them had really known Rachel. She refused to exercise. She was five-nine and had never gained weight. Adria was nine inches shorter. Adria had to work at staying in shape. She could never convince Rachel to go to the club.

Adria asked all the people to go away. Their kind intentions, their helpfulness, their sorrow, it was all more than Adria could deal with. She needed to be alone, wanted to be alone. She wasn't ready for company, no matter how well intentioned.

Adria told no one about her delusion. There was no such thing as mermaids, or mermen. She didn't want to see pity and knowing looks among their friends.

When the flock of mourners had been chased away, Adria lay down on the couch and waited for the tranquilizer to give her sleep.

She woke, gasping in the darkness, strange dreams vanished. Nightmares fading. She had vague images of ocean and strong hands trying to drown her.

Darkness lay pressed against the sliding glass doors. Moonlight shivered through the closed drapes. Adria sat up, abrupt, and felt dizzy and awkward. She couldn't remember closing the drapes. Her head felt like cotton, her throat horribly dry. Too many pills, she felt detached, the rush of fear dying under the dregs of the tranquilizer.

A shadow fluttered against the drapes. Adria stood, a little unsteady. Was it a man's shadow? She touched the drapes, soft, cool. Fear was back, adrenaline chasing the tranquilizer away. The sound of her own heart was obscenely loud. Adria shoved the drapes back, sudden, and he was there. He stood naked and beautiful on the other side of the glass. She tried to scream but couldn't, not while looking into his eyes, dark and peaceful.

He put a hand against the glass, spread it flat. There was webbing between his fingers like a frog's. Adria touched fingertips to the glass. The webbing began to shrink, smaller and smaller, until it melted away, like a moonlit dream. He smiled then, and she felt his need like a physical touch. His hand touched the door lock. Adria jerked back, startled, frightened, awake. The drapes fell shut – the moonlight gleamed empty.

Adria peeked round the drapes, hand shaking. There was nothing there. Had she dreamed it? She had been dreaming of him, of strong hands pushing her under the water. Adria stared at the empty deck. Moonlight glittered off something. She knelt against the glass and stared. There was a puddle of water on the deck. There was no rain this time of year.

Adria was halfway to the phone to call the police when she stopped. What could she say? 'I saw webbing between his fingers, and it melted away.' They wouldn't believe her, and he had known they wouldn't. He had come to taunt her, or to kill her. Adria remembered the feel of him inside her mind, slick, and cold and warm, like nothing she had ever felt. She wondered what he could have done if she hadn't been on the pills, half dead to the world. If he had opened the door . . .

Adria knew now how he had gotten Rachel down on the beach. He had called her, lured her, with himself as bait. The police wouldn't find him, because he could go places they couldn't, places they would never dream of going.

Adria knew the truth, but no one would believe her. It was crazy.

If she'd had her gun tonight she could have given him a surprise. Would bullets hurt a triton? They didn't hurt vampires, did they?

Adria couldn't remember any stories about how to kill a mermaid. Just fairy tales.

The morning paper showed another victim, miles from Adria. Adria drank morning coffee with a gun lying on the table. She had bought it years ago when her ex-husband had traveled a lot and left her alone. It was cleaned, oiled, and loaded. The hammer rested on an empty chamber. If five bullets weren't enough . . . well, Adria didn't think it would matter.

The triton didn't come back, but he killed two more women. The police were baffled, looking for lifeguards, triathletes. They weren't even close.

Adria stayed safe and warm and dry. And another woman died. He was killing almost every other night. The police were frantic; everyone on the beach was terrified.

When Rachel had been dead almost four weeks, Adria dreamed of the triton again. Strong webbed hands caressed her skin; she swam under water and breathed. She woke halfway across her bedroom floor. Her feet were tangled in a pair of discarded old jeans. Almost tripping had woken her. Adria swallowed, tried to breathe, tried to think. She heard his song then, inside her head. Music that cried and wept, that rolled and roared, lonely as the sea, vast and deep, promising miracles. She stood frozen for a moment, listening.

Adria stumbled back to her bed and sat on the edge of the rumpled sheets. She could not go to him, should not, would not. The song sighed and eased her mind, until she was standing. His need was in the music, strong and deep, careless as the ocean itself, and as unstoppable. She picked up her robe from the floor and slipped it on. It felt real and soft. She picked up the gun from the bedside table and put it in the robe pocket. It hung heavy and awkward, bumping her leg as she walked. She could not deny him, but she might be able to surprise him.

The moon rode high and almost full, shimmering silver on the rolling waves. The sea whispered, adding to the triton's song. Music and ocean hissed and roared until Adria could not be sure who was singing to her. Was it the sea? Did the sea itself want to touch her, to hold her? Yes, the sea wanted her. It was not love the sea offered, but violent need, a need so great it filled the world with crying.

She walked at the edge of the wet sand, as the lips of curling waves sloshed over her ankles. High tide was spilling inland.

She waded ankle deep to the rocks, the water soaking the edge of her robe, pulling, tripping. The song said, *Leave it.* But Adria climbed the rocks with the heavy robe still on. She didn't remember why it was important to keep it on, but there was a reason. The beach was bigger on the other side; part of it stayed dry. She thought of Rachel, and fear, grief filled her mind, but the sea took her terror and her sorrow and wove it into its song. Her throat was tight with fear, heart threatening to choke her. She slipped down to dry sand and waited, waited for the sea to come.

A chill wind blew off the ocean. She shivered, and the song took the thread of her chill, for the singer had never been cold. There was something heavy in her pocket that pressed against the damp robe, but it didn't matter. Nothing mattered but the sea.

Something bobbed out in the surf, dark and small, a sea lion maybe. The head disappeared and surfaced closer to shore. It wasn't a seal.

The triton let the waves sweep him up on shore, tumbling. His upper half was the muscular paleness she remembered, except for the long dark hair. Below the waist, he was a soft grayish black, abrupt against the white skin, as if somebody had pieced together two different creatures. There was a small ridge along his spine like a whale's humped back. His tail flukes whipped up and down, a dull half moon. He lay on his stomach in the surf and watched Adria with eyes so huge and luminous, they seemed to have a light of their own.

Tail began to melt, like wax exposed to heat, the tail flukes became blunt, the main trunk began to shrink, growing tight, and the shadow of legs pressed against the shrinking skin.

His face flickered in pain, and that fed into his song. It hurt to change over. Adria felt his pain, crumbling to her knees, staring, waiting, needing. He stood, nude, and human, his dark hair hanging in wet curls round his face. He called out to her, inside her head, the music sliding and seducing. She went to him.

He was tall. She came only to the middle of his chest. When he reached for her, moonlight glistened through the webbing on his hands. Adria took a step back, away. He frowned, and the song roared inside her until she could hear only that. She watched him come closer. He undid her robe, pushing it open. She shivered as the wind blew against her nightshirt. His hands cupped her breasts, water soaking through the shirt, cold. His face bent over her, eyes huge and drowning deep. Terror flashed through her; she shook her head, violently, tried to step back. He grabbed her, pressing her against the hard cold of his body. The song roared in her head, but her fear rode the waves. The sea had come to drag her down, and she was afraid.

His mouth closed over hers, probing. His lips nibbled down her neck. Adria tried to scream, but she couldn't. She was afraid, afraid of the song, afraid of the sea, afraid of this thing touching her, but she could not scream, could not move. He spilled her back onto the sand. Strong hands tore her nightshirt, leaving her gasping and half naked. Waves rushed in, spilling over her breasts, curling between her legs. He knelt over her, staring down, arrogant, no pity, no doubts, the sea made flesh. She meant nothing to him, the song clanged through her mind, a roaring violence, a vast unknowing guiltless thing.

She whispered, 'No.'

He lowered himself on top of her, skin cold, so cold. Waves splashed over his back and spilled into her face. He still kissed and bit along her skin. The hardness of him rested against her panties.

'No.' Still only a whisper. She needed to shout, to scream. 'No.' Then she remembered the gun.

His hands ripped away her damp panties. He lowered his hips, eyes distant.

The gun clicked on the empty chamber. Adria pulled the trigger again. The gun fired through the robe pocket. The shot seemed to explode, so loud. His body jerked, eyes staring at her, seeing her for the first time. She pulled the trigger again. He jerked and then slumped over her.

The song ended abruptly, jarring. Adria's breath came in ragged gasps. She tried to push him off her, but couldn't. He was too heavy. She panicked, beating at his arms and chest. His blood flowed warm onto her skin. She took a deep breath that quavered, and let it out. 'I'm all right. I'm all right.' She began to crawl out from under him, his body dragging along her skin as she wiggled free. She was crying now, sobbing. She began screaming, low tiny screams. The screams frightened her because she couldn't stop them.

She crawled free of him and clawed through the sand until she was free of the water. She sat in the dry sand, letting it cake the wet robe. She held the gun in her hand, loosely.

A wave washed over him, and his hand waved limp, moved by the water. An image of Rachel flashed through her mind. She put a shaking hand against her mouth to stop the awful whimpering screams.

His hand clenched. Adria stopped breathing for a moment. He raised his head. She felt his mind reach out for her. It was like the slow drag of the sea when you're tired and it would be better, easier to rest, to let the water take you down. He got to his feet.

Adria raised the gun two-handed. Blood flowed from two wounds in his stomach, but he never hesitated; the sea did not acknowledge death. Blood blossomed in his chest. He staggered, but kept coming. Adria fired, watching the bullets explode into his chest, ears ringing with the noise. He fell to his knees and then slid to one side, slowly so slowly.

He lay on his side in the dry sand, staring at her. His dark eyes were patient as the sea, nothing in them that she could read, or understand. He didn't seem to be able to move. His chest was a bloody mess. He lay only an arm's length from her. She watched his life pour out into the sand. He blinked. Adria pointed the gun at those eyes and squeezed the trigger. The gun bounced in her hands. A neat red hole appeared in his forehead, blood leaking into his eyes. His eyes stared sightless, the light gone out of them.

Adria did not check his pulse to make sure he was dead. She backed off, the empty gun still in her hand, and began running for home. She looked back once from the top of the rocks. The body lay pale and dark, shadow patched. Nothing moved.

Adria ran.

She heard police sirens a long way off. The strobe lights flickered outside her windows, colored shadows against the curtains. The police found blood on the sand but no body.

'The Beach Rapist' did not strike again. Was he really dead? Or had he just started hiding the bodies, letting the ocean take the evidence away? Adria couldn't sleep with the sea whispering outside her window anymore.

She sold the house for a nice price, even with the murders. Beachfront property was dear. Adria moved inland, far from the sea. But there are nights when the rustle of leaves outside her window becomes the rushing of the sea. And there is an echo in her head, a hiss of distant music.

Adria is looking for some place out of state. Some place where the sea does not touch the land for hundreds of miles on any side. Surely, there she will be safe.

# A SCARCITY OF LAKE MONSTERS

*I have a degree in biology. Wildlife biologist was one of the few other careers I dreamed about besides writing. This story comes out of wondering if the monsters of fable existed, then how would we deal with them? What if lake monsters were real? It's another example of my continuing theme of taking the fantastic and dropping it into the middle of the real.*

I WAS DREAMING of sea monsters when the phone rang. I dragged the phone under the sheets with me and said, ' 'Lo.'

'Did I wake you, Mike?'

Why does everyone ask that when the answer is obviously yes? And why do we lie automatically? 'No, no, what's up, Jordan?'

'It's your damn lake monster. He broke through the barricade again.'

I groaned. 'What's he doing?'

'Chasing speedboats, what else?'

'We'll be right there.'

'Make it quick, Mike. The skiers are about to wet their pants.'

I hung up the phone and sat up, pushing back the covers. Susan was still deeply asleep. Her shining black hair lay in a fan across the pillow. Her face was an almost perfect triangle. The firm jaw was the only hint a person had that this pretty, delicate-seeming woman was one of the toughest people I'd ever met. She was a fanatical champion of lost causes. Right now, it was lake monsters, and our monster was loose.

I touched her tanned shoulder gently. 'Come on, wife, duty calls.'

She muttered something unintelligible, which meant she wasn't awake at all. She's the only person I know who hates morning more than I do.

'Come on, Susan, Irving broke out of his barricade and is terrorizing the tourists.'

She turned over, blinking at me. 'He won't hurt them,' she said thickly.

'No, but they don't know that.'

She laughed, a rich, dark sound like good wine. 'Do you think they'd believe he was a vegetarian?'

'Not with all those teeth,' I said. 'Come on, we gotta go herd Irving back inside and repair the barricade.'

'You know,' Susan said, 'Irving used to be almost exclusively nocturnal, but lately he's active at all hours. I wonder why?'

I shrugged and ran a comb through my hair. 'Unknown,' I said.

*Unknown*, a good word for lake monsters. Nobody knew much about them, and now they were endangered, nearly extinct. Two lake monsters had died in the last fifteen years, both killed by pollution. To make the tragedy worse, both monsters had been pregnant. The babies had been fully formed, but the pollution had gotten them, too. Lake monsters need nearly pristine conditions, and as man spreads out, pristine gets pretty rare.

The question that no one could answer was, how had the two dead females gotten pregnant? Sexual reproduction is a little hard without a mate. There are wonderful theories about secret tunnels connecting the lakes, but no one had found any tunnels. Another idea was that male lake monsters look so different from females that they had been classed as some sort of fish or . . . something. But Irving, and two other monsters, had male genitalia. Irving didn't look anything like a fish.

Susan had come here three years ago to study Irving, the lake monster. I was a forest ranger with a master's degree in cryptozoology, a nice degree if you work in the Enchanted Forest National Park. I was assigned to help Dr Susan Greco, noted cryptozoologist, look into a possible breeding program for our lake monster. A female lake monster in New England was being studied as well. The idea was to transport her to Irving, maybe. There was always the chance that the two monsters would fight and kill each other. No one had ever seen two monsters together.

Three years later, married to each other for almost two years, and we still didn't know a damn thing about the sex life of the greater lake monster. Whether there was such a thing as a lesser lake monster was a matter of great debate. Were the two small monsters in other states just younger greater lake monsters, or were they a separate species? How long did lake monsters live? We could reach up and rub Irving between the eye ridges, and we still didn't know how old he was.

Twenty minutes later we were bouncing across the lake in a small boat. The sky was milky blue with cumulus clouds like white cotton candy. The water was the usual mirror brightness, reflecting the straight cones of pines, and the distant rise of mountains. Two boats passed us at full throttle; the passengers waved and yelled. I caught one word: 'Monster!'

Jordan guided our boat. He was one of the junior rangers. He looked like his name: blond, handsome in a California surf-boy kind of way. Susan said he was cute. If Jordan hadn't been such a hard-working nice guy, I could have disliked him. Jordan drove the boat so Susan and I could slip into diving gear. If you've ever tried to get into a wet suit while riding full tilt in a small boat, *slip is* not quite the word – *struggle* maybe. When I was encased in latex from ankle to neck, I took a quick peek through binoculars at our lake monster.

Irving looks like a cross between a Chinese dragon, an eel, and an oil slick. His head is the most dragonlike, with slender horns and rubbery spikes bristling around very square jaws. Most of his thirty-foot length is all slick and slightly flattened; eel, not land snake. His fringelike dorsal fin extends nearly the length of his body. Overall, his color is black, but he glistens in sunlight like an oil slick; rings of color flash and melt along his skin. The rainbow only shows up at close range, though. Most people aren't much interested in how pretty he is when they're that close.

Irving's head was keeping pace with the last water-skier. It was a man in a bright orange ski vest. Though through my binoculars his tanned face looked bloodless. Irving's mouth was half open, exposing a dazzling display of teeth. The boat was going full out, motor screaming. The skier was riding the white foam of the wake like his life depended on it.

The faster the boat went, the faster Irving swam, but quiet, no foaming wake for the lake monster. He could glide at incredible speeds nearly silent and waveless. The only reason we saw so much of Irving was because he liked people. He wanted to be seen. Most lake monsters gave a new definition to the word *shy*.

The skier fell into the water. He bobbed to the surface, trapped in his life vest. I could see him screaming and waving his arms.

The lake monster blew bubbles at him, then stretched his neck up ten feet and gave a great honking sound. It's his version of human laughter.

If Irving had been human, he'd have been your obnoxious Uncle Ned – the one who makes really bad jokes, wears loud plaid, and slips you twenty dollars when your parents aren't looking. Irving had a good heart, but his sense of humor was a little sadistic.

Susan waved and called, 'Irving!'

His great head swiveled and looked at our boat. He gave a loud snort and dived under the water. The skier started to paddle frantically for his boat.

Irving surfaced about five feet from us. Jordan cut the motor and let us drift while the monster moved up alongside. I struggled with my diving gear while Susan coaxed Irving. He finally let her rub the bristles on his chin and then snorted into her wet suit, splashing her with water and making a happy *humph* sound. She laughed and rubbed his eye ridges.

Jordan started the boat again, and we began moving slowly toward the barricade and Irving's part of the lake. Our walkie-talkies squawked to life. Someone was calling me. Jordan took it because I was still fastening air tanks into place. It was hard to hear anything over the whine of boat and happy monster noises.

'It's Priscilla. She and Roy are at an abandoned campsite. A whole troop of Girl Scouts plus two of their leaders are missing.'

'How long have they been missing?'

'Unsure.'

'Damn. Any signs of a struggle?'

Jordan asked, then shook his head. 'Looks like they just walked away.'

'Where were they camped?'

'Near Starlight Ridge.'

'What genius let them camp that far up?'

'You know how it is, Mike, they pick their own campsite.'

'But it's June,' I said.

Jordan just frowned at me, but Susan let out a slow whistle.

'What?' asked Jordan.

'No all-female groups are allowed to camp above Bluebell Glade between May thirteenth and June thirtieth.'

'But . . .' Then the light dawned. 'Oh, shit.'

I nodded. 'Satyr rutting season. Have them check Satyr Glade. And find out who the hell OK'd the campsite.'

Susan said softly, 'Somebody's going to get sued over this one.'

All I could do was nod. I wasn't usually in charge of anything but the monster. Unfortunately, our chief ranger was on the injured list for at least three weeks. I was acting chief ranger at the height of the tourist season.

The barricade stretched across the most narrow part of the lake, from pine-covered shore to rocky outcrop. It was a deluxe steel net, enough give and no sharp edges so Irving wouldn't be able to break it. The barricade had been the single most expensive item of the Lake Monster Breeding Program.

The net stretched smooth and unbroken, which meant the damage had to be below the water line. Irving had learned that if he damaged the visible part of the net, we'd discover his escape sooner, but underwater we wouldn't notice the breakout until we spotted him.

The water was cold even in June, not uncomfortable but cool, and it closed around me on all sides. Air may be all around you on land, but it doesn't have the invasive push of water. Water lets you know it's there. On a good day the visibility is twenty feet. Today wasn't a good day.

A swirl of water and Irving coiled through the silver trail of my air bubbles, the thickness of his body looped against my back. I brushed a hand down his side as he eased past me. I expected monsters to feel like dolphins, rubbery and somehow unreal, or snakes with their dry, soft brush of scales, but monsters feel like . . . monsters. Slick, wet but soft like pressed velvet. And underneath it all, even when you can't see most of him, just a glimpse of shining, black coils, there is the feeling of immense power. Even if you can't see him, you know he's big. You know he could flatten you if he wanted to, but Irving is like some of the great whales. He seems to know he's big and that you're small. He's careful around us.

The lake monster swam in and out of the wavering sunlight that pierced the water. Susan and I stayed within touching distance of each other. At twenty-five feet, we lost all light. Only my grip on the net let me know which way was up. I've been in caves where it was so dark you could touch your own eyeball and not see your finger. It was like that down here except the water gave the darkness weight and movement as if it were something alive. The water swirled, and something large rubbed against me. It had to be Irving, but my breathing seemed very loud. Even, deep breaths, that's it. I'm not afraid of water, and I'm not afraid of the dark, but combine the two and I am not a happy camper.

I switched on my flashlight and Susan followed suit. Her beam flashed into my eyes and I gave her the OK sign. She returned it, and we continued down into the blackness. I had to let my flashlight swing on the little loop around my wrist so I could use both hands to hold the net and feel for looseness. The light swung bizarrely, a slow-motion liquid dance of light and darkness.

The net wobbled under my hands, loose. I waved my light at Susan, and she swam over to me. Together we found the hole that

Irving had pushed under the net, tearing out two mooring lines. He was thirty feet long, but he had a snake's ability to squeeze through the darnedest holes. I would have bet a month's pay he couldn't have slipped through the opening. After we fixed one, we'd make sure there were no others, but usually it was just one. Irving is a lazy monster and doesn't do more work than he has to.

First, of course, we had to get Irving back through that little hole.

Susan swam through the hole, raising a cloud of silt that floated like a brownish fog in the flashlight's beam. Now even with the light I couldn't see anything. But Irving's smooth bulk eased past my leg. Nothing else in the lake could displace water like our monster. He stopped and I put a hand on his side. I still couldn't see, or feel his tail end. With a convulsive wriggle, Irving began to back out of the hole. It stopped almost as soon as it began, and I knew Susan was bribing him with some of the fish we'd brought. The way to a lake monster's heart is through his stomach.

Two hours later, the barricade was temporarily secure. We were making our last dive and had stopped at fifteen feet for our decompression stop. If you go up too fast, the air in your lungs doesn't have time to adjust to the pressure as you swim toward the surface. Swim directly up with no decompression stop, and you'll get 'the bends' — decompression sickness. The nitrogen in your blood will bubble like soda pop, causing, among other things, unconsciousness and death. That is the worst case, of course. Susan says I dwell too much on the things that can go wrong when you dive. I prefer to think of it as being cautious.

Irving butted me gently in the ribs, blowing bubbles at me. It's hard to laugh with a regulator in your mouth, but Irving will make you do it. Sunlight hovered in the water at this depth, making the monster's coils shimmer. He wrapped us both in his velvet muscled body, not tight, but to let us know he had us. Then he was gone, swimming away into dimness.

Susan's fingers brushed mine, and I took her hand. We kicked for the surface, turning slowly together, caught in the soft, hovering brightness of light and water.

We spent the rest of the afternoon searching for the lost Girl Scout troop. We found them asleep, drugged with music. They were curled around a sign that said, 'No All-Female Groups Beyond This Point. Satyr Breeding Area.' Satyrs have a peculiar sense of humor.

I had found the orders for their campsite. They hadn't camped where we told them. The park was not liable for their mistake. Honest.

That night Susan, as usual, was asleep first. She lay on her side, half curled against my stomach. My face was buried in the back of her neck. She smelled of shampoo and perfume and warmth. Nothing felt as good as going to sleep with Susan's body pressed against mine. The soft rise and fall of her breathing was one of my top three favorite sounds in the world. The second is her laugh, and the first is the little sound she makes, deep in her throat, when we make love. It is a personal sound, just for us, no sharing. I've never been in love. Does it show?

The phone rang and Susan stirred in her sleep, but didn't waken. I rolled over and grabbed the receiver. 'Hello.'

'Mike, it's Jordan again . . .' His voice trailed off.

'What's wrong?' I asked.

'It's Irving. A couple of drunks dragged their boat into his part of the lake. Said they just wanted to swim with the monster.'

I pushed the cover back and crouched on the edge of the bed. 'What happened, Jordan?'

Susan touched my shoulder. 'What's wrong?'

I shook my head. 'Jordan, talk to me.'

'They hit Irving with the propeller. It looks bad. I already called the vet. He's out on a call, but he'll get here as soon as he can.'

We drove in silence toward the lake. The sky was black and glittered with the cold light of stars. So many stars. Susan's tanned face was pale, her lips set in a tight angry line. Her eyes turn nearly black when she is really angry. They glittered like black jewels now.

I just felt sick. It was too ridiculous, too stupid for words, that all our work was going to be screwed up by some drunks in a boat. How bad was he hurt? The questions kept running through my head like a piece of song. How bad was he hurt?

It was Roy who met us with a boat. His thinning brown hair was rumpled; he'd forgotten to comb it. There was a smear of something on his glasses, too dark to be mud. We struggled into the diving gear while Roy talked above the roar of the engine. 'Priscilla's in the water with Irving. She swims like a fish. She's keeping him at the surface. Jordan's got our two drunks on the shore.'

'How bad is it?' I asked.

'Bad, Mike, real bad.'

Susan looked at me. I could see her jaw tighten by starlight. I felt the first warm flush of anger gliding up from my stomach to tighten my throat. Moonlight lay in a shining silver line across the lake. It was all so damn beautiful, so peaceful.

As the boat got close to the barricade, Jordan yelled, 'He's sinking. Priscilla can't hold him!'

'Cut the motor, Roy. We'll go in over the barricade,' I said.

The boat drifted against the netting with a soft bump. Susan and I pushed regulators into our mouths and grabbed for the barricade. Climbing netting while wearing fins is nearly impossible, but Susan spilled over the top first, using just her arms. I followed, plunging into the night-black water.

I couldn't see Susan's flashlight. I couldn't see anything, then I heard it, an echoing tap. The sound repeated, and I began to work my way toward it. Susan was tapping her air tank with the flashlight, guiding me to her.

Irving's body loomed out of the darkness first. She'd found him. I stroked my hand on his side and felt him shiver. My hand found a gash in his side. His dorsal fin had been half cut away, and I realized that part of what was making the water dark was blood. I swallowed hard around my regulator and swam toward Irving's head.

Susan was cradling his great head, and Irving leaned against her. She was rubbing his eye ridge. The whole left side of his face had been ripped open. The left eye was gone in a mass of meat and exposed bone. I swam up so Irving could see me out of his good eye. He nuzzled his nose against my chest and blew a thin stream of bubbles. There was a backwash of air and blood from his exposed jaw and underneath his body. I swam down to find a rip just in back of his head. His spine gleamed pale and unreal in the beam of my light. There was another rip in back of it. His stomach was half hanging into the water. At least, I thought it was his stomach.

There was no way the boat could have just hit him once. The first blow had to have been the head, stunned him, but the rest . . . They had to have driven back and forth over him, slicing him over and over.

I started to swim back to Susan when the stomach twitched. I shone my light on it and found a tiny lake monster moving inside a membranous sack. Irving was about to give birth!

The sack split and spilled about four feet of baby lake monster into the water. I cradled the little monster to my chest and swam for the surface. Irving was an air breather; it meant the baby probably was too. We were almost to the surface when I realized I had no idea how far down we'd been. Did I need a decompression stop? The little monster began to thrash in my arms. I let it go, and it popped to the surface. Decompression or not, it was too late. I said a silent prayer and surfaced.

The little monster made a loud happy snort as it gasped in air. It blinked at me; tiny bristling horns covered a dragonlike head. It was a perfect replica of Irving. Susan surfaced near me and just stared for a minute.

I wasn't in any pain, no tightness of chest, no muscle cramping; no decompression sickness, lungs OK. We couldn't have been down more than forty feet for a few minutes. Maybe I worry too much.

I rubbed my hand along the baby's back, like wet silk. I reached up to scratch a miniature eye ridge. The monster bit me, sinking needle teeth to the bone. I screamed around the regulator that was still in my mouth. The baby vanished into the water, gone.

Susan stared at the spot where it had been, then said, 'Irving's dead. His body started to float down. How the hell did he get pregnant?' She lowered her mask to hang like a necklace. 'My God, do you realize we've just seen the first birth of a lake monster ever?' Her voice held that hushed awe that you reserve for cathedrals and hospitals.

I held my bleeding hand up out of the water and didn't know quite how to feel. Irving was dead, and the way he died was awful, but I had held a newborn monster in my arms. I would have the scars to prove that. Even if we couldn't find the baby to get pictures, the bite radius would prove how small it was. I laughed then, spitting out my regulator. Sometimes I think I've been around Susan too long. It hadn't even occurred to her yet that I was hurt.

Something else had occurred to her, though. She turned in the black water, looking toward shore. The humor, the awe had left her face. Her face was stiff and pale with anger, eyes like black holes.

'Susan,' I said, reaching out to her, trying to touch her shoulder. She moved out of reach, with a smooth flow of ripples. 'Susan, what are you going to do?'

She turned onto her back as much as the air tanks would allow, kicking backward. 'I'm going to hurt them.'

'You can't do that,' I said.

'Watch me.'

I started paddling after her, but she was going to get to shore first. My adrenaline rush was over: Irving's death, the birth, and the bite wound. Blood was running down my hand, and with the blood, pain. I was tired. Susan was still running on rage.

She was sitting down in the shallows taking off her flippers.

Priscilla, the other junior ranger, moved over to help Susan take off the tanks.

Priscilla towered over Susan, heck, she towers over me. Priscilla is six foot one and has the strength to match the size.

Susan was free of the tanks and going toward the prisoners. I yelled, 'Stop her!'

Priscilla looked toward me, but didn't move.

'Stop her! Susan!'

Priscilla laid the tanks on the ground and moved toward my wife.

I lay panting in the shallows, struggling one-handed to get out of my diving gear. The shot echoed, loud enough to make me jump. I twisted around, one flipper on and one off.

Susan had Jordan's rifle. She was pointing it at the two men. Another shot rang out, and the men started screaming. She was shooting into the ground, right next to them.

Jordan was trying to talk to her, but she motioned him away with the rifle.

Priscilla knelt beside me in the water, undoing the last strap of my equipment. 'Talk to her, Mike. Somebody's going to get hurt.'

I nodded, shrugged out of the buoyancy vest, and walked toward Susan. She was firing into the ground, in a pattern around them. So far, I don't think she had hit either of them, but only skill and plain luck had saved them. Luck would run out. Part of me wanted them bleeding, hurt. Maybe we could hang their dead bodies near the entrance to the park with a sign: 'These Men Killed One of Our Animals.' Yeah, maybe that would convince the tourists to behave.

'Susan, give the rifle back to Jordan.'

'They killed him, Mike. They killed Irving.'

'I know.'

One of the men said, 'She's crazy.'

'Shut up,' Susan said.

'I'd do what she says, mister,' I said.

The man huddled against his companion. Both of them looked white in the moonlight. They stank of beer and urine.

'They slaughtered him,' Susan said.

'Give me the rifle, Susan, please.'

'What's going to happen to them? If I don't hurt them, what will the law do?'

'A hundred-thousand-dollar fine, or a mandatory ten-year prison sentence.'

'Do either of you have a hundred thousand dollars?' she asked.

The men looked at each other, then at me. 'Answer her,' I said.

'Hell, no. We haven't got that kind of money.'

Susan gave a thin, tight smile, and handed the rifle to Jordan. 'You better pray you get ten years apiece, because if you don't . . .' She knelt beside them. 'I'll hunt you down and shoot you both.'

'Hey, lady, it was just an animal.'

I grabbed Susan and pulled her to her feet before she could slug him. Jordan said softly, 'I'll let you have the rifle again.'

Susan leaned into me. 'You're bleeding.'

'A present from Little Irving.'

She held my hand in her smaller ones, but I knew she wasn't trying to stop the blood flow; she was looking at the bite radius. My wife the scientist.

I missed Irving when we went down to the barricade. No happy snorts, no bubble blowing, no dragon head butting your ribs. It was lonely. Baby Irving is like most of the monsters, shy. The best picture we have is a night shot of ripples on the water. My bite mark did prove our point. Pictures of my hand will make up part of Susan's report.

Susan now thinks that all lake monsters are capable of cloning themselves by parthenogenesis. The clone is born at the death of the parent. That would explain why no one has ever seen more than one lake monster at a time. It also explains why both lake monsters that had been autopsied in the past had unborn babies. Pollution killed them all. Irving died from injuries, so his baby lived.

The problem is that cloning leads to mutation and genetic drift. You need sexual reproduction in a vertebrate to keep the species healthy. Maybe centuries ago the lakes were all connected, but as the land closed in and isolated the monsters, they had to survive long enough to reproduce, so they cloned themselves. The individual genotypes were saved, but there is no known natural way for lake monsters to find mates. Without help from man, lake monsters are probably a dead end. If we don't kill them off first, that is.

Little Irving's birth put a stop to the Lake Monster Breeding Program. Susan was out of a job, but since she is already living in the Enchanted Forest National Park and has full cooperation of the park service, she has a good shot at new grant money. If she gets it, we'll be studying the sex life of the red-bearded leprechaun. The real question is, are there any female leprechauns? No one has ever seen one. This problem sounds vaguely familiar.

Susan is happy off on another project to save yet another endangered creature. But I miss Irving, and though Susan would laugh at me probably, I like to think that Irving is somewhere chasing angelic speedboats, or maybe he's got his own wings. Surely, even God needs a laugh now and then, and Irving is a funny guy, for a monster.

# SELLING HOUSES

*This story is set in Anita's world, but Anita isn't in it. None of the main or even minor characters are in it. One day I wondered: What are people with less dangerous jobs doing in Anita's world now that vampires are legally alive? How has it changed other jobs? For instance, real estate . . .*

THE HOUSE SAT in its small yard looking sullen. It seemed to squat close to the ground as if it had been beaten down. Abbie shook her head to clear such strange notions from her mind. The house looked just like all the other houses in the subdivision. Oh, certainly it had type-A elevation. Which meant it had a peaked roof, and it had two skylights in the living room and a fireplace. The Garners had wanted some of the extra features. It was a nice house with its deluxe cedar board siding and half brick front. Its small lot was no smaller than any of the other houses, except for some of the corner lots. And yet . . .

Abbie walked briskly up the sidewalk that led through the yard. Daffodils waved bravely all along the porch. They were a brilliant burst of color against the dark-red house. Abbie swallowed quickly, her breath short. She had only talked to Marion Garner on the phone maybe twice, but in those conversations Marion had been full of gardening ideas for their new home.

It had been Sandra who had handled the sell, but she wouldn't touch the house again. Sandra's imagination was a little too thorough to allow her to go back to the place where her clients were slaughtered.

Abbie had been given the job because she specialized in the hard-to-sell. Hadn't she sold that monstrous rundown Victorian to that young couple who wanted to fix it up, and that awful filthy Peterson house? Why, she had spent her days off cleaning it out so it would sell, and it had sold, for more than they expected. And Abbie was determined that she would sell this house as well.

She admitted that mass murder was a very black mark against a house. And mass murder with an official cause of demon possession was about as black a mark as any.

The house had been exorcized, but even Abbie, who was no psychic, could feel it. Evil was here like a stain that wouldn't come completely up. And if the second owners of this house fell to demons, then Abbie and her Realtor company would be liable. So Abbie would see that the house was cleansed correctly. It would be as pure and lily-white as a virgin at her wedding. It would have to be.

The real problem was that the newspapers had made a horrendous scandal of it all. There wasn't a soul for miles around that didn't know about it. And any prospective buyer would have to be told. No, Abbie would not try to keep it a secret from buyers, but at the same time she wouldn't volunteer the full information too early in the sales pitch either.

She hesitated outside the door and said half aloud, 'Come on, it's just a house. There's nothing in there to hurt you.' The words rang hollow somehow, but she put the key in the lock and the door swung inward.

It looked so much like all the other houses that it startled her. Somehow she had thought that there would be a difference. Something to mark it apart from any other house. But the living room was small with the extra vaulted ceiling and brick fireplace. The carpet had been a beige-tan color that went with almost any décor. She'd seen pictures of the room before. There was bare sub-flooring, stretching naked and unfinished.

The flooring was discolored, pale and faded, almost like a coffee stain, but it covered a huge area. Here was where they had found Marion Garner. The papers said she had been stabbed over twenty times with a butcher knife.

New carpeting would hide the stain.

The afternoon sunlight streamed in the west-facing window and illuminated a hole in the wall. It was about the size of a fist and stood like a gaping reminder in the center of the off-white wall. As she walked closer, Abbie could see splatters along the wall. The cleanup crew usually got up all the visible mess. This looked like they hadn't even tried. Abbie would demand that they either finish the job, or give back some of the deposit.

The stains were pale brown shadows of their former selves, but no family would move in with such stains. New paint, new carpeting; the price of the house would need to go up. And Abbie wasn't sure she could get anyone to pay the original price.

She spoke softly to herself, 'Now what kind of defeatist talk is that? You will sell this house.' And she would, one way or another.

The kitchen/dining room area was cheerful with its skylight and back door. There was a smudge on the white door near the knob but not on it. Abbie stooped to examine it and quickly straightened. She wasn't sure if the cleanup crew had missed it or just left it. Maybe it was time to hire a new cleaning crew. Nothing excused leaving this behind.

It was a tiny handprint made of dried blood. It had to belong to the little boy; he had been almost five. Had he come running in here to escape? Had he tried to open the door and failed?

Abbie leaned over the sink and opened the kitchen window. It seemed stuffy in here suddenly. The cool spring breeze riffled the white curtains. They were embroidered with autumn leaves in rusts and shades of gold. They went well with the brown and ivory floor tiles.

She had a choice now, about where to go next. The door leading to the adjoining garage was just to her right. And the stairs leading down to the basement next to that. The garage was fairly safe. She opened the door and stepped onto the single step. The garage was cooler than the house, like a cave. Another back door led from the garage to the backyard. The only stains here were oil stains.

She stepped back in and closed the door, leaning against it for a moment. Her eyes glanced down the stairs to the closed door of the basement. Little Brian Garner's last trip had been down those stairs. Had he been chased? Had he hidden there and been discovered?

She would leave the basement until later.

The bedrooms and bath stretched down the long hallway to the left. The first bedroom had been the nursery. Someone had painted circus animals along the walls. They marched bright and cheerful round the empty walls. Jessica Garner had missed her second birthday by only two weeks. Or that's what Sandra said.

The bathroom was across the hall. It was good-sized, done mostly in white with some browns here and there. The mirror over the sink was gone. The cleanup crew had carted away the broken glass and left the black emptiness in the silver frame. Why replace anything until they knew for sure the house wasn't being torn down? Other houses had been torn down for less.

The wallpaper was pretty and looked undamaged. It was ivory with a pattern of pale pink stripes and brown flowers done small. Abbie ran her hand down it and found slash marks. There were at least six holes in the wall, as if a knife had been thrust into it. But there was no blood. There was no telling what Phillip Garner thought he was doing driving a knife into his bathroom wall.

The master bedroom was next with its half bath and ceiling fan. The wallpaper in here was beige with a brown oriental design done tasteful and small. There was a stain in the middle of the carpet, smaller than the living room's blood. No one knew why the baby had been in here, but it was here that he killed her. The papers were vague about exactly how she had died, which meant it was too gruesome to print much of it. Which meant that Jessica Garner had glimpsed hell before she died. There was a pattern of small smudges low along one wall. It looked like tiny bloody handprints struggling. But at least here the cleanup crew had tried to wash them away. Why hadn't they done the same in the kitchen area?

The more Abbie thought about it, the madder she got. With something this awful, why leave blatant reminders?

The little bathroom was in stainless white and silver, except for something dark between the tiles in front of the sink. Abbie started to bend down to look, but she knew what it was. It was blood. They had gotten most of it up, but it clung in the grooves between the tiles like dirt under a fingernail. She'd never seen the cleanup crew so careless.

The boy's bedroom was in the front corner of the house. The wallpaper was a pale blue with racing cars streaking across it. Red, green, yellow, dark blue, the cars with their miniature drivers raced around the empty walls. This was the only carpeting in the house that had some real color to it; it was a rich blue. Perhaps it had been the boy's favorite color. The sliding doors to the closet were torn, ripped. The white scars of naked wood showed under the varnish. One door had been ripped from its groove and leaned against the far wall. Had Brian Garner hidden here and been flushed out by his father?

Or had Phillip Garner only thought his son was in here? For it was certain the boy had not died here. There were no bloodstains, no helpless handprints.

Abbie walked out into the hallway. She had walked into hundreds of empty houses over the years, but she had never felt anything quite like this. The very walls seemed to be holding their breath, waiting, but waiting for what? It had not felt this way a moment before, of that Abbie was sure. She tried to shake the feeling but it would not leave. The best thing to do was finish the inspection quickly and get out of the house.

Unfortunately, all that was left was the basement.

She had been reluctant to go down there before, but with the air riding with expectation she didn't want to go down. But if she couldn't even stand to inspect the house, how could she possibly sell it?

She walked purposefully through the house, ignoring the blood-stained carpet and the handprinted door. But by ignoring them she became more aware of them. Death, especially violent death, was not easily dismissed.

Rust-brown carpet led down the steps to the closed door. And for some reason Abbie found the closed door menacing. But she went down.

She hesitated with her hand almost over the doorknob and then opened it quickly. The cool dampness of the basement was unchanged. It was like any other basement except this one had no windows. Mr Garner had requested that, no one knew why.

The bare concrete floor stretched gray and unbroken to the gray concrete walls. Pipes from upstairs hung from the ceiling and plunged out of sight under the floor. The sump pump in one corner was still in working order. The water heater was cold and waiting for someone to light it.

Abbie pulled on all three of the hanging chains and illuminated all the shadows away. But the bare lightbulbs cast shadows of their own as they gently swung, disturbed by her passing. And there in the far corner was the first stain.

The stain was small, but considering it had been a five-year-old boy, it was big enough.

There was a trail of stains leading round the back of the staircase. They were smeared and oddly shaped as if he had bled and someone dragged him along.

The last stain was in the shape of a bloody pentagram, rough, but recognizable. A sacrifice then.

There was a spattering on one wall, high up without a lower source. Probably where Phillip Garner had put a gun to his head and pulled the trigger.

Abbie turned off two of the lights and then stood there with her hand on the last cord, the one nearest the door. That air of expectation had left. She would have thought that the basement where the boy was brutalized would have felt worse, but it didn't. It seemed emptier and more normal than upstairs. Abbie didn't know why but made a note of it. She would tell the psychic that would be visiting the house.

She turned off the light and left, closing the door quietly behind her. The stairs were just stairs like so many other houses had. And the kitchen looked cheerful with its off-white walls. Abbie closed the window over the sink; it wouldn't do to have rain come in.

She had actually stepped into the living room when she turned back. The handprint on the back door bothered her. It seemed such a mute appeal for help, safety, escape.

She whispered to the sun-warmed silence, 'Oh, I can't stand to leave it.' She fished Kleenex from her pocket and dampened them in the sink. She knelt by the door and wiped across the brownish stain.

It smeared fresh and bloody, crimson as new blood. Abbie gasped and half-fell away from the door. The Kleenex was soaked with blood. She dropped it to the floor.

The handprint bled, slowly, down the white door.

She whispered, 'Brian.' There was a sound of small feet running. The sound hushed down the carpeted stairs to the basement. And Abbie heard the door swing open and close with a small click.

There was a silence so heavy that she couldn't breathe. And then it was gone, whatever it was. She got to her feet and walked to the living room. *So there's a ghost*, she told herself, *you've sold houses with ghosts before*. But she didn't pick up the soggy Kleenex and she didn't look back to see how far down the blood would go before it stopped.

She was out the door and locking it as fast as she could and still maintain some decorum. It wouldn't help things at all if the neighbors saw the real estate agent running from the house. She forced herself to walk down the steps between the yellow flowers. But there was a spot in the middle of her back that itched as if someone were staring at it.

Abbie didn't look back, she wouldn't run, but she had no desire to see Brian Garner's face pressed against the window glass. Maybe the cleanup crew had done the best they could. She'd have to find out if all the marks bled fresh.

The house would have to be re-blessed. And probably a medium brought in to tell the ghost that it was dead. A lot of people took it as a status symbol to have a ghost in their house. Certain kinds of ghosts, though. No one liked a poltergeist, no one liked bleeding walls, or hideous apparitions, or screams at odd times in the night. But a light that haunted only one hallway, or a phantom that walked in the library in eighteenth-century costume, well, those were call for a party. The latest craze was ghost parties. All those that did not have a ghost could come and watch one while everyone drank and had snacks.

But somehow Abbie didn't think that anyone would want Brian's ghost in their house. It was romantic to have a murdered sixteenth-century explorer roaming about, but recent victims and a child at that . . . Well, historic victims are one thing, but a ghost out of your morning paper, that was something else entirely.

Abbie just hoped that Brian Garner would be laid to rest easily. Sometimes the ghost just needed someone to tell it that it was dead. But other times it took more stringent measures, especially with violent ends. Strangely, there were a lot of child ghosts running around. Abbie had read an article in the Sunday magazine about it. The theory was that children didn't have a concept of death yet, so they became ghosts. They were still trying to live.

Abbie left such thinking up to the experts. She just sold houses. As soon as the car started Abbie turned on the radio. She wanted noise.

The news was on and the carefully enunciated words filled the car as she pulled away from the house. 'The Supreme Court reached their verdict today, upholding a New Jersey court ruling that Mitchell Davies, well-known banker and real estate investor, is still legally alive even though he is a vampire. This supports the so-called Bill of Life, which came out last year, widening the definition of life to include some forms of the living dead. Now on to sports . . .'

Abbie changed the station. She wasn't in the mood for sports scores or news of any kind. She had had her own dose of reality today and just wanted to go home. But first she had to stop by her office.

It was late when she arrived and even the receptionist had gone home. Three rows of desks stretched catty-corner from one end of the room to the other. Most of the overhead lights had been turned off, leaving the room in afternoon shadows. A thin strip of white light wound down the center and passed over Sandra's desk. Sandra sat waiting, hands folded in front of her. She had stopped even pretending to work.

Her blue eyes flashed upward when she saw Abbie come in. The relief was plain on her face and in the sudden slump of her shoulders.

Abbie smiled at her.

Sandra made a half smile in return. She asked, 'How was it?'

Abbie walked to her desk, which put her to Sandra's left, and two desks over. She started sorting papers while she considered how best to answer. 'It's going to need some work before we can show it.'

Sandra's high heels clicked on the floor, and Abbie could feel her standing behind her. 'That isn't what I mean, and you know it.'

Abbie turned and faced her. Sandra's eyes were too bright, her face too intense. 'Sandra, please, it's over, let it go.'

Sandra gripped her arm, fingers biting deep. 'Tell me what it was like.'

'You're hurting me.'

Her hand dropped numbly to her side and she almost whispered, 'Please, I need to know.'

'You didn't do anything wrong. It wasn't your fault.'

'But I sold them that house.'

'But Phillip Garner played with the Ouija board. He opened the way to what happened.'

'But I should have seen it. I should have realized something was wrong. I did notice things when Marion contacted me. I should have done something.'

'What, what could you have done?'

'I could have called the police.'

'And told them that you had a bad feeling about one of your clients? You aren't a registered psychic, they would have ignored you. And Sandra, you didn't have any premonitions. You've convinced yourself you knew beforehand, but it isn't true. You never mentioned it to anyone in the office.' Abbie tried to get her to smile. 'And get real, girl, if you had news that important, you couldn't keep it to yourself. You are the original gossip. A kind gossip, but still a gossip.'

Sandra didn't smile, but she nodded. 'True, I don't keep secrets very well.'

Abbie put her arm around her and hugged her. 'Stop beating yourself up over something you had nothing to do with. Cut the guilt off; it isn't your guilt to deal with.'

Sandra leaned into her and began to cry.

They stayed there like that until it was full dark and Sandra was hoarse from crying.

Sandra said, 'I've made you late getting home.'

'Charles will understand.'

'You sure?'

'Yes, I have a very understanding husband.'

She nodded and snuffled into the last Kleenex in the room. 'Thanks.'

'It's what friends are for, Sandra. Now go home and feel good about yourself, you deserve it.'

Abbie called her husband before locking up the office, to assure him that she was coming home. He was very understanding, but he tended to worry about her. Then she escorted Sandra to her car and made sure she drove away.

It was weeks later before Abbie stood in the newly carpeted living room. Fresh hex signs had been painted over the doors and windows. A priest had blessed the house. A medium had come and told

Brian Garner's ghost that it was dead. Abbie did not know, or want to know, if the ghost had been stubborn about leaving.

The house felt clean and new, as if it had just been built. Perhaps a registered psychic could have picked up some lingering traces of evil and horror, but Abbie couldn't.

The kitchen door stood white and pure. There were no stains today, everything had been fixed, everything had been hidden. And wonder of wonders, she had a client coming to see it.

The client knew all about the house and its history. But then Mr Channing and his family had been having difficulties of their own. No one wanted to sell them a house.

But Abbie had no problem with selling to them. They were people, after all; the law said so.

She had turned the lights in the living room and kitchen on. Their yellow glow chased back the night. Charles had been unhappy about her meeting the clients alone, at night. But Abbie knew you couldn't sell to people if they didn't think you trusted and liked them. So she waited alone in the artificial light, trying not to think too much about old superstitions. As a show of great good faith, she had no protection on her.

At exactly ten o'clock the doorbell rang. She had not heard a car drive up.

Abbie opened the door with her best professional smile on her face. And it wasn't hard to keep the smile because they looked like a very normal family. Mr and Mrs Channing were a young handsome couple. He was well over six feet with thick chestnut hair and clear blue eyes. She was only slightly shorter and blond. But they did not smile. It was the boy who smiled. He was perhaps fourteen and had his father's chestnut hair, but his eyes were dark brown, and Abbie found herself staring into those eyes. They were the most perfect color she had ever seen, solid, without a trace, falling. A hand steadied her, and when she looked, it was the boy who touched her, but he did not meet her eyes.

The three stood waiting for something as Abbie held the door. Finally, she asked them in. 'Won't you please come inside?'

They seemed to relax and stepped through the door with the boy a little in front.

She smiled again and put a hand out to Mr Channing and said, 'It's a pleasure to meet you, Mr Channing.'

The three exchanged glances and then polite laughter.

The man said, 'I'm not Channing; call me Rick.'

'Oh, of course.' Abbie tried to cover her confusion as the woman introduced herself simply as 'Isabel.'

It left Abbie with only one other client, but she offered her hand and her smile. 'Mr Channing.'

He took it in a surprisingly strong grip and said, 'I have looked forward to meeting you, Ms McDonnell. And please, it's just Channing, no Mr.'

'As you like, Channing. Then you must call me Abbie.'

'Well then, Abbie, shall we see the house?' His face was so frank and open, so adult. It was disconcerting to see such intelligence and confidence in the eyes of a fourteen-year-old body.

He said, 'I am much older than I appear, Abbie.'

'Yes, I am sorry, I didn't mean to stare.'

'That's quite all right. It is better that you stare than refuse to see us.'

'Yes, well, let me show you the house.' Abbie turned off the lights and showed the moon shining through the skylights. The brick fireplace was an unexpected hit. Somewhere Abbie had gotten the idea that vampires didn't like fire.

She did turn on the lights to show them the bedrooms and baths. They might be able to see in the dark, but Abbie didn't think it would impress them if she tripped in the dark.

The female, Isabel, spun round the master bedroom and said, 'Oh, it will make a wonderful office.'

Abbie inquired, 'What do you do?'

The woman turned and said, 'I'm an artist, I work mostly in oils.'

Abbie said, 'I've always wished I could paint, but I can't even draw.'

The woman seemed not to have heard. Abbie had learned long ago that you didn't make conversation if the client didn't want to talk. So they viewed the house in comparative silence.

There was one point in the master bathroom, when the three had to crowd in to see, that Abbie turned and bumped into the man. She stepped away as if struck and to cover her almost-fear she turned around and nearly gasped. They had reflections. She could see them just as clearly as herself. Abbie recovered from the shock and went on. But she knew that at least Channing had noticed. There was a special smile on his face that said it all.

Since they had reflections, Abbie showed them the kitchen more thoroughly than she had been intending. After all, if one myth was untrue, perhaps others were; perhaps they could eat.

The basement she saved for last, as she did in most of her houses. She led the way down and groped for the light pull cord but did not turn on the lights until she heard them shuffle in next to her. She said, 'You'll notice there are no windows. You will have absolute privacy down here.' She did not add that no sunlight would be coming down because after the mirror she wasn't sure if it was pertinent.

Channing's voice came soft and low out of the velvet dark. 'It is quite adequate.'

It wasn't exactly unbridled enthusiasm, but Abbie had done her best. She pulled on the light and showed them the water heater and the sump pump. 'And the washer and dryer hookups are all set. All you need is the machine.'

Channing nodded and said, 'Very good.'

'Would you like me to leave you alone for a few moments to discuss things?'

'Yes, if you would.'

'Certainly.' Abbie walked up the stairs but left the door open. She went into the living room so they would be sure she wasn't eavesdropping. She wondered what the neighbors would think about vampires living next door. But that wasn't her concern; she just sold the house.

She did not hear them come up, but they stood suddenly in the living room. She swallowed past the beating of her heart and said, 'What do you think of the house?'

Channing smiled, exposing fangs. 'I think we'll take it.'

The smile was very genuine on Abbie's part as she walked forward and shook their hands. 'And how soon will you want to move in?'

'Next week, if possible. We have had our down payment for several months, and our bank is ready to approve our loan.'

'Excellent. The house is yours as soon as the papers are signed.'

Isabel ran a possessive hand down the wall. 'Ours,' she said.

Abbie smiled and said, 'And if any of your friends need a house, just let me know. I'm sure I can meet their needs.'

Channing grinned broadly at her and put his cool hand in hers. 'I'm sure you can, Abbie, I'm sure you can.'

After all, everyone needs a house to call their own. And Abbie sold houses.

# A TOKEN FOR CELANDINE

*This story is set in the world of my first novel,* Nightseer. *It's set on a continent hundreds of miles away, but it's still the same world with the same magic system. Marion Zimmer Bradley rejected the story by saying that I'd done a pastiche of Tolkien, and elves really should be left to him, but do send another story and try again. I disagreed about elves being left to Tolkien and sent the story out again. It sold next time out, to* Memories and Visions. *And I would send Ms Bradley my next story, and have the pleasure of her buying it. No elves in that one.*

THE PROPHET WAS an old man crazed with his own visions. He crouched against the dark wood of an elm. His fingers dug into the bark as if he would anchor himself to it. He gasped and wheezed as he drew in the morning air.

We had been chasing him through these woods for three days. And I was tired of it. If he ran this time, I was going to put an arrow in his leg. Celandine could heal him of the wound, and she could finally ask her question. I had not mentioned my plan to the healer. I thought she might object. The old man looked into a bar of dazzling sunlight. The glow showed his eyes milky with the creeping blindness of the very old and the very poor.

He was sick, blind, and crazy, and he had eluded me for days.

His prophecy protected him or perhaps the voices he called out to told him I was near. He turned his head to one side as if he were listening. I heard nothing but the wind and a small animal scuttling in the brush.

He turned his blind eyes and looked directly at me. The flesh along my back crawled. He could not see me, but I knew he did.

His voice was an abused cackle that never seemed to finish a thought completely. I had listened to him rant, but now he spoke low and well. 'Ask,' he said.

It was Celandine's question, but while he was in the mood to answer, I asked. Not all prophets are able to answer direct questions. Those that do tend to answer only one question for each person. 'How do I find the token which Celandine the Healer seeks?'

'The black road must take. Demons help you. Fight in darkness you will.'

I heard the whisper of cloth that announced the healer.

She came up beside me, white cloak huddled round her body.

Without taking my eyes from the old man I asked, 'Did you hear what he said?'

'Yes.'

'Ask him something.'

'Where is the token I seek?'

'Demon, demon inside.' He coughed, his body nearly doubled over with the violence of it. Bloody foam flecked his chin. Celandine stepped forward. 'Let me heal you.'

His eyes went wide. 'Death want, death seek, no heal.' And he was gone, vanishing into the underbrush noiseless as a rabbit.

Celandine stood there, tears glistening in her eyes. 'He'll die.'

'He wants to die.'

She shook her head, and one teardrop slid from crystalline blue eyes down a flawless white cheek. 'He doesn't know what he's saying.'

I touched her arm. 'Celandine, no healer can cure the madness of prophecy.'

She nodded and pulled the cloak's hood to hide her face. A strand of black hair trailed across the white cloth like a stain.

I said, 'This is the seventh prophet, Celandine. We must trust the information and act upon it.'

She spoke in a low voice that I had to strain to hear.

'Aren't you afraid, Bevhinn?'

I debated with myself whether she wanted truth or for me to be strong for her. I decided on truth. 'I fear the black healers of Lolth. I fear being a female trapped behind their dark border.'

'And yet you will go?'

'It is where our quest takes us. We must go.'

She turned to me, face framed in shadowed hood. 'It is death by torture for me if I am caught.'

I had heard the stories of what Loltuns did to white healers. They were tales to curdle the blood round winter fires.

'I will die before I let them take you. You have my word.'

She spun round as if she would find an answer in the spring morning. 'I have your word.' She turned back to me, blue eyes hard. 'What good is your word? You aren't human. You don't worship the Goddess that I serve. Why should I trust you to give your life for me?'

I clamped a six-fingered hand round sword hilt. Five months I'd traveled with her. Five months of living off the land, killing that we both could eat. I had slain winter-starved wolves and fought bandits. I had guarded her back while she healed the sick. I had been wounded twice, and twice she had healed me. And now this.

I let the anger flow into my face. I stared at her with my alien purple eyes, but I kept my voice low with menace. I had no desire to shout and bring men or a wild beast upon us. 'Your fear makes you foolish, Celandine. But do not fear. Your father paid me well to guard you on this exile's quest.'

'You sell yourself for money like some harlot.'

I slapped her hard, and she fell to the ground. She looked startled. I had never offered her violence before. 'Your father bought my sword, my magic, and my loyalty. I will lay down my life to protect you, but I will not be insulted.'

'How dare you. I am a white healer . . .'

I finished for her, 'And bastard daughter of the King of Celosia. I know all that. He hired me, remember.'

'You are my bodyguard, my servant.'

'I'm not the reason we're out here in this godforsaken wilderness. You killed a man. You took that pure white gift of yours and twisted it. You used black healing and took a life.'

She was crying now, softly.

'The only way to end this exile is to follow the prophet's advice and go to Lolth.'

'I'm afraid.'

I grabbed her upper arms, pulling her to her feet. 'I'm afraid, too, but I want this over with. I want to go back to Meltaan. I want a bed and a bath and decent food. I want someone to guard my back for a change.' I let her go, and she stumbled back, sobbing.

'I will not let your fear keep me out here forever. Your father didn't pay me that much.'

'You can't leave me.'

'I could, but I won't. But tomorrow we travel the dark road.'

Morning found us on the bank of Lake Muldor. A blue cloak to match her eyes replaced the healer's cloak Celandine usually wore. She kept it pulled close around her though it was very warm for spring.

The sun was warm on my face. The light shattered diamond bursts off the lake water and the silver of my armor. I had bound my breasts tight under the scale mail. I was counting on the fact that most humans think male Varellians look effeminate. And that they would look at sword and armor and think me male.

Celandine would simply go as my wife. It was rare, but it was done. That would explain my exile. The problem was that we both stood out. We could not simply blend with what few travelers there were.

Celandine was too aware of her royal heritage to play the common wife. She had no talent for lying or being false. I could have wasted magic to disguise myself as human, but it wouldn't have been safe. I was earth-witch, not illusionist, and disguise was not one of my better spells. So I rode as a Varellian. My hair was spun snow with a purity of color that few humans achieved. The hair could have been dyed, the odd-shaped ears hidden, but a sixth finger was something else. It was considered a mark of good fortune in Varell but not among the humans. And, of course, my eyes gave me away. Purple as a violet, the color of a grape.

We were not your usual traveling couple. I rode a unicorn, which was very hard to hide. The unicorns of Varell are as big as a warhorse. They were the mounts of royalty and of the royal guard. Once a unicorn and a rider are bound, it is a lifelong binding. So through no fault of his own, Ulliam shared my exile among the humans and the horses.

But he also shared my magic, though he can only feel it and not perform it. His great split hooves danced on the damp meadow grass. The earth-magic of spring was calling. My power was tied to the ground and that which sprang from it. Every meadow flower, every blade of grass, was hidden power for my magic. My power called to other things. I shared the joy of the swallow as it turned and twisted over the lake. I froze in the long grass with the rabbit waiting for our horses to pass. Spring was one of the most powerful times for an earth-witch, as winter was one of the worst. And Ulliam danced with me on his back, feeling the power. I hoped I would not need it.

Celandine rode silently, blue cloak pulled over a plain brown dress. Visions of torture still danced behind her eyes. Her fear was an almost palpable thing. She rode one horse and carried the lead for a second. She would need a fresh mount if we were to make good time. I would have liked to rest Ulliam, but warhorses were not easily found in the wild lands. I would not ride less. You could not fight off the back of a normal riding horse. The clang of metal, the swinging shield, even drawing bow and arrow, could send a horse racing in fright. And you couldn't afford that in battle. A war steed had to be trained to it from birth; there was just no other way. Ulliam and I had been trained together. No other mount could have known my mind as he did.

I had used magic to make him less noticeable. Most would see a great white horse and nothing more. If a wizard concentrated, then perhaps he would see past the glamour, but it was the best I could do. In Lolth they sacrificed unicorns to Verm and Ivel.

I asked Celandine, 'Have you ever worshipped Ivel?'

She made the sign against evil, thumb and little finger extended near her face. 'Don't use her full name.'

'As you like. Have you ever worshipped Mother Bane?'

'Of course, you must not ignore any of the three faces of the Great Mother.'

I didn't argue theology with her. We had found we did not agree on matters of worship. 'You've never spoken of Mother Bane as one of your Gods.'

'Because it is not wise to do so.'

'Why do the Loltuns sacrifice women to Her altar?'

'It is a matter of theological interpretation.'

'Interpretation?'

'Yes.' She seemed reluctant to speak further, so I let the subject drop. Celandine was not happy that I could argue her into a corner using her own sacred tomes.

The black road erupted from the damp meadow grass without marker or warning. It seemed to be made of solid rock, black as if the earth had bled. Legend said that Pelrith of the Red Eye forged the road. And seeing it lying there on the shore of the lake, I believed in demigods calling things forth from the earth. I urged Ulliam forward.

The moment his hooves hit the road, I felt it. The road was dead; no earth-magic sang through it. The horse Celandine was leading shied at the black surface. I moved Ulliam to calm it before the horse she was riding could bolt as well. We rode into Lolth three abreast, with the skittish horse in the middle.

I noticed bumps in the smooth surface of the road, but there was no pattern to them. I dismounted and walked Ulliam until I came to a bump that seemed higher than the others. I knelt and ran a mailed hand over the blackened lump. My eyes could not puzzle it out at first, then suddenly, it was clear. A human skull gaped from the road, barely covered in the black rocklike stuff. And I could not force the image from my mind.

Celandine called, 'What is it?'

'Bones. Human bones.'

She made the sign against evil again.

I mounted Ulliam, and we rode on. My eyes were drawn with a horrible fascination to each half-hidden shape as we rode. We traveled on the burial mound of hundreds.

We came to the border guard then. There were only four of them, but two shone magic to my eyes. And I knew that I shone as well. But there was nothing illegal about being a wizard; at least I didn't think there was. A female wizard might have been stopped, but healers do not shine like wizards. Celandine would seem merely a woman until she healed someone. When she laid hands, she glowed like the full moon.

One man came from behind the wooden gate. He stood in front of me. 'Well, you must be an ice elf.'

It was a rather rude way to begin, but I had been prepared for that. It was a killing insult in Varell, but I had been five years from there. It wasn't the first time someone had called me elf to my face. It would not be the last. 'I am Bevhinn Ailir, and this is my wife, Celandine.'

His eyes turned to the healer, and he said, 'Oh. She's a beauty.' He walked over to her and put a hand on her knee, massaging it. Celandine glared at him.

The hand began to creep up her thigh, and she yanked her horse backward. It bumped the man, and he backed away smiling. He said, 'You could make money off this one. She would bring a fair price every night you stay in our country.'

'She is a wife, not a whore.'

He shrugged. 'There isn't that much difference, now, is there?'

'There is where I come from.'

'Yes, the Varellians and their reverence for females. You and your queen.'

I had had about enough of this. 'Can we pass, or must we stand here and be insulted?'

He frowned at that and said, 'I'd keep that fancy armor hidden. There are those who would take it from you.'

I smiled at him, forcing him to stare into my alien eyes. 'It is good armor, but surely men aren't eager to die for a suit of armor they would never fit into.'

He returned the smile and said, 'I would love to see one of your Varellian women. You're pretty enough to eat yourself.'

I said, voice low, 'Your two friends over there can tell you I'm a wizard. And this wizard has grown very tired of you.' I flexed a hand for dramatic emphasis, and he backed away. Truth was, an earth-witch wasn't big on instant magic, but they didn't know that. With my power tied to the spring, I sparkled like a sorcerer. It was a good time of year to bluff.

The gate opened, and he called after us, 'May you run afoul of a black healer.'

I answered back over my shoulder, 'And may the next wizard you torment blow your head off.'

Forest stretched on either side of the road. The birds and beasts didn't know they had crossed a border. In truth, it looked much like the wild lands where we had spent the winter, except for the road.

Farmland opened on either side of the road, fighting back the trees; the smell of fresh-plowed earth was strong and good. The soil was a rich black. I felt an urge to crumble the dirt in my hands and feel its growing power, but I resisted. Ulliam danced nervously under me.

Forest returned, hugging each side of the road. But no blade of grass, no wildflower dared to encroach upon the black road. It was late in the day when we heard a loud cracking noise, like a cannon-ball striking wood. The horses pranced in fright, and even Ulliam shivered under me. There was a tearing sound, as if the earth itself were being pulled apart. We rode cautiously toward the sounds.

A wide path had been freshly cleared from the forest. Trees with jagged trunks lay in heaps on their sides. Stumps lay in a second heap, earth-covered roots bare to the sky. Stooping to pull another great stump from the ground was a demon. His skin was night-black.

Muscles bulged along his back and arms. His ribbed bat ears curled tight with his effort as he strained upward. The roots ripped free of the earth. He put the stump in the pile with the rest. He caught sight of us on the road, and we all stared at each other. A silver necklace glittered round his neck. The cold eye of a diamond the size of a hen's egg winked out from it. From here it glowed with magic.

Celandine looked at me. Was this our demon's help, or was the token inside the demon? I hoped it wasn't the latter. I didn't see myself slitting the gullet of a greater demon.

A man stepped out of the trees. He was thin, and a scraggly beard edged his pointed chin. He said, 'Be on your way. You're distracting him.'

'I am sorry, good farmer, but I have never seen a greater demon before.'

A look of incredulity passed over his face. 'You swear by Loth's bloody talons that you've never seen a greater demon?'

'I swear.'

He smiled then, friendly. 'Well, you have started out with a greater demon named Krakus. He's been ensorcelled to the farmers hereabout for over fifty years. He's cleared most of the fields along this road.'

I stared at the demon, and there was something in his smooth yellow eyes that said hatred. A hatred deeper than anything I could feel.

'Good farmer, are you never afraid of him breaking free?'

'No, the enchantment on him is strong enough.'

'What would happen if he ever was freed?'

The farmer looked back at the demon, the smile gone. 'Why, he'd kill me and everyone else he'd worked for.'

'Where do you keep the demon when he's not working? Does he go back to the pits from which he came?'

The man found the question very funny. 'Why, you don't know anything about demons. An ensorcelled demon can't leave the place he's been put, just can't leave. We keep him chained at night near where he's working.'

I shivered under the gaze of those sullen yellow eyes. 'I hope you keep a guard on him at night, farmer.'

'Oh we do, but nothing to worry about. He'll still be pulling stumps fifty years from now.' The farmer walked back into the cleared area and slapped the demon lightly on the arm. 'No, we couldn't lose such a good worker. Get back to work, Krakus.' The demon turned without a word or a snarl and stood before a full-grown tree. With one gesture and a flash of sorcery he felled the tree, blasting it off a few feet above the ground. The farmer went to sit in the sunshine. Our interview was over.

Celandine and I rode in silence for a short time, then she asked, 'Do you think that is the demon who will help us?'

'I don't know.'

'You don't know. Then what are we doing here? What good is prophecy if you don't know what it means?'

'None, I suppose.'

'Then what are we risking ourselves for?'

I grabbed the reins of her horse and said, 'The only way to understand prophecy is to do what it says. Now stop sniveling.'

She glared at me but kept her peace. Her fear kept her silent more than I did.


Twilight had fallen, spreading a blue haze across the trees. An inn sat in a small clearing. In the dim light I made out a sign. It had a crude drawing of the demon we had just seen, and words proclaimed it the Black Demon Inn. Krakus had been here a long time.

I tied the horses up outside, and we entered. The place smelled stale. The windows were open, and the spring wind blew through the place, but it would take weeks for the sourness of winter to be blown away. When my eyes adjusted to the dim lighting, I saw the place was almost empty.

Only three of the small scarred tables were in use. A group of five farmers sat drinking and laughing. Two men in chain mail sat eating at another table. Their swords were out on the table beside them, sheathed. And a young man dressed all in black sat at the last table near the stairs. A young girl no more than twelve sat with him. Her eyes were downcast, and she was obviously afraid.

Celandine stiffened beside me. She had recognized the robes of a healer, a black healer. The host came over to us, smiling, 'And how may I help you this night, travelers?'

'Food, stabling for the horses, and a room for the night.'

'One gold ducat will get you all you desire.' His leer was obvious. I looked blankly at him. He explained patiently, 'All our guests have the choice of three fair ladies to keep them company for a time.'

'No, thank you. My wife and I are quite fine, alone.'

He shrugged. 'As you wish, but if I were you I'd have my wife pull up her hood. And have her lower her eyes.'

'She is fine as she is.'

He shrugged again. 'Just trying to help. The stables are to the left. My boy will see to them. When you return, I will have your dinners waiting.'

We went out and led the horses and Ulliam to the stables. They were cramped, and a dirty boy of about ten scuttled up to take the horses. He did not try to take Ulliam, and I did not offer. While he brushed down the horses, I tended the unicorn. The boy was dirty and perhaps not quite bright, but he brushed the horses well, and the feed he gave them was good quality.

We took a small table near the wall so I could watch the room. It was then that I noticed a small demon, barely three feet high, cleaning tables. He balanced the dirty dishes above his head with impossibly long arms. He was bright green in color and scaled rather than skin-covered. Celandine and I stared after him as he disappeared into the back.

She stared at me, and I shrugged. In the end it would be Celandine who said what the token was and where it was. My job was just to help her get it.

The little demon also brought our food. Neither of us spoke as it put down bowls of stew, thick slices of brown bread, and tankards of some liquid. He seemed accustomed to silence and raced back through the tables with his empty tray.

The stew was hot, the meat and vegetables a little stringy, but it had been a hard winter. Stores were running low everywhere, but the bread was fresh and good. One of the farmers I had noticed earlier came to stand beside us. He bumped into our table, unsteady on his feet. He smelled of beer. 'Is this pretty thing your wife, Varellian?'

'Yes.'

'How much for a night with her?'

I stared at him a moment, not sure I had understood. 'I said she is my wife.'

'I heard you. How much for the night?'

'We are new to Lolth and do not understand all the customs. Are you saying that Loltuns sell their wives for money, like whores?'

'You brought her in here, with her face showing. She looked at every man in the place, bold as a basilisk. What else would you be doing but selling?'

I understood the host's warning now, but it was too late. 'We are not Loltun, and I am not selling my wife.'

He scowled at that. 'The other three women are busy, and I don't go near a black healer. I have need of a woman, and she is the only one available.'

'You'll have to wait then.'

'Loltun men do not wait for women.' He grabbed at Celandine surprisingly fast and jerked her to her feet.

My sword was out before I had time to think. 'Let her go, or die.'

The sight of naked steel seemed to catch his attention. He let go of her, and she sank back into her seat. The man stared at the end of my sword, and finally said, 'Well, if you don't want to sell, then have her keep her eyes to herself. You could get a man killed over a mis-understanding like this.'

I said nothing as he shuffled back to his companions. Celandine pulled up her hood without being asked. I resheathed my sword, and we ate in silence. But there was another scene taking place.

The black healer and his girl were having a fight of sorts. He would touch her and then laugh, and she would scream. And then he would touch her again and laugh. I asked Celandine, 'What is he doing?'

She swallowed. 'I think he is hurting the girl and then healing her.'

'To what purpose?'

'Many black healers are insane. They pervert their healing power into harm, and it contaminates them.'

The girl was pretty. She had long yellow hair and light eyes that I guessed were blue, but couldn't be sure at this distance. Her body had just begun to swell to womanhood, but she was still more child than woman. A bleeding scratch appeared on her cheek. He touched it, and the cut vanished.

'How did that cut appear? He didn't touch her.'

'He is a very powerful black healer. He has a gift similar to sor-cery.'

'As you have.'

She nodded. 'As I have, but I must not use it again on peril of my soul.'

That was what the quest was all about. The token, whatever it was, would cleanse the healer's soul of the stain of black healing.

The girl screamed, a full-blown shriek. She stood, knocking her chair backward. Even in the dim light I could see the open sores on her arm.

Celandine started to rise, and I gripped her arm. It was automatic for her to help the sick, but not here. My grip seemed to remind her of her fear, and she sat down.

I had seen this sudden bravery many times. It came from her

healing. She was afraid of so many things. But her healing made her different. I had seen her risk death to save a drowning child. Many times she had walked among bandits to heal their sick. It was as if all her strength, all her bravery, went to healing, and there was none left for Celandine herself.

The black healer caught the girl-child. She struggled as he clutched the diseased arm. She broke away from him and stared at the now-healed arm. He laughed.

The host went up to him, and his voice carried in the sudden silence. 'Sir, we are honored at your business, but your lady friend is upsetting the other guests. Would it please the most honorable healer if he would take her up to his room?' The man had bowed low but never took his eyes off the healer.

What would the host do if the healer moved to touch him? The healer laughed again. 'You should be honored that I come to this piss hole of an inn. I am of the highest rank of healer. I talk to your Gods for you. I face them when you cower in fear.' He was addressing the entire room now. 'I hold the power that pacifies the Gods themselves. I consort with the demons of the pit. I do things that would crack your minds like brittle kindling.' And he walked over to the now-quiet farmers. 'But you turn away from me when I show power. Oh, heal me, please, heal me. But then leave us alone. That's how it is.'

He went back to the girl, and she backed away crying. She begged him, 'Please, let me go, please.'

'Come, girl, it is time someone here learned what it is to embrace a black healer.' She screamed as he grabbed her. He pulled her toward the stairs. Her hand gripped the banister, and he tugged her. Her fingers slipped, and he grabbed her close to his body. He carried her like that up the stairs and paused at the very top. He yelled at the host, 'Which room is mine?'

The host made a half bow and said, 'Turn to your right. It is the last door on that side. It is the nicest room in the inn.'

'And it will be poor,' the healer said and walked from sight with the struggling girl in his arms.

My fingers bit deeply into Celandine's arm. Her blue eyes glowed with anger. But I thought some of it was directed inward at her own fear. There were white healers I knew who would have challenged him regardless of the cost. They would not let such evil go unquestioned. For once I was glad that Celandine was not so zealous. She would be killed for being a white healer, and I would be killed defending her. It was not the way I wanted to die.

The first shriek sounded from upstairs. It cut through the fresh conversation and killed it. Everyone downstairs sat, waiting. A second scream came, piteous, all hope gone, choking sobs followed it.

The farmers got up and paid their bill. Only the two fighters were left. And they, like us, were travelers with no other place to go.

Celandine nodded. I motioned to the host, and he came over. There was a light dew of sweat on his face.

'Good sir, we are ready for our room.'

'Was the stew to your liking?'

'The food was good, but we seem to have lost our appetites.'

'He is a high priest of our people. But to strangers, who do not understand, well . . . he may seem extreme.'

'On the contrary, mine host, I do understand. Even in other lands some magics drive the sense from a man.'

The host looked nervously about as if someone might overhear. He said, 'As you wish. Your room is to the right, the first door. It is as far away from the noise as I can put you.'

'We appreciate that.'

He nodded, and we stood. Celandine followed me, hooded, eyes down, more to hide her anger than to hide her face.

We mounted the stairs to the sounds of screams. The screams became words, a prayer. I didn't need to look behind me to know Celandine was stiffening. The girl was praying to Mother Blessen. She was praying to Celandine's God.

The prayer was cut short as if she had been cuffed. We stepped into the dark hallway, and both of us simply stood as if waiting. The child's voice rose again in prayer. He was beating her. But she had decided that she would probably never see daylight. So she prayed, and he hit her. Celandine let her hood slip back. She turned to me wordlessly, and I met her eyes.

I whispered, 'The token?'

She nodded.

There was logic to it. The girl was inside the Black Demon Inn. The token was inside a demon just as the prophets had told us it would be. My sword sighed from its sheath, and I hefted my shield, balancing it on my arm. She smiled at me then. Fear danced in her eyes, but that curious strength that she had when healing, it was there, too.

She whispered to me, 'You must cut off his head, or take out his heart. He will simply heal himself otherwise. And you must kill him as quickly as possible, for he can do us all great harm.'

'Surely he has used most of his power already tonight.'

'He is high in the favor of the dark Gods. He may have more than his own power to draw from.'

I prayed silently. 'Balinorelle, let it not be so. Guide my hand and allow me to slay this demonmonger.'

Celandine waited for me, and we walked to the room. She opened the door quietly, for we didn't want to alert the men down below. I went in ahead of her, shield held close, wondering if it would help.

The girl lay on the bed partially nude. Her small breasts and entire upper body were covered with the green spreading sickness. It was something that killed thoroughly and quickly. The black healer lay next to her fondling her diseased body. Celandine closed the door behind us.

The man said, 'What do you want?'

He spied Celandine behind me and leered. 'Have you come to offer a gift? For a gift as fair as she, you could have much.'

'I have come to ask if you will sell the girl to me.'

He stared down at the dying girl and laughed. With a careless hand, he healed her, the disease absorbing into his skin, where the green sickness faded away. She was pure and unblemished once more. 'I don't think I'll sell her to you, elf. But I might trade.'

I shook my head. 'No, black healer, no trade.'

He knelt on the bed and said, 'Then you can fight me for her.' A thin smile curled his lips. He gestured, and I felt claws sink into my cheek. Blood trickled down my face, from under my helmet.

He laughed. 'How badly do you want her?'

I wiped the dripping blood with the back of my hand and said, 'Badly enough.'

I advanced, holding shield and weapon up, but another claw raked me across the ribs as if my armor were not there. Stealth gained me nothing, so I rushed him. He motioned, and my sword hand was cut and bleeding.

A sorcerous claw raked over my eyes. I shrieked and fell to my knees. I gripped shield and sword in the crimson dark. Blind, I fought the pain and the panic. I had been trained to fight blind-folded: darkness was darkness. The pain was overwhelming, and I crouched and tried to think past it, tried to hear past it.

A sound, footsteps. The girl's scream. A rush of cloth that was Celandine's dress. The heavier sloppy footfalls of the black healer.

'It seems I will enjoy two beauties tonight.'

Celandine backed away from him but kept close to the bed and the girl. She called out to me, 'Bevhinn!'

He moved round to the foot of the bed to come at Celandine. I had to make my first strike deadly or all was lost. I listened to his breathing and his movements. I would go for stomach and chest, not knowing if he was facing me or not. Then he spoke again. 'Such a pretty pair.' He was facing away from me.

I rose and struck. The blade sank into flesh. I pulled it free and struck point first through his neck. The blade grated on bone and was through to open air. I knew where everything was now. I took five strikes to cut off his head. The smell of blood was thick and violent.

Celandine said, 'Bevhinn, you've killed him.'

She was beside me lifting off my helmet. I felt her fingertips touch my eyes. I felt the pain again like a lance through my brain, and it was gone. I blinked.

The black healer lay sprawled on the bed. His head was a short distance from his body. Blood soaked the bedclothes to drip on the floor. The girl looked up and smiled her gratitude at me. She paled only a little at the sight of the headless body. She had probably seen worse things in her stay in Lolth. Celandine retrieved the girl's cloak and spread it over her torn dress.

I cleaned my sword on the edge of the sheets and sheathed it. I forced open the wooden shutters on the window. I strapped my shield to my back, and scrambled out to kneel on the sloping roof. The girl crawled out to me, and Celandine followed.

We slipped unseen and, hopefully, unheard to the ground. I led the way to the stables. We entered, and the boy scrambled down from the loft where he probably slept. I said, 'Come here, boy.'

He came, but he was afraid. I gripped him quickly and put a hand over his mouth. 'Find some rope and cloth for a gag.'

Celandine and the girl moved to obey. The boy's eyes were huge with fear, showing the whites of his eyes. 'Boy, we will not harm you.' He wasn't convinced, and I didn't blame him.

When he was tied with some good-quality rope and gagged with a questionably dirty rag, I shoved him up in his loft. Hopefully, no one would find him before morning.

We saddled the horses while the girl kept watch. So far no alarm had been raised. But sooner or later the host would raise courage enough to check the strange noises from the healer's room. We had to be away before that.

We led Ulliam and the horses out onto the road, but I motioned for them to follow me back the way we had come that day. When we felt it safe to talk, Celandine asked, 'Why are we going back?'

'We cannot go on to the next inn. You and the girl might be able to disguise yourselves, but Ulliam and I are not so easily changed. We could run back to the wild lands, but the Loltuns would chase us down. We are at least five days from the Meltaanian border. Every hand will be against us by morning. We must leave Lolth tonight.'

'But how?'

'We're going back to the demon, Krakus.'

'The help of demons?'

'Let us hope so.'

The girl rode our spare horse, and she rode well enough. We raced through the night, riding the horses hard because we wouldn't be needing them much longer.

We came at last to an area of newly cleared land. The demon's shattered stumps and trees were piled high on either side of the road.

I left Celandine and the girl-child with Ulliam and the horses. And I crept through the woods toward the two men who were guarding the demon. One was simple, a dagger thrust in the throat when he went to relieve himself. But the other stayed near the fire and kept his sword naked and near at hand. Guarding a demon seemed to make him nervous. Every time Krakus rattled his chains, the man kept staring back at the demon. I stepped up behind him and put my sword through his throat. I cleaned the blade in the tall grass and sheathed it. The demon was watching me with eyes that caught and reflected the fire.

Heavy chains bound Krakus, but the keys to those chains glinted at the dead man's belt. Celandine and the girl entered the clearing with the horses and Ulliam. The demon's eyes flicked to them and then settled back on me. I said, 'I would bargain with you, Krakus.'

His voice was deep and seemed to come from a long way off, as if from the bottom of a well. 'What manner of bargain?'

'You teleport the three of us and the unicorn just across the

Meltaan border at the city gates of Terl, and I will free you from your enslavement.'

'I like this bargain, elf. Free me, and I will do as you ask.'

'Not yet, demon. First we take blood oath so I know you will not desert us, or teleport us to a harmful place.'

'Why would I do that to the ones who free me?'

'Because you are a demon.'

He laughed, baring white fangs. 'I like you. You understand the way of things.'

His voice sank even deeper until it was almost painful to hear. 'But what blood oath could bind a demon?'

'One to the hounds of Verm and the birds of Loth.'

The smile vanished from his face, and he said, 'Have you ever made blood oath with a demon?'

'No.'

He laughed again. 'Then let us proceed.'

I cut my right hand in a diagonal slash. The blood was bright red and poured in a sheet down my palm. It stung with the sharp pain of all shallow cuts. The demon extended his left hand, and I sliced it. The blood was black and slow to ooze.

We clasped hands and suddenly I felt dizzy. I stared up into those intent yellow eyes and said, 'What is happening, Krakus?'

'What always happens when you bargain with demons, warrior. I am taking blood price. But because this oath holds us both, you are getting my blood in return.' He hissed, 'You are demon kin now, elf. Those who have the power will see the taint and act accordingly.'

It felt as if someone had thrust a red-hot poker into my hand. Fire filled my veins. I fell to my knees, gasping in the cool night air. I could not afford to scream. If we were being chased, screams would bring them. That was the last thought I had before blackness engulfed me.

I heard Celandine from a distance. 'What if she dies?'

'Then you will still be a prisoner because only she can free you.'

The demon's voice came. 'It is the way of demon bargains, healer. The mortal must risk more than the demon. I cannot change my nature, not even to save myself.'

I woke with the sky clearing toward dawn. The cut on my hand had been burned shut and formed a scar across my palm. It had not been Celandine's magic that had closed the wound.

She was there beside me. 'How do you feel?'

'Good enough.' I sat in the morning-damp grass, waiting to feel whole again. I got tired of waiting and called to my magic.

It answered but with a difference. It seemed sluggish, as if it moved through thick air to reach me. My magic felt tainted, but there was no time to worry about it. I had to free the demon.

The spring dawn was close, and the spring night still here. The world was poised between the two, so I called upon both. I drew the cool spring darkness and the soft call of an owl. I breathed in the first hint of dawn on the wind.

A rabbit stirred in its sleep, and I took its dreams and wove them into my spell. The bark of a fox and the fleeting shadow of a nighthawk mingled with the aroma of fresh-turned earth. The power stretched like a second moon, swollen with spring's bounty. I stood and cupped my hands, letting the magic fall into my palms like moonshine. I engulfed the diamond of the demon's necklace in white magic. I felt the enchantment snap. Krakus bowed his head, and I slipped the necklace free of him. The diamond still glittered like warm ice, but it would take an enchanter to reactivate the necklace. For now it was only a piece of jewelry.

He rose to his full seven feet and stretched. The chains fell away without benefit of keys. He leered down at us. 'Let us go and fulfill my part of the bargain.' He offered me his left hand, and I saw the matching burn scar across his great palm. I took his hand, and Ulliam shied but came to stand on the other side of me. Celandine touched his white flank, and the girl clung to her. We were an unbroken chain. The world shifted, and we were before the gates of Terl. It was already dawn there, and a farmer with his load of chickens fought his mule to keep it from running away. It did not like the smell of demons.

Krakus let go of my hand and said, 'I am sure I will not be the last demon you see, earth-witch; blood calls to blood.' He vanished.

Later that day we stood before the High Priestess, and she welcomed Celandine back into the fold of the white healers. The girl-child had some healing magic and was being sponsored as an apprentice healer. She was a worthy token for such a quest.

Celandine's father held a great feast, and I was invited. I had the gratitude of the most powerful petty king in Meltaan. And I had a diamond only slightly smaller than my fist. It would be a long time before I was forced to guard someone else's treasures again.

Celandine was in her element, bejeweled and dressed in white silk. She did not look my way. She was cleansed, and her soul was her own again. And I was a reminder of less pleasant times.

I watched the girl we had saved, laughing with the other young healers. I felt good at having saved her, but my eyes were drawn back again and again to the burn scar on my palm. Celandine had done nothing on this quest. Yet she was cleansed, and I was tainted. I wondered, was there a cleansing ceremony for the demon-touched?

# A CLEAN SWEEP

*My daughter was a very small baby when I got the invitation to join this anthology. I was getting very little sleep, and the house was a disaster so when asked to write a superhero story, I knew the superhero I most wanted to see on my doorstep.*

CAPTAIN HOUSEWORK MATERIALIZED on the doorstep of 11 Pear Tree Lane. His emergency beeper had awakened him, code red. Was it his nemesis, Dr Grime, or the infamous Dust Bunny Gang, or perhaps Pond Scum, the destroyer of bathrooms?

He had to levitate to reach the doorbell. As crimefighters go, Captain Housework was on the short side. His white coveralls, silver cape, and mask – formed of a billed cap with eyeholes – were gleamingly clean. He stood on the top step shining as if carved from ivory and silver.

He looked perfect, crisp, and clean. And he liked it that way.

The door opened, and a woman dressed in a bathrobe stared down at him. 'Oh, it's you. Please come in.' She held the door for him, waving him in eagerly.

He stared up at her, a grim smile on his face. 'And what dastardly villain is plaguing your home, dear lady?'

She blinked at him. 'Dastardly villain?' She gave a small laugh. 'Oh, no, it's nothing like that. My husband made the call. Did he say we had a supervillain in the house?'

Captain Housework drew himself up to his full three feet and said, 'It was a code red, madam. That means a supervillain has been spotted.'

The woman laughed again. 'Oh, dear, no. I've got a party of twelve people coming at six o'clock and my maid canceled.'

'You called the superhero hotline because your maid canceled.' His voice had a harsh edge to it that the woman didn't seem to notice.

'Well, my friend Betty had you over when her kids threw that wild party. You did miracles with her house.'

'I remember the incident. I made it clear that it was an exception to the rules that I aided her.'

'But you've just got to help me, Captain Housework.' The woman went to her knees, gripping his arms. 'Please, it's too late to turn to anyone else.' Tears glittered in her eyes.

Captain Housework crossed his arms across his thin chest, his mouth set in a firm line. 'Madam, I am a superhero, not a maid. I do not think you realize how terrible my foes can be. Have you ever had a wave of black mildew engulf your husband and eat him to the bone before your eyes?'

She blinked at him. 'Well, no, but surely that doesn't happen all that often. In the meantime, couldn't you help me, just this once?'

It was true that his archenemies had been lying low for a while. Work had been slow. He stared into her tearstained face and nodded. 'All right, but only this once.'

She hugged him, crumpling the bill of his mask. He pushed away from her, straightening his costume. 'That will not be necessary. I will get to work at once, if that is all right with you?'

'Oh, that's wonderful. I'll just go get dressed.' She raced up the stairs, trailing some floral perfume behind her.

Captain Housework sniffed. He preferred the cleaner scents of household air fresheners. Pine was his favorite.

He sighed and walked into the living room. For a moment his heart beat faster; surely such destruction could only be the work of the Dust Bunny Gang. Sofa cushions were scattered across the floor. A vase had fallen on its side, spilling water.

Dying flowers made a sodden mess on the gray carpet. The fireplace was choked with ash and the partially burned carcass of a doll. Toys covered nearly every inch of the floor. Children. The only natural disaster that could rival Dr Grime. Perhaps children weren't as deadly, but they were just as messy.

This was the fifth time in a month that he had been called in and found no archvillain but only bad housework. His name was being traded around like that of a good maid. He, Captain Housework, had been reduced to drudgery.

He, who had fought the great dust invasion of '53, would have no problem with this mundane mess. His superhuman speed would make short work of it all. But that wasn't the point. People did not call the Purple Avenger to change a tire. They called him to save their lives.

Once they had called Captain Housework for the same thing. Dr Grime had nearly engulfed St Louis in a giant rain of grease. All cars, trains, and planes had come to a slippery halt. Pedestrians caught in the first greasy rain had melted into puddles of sizzling goo. They had called for Captain Housework then, and been glad to have him. But that had been ten years ago.

Dr Grime had retired. The Dust Bunny Gang had split up over contractual differences. There just weren't that many supervillains who specialized in true dirty work.

It wasn't really the mundane cleaning that bothered him. It was the repeat business. People had been calling him back; again and again to clean up after them. He'd get a house spotless, perfect, and they'd mess it up again.

It was a never-ending drudgery. Even with superpowers over dust and dirt, he was tired of it. They were taking advantage of him. But without any supervillains to fight, a superhero had to fill some need. It was in his contract that he had to be useful to mankind, just as a supervillain had to harm mankind. If all the villains needing his special powers to thwart them had retired, he had to answer the call of need. Captain Housework sighed and waved a white-gloved hand. The sofa cushions danced back in place, fluffing themselves before snuggling down. 'I am a glorified maid,' he said softly to the empty room.

The kitchen was the worst. Dishes were stacked nearly to the top of the windows, thick with grease and moldy food. He conjured a superscouring wind and cleaned them with the force of a hurricane without cracking a dish.

When every room was spotless, he appeared before the woman who had summoned him. 'The house is clean, madam.'

'Oh, gee, thanks.' She held out money.

Captain Housework stared at the offending hand. 'I am a super-hero, not a servant. I don't need your money.' His voice was very tight, each word bitten off.

'No offense. I'm grateful.'

'Be grateful and don't call me again.'

'But I want you to come back after the party and clean up,' she said.

'You what?'

'The maid can't come tonight at all. I thought you'd clean up after the party. The superhero hotline said you would.'

'They said I would?'

She nodded. 'The operator on the hotline said you would be happy to be of service. She said something about superheroes need-ing to be of service to mankind.'

Captain Housework stared at the woman for a few heartbeats. He saw it all then, his future stretching out before him. An eternity of cleaning up after parties, repairing the damage of crayon-wielding tots and unhousebroken dogs. He saw it all in the blink of his sparkling eyes. It was intolerable, a hell on earth, but the woman was right. A superhero had to serve mankind. If all he was good for was maid service, then so be it.

The woman had been putting on red nail polish. She reached back to tighten the lid, but was unwilling to grip it with her wet nails. The bottle went spinning. Bright red liquid poured out onto the white carpet, trickled down the newly polished vanity.

'Oops,' the woman said. 'You'll get that, won't you? I've got to finish getting ready; the guests will be here any minute.' She stood, waving her nails to dry them. She left him staring at the spreading red stain on the carpet he had just shampooed.

His tiny hands balled into fists. He stood trembling with rage, unable to utter a word. An eternity of this — it was intolerable! But what else could he do? Talk Dr Grime out of retirement? No, the villain had made millions off his memoirs.

*Memoirs of the Down and Dirty* had been a bestseller. Captain Housework stared at the slowly hardening stain, and a great calmness washed over him. He had an idea.

The police found fourteen skeletons at 11 Pear Tree Lane. The bones were neatly arranged, sparkling with polish, lacquered to a perfect finish. The house had never been so clean.

# THE CURSE-MAKER

*I would set myself goals of magazines, or editors, to sell to.* Dragon
Magazine *was one of those goals. They published only one fiction piece
an issue, so it was a tight market. I made it with this story. It's the second
appearance on paper of Sidra and her semifaithful magical sword, Leech.
You'll get to meet most of her small band of mercenaries in this story.
They are her family, and she theirs. I still have a soft spot for Sidra and
her gang, and Leech was always a lot of fun to write.*

MILON SONGSMITH WAS dying. Brown hair clung to his face in limp, sweat-soaked strands. His skin was gray-tinged, like dirty snow. Breath was a ragged choking sound, his body trembling with the effort to draw air into his lungs.

Sidra Ironfist stood looking down at her friend. Her strong, callused hands gripped the hilts of her swords until her hands ached. Sidra's solid gray eyes stared down at her friend and willed him to live. She ran a hand through long yellow hair and turned to the wizard leaning against the wall.

Gannon the Sorcerer was tall, as tall as Sidra. His hair was yellow, his eyes the fresh blue of spring skies. But his face was set in cynical lines, as if he had seen too much of the world, and it all disappointed him. Today his eyes held anger and sorrow.

'I will not let him die like this,' Sidra said.

'It is a death curse, Sidra. You cannot stop it. The bard is a better friend to me than any man alive, and I am just as helpless,' Gannon said.

'Can nothing stop it?' Her eyes searched his face, demanded he give her some hope.

'It is the most powerful death curse I have ever seen. It would take days for another curse-maker to remove the spell. Milon has only hours.'

Sidra turned away from the sorcerer and his compassionate eyes. She would not let Milon die. He was her bard. They had ridden together for eight years. Even with a bard's safe conduct, accidents could happen. If you rode into battle, unarmed, you took your chances. But this – this was a coward's way of killing. By all laws, Milon should have been safe in the tavern. Harming a bard, save in self-defense, was punishable by death.

Someone had hated him enough to risk that. But who? And why?

Sidra Ironfist knelt by the bed. She reached out to touch Milon's forehead with one scarred finger. She could feel the heat before she touched his skin. The magical fever was eating him alive.

She whispered to him, though he could not hear her, 'I will not let you die.' She turned to the sorcerer. 'What of the curse-maker who placed the curse?'

Gannon frowned. 'What of him?'

'Could he remove the curse?'

'Well, yes, but why would he?'

Sidra smiled, tight-lipped. 'I think we could find ways to persuade him.'

Gannon nodded. 'We might at that, but how to find him in such a short time?'

There was a knock on the door. Sidra pulled her long sword from its sheath and called, 'Come in.'

A woman hesitated at the doorway. Her hair was streaked with gray, and she wore the robes of a white healer. 'I was told you had an injured man.' She caught sight of the bard and stepped into the room past Sidra's bare steel. 'That is not a wound.'

Sidra sheathed her sword. 'Tell her, Gannon.'

He explained briefly. Outrage showed on the healer's face, then anger, a white burning anger that Sidra found comforting and frightening all at the same time. 'By all the civilized laws, bards are sacred. A death curse on one such as this is an insult to all we hold dear.' The healer asked, 'Who has done this?'

'Unknown,' Gannon said, 'but we will find out.'

Sidra said, 'Yes, we will find out.' There was something – in her voice, in the steel gray of her eyes – that was frightening.

The healer stepped away from the tall warrior woman. 'You look like calm death, warrior.'

'Can you keep him alive until we return?'

'I will keep him alive, but be swift. There will come a point from which no one can bring him back.'

Sidra nodded. 'Keep him alive, healer. He's important to me.'

'That I knew when I saw your face, warrior.'

Sidra looked away from the healer's wise face. She was uncomfortable that anyone could read her so easily. 'Come, Gannon.' She was through the door and on the stairs before Gannon had time to move. He jogged to catch up with her. 'Where do we begin?'

'Malhari.'

Malhari was a big, beefy man. The muscle of his mercenary days had run to softness but not to fat. He was still a formidable man. His black hair was close cropped, framing a nearly perfect roundness of face. His right arm ended abruptly a span above the wrist. A metal-studded leather sheath hid his stump. It had given the tavern its name: The One-Armed Man. His dark eyes caught them as they came down the stairs; no words were needed. He called one of the bar-lads over to pour drinks and motioned them into his office – small, neat, and orderly, the way Malhari had run campaigns years ago.

He eased his big frame into a chair and motioned them to sit. They remained standing. 'What has happened to your bard, Sidra?'

'A death curse. He has only hours to live.'

Malhari's eyes went wide. His fingers curved over the metal studs as another man might drum his fingers. 'Why come to me?'

'Where in Selewin do you go for a death curse?'

'I go nowhere for such things. Curse-makers are unlucky, Sidra. You know that.'

She sat down across from him, hands spread on her legs. Gannon remained standing like a guard at her back. Sidra said, 'You did not pay for that splendid house in the hills from this small inn. You are the person in Selewin to come to for information, for a price. Tell me what I need to know, Malhari. Do it for friendship or money; I don't care which.'

'If I am what you say I am, and if I had your information, how much would it be worth to you?'

Sidra's eyes narrowed, as if from pain. 'Not friendship, then, but money.'

'You cannot spend friendship on a cold winter's night.'

'I think you would be surprised what you can do with friendship, Malhari.' She did not wait for the puzzled look on his face to pass but threw a leather pouch on the desk. 'Gold, Malhari, twenty-five pieces.'

'And,' he said.

Sidra hesitated.

'You would quibble over the life of your friend?'

Sidra pounded her fist into his desk twice – violent, painful, but it helped the anger. It kept her from drawing steel and slitting his throat. Her voice came low and soft, the whisper of steel through silk. 'That is three times your usual pay.'

'This is a seller's market, Sidra. Supply and demand.'

'Our friendship is no more, Malhari.'

'I know.'

'If Milon dies because of this delay, I will kill you.'

'You will try,' he said.

Sidra leaned toward him, and suddenly Malhari was staring at six inches of steel. The knife caressed his throat with no pain or blood, yet. He did not try to move, though he had several secreted blades of his own. He knew better than to try.

Sidra's words came careful and neat, soft and angry. 'You have grown soft, Malhari. In the old days, I could not have taken you without your at least clearing a blade of your own. I will kill you if I want to.'

He said nothing but felt the blade dig into his throat as he swal-

lowed. 'You have paid a fair price. The one you seek is Bardolf
Lordson. I saw one of Bardolf's lackeys talk to your bard tonight.
Bardolf is powerful enough to have done the spell.'

Gannon cursed. 'When we worked for Duke Haydon, I detected
magic on Bardolf. I thought that it was not quite enough to warrant
training as an herb-witch. But a curse-maker! It suits him.'

Sidra nodded. Bardolf had thought to bed a warrior. Sidra had
broken his arm for the insult. Neither she nor Bardolf mentioned the
incident to Duke Haydon.

'He is Duke Haydon's favorite son, bastard or not. We cannot kill
him after he has cured Milon. I will not risk everything we have
worked for in one act of vengeance. If Milon dies, things are different. But our true purpose is to save the bard, not to get revenge.'

Gannon said, 'Agreed. We save the minstrel. If the curse-maker
just happens to perish,' he smiled, 'well, that is an added bonus.'

Sidra smiled. 'Even a duke's son can have an accident.'

She bent close to Malhari's face. 'Tell me where he is.'

'You wish more information from me, Sidra? I am a business-
man.'

'You are a fool,' Gannon said.

The blade tip bit into Malhari's neck. Blood trickled down his
throat. Sidra said nothing.

The innkeeper's breath caught in his throat. 'For you, Sidra.
Bardolf has a house on Silk Street.' He stared into her eyes and saw
death. 'Take the money, Sidra. I give you this information freely.'

She smiled then. 'No, Malhari. If it was a gift, then the bonds of
friendship would constrain me. This way it is only money, and I
owe you nothing.'

He tried not to swallow around the point of the knife. 'I don't
want you to sell this information to anyone else,' Sidra said.

Malhari was having trouble talking. 'I give you my word, I will
not.'

'Your word means nothing. Gannon, if you please.'

'With great pleasure.' The sorcerer smiled. There was something of fearful anticipation in that smile.

Sidra stepped back from the man, quick and careful.

'Please, Sidra, I would not tell. I swear to you.'

Gannon made a broad sweeping gesture, hands upraised to the ceiling, and brought his hands down in a fast clap, pointed at the man.

Where Malhari had sat there was a large black tomcat missing one front paw. It yowled once and fell silent. Sidra had never seen horror on a cat's face, but she saw it now.

Gannon said, 'It is a permanent shapechange, Malhari, unless I remove it.' He knelt, eye level with the cat. 'It is almost a curse, but not quite.'

The big cat just stared at them, yellow eyes dazed.

Sidra said, 'Come, we haven't much time.'

Precious minutes had passed before they stood in an alley that spilled into Silk Street. They were in a wealthy part of town. It was well known that Bardolf was the duke's favorite son, and the grand house showed it. The wealthy could afford magical guardians, things that normal steel could not touch. Sidra's long sword was such ordinary steel. The short sword was not.

Sidra unsnapped the locks on the hilt, and the short sword sprang to her hand, rising of its own accord. The sword said, 'Ah, free.' Without moving, it gave the impression of catlike stretching.

'I may have work for you tonight,' Sidra told it.

The sword hissed, 'Name me.'

'You who were Blood-Letter when the world was new. You who were Wound-Maker in the hands of a king. You who were Soul-Piercer and took the life of a hero. You who were Blood-Hunger and ate your way through an army. I name thee blade mine, I name thee Leech.' For every name the sword had taken, the legend had ended with the blood blade slaying its wielder.

The sword chortled, 'I am Leech, Leech. I am the bloodsucker.' The sword's voice dropped to a whisper. 'Feed me.'

Sidra pressed the naked steel against her bare forearm.

The sword felt like any steel against her flesh. Gannon assured her that, once activated, Leech gave off an aura of evil. 'Feed gently, Leech, for we have much work to do.'

There was always the chance that Leech would take too much and kill her. It had happened to others, great heroes. But the sword bit once into her arm. Blood poured in a sharp painful wash down her skin. The blade said, 'Sacrifice made, contract assured.'

Sidra ignored the wound. It would heal in a moment or two to join the dozens of shallow white scars that crisscrossed her hands and arms. She did not bother to clean the blade. All blood was absorbed cleanly. It truly did feed.

Gannon stepped close, and the sword struck at him.

Sidra held it two-handed, saying, 'Behave.'

'You don't frighten me, little knife,' the sorcerer said.

'Not afraid,' the sword whined. 'No fun.' The sword turned in her hands as if looking for something. 'Where is bard? Bard fears Leech. Baard,' the sword called, drawing the word out in a singsong, 'Baard.'

'Silence, Leech.' Sometimes the blood blade seemed aware of everything that went on. It would spring from its sheath ready for action. At other times it acted as if it had been asleep until called. Sidra wondered what, if anything, the blood blade dreamed of. She doubted she would enjoy the answer, and she knew Leech would lie about it anyway. Blood blades were notorious liars.

She told the sword only that the bard was away. If the sword knew that Milon's life was at stake, it would demand a larger blood price.

Sidra sheathed Leech but left its locks undone in case she needed it quickly. The blade did not fight being sheathed; it was strangely content tonight. It hummed one of Milon's own tunes – Leech's favorite – 'Lord Isham and the Goose Girl.' There were two versions: one for the taverns and one for the prince's halls. Leech, of course, preferred the bawdy version.

She persuaded the blade to stop humming and scouted the house. She was a flicker of shadow, gone before you could look directly at it.

She returned to Gannon. 'Two doors: this one and another that leads into a small yard. Both doors are posted with warning signs. They're both warded.'

It was the law in Selewin that you had to post signs for wardings. There had been too many innocent people killed.

'All windows are barred, no traps that I could see.'

She asked Gannon, 'What kind of warding is on the front door?'

He concentrated a moment, staring at the door, and then said, 'Fire, powerful enough to kill whatever touches it.'

Sidra gave a low hiss. 'I thought death wards had to be marked as such?'

'By law they do.'

'Can you get us past it?'

'Yes, but stay well back while I'm testing it.'

Sidra knew what would happen if he failed to negate the warding. He would die, and he didn't want to risk her life as well. But Gannon had risked himself before, as had they all.

Sidra nodded, and Gannon walked alone into the street. He pressed his hands wide and moved them toward the door. Leech began to hum a drum roll. 'Brrrrrm, brrrm.'

'Hush.'

The sword did not stop but only hissed an accompaniment as the sorcerer touched the door. Gannon's back bowed outward, and the sword hissed a crescendo. Sidra slapped the sword's sheath, and it made a muffled sound and fell silent.

Gannon was walking toward them, cape pulled close about him. The door looked just the same to Sidra. A sorcerous ward was always invisible until you tripped it, unless you had eyes that could see magic.

The sorcerer stepped into the alley, and Sidra said, 'Let me see your hands.'

He hesitated only a moment, then drew them from inside his cloak. The palms were scorched and hung heavy with huge watery blisters.

Sidra drew a hissing breath. 'Gannon, can you go on like that?'

He shrugged and grimaced. 'There will be many sorceries I cannot do with injured hands. I can still levitate and teleport, but not much else.'

'Our luck is low tonight.' She touched his shoulder. 'It is up to you, Gannon. I cannot ask you to go on.'

'No one asked me to come.'

She nodded. It was his choice, and she would not tell him to stay behind.

The door looked ordinary enough except for the sign next to it that read, 'Warning. WARDINGS in place. Please ring bell.' A brass bell hung from a bracket by the door, its cord swinging uneasily in the night wind.

Sidra knelt beside the door and touched the rough wood. No fire, no warding – Gannon had done his job. The lock was cheap and easily picked. All that money on a sorcerous ward, then skimping on the lock itself. Bardolf wasn't spending his money wisely.

She reached for Leech, and it leapt to her hand. Shield held close, she pushed open the door. They had just stepped into the inky blackness when Gannon said, 'Someone teleports nearby.'

There was no time for stealth. If they hoped to trace the teleport, they had to find the point of departure quickly. Gannon said, 'This way.' Against all caution, she let the wizard lead in a mad flight up the broad stairs. Two dim lanterns threw pools of shadow and light on the steps. She glimpsed her own reflection in half a dozen gilt-edged mirrors. Glass and gold were both rare and costly. Bardolf was well off indeed.

Light spilled from a room at the end of a long hallway. Dark rooms with closed doors led up to that one shining door. Sidra pushed past Gannon so she could enter the room first.

It was a bedroom. Silks and pillows were strewn over the carpet like a child's toys, used and carelessly forgotten. A huge candelabra hung from the ceiling, and it sparkled like pure gold. A sobbing woman knelt on the carpet. Her raven-black hair was thrown over her face, and she curled naked near a pile of clothing.

Gannon strode to the middle of the room and picked up a now-blank scroll. He sniffed it as if he were a hound on the scent of a fox and said, 'I have it.'

There was no time, and Sidra stood beside the sorcerer. As the woman glanced up, Sidra had a glimpse of a lovely pale face that was bruised and battered.

The world spun and Sidra caught her breath. They faced outward, back to back. Sidra crouched, sword and shield ready. Then she recognized the throne room of Duke Haydon. Bardolf had run home to his daddy. Someone shouted orders, and the room was suddenly full of the red and silver of Duke Haydon's guards. Sidra wondered if they would have time to explain before someone died.

It was the head of the guards, Jevik, who recognized them and called, 'Hold!' He strode forward through his men and stood before Sidra. He sheathed his sword, and she did likewise. Leech complained about missing such a lovely sight.

Jevik only blinked. He had fought beside her and tasted the sword's humor before. 'Why are you here like this, Sidra?'

'It is a long story, Jevik. But we give chase to an outlaw.'

'What sort of outlaw?'

'One who would kill a bard.'

'Did this bard give up his safe conduct?'

'He never had the chance. He was attacked in his room, alone.'

Jevik waved the guards back and said, 'And how did you trace this outlaw here?'

'Gannon traced a teleport.'

'Come, we will talk to the duke,' Jevik said.

The guards had formed a wary but respectful line to either side of the newcomers. Lord Haydon himself sat upon his throne. His beard was still as full and gray as before. He did not shave because it was court fashion to be smooth-faced. And he did not waste sorcery on looking younger than his years. He smiled a greeting at them and extended his hands.

'Sidra Ironfist, you who saved my castle and all that I own.' She bowed and took his hands. He touched hands with Gannon and saw the sorcerer wince. The duke drew a sharp breath when he saw Gannon's hands. 'Go with one of the guards and use my own healer.'

Sidra did not like the idea of Gannon being separated from her. He looked at her a moment, smiled, and followed a guard from the room. He was right, of course. When a noble offers you hospitality, you do not refuse it.

'Now, Sidra, tell me what has brought you here so unexpectedly.'

She told the story quietly, leaving out only the name of the curse-maker.

Haydon's eyes were a glittering icy blue when she finished. 'It is against all civilized laws to harm a bard. How are we to hear of the great deeds of heroes if bards are not safe in battle?' He asked her then, 'And do you have a name for this outlaw?'

'Yes, my lord. It is Bardolf the Curse-Maker.'

He opened his mouth, then closed it. An angry flush crept up his neck. 'These are grave accusations, Sidra. If you leave now and say no more of this, I will let it pass.'

'It pains me to have to bring you such news, Duke Haydon, but it is the truth. I swear it.'

He took a deep breath that shook with rage and perhaps a touch of apprehension. Sidra wondered if others had come before her and told tales of evil against Bardolf. If so, they had been bullied into silence. Sidra would not be bullied. She did not want to believe that Haydon would simply kill her out of hand, but if that was the case, she would not die easily.

At last the duke said, 'You will persist in this lie against my son?'

'It is not a lie, my lord.'

'Jevik, have my son sent to me now.' The guardsman half-ran from the room.

Gannon was back with his newly healed hands before Bardolf was escorted in.

Bardolf strode in just ahead of Jevik. He was short, with the soft lines of a man who has never done physical labor.

His sensual pouting mouth was set in a confident smile. He was dressed all in brown silk worked with black pearls. When he saw Sidra and Gannon, his smile vanished. Jevik led him in front of the duke, then stepped back, leaving Sidra, Gannon, and Bardolf in a semicircle around the throne.

Bardolf greeted his father first and then very correctly turned to Sidra and Gannon. 'Sidra Ironfist and Gannon the Sorcerer. How good to see you again.' He stared up at his father, eyes unreadable. 'Father, what is this all about?'

Haydon sat very still upon his throne and kept his face blank. He was a noble and knew how to hide his emotions. He told his son of the accusations. Confusion, then anger crossed Bardolf's face. Sidra would almost have believed the act herself. Some people had a true talent for lying.

'Would you convict me of such a vile crime on the word of an information peddler?'

The Duke smiled. 'No, Bardolf, not on that alone. I want you to take an oath for me.'

'Of course, Father.'

'Swear by the birds of Loth and the hounds of Verm that you did not harm Milon Songsmith.'

'I have never taken such an evil oath!'

'It is only evil if you have something to fear. Swear, Bardolf, swear to it.'

'If you insist.'

'I do.'

'I swear by the birds of . . . I swear.' He stared up at his father, a sort of pleading look upon his face.

Haydon's noble mask slipped, showing pain in his eyes.

'Swear.' His voice held a note of begging.

'I cannot, Father.'

'If you are innocent, the oath means nothing. You are guilty, then.'

'I cannot take the oath you ask. Perhaps another to Mother Gia.'

Haydon looked down at the floor and drew a deep breath. He seemed suddenly older than he had a moment before. 'Only the oath to Loth and Verm is binding enough for this. Will you swear?'

'No, Father.'

The duke's face seemed to crumble. The tears that threatened in his eyes were chased away by anger. The same anger he had been willing to use against Sidra, to protect his child, now turned against his son. 'Why, Bardolf? Have I not shared my wealth with you?'

'Yes, Father.'

'Then why?' He stood and walked the few steps to stand before his son – the son who could still look him in the eye and lie, even now.

Bardolf said, 'You gave me crumbs from your table, Father. I wanted my own table. My own money. My own lands.'

'I have given you all that and more.'

Bardolf shook his head. 'They are mine until I anger you. Then you take them away as a punishment, as if they were sweets and I were a child.'

'There are honest ways to make money!'

'Not enough money.'

'Not enough, not enough!' Haydon raised a hand as if to strike him. Bardolf cringed, throwing up a hand. The duke stepped back. Sidra watched the man gain control of himself. It was a painful thing to see. When he spoke again, his voice was soft and controlled. 'Do you know the penalty in Meltaan for killing a bard?'

'Yes.'

'You will be executed, and your blood money will do you no good.'

'Father, even if I cured the bard and gave back the money, my client would see me dead.'

'Who, who will see you dead? Who ordered such a vile deed?'

'I cannot say. As your son, I beg that you do not ask me again.'

Duke Haydon said, 'No! No son of mine would do such a thing.' A soundless tear trailed down his face; his voice remained firm, but he cried.

Sidra looked away.

Bardolf's face showed fear. 'Father?'

Haydon turned to Sidra. 'Do with him as you see fit. Let all here be witness. Bardolf Lordson is no son of mine.' Tears flowed in silver streaks down Haydon's cheeks. Everyone in the room was pretending not to see. Bardolf knelt before the lord, touching the hem of Haydon's robe. A tear trailed down his face. 'Father, please. If I cure the bard, I will be killed.'

Duke Haydon jerked his robe free of the man and left the room. All but two guards left with him. Sidra had wanted to call after the duke, but what could she say? 'Thank you, Duke Haydon, for being just and law abiding'? The man had just signed the death warrant of his favorite son. 'Thank you' did not even come close to covering that.

Bardolf stood slowly, rubbing his eyes. Sidra and Gannon moved to stand beside him. Bardolf tensed to run and found himself entangled in a spell. He could not move his arms or legs. Sidra said, 'Nicely done, Gannon.'

The sorcerer shrugged. 'Healed hands do wonders for a person's magic.'

Sidra stepped near him and asked, 'Do you know what a blood blade is, Bardolf?'

The younger man's eyes flared wide, showing white. She could see the pulse in his neck jump.

Gannon hissed near his face, 'Answer the question.'

'Yes,' he whispered.

Sidra said, 'What is it?'

'An evil sword that can suck a man's soul.' All the color had drained from his face.

She leaned against the cool marble throne and asked, 'Have you heard the song "Blade Quest"?'

Bardolf whispered, 'Yes.'

'I think Milon captured the essence of a blood blade in that song: dark, hungry, evil.' Leech chuckled.

Sidra drew the sword. It gleamed in the torchlight. She said, 'Leech, I want you to meet Bardolf the Curse-Maker.'

The sword hissed, 'Fresh blood, yumm.'

Sweat beaded on Bardolf's face, but his words were brave. 'You can't feed me to that thing.'

'I think I can.' She bent close to him, the naked blade quivering near his neck. She held it two-handed, not trusting it. She spoke low and close to his frightened eyes.

'The duke, your father, has decreed that I can do anything I want to you. Up to and including taking your soul.'

'No, please.'

'Gannon.' Gannon unlaced Bardolf's sleeve and began to roll it upward. The skin was pale.

Leech crooned, 'Blood, fresh blood, new blood.'

The man struggled until sweat dripped down his face, but he could not move. Only his head was free to thrash from side to side.

'Please, please don't let it touch me.'

'Tell us who hired you, agree to cure the bard, and you will live.'

'I won't live. He'll kill me. Or have me killed.'

'But he is not here, and I am. I'll kill you now.'

Bardolf shook his head and closed his eyes. 'Please, he'll kill me.'

Leech hovered over the flesh and said, 'Blood.' Bardolf opened his eyes and watched the blade come closer to his arm. 'No!' The point bit into his flesh and he screamed. Blood spurted out from a cut artery. Leech chortled in a rain of blood. Bardolf cried, 'Lord Isham! Lord Isham hired me!'

Sidra didn't remove the sword but watched it lapping his blood.

'Get it away! Get it away!'

'Why would Lord Isham want Milon Songsmith dead?'

Bardolf swallowed, closing his eyes against the sight of the sword in his arm. He looked as if he might faint. When he finally spoke, his voice was as pale as his skin. 'The song that Milon wrote about him. Lord Isham took insult.'

Sidra asked, '"Lord Isham and the Goose Girl"?'

'Yes. Now, please, get that thing away from me.'

Sidra drew Leech back from the wound, but it did not want to come. She fought the sword two-handed as it struggled and cursed. 'Not enough, not enough. Fresh blood, not enough.'

The sword was quivering, fighting against her, and she could not sheath it. Gannon said, 'Sidra.' He bared his arm.

She said, 'No.'

Leech stopped shrieking and began to wheedle, 'Just a little more, a taste, fresh taste.'

It was a very unhealthy habit to disappoint a blood blade.

Sidra held the blade carefully and said, 'Gannon, I would not ask this.'

'You did not ask. Do it. I have often been curious.'

She laid the blade tip against his arm, and it bit deep into muscle. The wizard winced but stared as the blade wiggled in the wound like a nursing calf.

Sidra pulled Leech free of the wound, and the sword said, 'Ah, good, yumm.' Gannon ignored the sword and stared curiously at his wound as the edges knit together. Soon there was nothing but a whitish scar.

She sheathed the short sword and turned to Bardolf. 'Are you willing to cure the bard now?'

Bardolf nodded weakly. 'Anything you want. Just keep that sword away from me.'

Leech chuckled.

Gannon stood on one side of him and Sidra on the other. Then Gannon released the spell hold, and Bardolf nearly fell. With Gannon steadying him against the dizziness, they teleported to the inn.

The three appeared in front of Milon's bed. His skin was gray, his eyes sunken and black-smudged. If he was breathing at all, Sidra could not tell it. The healer gasped.

Sidra's heart felt like lead in her chest. 'Are we too late?'

The healer shook her head. 'There is time.'

Sidra pushed Bardolf forward against the bed. 'Cure him or the blood blade will taste your soul.'

Bardolf half-fell to his knees beside the bed. He laid a hand on Milon's forehead and over his heart. The curse-maker's face went blank. It was the tranquility Sidra was accustomed to seeing on a healer's face. She found it strange for a curse-doer.

Milon took a deep, shuddering breath, then his chest rose and fell. Bardolf stood up, looking relieved. Gannon forced him to stand back from the bed.

The healer touched the bard's forehead. 'The fever has broken; he sleeps. With a few days' rest, he will be well.'

Sidra asked Gannon, 'Can you take that one to the jail?'

'I think I can manage.' Gannon placed a hand on Bardolf's forehead and spoke one strange syllable. The curse-maker's eyes went blank, and he followed obediently as Gannon moved to the door. He turned back and asked, 'What of our feline friend?'

'Do as you think best.'

Gannon smiled, a broad cheerful smile. 'I will attend to it with pleasure.' He left with Bardolf following behind.

Sidra knelt by the bed and smoothed the sweat-darkened hair from Milon's forehead. The healer moved a short distance away, giving them privacy. Sidra whispered to the bard, 'I did not let you die.'

Leech was singing softly in its sheath. The words came up faint and hollow. 'Lord Isham went a-riding, a-riding, a-riding. On his great bay stallion he went riding over his land. First he met a milkmaid, a milkmaid . . .'

Sidra asked, 'Leech, have you ever tasted the blood of a province lord?'

The sword stopped in midsong and whispered, 'Never, but I hear they're quite tasty.'

'We will be visiting Lord Isham.'

Leech asked, 'When?'

'Very soon.' Sidra fought the urge to smile. One should never smile when contemplating another's death. The sword giggled, and Sidra found herself laughing with it. She saw the healer make the sign against evil. Sidra sighed. Evil had many faces. Some were just more obvious than others. She brushed her lips on Milon's forehead and whispered, 'Very soon.' She made it sound like a promise.

# GEESE

This is the only story that I ever wrote through pure inspiration. My first apartment in the St Louis area was on the edge of a lake. It had Canada geese on it. I took the trash out one night with the sunset spread across the sky and the geese settling down for the night. I stood there in the coming darkness, watching the geese, and the first line of the story came into my head. By the time I got back inside to the computer, the first paragraph was in my head. All I had to do was sit down and type fast enough to write the story. It was amazing, this rush of ideas, character, a whole story from beginning to end. I have never had this happen again. I've had moments of inspiration, but never so complete.

THE GEESE LAY in the long shadows of afternoon, gray lumps, with rustling feathers and flapping wings. I dozed, long neck tucked backward, black bill buried in my feathers. I watched the other geese through black button eyes. Soon I closed my eyes and gave myself to the peace of the flock.

Perhaps I had been a goose for too long. Perhaps it was time to become human again, but the desire was hazy. I was no longer sure why I wanted to be human. I could not quite remember the reason I had hidden myself among the geese.

I realized I was losing my human identity, but it had borne so much pain. This was better. There was food, the freedom of wings, the open sky, and the comfort of the flock. I did not remember humanity as being so simple, so peaceful, so restful. I had lost the desire to be human, and that should have frightened me. That it did not was a bad sign.

Beside me, head nearly lost in the feathers of his back, was Gyldan. That was not his real name, but a human name I had given him. One of the last things to leave was this need to name things. It was a very human trait.

In my own mind I still called myself Alatir. As long as you had a name, you were still human.

Gyldan was a young gander, but he had been with me for two seasons. He was a handsome bird; jet black, cloud gray, buff white, all markings distinct and artificial in their perfectness.

He had chosen me as his mate, but I offered only companionship. I was still human enough not to wish to bear goslings.

He had stayed with me, though there were other females who would have taken him. We had spent long summers on empty lakes, claiming our territory but never going to nest. If I did that, I would never be human again. The thought came that I wanted to be human, someday, but not today.

The children came then, peasant children with their dark hair and eyes. They came from a prosperous household, for they fed us scraps of vegetables and bread. They had almost tamed us, almost.

The oldest was a girl of about fourteen, her black hair in two thick braids around a slender face. The next oldest was a boy of perhaps eleven. The rest were all sizes, with laughing brown eyes and gentle hands.

I had flown over their father's mill many times. I had watched them help their mother in the garden and play tag in front of their house.

They came earlier by human standards, for the days were growing autumn short. By geese standards, the sun was in the same place.

The bread was day-old, crisp, and good. I remembered other bread, formed in curves and sculpted for feast days. Gyldan did not press me to share my bits of bread. He sensed my mood and knew my temper was short. There was a sound of horses riding along the road. All of us craned our necks to hear, to see danger. The oldest girl noticed it and asked us, 'What's wrong?' as if we could speak.

We thundered skyward as the horses rode out beside the lake. The children were still stunned by our beating wings, afraid. The girl recovered and screamed, 'Run, hide!'

The children scattered like wild things. The girl was cut off by one prancing horse, and the oldest boy would not leave her.

I circled back, Gyldan beside me. I settled at a safe distance and listened. It took magic for me to hear them, and I found the knowledge to stretch my senses came easily.

The men wore the livery of the Baron Madawc, a white bull on a background of silver, a sword through its heart. I knew Lord

Madawc well. Human memories tore through my mind. Blood running between my mother's dead eyes. My father's chest ripped open, so much blood. I had been but newly made a master of sorcery when Madawc slaughtered my family and took over our lands. Five years ago, I had been a child, though a powerful one. Lord Madawc had mocked me when I challenged him to a duel. He had let me live and put a geas on me, a geas to kill him, thinking that it would surely mean my death. Having a geas-ridden child seek the death of a powerful sorcerer amused him.

So I had hidden myself in a form that the geas would not touch. My human mind roared through my animal body. I remembered. I remembered.

One soldier had placed the girl across his saddlebow. 'Our lord will be pleased with this.' He slapped her buttocks. She was crying.

The boy said, 'Let go of my sister.' Another soldier swooped down on him and carried him, struggling, to the front of his saddle. He said, 'There are those at court that like a bit of little boy. You can come along if you like.'

I could not let this happen, and I could not stop it as a bird. I hid myself in some reeds. Gyldan felt the magic begin. He hissed but did not leave me.

Human form was cold. I found myself crying. Crying, for the family I had forgotten. I huddled in the reeds, in the mud. My skin was pale; my black hair, waist-long. I know my eyes were blue, the pale color of spring skies.

I could pass for a lord's bastard daughter just as easily as a true aristocrat. Peasant blood was peasant blood, to some.

Gyldan touched my shivering skin with his firm beak. He croaked softly at me, and I touched his feathered head. 'If I live, I will be back to say a proper goodbye, I promise.'

I walked up the sloping bank toward the soldiers. He followed me on his thick, webbed feet, but he stopped before I reached the men. He launched skyward in a thrust of feathers and fear.

The soldiers saw only a naked woman walking toward them. I had grown older and was no longer a girl, but a woman. I doubted Madawc would recognize me. But because of his own magic, I was compelled to find him and slay him, if I could. Fear tightened my stomach, yet there was no time to be afraid. I had to help the children now.

'Let the children go.'

'Oh yes, my lady . . .' They laughed.

I gestured, a bare pass of wrist and hand. The children were set upon the ground, and the soldiers said one to another, 'Children – who needs children? We will take a woman to our lord.' Freeing the children was their own idea now.

The children were frightened and huddled near me. I whispered to them, 'Go home; do not be afraid. I may come there seeking shelter later.'

The girl dropped a clumsy curtsey and said, 'You are most welcome, my lady. Be careful.'

I nodded, and one of the soldiers gave me his cloak as a damp autumn drizzle began to fall. It was his idea to let me ride in front of him, covered, a special gift for Lord Madawc. He was their captain, and the only one I had to control. I had been lucky that none of these soldiers was a spell caster. It would never have gone so smoothly with magic to fight.

It was miles to the castle, and by the time we arrived, the captain believed it was his idea. No magic was required to maintain my safety.

The castle gate was brilliant with torchlight. Our group was one of dozens. Many had brought children, both male and female. One little boy was perhaps six, frightfully young. He clung, crying, to the soldier that held him. The soldier looked decidedly uncomfortable. I marked him for later use, though if I needed help, it would probably be too late. Too late meant dead. I took a deep calming breath. If I panicked, I would be useless.

Somehow I would kill Madawc. Even if it meant my own death.

We were escorted through the main hall, where there was a party going on. I heard one of the soldiers murmur, 'Pigs, all of them.'

The captain whispered, 'Don't let Madawc hear such talk. He'll skin you alive for entertainment.'

Another said, 'I'm leaving this foul place when my contract is up.' There was a lot of head nodding.

Five years without my father to stand guard against him had not made Madawc popular.

The place smelled of spilled wine, vomit, and sex. Drunken voices, both male and female, called out bawdy suggestions. There was a young man of about fifteen, chained to the center of the room. A line of silk-clad ladies were taking turns with him.

I turned away, and the captain jerked me roughly forward. Fear knotted in my belly, and for the first time I felt naked under the cloak. I had magic, but so did Madawc, and he had beaten me before.

The little boy was given over to an older man. The soldier looked near tears himself as he pried the boy's fingers from him. The old noble offered the child sweetmeats and held him softly. He would gain the child's confidence first. I recognized Lord Trahern. He had been thrown out of my father's court for being a child-lover.

The captain led me by the arm through the crowd. Hands pulled at the cape, saying, 'A beauty, did you taste her before you brought her here?'

He ignored them and went to the front table. Madawc had not changed, except to grow thicker around the middle. His black hair was dark as any peasant's, but his eyes were the cool blue of autumn skies.

Anger flashed through me warm and whole. Hatred. Memories. My mother's cries for help. Her screams, 'Run, Alatir, run!' But there had been no place to run. I needed no geas to want him dead.

The captain went down on one knee and pulled me down as well. We waited, kneeling, faces hidden from the man. Would Madawc recognize me? I was afraid and didn't try to hide it. I was just another victim, a bit of meat. I was supposed to be afraid. Finally, Madawc said, 'Yes, what is it?'

'A special treat for you, Lord Madawc.' He pulled my head back, so my face showed.

Madawc said, 'Ah, blue eyes. Did you find another one of my own bastards for me?'

'I believe so, my lord.'

He smiled and traced my face with his hand. 'Lovely. You have done well, Captain. I am pleased.' He held out a ruby and gold ring. The captain bowed and took it. I was left kneeling.

Madawc pulled aside the cloak. It fell to the floor. I hunched forward, using my long hair as a screen. Fear thudded in my throat. He laughed. 'Naked, all pleasures bare, as I like my women. And modest, I like that as well.' He touched my breast, and I jerked away with a small gasp. I would not let him touch me. I would destroy myself first. No, the geas would not allow that. I had to try to kill him. But I could not perform death-magic here and now. He was not drunk; he would break my concentration long before I completed a spell. I could damage him but not kill him. I needed to get away from him; I needed time.

It came to me then what I needed to do. I had been too long away from the nobility; I had forgotten how silly even the best of them could be. Even Madawc, tainted as he was, would not refuse challenge, especially from a woman he had defeated before.

I draped the cloak around my shoulders and said, 'I am Alatir Geasbreaker, as you named me. Daughter of Garrand and Allsun.' I stood, cloaked in deepest blue and the mane of black hair. I was ivory skin and eyes of sapphire. I felt the magic of true challenge flow through me, born of anger, righteousness, and five years of magic almost untapped. Fear was gone in a rush of magic.

Madawc knocked his chair backward to scrape along the marble floor. 'What trick is this?'

'No trick, Madawc of Roaghnailt. I am Alatir Geasbreaker, and I challenge you to battle.'

If it had been another who was trained in sword as well as magic, it would have been a foolish challenge. I knew nothing of weapons, but neither did Madawc. He was of the belief that magic was always enough. Now we would see.

A hush ran through the throng. They turned eyes to their honored lord. He could not refuse, for to do so, even in front of this silken rabble, would be to lose all honor. A lord without honor did not get invited to the king's courts. A lord without honor became the butt of songs by bards known for their comedic talents and biting wit.

I was remembering what it meant to be human and a Meltaanian noble

'I accept challenge, of course, but you cannot be Alatir, daughter of Garrand. I put a geas on you that would have forced you to kill me years ago.'

'It was your spell. Test it; see if it still holds me.'

I felt a tentative wash of magic, a mere butterfly's wing of power. 'You bear my spell, but how have you hidden from it?'

'Shapeshifting, Madawc. Even as a child, shapeshifting was my best spell, and animal cannot answer geas.'

'What brought you back?'

'You called me. You might say, I am what you made me: someone who hates you, someone who has to kill you, at risk of her own life if necessary. I am under geas to see you stretched dead before me.'

His jaw tightened; the shock and fear were gone. 'I defeated you once, easily. I will do so again. This time I will not leave you alive.'

'This time,' I said, 'you will not have the chance.'

Meltaanians love spectacle more than anything. In short order, torches were set in a circle outside the castle grounds. You never let sorcerers fight within walls. The walls had a tendency to tumble down. Even that thought did not frighten me. The magic of challenge still held me safe. Fear was a muted thing, for now.

One of the ladies had found me a dress to wear. It was blue silk and matched my eyes. My hair was braided down my back and threaded with silver ribbons. Silver was echoed at bodice, sleeve, and dress front. It was a very simple dress by Meltaanian standards, but the people needed to be impressed, needed to remember what was about to happen.

Madawc faced me in black, run through with silver threads. He glittered like ice in the sun when he moved. He spoke to me as we stood, waiting. 'You are Alatir.'

'Did you doubt it?'

'I thought you long dead.'

'You thought wrongly.'

He gave a half bow, a strange self-mocking smile on his face. 'I think, dear lady, that you are some lovely phantom come to haunt me.'

'I am flesh and blood and magic.'

Magic grew in the circle of torches. Magic ran along my skin and tugged at my hair, like an unseen wind. I called sorcery to me but did not want to commit its shape to any one spell. I wanted to know the measure of the man I fought. In my terror, he had been twelve feet tall, an endless fountain of magic. Now he was a man, and I was no longer a child.

Fire exploded around me, orange death. The air was choking, close, heat. The fire died, and I stood safe behind a shield. Lightning flared from his hands. The bolts struck my shield and shattered in an eye-blinding display of light.

I faded inside my shield, willing myself into another shape. I was small, thin, hidden in the grass. A green adder hidden in the uncertain torchlight.

I could feel the vibration as he moved over the earth, but I could hear his puzzled voice asking, 'Where is she?'

I felt his magic wash over me, searching, but I was a snake and had no real business with magic. He did not come too near the empty folds of the silk dress, but I slipped out a sleeve hole and began moving cautiously, thin and hidden, toward him.

I was a small snake and could not bite through his boots. As he passed me, put his back to me, I grew. I was an older snake, thick as a man's wrist. There were gasps from the audience. He turned, puzzled, and I struck. He screamed as my fangs tore his flesh, poison pumping home. His struggles flung me away to lie half stunned in the grass.

I began to shapeshift, slowly. He was yelling, 'Get me a healer, now!'

A soldier, the one who had brought in the littlest boy, said, 'You cannot be healed until the fight is over, Lord Madawc. That is the rule.'

'But I've been poisoned!'

The mercenaries whom he had bullied and made into whoremongers formed a wall of steel. 'You will not leave the circle until the fight is done. Isn't that right, Captain?'

The captain, who had brought me in, didn't have a problem with Madawc, but he licked his lips and agreed. He knew better than to go against all his men. 'You must wait for healing, Lord Madawc.'

'I will see you all flogged for this, no, hanged!'

It was the wrong thing to say. The soldiers' faces went grim, dispassionate. They waited for someone to die.

I stood naked and human once more. All I had to do was stay alive until the poison took effect, and that wouldn't be long.

Madawc turned on me with a snarl. 'I'll take you with me, bitch!'

He formed a soul-beast, made of magic, hatred, and fear. It was a great wolf that glowed red in the night.

I had never made a soul-beast before. It took great strength, and if it was destroyed, the spell caster died with it. I formed mine of power, vengeance, the memory of five years of unused magic, the quiet stillness of water, and the freedom of skies. It flowed blue and burst into being a moment before the wolf leapt. Mine was a thing of feathers and claws, no known beast.

I felt the power as never before. I rode the winds of it. It lifted me in a dance of death and joy. I was fanged claws and whirling feathers of gold and sapphire. I bit the wolf and raked his sides with claws. I bled under his teeth and staggered under the weight of his body.

The wolf began to fade. As it lost substance, I gained its magic. I drew its power like a hole in Madawc's soul; I drained him until I fell to my knees, power drunk, stunned.

The soul-beasts were gone. It was effort to turn my head and see Madawc on the grass. His body convulsed, and bloody foam ran from his lips. The green adder is a deadly thing.

I was stronger than five years ago, but all those years had been without training. Madawc might have killed me without the aid of poison. Then again, he might not.

The geas was gone, and I felt pure and empty of it. I had expected triumph; instead I felt relief, and a great empty sadness.

A voice declared the match over and Alatir the winner. There were hands, a cloak thrown over my nakedness, the warmth of healing magic, and a warm draught of tea.

Dawn light found me rested, healed, and in the bedchamber that had once belonged to Madawc. By Meltaanian law it was all mine now, both my father's lands which had been stolen and Madawc's. Madawc had never bothered to appoint an heir from his many bastards. No royalty would marry him.

There was a knock on the door, and the captain entered with the mercenary who had brought the little boy in. They both knelt, and the captain said, 'My lady, what would you like for us to do? We have weeks left on our contract, and our contract is now yours, if you want it.'

I asked, 'Have you a guard outside my door?'

The younger man spoke. 'Yes, my lady, some of the dead lord's friends are less than pleased at the duel's outcome.'

I smiled at that. 'Is Lord Trahern still within these walls?'

'No, my lady.'

I ignored the captain and asked the other man, 'What is your name?'

'I am Kendrick Swordmated.'

'You are now Captain Kendrick.'

The other captain sputtered, but I interrupted him. 'I want you gone from here and never come back. Take the four men who rode with you on search yesterday.'

There must have been something in my eyes that told him not to argue. He gave a stiff bow and left the room.

'Now, Captain, how long ago did Trahern leave?'

'Only moments, my lady.'

'Then take what men you think you need and find him. Relieve him of the peasant boy he got last night. The boy is to be healed, then taken back to his home. A gift of gold will be given to his family.'

He smiled. 'Yes, my lady.'

'And free all the others. They are my people now, and no one mistreats my people. No one.'

He bowed, grinning. 'All will be done as you ask, Alatir Lord-Slayer.'

'Lord-Slayer?' I questioned.

'Yes, my lady, from last night.'

'Go then, Kendrick.' I stopped him just before he left. 'I must attend some business and will be away perhaps until tomorrow. But I will return and expect everything to be done as I asked.'

'I will inform the castle staff of your absence and will do as you ask.' He bowed and left the room.

I stood at the open window and let the autumn wind shiver over my skin. I changed into a familiar form and took to the sky on gray wings.

I settled on the lake's dark waters and looked for Gyldan. I could not remain with the flock now. I remembered too much, but I had promised him a goodbye.

He called to me from shore, his voice different than any others. I paddled over to him and hopped up on the grass. Regardless of what shape I wore, I loved him. We caressed, touching necks and bills. How could I leave him behind? And how could I take him with me?

He stepped back from me, and I saw magic shimmer over him like silver rain. The flock awoke with cries of alarm and took to the safety of the sky. I watched him change, slowly, but his magic was strong and sure.

He lay, a naked man, pale, white hair like moonlight. Eyes sparkled black so they showed no pupil. He blinked up at me with wide uncertain eyes. His voice was deep and song-filled, full of rushing wind and the freedom of wings. 'I saw how you changed.'

I was human beside him, crying.

He ran hands down the length of his new body. 'I could not follow you as a bird, but as a man . . .'

I knelt and kissed his forehead. 'You are not a man.'

He gripped my hand. 'I am your mate. I will follow you, whatever form you take.'

We held each other as the sun rose and knew each other as a woman knows a man. Afterward he lay panting beside me with innocent eyes. How much he had to learn. I could take the memory of my magic, of his magic, away. I could leave him as I found him. I ran a fingertip down the sweat-soaked length of his body. He shivered. 'Your name is Gyldan, and I am Alatir.'

He tried the names on his human tongue, 'Gyldan, Alatir. Are they nice names?'

'Yes, I think so.' I stood. 'Come, we can take shelter at the mill for today. They will give us clothing and food.'

He nodded, and I helped him stand on his uncertain legs. I led him by the hand along the path that the children took to feed the geese. We shivered in the dim autumn sunlight. It was colder without feathers.

# HOUSE OF WIZARDS

*This is another story about domestic skills being more important than magic. I have no talent for organizing a household. None. Over the years I've come to realize that being able to cook, clean, and make order from chaos is a skill of the highest order. It is a different way of looking at the world, almost a polar opposite to the absent-minded artist thing I've got going. I wouldn't trade who and what I am, but sometimes I get glimpses into that other way of thinking, of being, and I think, wouldn't it be nice. But I am definitely one of the wizards making a mess, and more work for Rudelle.*

RUDELLE WAS A practical woman. The fact that she had married a wizard did not change that, though marrying Trevelyn Herbmage was the most impractical thing she had ever done.

Her husband was tall, as were most Astranthians. His eyes were the color of a Red-Breast's eggs. His hair was the yellow of early summer corn silk.

Rudelle knew she herself was not a great beauty. Her hair fell thick and wavy to her waist, was only the color of autumn-browned leaves. She wore it in a long braid, piled like a crown atop her head. Her eyes were plain brown, like polished oak. She was not tall, though she did possess ample curves, of which many men were fond. She was a good cook and tidy, laughed often and well, but had a sharp tongue. Her brothers learned early that she was not to be trifled with.

She had no idea why the tall, blond stranger had asked for her hand. And she found it a sense of wonder that his eyes shone with love when he looked upon her.

She knew she would be the only non-magic in the house full of wizards. Trevelyn was the eldest and would inherit the family estate. He tended the family magic shop already, freeing his parents so they could further their magical research.

So Rudelle and her husband would live with his parents, two sisters, and a brother. All were spell casters.

Rudelle would cook and clean and help tend the shop. She would raise fat children and fend for herself in a house of magic.

Her brothers had thought her mad to travel across the sea to

Astrantha. Calthu was a land where magic was rare and often perse-
cuted. What did she, a Calthuian farmer's daughter, know about
Astrantha — land of a thousand magics? Nothing.

But from the moment their boat docked Rudelle had loved the
City of Almirth, capital city of Astrantha. It was noise, the frantic
calls of multicolored parrots being unloaded from a boat, the high
neighing of unicorn-horses with their spiraling horns, the soft mum-
blings of spells as sorcerers lifted cargo boxes with word and gesture,
and the hum of any busy port.

Trevelyn said, 'Look up, there.'

She followed where he pointed but at first saw nothing against the
summer blue sky. Then something, something silver, flashed in the
sun. The silver point whirled and raced itself and was joined by a
flashing bit of gold. A third point of light, like a ruby winking in the
sun, joined the mad flight.

'What is it?' she asked.

'Dragons,' he replied, 'playing tag.'

Rudelle stood and stared until the point of light became a rainbow
of scattered stars, a dozen colored fireflies, high in the vault of the
day.

Trevelyn touched her shoulder gently. She turned, startled, and
winced. Her neck was stiff from looking up.

'My family is expecting us.'

'Oh, I'm sorry.'

He hugged her. 'Don't be sorry. I love the way you enjoy such
ordinary things.'

She blushed. 'I am a country bumpkin.'

'No, never. Most of these people would be lost without their
magic. They couldn't cook, or do business, or even marry without
magic. They would be just as amazed at ordinary things in your
world.'

Rudelle shook her head. 'If you say so, husband.'

He kissed her forehead. 'I say so.'

As they walked arm in arm through the bustling crowd, he warned her of his parents. 'They liked the idea of having children, but raising us didn't interest them much. Their primary interest is the study of magic not family.'

She frowned.

He squeezed her hand and smiled. 'That is one reason I did not wish to marry another wizard. I wanted a wife, and I wanted to be a real father.'

She smiled, then, and felt warm and whole in the shadow of his eyes.

The house was on a quiet street with large, fenced yards and tall, stately houses. There was a woman walking very fast from the house. Her shoes *clump-clumped* on the stone walkway. She nearly ran into them in her haste to get through the gate. She gasped, made a vague curtsey, and said, 'I resign my position. You can't cook in a kitchen that explodes,' and she was gone, half-running down the quiet street.

Rudelle looked at her husband.

'That was the maid,' he said, as if that explained everything.

Rudelle was about to ask for a more detailed explanation when the world swam for a dizzying moment and they were no longer in the yard.

Rudelle grasped his arm in a panicked grasp. 'Trevelyn, what's happening?'

'It's all right, Rudelle. Mother teleported us to her study. No harm done.'

Rudelle wasn't sure she agreed. Her stomach was twisting, and she was forced to breathe deeply of the stale unpleasant air. Rudelle hoped she would not embarrass herself by throwing up all over her new mother-in-law.

A tall, blond woman stood in a room. She could have been Trevelyn's younger sister, but Rudelle had been warned that sorcerers lived a very long time and aged accordingly. She was still grateful that Trevelyn was a mere herb-witch and herb-healer, and thus would age normally.

The woman was beautiful, like a princess. But her yellow-gold hair was straggling from a loose braid, and her blue gown, which matched her eyes perfectly, was stained with ink in a large smear from bodice to mid-knee.

The woman smiled; it was Trevelyn's smile. 'Welcome, wife of my eldest son.' She closed her eyes a moment and yelled, 'Gaynor, your son is home! Where is that man?'

Her voice seemed to echo in an unnatural way. Rudelle glanced at Trevelyn.

He said, 'The only way to communicate from Mother's study is by magic.'

Rudelle turned in a circle, searching for the door. There were only rough-hewn stone walls. 'There's no door.'

'No. In case one of Mother's spells goes awry, the house above us is protected.'

Rudelle stood in the middle of the room, trying to keep her face blank. A thick, gray coating of dust touched everything. Spider webs stretched across the room like garlands strung for a party. Broken bits of crockery lay on the floor. Ancient bits of food had dried to their surface.

His mother vanished to find his father. Trevelyn whispered to her, 'Mother never allows a maid to touch this room.'

'Why not?'

'It is her work room.'

'She works in this?'

He grinned. 'She never allows anyone to clean this room.'

'We shall have to see about that. It's filthy.'

His mother reappeared accompanied by a slightly older replica of Trevelyn.

Trevelyn said, 'May I introduce my mother, Breandan Spellweaver, and my father, Gaynor the Researcher. And to you, my parents, may I introduce my wife, Rudelle the Quick-fingered.'

Breandan asked, 'May one ask how you came to have such a name?'

'I am quick with needle and thread.'

'Oh, I suppose if you have no sorcery that sewing is a useful talent.'

His father interrupted, 'You are not a sorcerer, for you do not shine.' He squinted at her. 'She does not shine at all, Breandan.'

'She is a healer, Gaynor. Healers do not shine until they perform their magic.'

He nodded. 'Yes, a healer. We've never had one of those in the family.'

Trevelyn stopped them. 'Rudelle is not a healer.'

'Then what is she?' his mother asked.

'A woman and my wife.'

Neither parent understood, then his mother said, over slowly, 'You . . . mean . . . she . . . has . . . no . . . magic?'

'Correct.'

She flopped down into a dust-covered chair. 'You married a non-magic, a non-person? She can't even vote.'

'She can vote because she is married to me.'

'But if she wasn't your wife, she would be a non-person. A peasant.'

'Mother, please remember, she is my wife, and I love her.'

His father added, 'Son, why, why did you do this?'

Trevelyn took Rudelle's hand and drew her aside. 'This could take some time, my beloved. Why don't you go out in the garden for a time?'

'No, I will stand beside you.'

'It will be an argument. An argument with my parents means magic. I would rather have you settled in a few days before being turned into a frog.'

Rudelle's eyes widened. 'They could really do that?'

'My parents? Without a word or a gesture. Most sorcerers have to at least say a spell, to help their concentration, but not my parents.'

Rudelle swallowed. 'I'll remember that, and go wait in the garden.'

She paused before a blank wall and asked, 'How do I get there?'

He kissed her then, hard and full on the lips. 'Enjoy the garden. Mother, if you please, teleport her gently into our garden.'

His mother looked unhappy but waved her hand and the world vanished for a moment.

Rudelle appeared in the garden. Two teleports so close together were too much for her stomach. She vomited into the grass. At least she hadn't thrown up in front of anyone, but she decided then and there that she did not care for teleportation.

The garden was a contrast to the house. Neat, trimmed fruit trees formed a small orchard in the west. An herb garden formed an intricate green-leafed knot around a small garden. Flower beds were isolated and planted to be viewed from every side: carnations in pink and scarlet, delphiniums in shades of royal blue, and brown speckles over all, the pure white of crystal stars on their dainty nodding stems.

A vegetable patch opened behind a screen of hedges. Never had Rudelle seen such perfect red tomatoes, crooknecks so large and glossy yellow that they did not seem real. Bees hummed among the bean blossoms. The bean plants were rainbows of bean pods; purple, spotted and streaked, bright yellow and pale pink. Two short rows and every color Rudelle had ever heard of, and some she had not. No one grew them like this, for the eye's beauty more than the harvest.

Then Rudelle came to the rose garden. She stopped and simply stared. There was nothing else to be done. The reds were an eye-searing scarlet, pinks from the palest dawn's blush to deep coral, yellows the color of goldfinches and buttercups, and whites like crystal shining in the sun. Then she came to one of pale lavender. Another was orange like the rare fruit itself. The scent on the afternoon breeze was almost intoxicating. Then the sound of humming came to her ears. For a moment she thought the roses were singing, then she spied a young girl kneeling among the bushes.

Long yellow hair blew free in the wind. The white and silver of a party gown was bunched underneath her knees. She was working with a small hand trowel in the soil underneath a yellow rose.

Rudelle cleared her throat quietly. The humming stopped abruptly, and the girl turned, flinging her hair from her eyes. There was a smudge of fresh dirt on one cheek. Her eyes were the startled blue of an autumn sky.

They stared at each other a moment, then Rudelle said, 'I am Trevelyn's new wife, Rudelle.'

The girl smiled. 'I am Ilis, his youngest sister.' Ilis stood, bunching the silk of her dress in muddy hands.

Rudelle asked, 'Do you always garden in a party dress?'

The girl smiled down at the ruined cloth. 'Well, sorcery can fix it instantly, so it's not ruined. It is the last clean dress I have. Mother and Father have both been terribly busy with their research as of late.'

'Trevelyn tells me you're an earth-witch.'

'Yes.'

'And you made this garden.'

'Helped it.' Ilis stroked a rose bud, and it opened instantly, bursting with color and scattering scent both rich and welcoming.

'That rose, it opened when you touched it.'

'Of course it did. I am an earth-witch, and this is my special bit of ground.' Ilis looked at her new sister-in-law critically for a moment. Then she laughed, 'You aren't magic, are you?'

'No.'

'Oh, Mother must have had a fit.'

'Something like that, yes.'

'Where are you from?'

'Calthu.'

'Oh, no. No magic. You've never seen it, have you?'

'Not really.'

The girl laughed and grabbed Rudelle's hand. 'Come. I'll show you some real magic.'

Rudelle had to laugh. A feeling of such warmth, health, wholeness came through the girl's touch.

She let her pull her along the grass paths until they came to the center of the rose garden. There they stopped, still hand in hand.

There was a white painted arbor with a bench underneath. A rose climbed and fell and curved over the wood until it was like a small house. The roses were the size of cabbages, white like frost, the lip of each petal kissed with the palest pink, and outlined and ribbed with silver that sparkled metallic in the sun.

The girl walked forward, leaving Rudelle to gawk. Ilis touched the bending flower, larger than her own face. The flower nodded in response, moving all on its own. It rubbed against her cheek, like a cat.

'It moved.'

'This,' the girl said, 'is real earth-magic. Not just every earth-witch can animate a growing thing. It took me three years to get flower color and size, and only the last month has she lived for me.'

'She?'

'Yes. Blinny.' Ilis held out her hand. 'Come. She'll like you.'

Rudelle approached slowly, noticing now how the flower heads wavered independent of the wind. The ruffling of petals was a soft, sibilant sound. A half-opened rose nodded over her and touched pink-tinged lips to her face.

'Oh,' Rudelle said.

A lightning bolt struck near Rudelle. She screamed and Ilis dragged her to the ground.

Ilis tried to hide Rudelle underneath her, as a sound of explosions and lightning cracks got closer.

Rudelle struggled to raise her head and asked, 'What is happening?'

'Elva and Ailin are having a quarrel.'

'What . . .'

There was a roaring whine overhead; Ilis dragged Rudelle to her feet and screamed, 'Run!'

They ran, Ilis leading them toward dubious safety, as fire rained down from the sky. They huddled at the base of a small oak tree. Now Rudelle could see the combatants.

A young woman of about seventeen was shooting balls of greenish flame toward a boy of about ten. The green flame splattered harmlessly against nothing that Rudelle could see, as if there were an invisible shield around the child. The boy was flushed and sweating; the girl calm and unstained. She waved aside his attacks with a careless hand. Then, laughing, she vanished.

Ilis let out a sigh and slumped against the tree trunk.

'Where did the woman go?' Rudelle asked.

'Elva? She teleported. She'll stay gone until Ailin cools down.'

'You can't teleport, though?'

'No.'

'How do you hide from your brother when he's angry?'

'I stay out of his way as best I can.'

The little boy was furious. His pale face was flushed, and his hands balled into fists at his side. Rudelle could see him trembling with rage.

There was no sound in the garden but the boy's labored breathing. Then the climbing rose moved; a mere whisper of silken petals, but it was enough. Ailin pointed one small fist at the bush and began to chant.

Ilis cried, 'No, Ailin, no, please!'

Rudelle was uncertain what was happening, then fire like a furnace blast swallowed the climbing rose. Half the bush melted like hot wax.

Ilis screamed, wordlessly, and hid her face in her hands.

Rudelle was numbed at the careless cruelty of it. She wondered, briefly, if she had drawn attention to herself, if the boy would have melted her. Then she stood and strode toward the child.

Ilis called, 'Rudelle, don't!'

Ailin turned, still angry.

Ilis called, 'Ailin, this is Trevelyn's new wife, your sister-in-law. She doesn't mean any harm. Don't hurt her.' Ilis got to her feet, uncertain what to do.

Rudelle wasn't certain either, but one thing she knew, no ten-year-old boy was going to bully her. And no one had the right to destroy such harmless beauty.

Ailin said, 'I can blast you, just like I did that stupid rose.'

Rudelle kept moving.

'I can change you into a toad. I bet Trevelyn wouldn't like you so much then.'

Rudelle ignored the threats and kept coming. She was furious and let the anger show on her face.

Uncertainty showed in his eyes. 'I'll do it! I'll change you!'

His hands raised, and the first word of an invocation trickled from his mouth. Rudelle hit him hard, closed fist, against the jaw. He slid to the ground, boneless as a sack of wheat.

Ilis crept closer, a look of wonder on her face. 'Is he dead?'

'No, just unconscious.'

Ilis knelt beside the fallen sorcerer and looked up at Rudelle, her eyes shining.

'But didn't you know he could have killed you?'

Rudelle shook her head. 'I am the middle child of seven, all boys except for me. I am not about to start letting little boys bully me, magic powers or not. Once you let them think they have the upper hand, they do. And he doesn't have it with me.'

Elva reappeared. Ilis introduced them. Elva said, 'He'll kill you when he wakes up. No one insults Ailin like that.'

'You speak of him as if he were a grown man; he is not. He is a little boy, and little boys respect and need discipline.'

'Ailin is a sorcerer.'

'And a little boy.'

Elva shrugged. 'Have it your way, farmer's daughter.'

Trevelyn walked through the destruction, calling for Rudelle. He hugged her when he found her. 'I was worried when I saw the signs of battle.'

Ilis said, 'Did you see what Rudelle did?'

'No.'

Ilis told him, the deed growing a bit with the telling.

Elva spoke to Trevelyn as if Rudelle were not there. 'She won't live out the week.'

Elva vanished.

He hugged Rudelle tighter and said, 'I'll carry Ailin inside and put something on his face to keep the swelling down.'

'I'm sorry that I hit him.'

'I'm not,' Trevelyn said.

She asked, 'Ilis, can your rose be saved?'

The girl walked close to the wounded vine, tears glistening in her eyes. 'Yes, but she hurts.' The girl sat on the ground, and the surviving blossoms shivered and cringed above her head.

Trevelyn motioned for Rudelle to come with him and leave Ilis to her magic.

Rudelle asked, 'How are your parents?'

'Down in the caverns under the house. They have research to do and spells to prepare. They've neglected the magic shop. It'll take me weeks to catch up.'

'They don't like me very much.'

'No, but I love you, and that will be enough for them, eventually.'

Rudelle nodded, but was unconvinced.

Dinner preparations went forth in the only truly clean room in the house, the kitchen. The maid had kept up in there. Trevelyn watched through the open doorway. Ilis worked beside Rudelle. The girl wore a clean brown dress and clean undergarments.

Rudelle had even shown her how to mend rips without magic.

Ailin was nursing a wondrous bruise, but the boy was peeling potatoes, something his mother could never have gotten him to do. Of course, his mother wouldn't have been basting a turkey either.

Ilis watched everything Rudelle did with a kind of wonder. Ailin watched her with a wary and unusual emotion, respect.

Elva came to stand beside Trevelyn. 'What have you brought into this house, brother?'

He smiled. 'Peace, cooked meals, love, discipline.' He shrugged. 'Rudelle.'

'How did you know?'

'I went to a prophet and paid gold.'

Elva laughed. 'It looks like you're going to get your money's worth.'

He nodded. 'Rudelle will see to it.'

An explosion shuddered through the house. 'What was that?' Rudelle asked.

Ilis answered, 'Mother or Father, they are working spells.'

'Well, my cake is going to fall if they keep doing that. Go downstairs and tell them to please not rock the house until after dinner.'

Ilis looked like she'd lost her mind.

Elva saved her. 'I'll do it. Should I tell them you said so?'

'Please do, and tell them that if they can refrain from blowing up the house, we will have layer cake, turkey with walnut stuffing, candied orange breads, potato cakes, and fresh greens, courtesy of Ilis's magic.'

Elva grinned. 'You fixed all their favorites.'

Rudelle grinned back. 'Did I?'

Ailin said, 'Candied orange breads? Really? But it isn't a holy day.'

Elva gave a small bow in Rudelle's direction. 'I will tell my parents to stop rocking the house. If you can scold them like children, I can be brave enough to bear the message. Though I will have a sorcerous shield ready when I tell them.'

Rudelle said, 'Thank you, Elva.'

Elva laughed and hugged her brother. 'That new wife of yours may live out the week.' Then Elva vanished.

'People certainly leave rooms quickly here,' Rudelle said.

Ailin asked, 'May I have a candied orange bread?'

'Just one, or you'll ruin your dinner.'

The boy nodded.

Rudelle handed him the treat and said, 'You've done a wonderful job on those potatoes. You've been a big help, and you didn't waste a spell on it.'

He grinned, mouth full of orange bread, and mumbled, 'I don't need magic to peel any old potatoes.'

'Of course you don't.'

Ilis asked, 'Rudelle, the water's boiling, now what?'

'We cut up the potatoes and put them in.'

'Oh.'

Trevelyn listened to the rise and fall of voices, smelled the rich fragrance of cooking food, and smiled.

# HERE BE DRAGONS

*This is the only science fiction story I've ever completed. Hardware-oriented science doesn't interest the writer in me. It's the softer sciences that fascinate me on paper. Of course, just because it's soft science doesn't make it a soft story. One editor rejected this story by writing that it made her feel unclean. Cool.*

SOME PEOPLE ARE just born evil. No twisted childhood trauma, no abusive father, or alcoholic mother, just plain God-awful mean. Dr Jasmine Cooper, dream therapist and empath, believed that, knew that. She had spent too many years looking inside the minds of murderers not to believe it.

Bernard C. had been born evil. He was sixty, tall and thin, a little stoop-shouldered with age. Thick white hair fell in soft waves around a strong face. At sixty, he still showed the charm that had allowed him to seduce and slaughter sixteen women.

He wasn't your typical mass murderer. First, he was about fifteen years too old; second, until he started murdering people he had seemed quite sane. No abuse of animals, no child beating, no rages, nothing. Perhaps it was that very nothing that was the clue. Bernard had been the perfect husband until his wife died when he was fifty. He had raised two children, the perfect father. Everything he did was perfect, so squeaky normal that it screamed when you read it. Too perfect, too ordinary, like an actor that had his role down – to perfection.

Jasmine had studied the pictures; the basement slaughter room with its old-fashioned autopsy table. Bernard had been a mortician before he retired. Jasmine had found morticians to be some of the most stable and sane people she had ever met. You had to be pretty well grounded to work with the dead, day after day. As a mortician, Bernard had been the best, until he retired.

He brought sixteen women down his basement steps, ranging in age from forty-five to sixty-nine. He tapped them on the head, not too hard, strapped them to his table, and started the embalming process while they were still alive. Technically, most of them just bled to death. Bernard drained out their blood and pumped in embalming fluid, simple. They bled to death.

But Jasmine knew it was not simple, that they hadn't just bled to death, that they had strained against the tape over their mouths, struggled against the straps at wrist and ankle until they rubbed the skin away and bled faster. As you grow older the skin tears more easily, thin and fine as parchment.

And Jasmine was in charge of Bernard's rehabilitation. Dreaming. Images swimming, colored clouds floating across the mind. Brief glimpses of places, people, sharp glittering bits of emotion. The dreamer moved in his sleep, almost awake, dreams surfacing, spilling over his conscious mind. Bright memories of make-believe following his thoughts like hounds on a scent. He would remember. Jasmine would see that he never forgot.

Bernard C. woke screaming. It was the best that Jasmine could do. She had tried to make him remorseful, sympathetic to his victims, but Bernard was a sociopath; he didn't really believe in other people. They were just amusing things, not real, not like he was real. He had embalmed sixteen women alive because he had wanted to do it. It was pleasant – amusing.

She could not make him feel things he had no capacity to feel. His emotions were a great roaring silence. But he could feel fear for himself. He could feel his own pain. So every night when he slept, Jasmine hurt him. She strapped him to his own table and had his victims bleed him dry. She buried him alive; she closed him in the dark until air burned in his chest and he suffocated. She terrorized him night after night, until Bernard did feel one emotion. Hate. He hated Dr Cooper, not the burning hatred of a 'normal' person but the cold hate of a sociopath. Cold hate never dies, never wavers. Bernard's fondest wish was to strap Dr Cooper to a table.

Jasmine knew this, felt it. The therapy was working. And if Bernard C. ever got Dr Cooper alone, he'd do worse than kill her. He wasn't alone. If you asked most of the men in Clarkson Maximum Security Prison what they most desired in the whole world it was to have Dr Cooper at their mercy.

The Clarkson Prison had the highest rate of successful rehabilitation for violent criminals in the country, perhaps in the world. Some had found in their dreams the taste of other people's tears, sympathy for others, at last. Other dreams held the taste of blood, the pulse of their own hearts dying.

Distance is no protection against psychic ability. Dr Cooper knew what their dreams tasted of; she could find them wherever they would go. Only death would free them from her, and some of them weren't sure about that.

Dr Jasmine Cooper, empath/dream therapist, most hated and feared person in a building full of monsters, was at her desk doing paperwork when the phone rang. She ignored it, knowing the machine would pick up. It did. Her voice first and then, after the beep, a man's voice, 'Hello, Jasmine, this is Dr Edward Bromley, again.' Silence, then, 'Well, we have a problem at the school that requires your special touch. This is the fifth message I've left, Jasmine. Call me or a child's going to die.'

She picked up at the last moment. 'Dr Bromley.' Her voice was utterly neutral, a trick she'd picked up from some of her patients.

'Ah, yes. Jasmine. I'm glad you picked up. Can we have a visual to go along with the voice?'

She stared at the small credit-card-thin screen just above the phone. The screen was a blank silver-gray. 'No,' she said. 'What do you want, Dr Bromley?'

He sighed. 'Jasmine, or should I call you Dr Cooper?'

'That would be fine. What do you want?'

'I would really like to see your face when I tell you.'

'Why?'

'Damn it, Jasmine . . . Dr Cooper. Do you know how hard it was for me to come to you with this?'

'No,' she lied. His anxiety oozed over the lines, trembling with distance and electricity and a touch of fear. Something was very wrong.

'Tell me what you want, Bromley. What needs my special touch?' Her voice held a bite, sarcasm leaking through her professionalism. She could feel her face crumbling. She didn't dare let Bromley see her like this. She could feel the hate blazing through her eyes, trembling down her hands. He'd see it too. Even he wasn't that blind.

'There's a problem at the school.' He hesitated, only his breathing still hissing through the line.

'What sort of problem?'

'Bad dreams, no, nightmares. Freaking, bloody, awful nightmares. We've had one attempted suicide.'

'Student or teacher?'

'Student, but he was an advanced student. He had training, but the dreams just ate him alive. He slit his wrists because he didn't ever want to fall asleep again.'

Jasmine smiled. 'You've been doing this long enough, Bromley. You've got a powerful untrained dreamer in the school. Police yourself.'

'We tried, Jas.'

'No,' she said, 'no one calls me that anymore.' The old nickname crept along her skin, raising the hairs on her arms.

'Jasmine, then. Do you remember Nicky?'

'He was a dreamer a few years older than I was.'

'Yes. He's dead.'

She stared at the phone receiver wondering what Bromley's face looked like right now, this minute. A trickle of sweat oozed down her forehead; she wiped it with the back of her hand. 'What happened?'

'He tried to take care of the nightmares. We think he linked up with our rogue dreamer and a blood vessel in his brain burst. An embolism.'

Jasmine swallowed hard, hoped Bromley couldn't hear it. 'It happens.' Her voice was level, so bland she knew the strain showed.

'Not to fully trained dreamers. Nicky was almost as good as you were. People with that kind of talent don't burst their brains, not without help.'

'It is impossible to truly kill someone during a dream session. A bad heart, well it happens. Nicky didn't die in dream. He just died. Coincidence.'

'You don't believe that any more than I do.'

'Read any textbook on psychic phenomena, Bromley. You wrote the standard: no one can kill another person by dreaming them to death.'

'We both know that isn't true.'

'There is no record of it ever happening.'

'Because I destroyed the record, Jasmine. You owe me.'

There it was, bland and clear, and no ignoring it. 'Are you recording this?'

'No.'

'Don't be.'

'You think I'd get you to admit something on tape and then blackmail you with it?'

'Obligate me, maybe.'

'I'm not recording this, Jasmine. Talk to me, please.'

Maybe it was the *please* that did it, or perhaps the rushing sense of fear. 'So you've got another dreamer that can kill during dream. Someone at least as powerful as I was.'

'God, Jasmine, don't ever say it like that again. If someone should overhear . . .'

'You said talk, I'm talking. Do you know who it is?'

'We think so. A student who just arrived two months ago. A ten-year-old girl named Lisbeth Pearson.'

'Why do you think it's her?'

'We've only got one other dreamer in school right now. Malcolm hasn't got the control. Lisbeth's sucking him into everyone's nightmares. We're hiding all the sharp objects from Malcolm.'

'How old is he?'

'Fourteen.'

'Ten and fourteen, you're still a baby-raper, Bromley.'

'The school did OK by you, Dr Cooper. You're the most respected dream therapist in this country. I saw on the news, you've set up two sister programs in different states. Did you get an invitation to do the same in, what was it, France?'

'England.'

'Without this school, you wouldn't be where you are.'

Jasmine almost laughed, but it wasn't funny, it was pathetic. He was right. She was keeper of the monsters, thanks to Bromley and others like him. And she hated them all.

He had asked her something, but she hadn't heard.

'Excuse me, Dr Bromley, can you repeat that, please?'

'When can you get here?'

Her stomach tightened, palms sweating. 'I swore I'd never go back, Bromley.'

'I remember, Dr Cooper, but this is an emergency. If you don't come here and defuse the situation, I'll have no choice.'

'There are always choices, Bromley.'

'Not here, not now, Jasmine. I write up my report and they'll execute Lisbeth Pearson as a dangerous, uncontrollable psychic. Unless you can tame her, Lisbeth won't see her eleventh birthday.'

Using the child's name twice in a row – manipulation, a tug at the heartstrings. It worked like it was supposed to.

'I'll come. It will take me a few hours to divide my patients between my fellow therapists, then I'll be there.'

'Thank you, Dr Cooper.'

'Send all the material you have on the child. I'll give you my fax number. I'll study it all on the trip and be ready to work when I arrive.'

'It'll be to you as soon as we hang up.'

'One more thing. How do you know it's the child?'

'I told you we don't have any other students that could do it.'

Jasmine smiled, a bitter twist of lips. 'What about a teacher, a trained dreamer that's gone off the deep end?'

'We screen our workers, Jasmine.'

'I remember.'

'Dr Roberts was a fluke. It couldn't happen again. We see to that.'

'If you've got everything under such bloody good control, then what do you need me for?'

'Jasmine . . .'

'No, I don't want to hear any more. I'll be there as soon as I can.' She hung up the phone. Sweat was beading on her forehead despite the air-conditioned quiet of the room.

Dr Roberts had taken a butcher knife to two students, and Jasmine would always carry the scar where she had thrown up an arm to keep the doctor from slashing her face. A guard had shot Roberts then, and she had fallen forward on her knees, still whispering, 'Evil, you are all evil.'

Jasmine could control her dreams, but Roberts still accused her, questioned her at night before she could stop it. 'You're evil, aren't you, Jasmine? You know you are.'

'Yes, Dr Roberts, I know I am.' But Jasmine knew that everyone was evil, down deep when you scrape the skin away. Inside their heads everyone hunted, everyone killed, everyone was a monster.

The thought that Dr Roberts couldn't deal with was not the children's evil, but her own. That morning when she woke she saw a monster looking back at her from the mirror. She had set out to kill the monster and gotten killed for it.

Jasmine knew the truth. You couldn't kill The Monster. It was always there just behind your eyes. You could kill a *monster*, though. Jasmine was a great believer in the death penalty. It was the ultimate therapy. It cured everything. The first stirrings of fear crawled in her belly, low and real. It would get worse. Jasmine knew that it would get worse.

Dr Cooper cradled her face on her arms, cheek pressed into the coolness of her desktop, and cried. *The school*, that was all it was ever called, it had no other name. A lot of secret government projects had no names.

Thirty years ago, almost Jasmine's lifetime, psychic phenomena became a proven scientific fact. In fact, there were so many psychics that scientists started making jokes about pod people. It didn't stay funny for long. Most of the new breed were children. They had powers that were dependable and as testable as such phenomena ever would be. There were lots of theories as to why, suddenly, we had empaths and telepaths and dreamers coming out of the woodwork. The evolutionists said it was proof of their ideas; mankind was evolving. Others thought it was junk food, chemicals and preservatives in the American diet. The majority of talent did occur in industrialized nations. Maybe it was the pollution. Inoculations. The beginning of the Apocalypse. No one knew. Jasmine doubted anyone ever would.

But a few of the children had been dangerous, their powers so far beyond the dreams of normality that their families couldn't cope. In most cases the families were afraid of their children. Glad to give them up to someplace that would care for them.

Jasmine's family gave her up when she was five. Her mother cried and kissed her. Her older sister and brother hugged her dutifully. Her father said, 'Be a good girl, Jas.'

The smell of pipe tobacco could still bring back the memory of her tall, dark-haired father. A twinge of memory like a badly healed scar.

What she remembered most of her mother was the cool sense of fear. That red lipsticked mouth kissing her, laughing, and wiping the lipstick smear off Jasmine's cheek with a Kleenex. Laughing, golden hair, and the sick smell of fear. No perfume in the world could hide the stench from an empath.

But then maybe Mommy didn't know, maybe she didn't understand, maybe she had done her best. Maybe.

Lisbeth Pearson was small for ten, with coppery red hair, almost dark enough to be auburn, but not quite. The hair fell in thick waves to her shoulders. Her face was that peaches-and-cream skin that some redheads have; no freckles, just creamy skin. Her eyes were a pale brown, almost amber. She wore a dress that seemed too young for her, with lace-topped white socks and patent leather shoes.

She looked like she was dressed for Halloween, or like someone else had dressed her. She was playing alone with a dollhouse on the other side of a one-way mirror. Jasmine found that very funny. She remembered being on the other side of the glass. She had always known who was watching and what they were feeling. Always.

Lisbeth looked up and stared directly at the mirror, and smiled. Jasmine smiled and nodded back.

'Can she see us?' Dr Bromley asked.

'No.'

'You acknowledged each other, I saw it.'

'Did we?'

'Don't bullshit me, Jasmine.'

She turned to stare at the infamous Dr Bromley, protector and tormentor of her childhood. He was five foot eight, but the weight he had gained made him seem smaller. His curly brown hair was fading back from a gleaming expanse of scalp. His hands, which had once looked strong, now resembled uncooked sausages. His face was blotched with red. Was he sick? She stared into his small eyes and thought, *yes, maybe.*

Beth could have told Bromley if he was dying. She had had a feel for death. Beth was dead, had been for twenty years. Tall, laughing, gray-eyed Beth. She had been able to think people to death, a wasting illness. She hadn't meant to kill people, just didn't know how to stop it. Neither did anyone else. So they killed her.

'Jasmine . . . Jasmine.'

'I'm sorry, Dr Bromley, I was thinking about something.'

'Are you all right?'

'I was going to ask you the same thing.'

'Why?' he asked.

'You don't look well.'

He fidgeted, glanced away, and knew that it wasn't his eyes she could read. He laughed, abrupt and harsh. 'No, I'm not well. It's none of your damn business what's wrong, Dr Cooper. Let's get back to Lisbeth. You're here to save her, not me.'

'Could I save you?'

'No.'

'I'm sorry, Dr Bromley.' And Jasmine realized she really was sorry. She didn't want to be sorry for him, to feel anything but hatred and contempt, and fear. Not sorrow, not for Dr Bromley.

'Tell me what you think about Lisbeth Pearson.'

'I don't think anything yet. I want to talk to her alone.' Jasmine smiled. 'As alone as this place allows.'

'We have to monitor the children. It's part of the project.'

'I remember the arguments, Dr Bromley.'


Lisbeth was placing tiny gilt-edged chairs around a miniature dining room table when Jasmine entered. The child ignored her and continued to rearrange the furniture. She seemed completely absorbed in the task, but Jasmine felt the child's interest, her power, glide over her skin like a cold breeze.

'My name is Jasmine.'

Lisbeth looked up at that, one small hand cradling a flower arrangement. 'I've never met anyone named Jasmine before.'

'And I've never met anyone named Lisbeth before.'

The child grinned, perfect lips, eyes sparkling. 'No, you've never met anyone like me.'

Jasmine looked into those brown-amber eyes, shining with

humor, and felt the threat. The words were subtle; the power that emanated from the child was not.

The power climbed over Jasmine's skin, raising the hair on her body, like insects crawling, or a faint buzz of electric current. You could breathe in Lisbeth's power, choke on it.

The child smiled, even white teeth flashing, but her eyes didn't sparkle anymore. Games were over; Lisbeth didn't have to pretend to be 'normal,' so she didn't try. Jasmine stared into her eyes and found – nothing. Inside her head was a great roaring silence.

Jasmine had never met a sociopath at such a tender age. She knew that they were born broken, but to feel it, to feel that emptiness stretching inside this lovely little girl, to feel the void . . . was the most frightening thing she had ever felt.

The child laughed, sweet and joyful. 'You're afraid of me, just like all the others.'

Fear meant control. It meant Jasmine was controllable, so Lisbeth lowered her defenses; she allowed Jasmine to glimpse what was there. Or what wasn't.

Jasmine's power eased through the girl, along her mind, and found other things missing. She was an empath; no empath could be a sociopath and bring harm to people, because they would feel that pain as their own. Unless they couldn't feel anyone's pain but their own.

Lisbeth was blind to positive emotions; she could only absorb the negative. As far as she was concerned, she alone felt joy, happiness, love. Everyone else was full of hate, fear, shame, or nothing. It was an empath's version of hell. And the child had never known anything else.

The curling auburn hair had little pink barrettes that picked up the small pink design in the dress. Perfectly matched. Perfect. If she hadn't been a psychic, Lisbeth Pearson would have been the perfect daughter, the perfect student, the perfect worker, or wife, or mother, until the day that she broke. The day that The Monster came out.

But The Monster was too close to the surface in Lisbeth; there was almost nothing else left.

The child had gone back to her dollhouse, ignoring Jasmine. She no longer considered her a threat.

Dr Jasmine Cooper turned abruptly on her heel and walked out; the sound of her high heels was loud and echoing. She leaned against the door trying to breathe. She was shivering uncontrollably, fear soaking like frost into her bones. Jasmine tried to gain control of herself and knew that Lisbeth felt her falling to pieces. Knew that a closed door was no barrier at all.

An echo of the child's joy filtered through Jasmine's nerves like distant, mocking laughter.

Jasmine entered Bromley's office all cool professionalism. No seams showed; she had swallowed the fear whole. Years of practice.

Dr Bromley was sitting behind his paper-strewn desk when Jasmine entered. His eyes looked tired, wary. 'Well?'

'Just being in the room with her raises the hairs on my arms. You don't have to be an empath to know that.'

'She's evil,' he said.

'If you've already made up your mind, Dr Bromley, why did you bring me here?'

He stared at her, without saying anything.

'You want me to save her.'

He nodded once up, once down.

'Do you know what she is?'

He rubbed his fingertips over his eyes. 'She's a sociopath. She's an empath that can only feel negative emotions.'

Jasmine didn't try to keep the surprise off her face. 'If you know, why is she still alive?'

'Because, Dr Cooper, I'm tired of killing children. So many of them come through with talents we can't begin to understand. They can do things that make Lisbeth look safe. But most of the time we just don't understand them enough to help them. We destroy them because we don't know what else to do. But Lisbeth is like you were, in some ways; I hoped you could help her, understand her. Keep her alive.'

'And if I can't help her? If I think she's too dangerous?'

He shrugged. 'I fill out a form, submit it to my superiors, and in a month she'll be dead.'

'Just like that,' Jasmine said.

'Just like that,' he said.

She stared at the doctor, tried to feel what he felt. Sorrow, an almost unending sorrow. The school had eaten him alive, just as it had the children. There was nothing left of him but sadness, fear, and a dogged sense of duty. A fragile wish for hope, for meaning. He was looking for peace.

'I can't give you absolution, Bromley.'

He flinched. 'Is that what I want?'

Jasmine nodded. 'You're wondering if you played God, or were just a murderer.'

He gave a weak laugh. 'You are merciless.'

'I had good teachers.'

He nodded. 'All right, no absolution for me. Can you save this child?'

Jasmine knew she should say, 'Kill her.' Lisbeth Pearson was too dangerous for words. But she looked into Bromley's tired, sick eyes, and said, 'Maybe.'


Jasmine was walking to her room, down the familiar empty corridors. No matter how many children were in the school, there were never people in the hallways. Always there was the feeling of abandonment, emptiness. She walked the halls alone, tracked by the blinking red lights of cameras.

A woman came from around the corner; long yellow hair swept nearly to her knees. She had the height for the hair, slender and graceful. The face was dominated by pale blue eyes. Jasmine stopped and waited for the woman to come to her. A feeling of horrible déjà vu swept over her. An almost claustrophobic sense of time spinning backward. 'Vanessa?' It came out a question, though it wasn't meant to be.

The woman smiled, and held out her hands. 'Jasmine, it is you.' Vanessa hugged her tight, and Jasmine fought the urge to pull away. She relaxed into the arms of her best friend from childhood, and one of the most powerful telepaths the school had ever had.

When she could, Jasmine pulled back, and said, 'Are you visiting?'

Vanessa turned away. She hid her eyes, and her mind was as tight and closed as a locked door. She stepped back from Jasmine. 'No, I'm an instructor.' Her voice made it bright, cheerful.

'An instructor. For how long?'

'Since high school.'

'You went away to college, just like I did. We rode to the airport together.' Jasmine felt panic like a cold weight at the pit of her gut.

Vanessa paced back and forth, then whirled, smiling. 'I didn't finish college. They needed me here to help with all the little telepaths.'

Jasmine worked very hard at keeping her own mind locked tight. No empath's control can match a telepath, but she tried. Her face was absolutely blank, pleasantly so, practice, years of practice. 'Do you enjoy . . . teaching?'

'Oh, yes, I really feel like I make a difference – you?'

Jasmine nodded.

'You've done really well. My best friend, the famous doctor.' Vanessa laughed and hugged her again.

Best friend – they hadn't seen or talked to each other in ten years. Jasmine found herself crying, hugging the tall stranger who used to be her friend, and crying.

'Hey,' Vanessa said. 'Hey, what's the matter?'

She pulled away and shook her head. What could she say that wouldn't hurt Vanessa? *You betrayed our dreams. You gave up and came back here to hide. We swore an oath that we would never come here to hide, better death than this tomb.* Jasmine wanted to scream it all out. To find out why Vanessa had failed, the ultimate failure, she had come back here. Once you came back, you never left. No one ever left a second time. The words echoed in her head, and the walls seemed to be closing around her, narrow. Jasmine hadn't noticed how narrow the halls were. The roof was close enough to touch. The school was crowding her, crowding.

'Jasmine, what's wrong?'

She drew a deep, shaking breath. 'Panic attack.'

'Do you still get those?'

'First one in . . .' *Breathe deep and even, breathe.* 'Twelve years.'

'Open your mind to me. Jasmine, I can help. Remember.' Jasmine backed away until she hit the wall. She pressed against it. Vanessa took a step forward, reaching.

'No!'

'Let me help you.'

Her breathing was beginning to slow, pulse going down. The corridor was still hot and too close, but it was going to be all right. It was going to be all right. 'I'll be all right, Vanessa.'

'I can help you with whatever is wrong. Telepaths are great counselors.'

Jasmine stared into her eyes. 'You wouldn't like what I was thinking.'

Vanessa froze, hands still outstretched, smile sliding away from her face. It was one of those moments when you don't need empathy. When truth stretches between two people. Truth could be violent, could strip you of dignity and hope just as quickly as a gun.

It was one of those moments when you can look in someone else's eyes and see your own reflection so sharp and true that it slices like glass.

Vanessa turned away first and began to walk down the hall, then to run. Her footsteps thundered against the narrow walls.

Jasmine stared up into the watching monitor, red light blinking. She spoke to it. 'The monitor in my room better be disabled before I get there, Bromley. If it's not, I'm going to tear it out of the wall.' She took a deep shaking breath. 'You should have told me Vanessa was here. What else haven't you told me?'

There was no answer from the whirring monitor. She hadn't expected one. If Bromley had answered, she wouldn't have believed him anyway.

The room was like all the other rooms. It was rectangular with pale blue walls. A single bed was against the right-hand wall, white sheets, brown blanket. When Jasmine was a child, she had longed for colored sheets. The kind with animals and clowns on them. In her house were bright-colored sheets, and none of the rooms were painted blue.

There was a white bureau with mirror against the left wall, and a closet in the far wall. That was all. Small or not, the rooms always seemed empty.

There was a monitor up in one corner. The red recording light was off, no whirring, no moving to scan the room. Bromley had turned it off; supposedly that meant that Jasmine was alone, unobserved.

Jasmine pressed her palms on top of the perfectly clean bureau top. She leaned forward until she was almost touching her own reflection. The old litany came back, 'This is not the whole world. You will get out. You will make it on the outside. You can do it. This isn't forever.' How many nights had she told her reflection that? How many years?

This wasn't the whole world. She had gotten out. She had made it on the outside. She could do it. It hadn't been forever. And now she was back. To save another little girl. The thought came, *But does she deserve saving?*

Jasmine answered aloud, 'I save monsters all the time.' Fear had settled in the pit of her stomach, hard and thick. This place pressed so many of her buttons, so much shit to wade through here. And the child, that frightening, beautiful child. Why was so much evil pleasant, pretty on the outside, like poisoned candy? Most mass murderers were the nicest people.

Lisbeth Pearson was already in bed. It was an hour past dark. She would be out there in the dream network, hunting. For the first time someone would be hunting Lisbeth. Did the child suspect? No. There was one other trait of the serial killer that Lisbeth shared: arrogance. The predator never expects to be hunted.

Jasmine had never been hunted either. It would be a night of firsts.

That night Jasmine dreamed. Her own dreams first. Nothing pleasant; fears about the school, Lisbeth, Bromley, childhood nightmares, she brushed them away. Then the sensation that her skull evaporated and her mind eased outward like mist. She floated through one dream at a time. She could touch more than one mind at a time, bringing other people into the same dream, but they had to share a single dream. Multiple minds, but not multiple fantasies. No one was sure why that particular restriction. It was just the way it worked.

Jasmine swam through the colors of other people's dreams, searching. A boy played catch with his dead father, sorrow, things left unsaid; a woman held a stranger in her arms, naked, unafraid, private, lust flowed warm and felt like anger; Bromley dreamed of flowers surrounding a coffin, rage, hate. Jasmine moved on before she could see who was inside the coffin. She could have wandered all night from dream to dream like a butterfly in a field of fantastic flowers, but something burned through her mind, screamed along her nerves: terror.

Jasmine followed it like a beacon. The silent rush of fear called her as surely as a scream for help. She appeared in the dream with an almost physical jolt. She had rushed, hadn't taken her time; the reality of the nightmare was concrete, touchable, breathable, visible, real. A boy stood with his back to her. He was tall, slender, hair neatly buzzed next to his scalp, skin the color of dark coffee. He was struggling to lock the door to a dingy room. Windows leaked gray daylight through dirty glass. Wallpaper fell in strips from yellowed walls. The place reeked of damp, rot, urine.

The bolt slid home and he turned, leaning against the door, relieved. His eyes flew wide. 'Who are you?' His voice hadn't caught up to his tall, leggy body; it sounded like a child's voice.

'I'm Jasmine. I've come to help.'

'You're that new dream teacher.'

Jasmine started to explain that she was not a teacher, was not a part of the school, but standing there soaking up Malcolm's terror, she let it go. 'Yes.'

The smell was growing worse, a choking outhouse stench that was filling the room, coming from under the door. Malcolm backed away from the door, until he bumped into Jasmine. He jumped and she gripped his shoulders. He didn't pull away. His breathing was coming in short gasps. The whole dream focused on that door. Jasmine could feel the pull of it. Fear. Fear forced down their throat until more than anything in the whole world you didn't want that door to open. You didn't want *IT* to come through and get you. And you knew that that was exactly what was going to happen, and there was nothing you could do about it. The helplessness of nightmare, but Jasmine could do something about it. Nightmares were her specialty.

The girl's focus was strong and pure. Jasmine could not look away from the door. The sound of heavy footsteps scraped outside; the smell of rotting corpses, sweet and putrid, filled the room.

Jasmine concentrated, willing the walls to dissolve, the dream to end. Nothing happened. She took a deep breath and choked on the stinking air.

Malcolm's voice was thin with fear. 'Do something!'

She tried. Manipulating dreams was just a matter of will and concentration. Jasmine knew this wasn't real; if you knew that, you could change it. But she had never been inside the dream of someone who matched her powers so exactly.

'I can't break the dream.'

Malcolm made a small sound low in his throat. He sagged against her. 'Oh, God,' he said, 'oh, God.'

Jasmine swallowed the first rush of real fear, not Lisbeth's creation but her very own fear. She was as trapped as the boy. Trapped in the mind of a sociopathic child.

Then things began to melt from the walls. Hands, arms reached outward; rotted flesh falling away from white bone, rags of clothes. Things long dead crawled out of the rotting walls and began to drag themselves closer.

One man had half his face blown away; his tongue rolled between bone and raw meat, a large fat worm twisted round the corpse's tongue.

Malcolm screamed, one high shriek after another, as four of the things shambled toward them.

The faces were recognizable; a man, woman, two teenage children. They had been black; now they were the colors of old death.

Jasmine grabbed Malcolm's hand; his fingernails dug into her palm. His screams became words. 'My father, my father! Noooo!'

Of course, the dead things were Malcolm's family. They were horrible, paralyzingly so to the boy, because this nightmare was designed with him in mind, not Jasmine. The dead things were slow; little pieces of them fell away as they walked, slow.

Jasmine dragged Malcolm toward the door. He fought her, the dead things turned toward them, but Jasmine was at the door with the boy screaming, tugging at her hand, trying to get free, to run, but there was nowhere to run.

Jasmine couldn't break the dream, but maybe she could manipulate it. She unlocked the door and flung it open. The dream lurched; the dead things wavered. There was nothing on the other side of the door. *Sloppy, Lisbeth*, Jasmine thought. There was a sensation of vertigo, then Jasmine filling the emptiness with a stairway, leading down.

She dragged Malcolm onto the stairs and shut and locked the door behind them, with a thought. Malcolm was running now, still gripping her hand as if afraid she would vanish and abandon him. They clattered down the stairs; suddenly there were walls on either side. The stairs led downward, but now there were walls to hold them, rotting yellow walls.

Hands grew out of the wall, pale arms, they fluttered, hands wringing. A hand grabbed Jasmine's wrist. The flesh was too soft, doughy, rubbery, but strong.

Malcolm screamed as hands grabbed his shirt.

Jasmine needed to be free of the hand; she thought of a sword. It levitated over the hand, and sliced downward in a glittering arc. The arm flopped, spraying warm blood into her face. The hand still clung to her wrist, but she pulled Malcolm free of the bloated hands, and they ran.

Jasmine sprayed the walls with blood from the sword as it sliced the hands in front of them like a thrasher, cutting wheat. The stairs were littered with pale hands that twitched and bled.

The stairs spilled onto a landing, and the walls closed in, dead end. Jasmine had been concentrating too much on the sword and the hands to maintain the stairs. The smell of rotting corpses began to fill the air.

'Malcolm, is this the same dream every time?'

'No.'

'Is there anything that is the same every time?'

'My family, she always kills my family.' Both of his hands dug into her arm. His fear was nearly choking her. Her fear was nearly a cold heat on her skin. The bloated hand had fallen off in the running. She and Malcolm stood alone on the landing, as the stench became stronger. The dead things were coming.

Malcolm's family, turned into rotting corpses that would tear the boy apart, maybe eat parts of him alive while he watched.

Yes, that would be what Jasmine would do, if she really wanted to terrify. To horrify. If she really hated someone.

That was it: hatred. Jasmine called out, 'Lisbeth, I know why you hate Malcolm. I know.'

The first rotted corpse began to pull itself from the wall. 'You're jealous of his family. Malcolm's family loves him. They love him, Lisbeth. Malcolm's father loves him. His mother loves him. His sister loves him. His brother loves him.'

The corpses had pulled free of the wall and were reaching for them, but the smell was fading. 'Your family hates you, Lisbeth. Your mother is afraid of you, Lisbeth. I read your file. Your father tried to kill you, and you punished him for it. Didn't you? Didn't you!'

The dead things began to melt. There was the sensation of something large sliding through the nightmare, like a whale swimming next to you in the dark. Lisbeth's power.

'No one loves you. They hate you, Lisbeth. Everyone hates you. Even your own family.'

Silence, not of the ear, but sensation of feeling, silence more profound than soundlessness.

The dream broke and Jasmine was spilled back to wakefulness. She sat up in bed, heart hammering in her chest. That was it. Lisbeth had never been loved, not by anyone, ever. Even sociopaths need the illusion of acceptance from someone. Lisbeth needed to be loved.

That morning Jasmine went to Malcolm. They met for the first time in the flesh. She promised him that Lisbeth would never hurt him again. One way or another Jasmine meant to keep that promise.

Lisbeth was playing with a nearly life-size doll when Jasmine walked through the door. She knew that Bromley was on the other side of the one-way glass. She no longer cared.

'Nice doll,' Jasmine said.

'My mommy sent it to me.'

'Why?'

Lisbeth frowned up at her. 'Why what?'

'Why did your mommy send the doll to you?'

'What do you mean?' Lisbeth asked. The lovely, golden-haired doll lay very still in the child's lap.

'Why did your mother send you a doll? Why would she send you anything? Most parents never contact their children once they come to the school.'

Lisbeth gave a lovely smile, eyes shining. 'Because she loves me,' she said, very matter-of-fact, very sweet, and as soon as she said it, Lisbeth knew it had been a mistake.

Jasmine laughed, then the laughter died. She stared down at the child, met her brown eyes, and did not look away. 'No one loves you, Lisbeth; you and I both know that.'

'I hate you,' Lisbeth said, voice quiet and precise.

'I know,' Jasmine said. 'Why did you kill Nicky?'

'Didn't.'

'Why, Lisbeth?'

'Why what?' the child said, voice sulky.

'Why did you kill Nicky?'

'I could have killed you last night.'

'Then why didn't you?'

'Get out! Get out!' She stood, screaming. Lisbeth began to beat the doll against the floor. Bits of plastic began to shatter onto the floor. One blue eye lay winking to itself, naked against the floor.

'Why did you kill Nicky?'

'Because he wouldn't let me do what I wanted to do. Just like you won't let me!'

'No,' Jasmine said, quietly, 'I won't.'

Jasmine waited the following night, waited until the children had been asleep for a couple of hours. Malcolm wasn't sleeping tonight. Vanessa was sitting up with him, keeping him awake, at Jasmine's request. He would be safe tonight, she could see to that.

Tomorrow night was another problem. Jasmine had made her decision; either Lisbeth was 'tamed' tonight, or the child would die. There was one more possibility: that Lisbeth would kill her.

The thought flowed over her skin like a cool breeze, tickling the hairs on her arms, sliding down her spine like an ice cube. Fear; it was an old companion. Dr Cooper wouldn't know what to do if she wasn't afraid of her patients.

Jasmine flowed from dream to dream; bright glimpses of color, motion, thoughts, feelings. She pushed forward like a swimmer, concentrating on getting to the other shore. Then it came, terror, it screamed along Jasmine's nerves, opened her mind, called to her.

She didn't enter the dream this time, she pushed at it from the outside, shoved the fear aside. Lisbeth's anger flared over her, but there was nothing for the girl to use to trap Jasmine. Outside of dreams, you were safe. 'No, you can't. You're afraid of me, like all the others.'

Jasmine smiled. 'You made the mistake they all make. Just because I'm afraid of you doesn't mean you shouldn't be afraid of me.'

Lisbeth began to gather her forces. Jasmine could feel it, like a thunderstorm building in the distance. She might break the dream, or at least change it. 'How would you like to visit one of my patients?'

The girl hesitated, power swirling around her. 'Patients?'

Jasmine explained what she did; by the time she finished Lisbeth was smiling, that same angelic twist of perfect lips. Lovely and meaningless as a lifelike doll.

'Would you like to see one of their dreams?'

'Do you mean it?' Lisbeth asked.

'Yes.'

Lisbeth licked her lips, breath easing out. It was almost a lust reaction, anticipatory, and far too old for the child. But then in many ways Lisbeth was no longer a child; she had haunted people's dreams too long for that. 'I'd like that.'

'All right.' Jasmine paused as if thinking. 'We'll visit William. You'll like William, and I know he'll get a kick out of you.'

Lisbeth giggled, the first real little-girl sound Jasmine had heard her make.

'I can hold on to you and take you to his dream, if you stop fighting me.'

Lisbeth frowned at that. 'What does that mean?'

'Just relax and let me do the work. Be the passenger for once instead of the driver.'

'You promise to take me to this William. Promise I'll get to see a real killer's dream.'

'Promise,' Jasmine said.

Lisbeth nodded, and lowered her protection. Jasmine felt Lisbeth's consciousness slide against hers, almost a faint bump as the child released all control. An adult empath would never have lowered everything, but Lisbeth didn't have the experience in dealing with people who were her equals. Until now she had had no equal. Ten was still very young.

William was asleep, and he dreamed, as he often did, of past glory. He was lying on a twin bed with a little girl. She was wearing blue shorts and a red tank top with cartoon figures on it. Jasmine remembered the clothes from photographs. This was six-year-old Caitlin, and it was William's version of a wet dream.

Lisbeth sighed. 'Oh, this is great.'

The child was crying, saying, 'I want to go home now, please.'

'Not yet,' William said, voice soothing, as his hand rubbed the tiny bare leg. 'Not yet, soon. If you do everything I say, I'll take you home.'

'You said there were kittens here. Where are the kittens?'

'I'll show them to you.'

'I don't want you to touch me. Don't!' The child's fear stabbed outward like her words. A sharp gut-jerking cry.

Lisbeth hovered as close as Jasmine would allow, soaking up the terror. Feeding off the child's small body. The cries for help, the pleading; Caitlin would ask about the kittens William had promised to show her just seconds before he placed one hand around her slender baby neck and squeezed. He would crush her windpipe. He was a very strong man.

Her small, nude body lay beside the man, dead. Her head was thrown to one side; eyes mercifully closed. She looked like a broken doll, skin perfect and flawless.

Jasmine brought herself and Lisbeth into the dream. The broken little girl vanished, and William was suddenly fully clothed again.

He stared up at her, fear plain on his face, his fear crawling along Jasmine's body. She enjoyed his fear, enjoyed making him suffer.

Lisbeth said, 'He's afraid of you.'

'I know.'

'I been good,' William said. 'I done everything you told me to. Why should I be punished? What'd I do wrong?'

'Oh,' said Lisbeth, 'he's so afraid.' She walked closer to the bed, and he shrank back from her, eyes shifting from Jasmine to this new little girl.

'I'm not here to punish you, William. I want you to help me.'

'Anything, anything you want, Dr Cooper. You just name it.'

Lisbeth reached for him, and he jerked away as if she had burned him.

'Did you enjoy William's dream, Lisbeth?'

'Oh, yes, it was great.'

'Would you like to see another?'

Lisbeth turned, eyes shining, genuinely excited. 'Oh, please, yes.'

Jasmine nodded. 'She's yours, William.'

'Wh-what!' he gasped.

'It's the girl that needs punishing, not you. I'm giving her to you.'

'You can't scare me,' Lisbeth said.

'Is she real?' he asked.

'Very.'

'You think threatening me with him will scare me. It won't. I can make him disappear.'

'I control this dream, Lisbeth.'

William grabbed her wrist. She turned, completely confident that she would destroy him. Jasmine held William's mind and protected it.

The first trickle of fear rose out of Lisbeth. Fear for herself. She struggled to get her hand free. 'You won't let him hurt me. You're not bad. Only bad girls let people get hurt.' The fear was still in check, because she believed what she said. Jasmine was a teacher, a doctor, an adult, and would not really hurt a child.

'I'm not a good girl, Lisbeth, never have been.'

William dragged her against his chest. 'NO!' Lisbeth yelled it, anger still stronger than fear. 'You can't scare me. You can't make me behave. I'm not like the other children.'

'No,' Jasmine said, 'you are not, and neither was I.' Jasmine vanished from the dream, leaving Lisbeth to the man's tender mercies. She did not want to see it happen, but she was drawn to feel it. Fear at last, full-blown and wonderful. Lisbeth terrified. Lisbeth feeling the only thing she could feel, her own pain. Dr Jasmine Cooper hovered on the edge of the dream and fed off the fear, the lust, the horror. She drank the sweet breath of evil, and it filled her up. Jasmine, like the child, not only was attracted to darkness but fed off it.

She broke the dream before William was finished but long after Lisbeth had begun to cry. Jasmine woke and went down the dark hallways to Lisbeth's room. She opened the door to find the child gasping and sweat-soaked. She cringed when she saw Jasmine.

'You're like me, aren't you? You're like me.'

'Yes, Lisbeth, I'm like you.' Jasmine sat down on the edge of the bed.

'I don't want to be punished anymore.'

'Then you've learned your first lesson. I'll show you how to stay alive, Lisbeth. They won't kill you now, not if you let me teach you.'

Jasmine leaned close to the child, whispering so the monitor would-n't hear her, 'I'll show you how to feed off them, so that they don't know. You can do what you like with them within limits. You can tor-ture and get paid for it.'

Lisbeth's breathing had slowed to almost normal. 'You are just like me.'

Jasmine nodded and reached a hand out to the child. Lisbeth came to her, small arms hugging her. They sat together in the dark, hold-ing each other. Lisbeth couldn't love, not really. But every child needs love, whether they can give it or not.

'You won't leave me?' Lisbeth asked in a small voice.

'I won't leave you. You can come visit me during holidays.'

'You're still afraid of me, aren't you?'

'Yes.'

'But now I'm afraid of you.'

'Yes.'

The child leaned her back against Jasmine, small hands holding the woman's arms around her. Every child needs to be held.

She rested her chin on top of Lisbeth's head, and rocked her gently, comforting herself as much as the child. *From one monster to another*, Jasmine thought, *I'll show you how to stay alive. I'll show you how to drink tears and spill blood. We'll carve them up and feed off their fear, and no one will know but us.*

Jasmine glanced up at the room's monitor. *Are you there, Bromley?* she thought. *Are you there?* Maybe he knew, maybe he had always known. *Why did you keep me alive, Bromley? Why?*

She hugged Lisbeth, and felt the first hot trails of tears on her own cheeks. Jasmine whispered into the child's hair, 'Monsters beware, here be dragons.'

# WINTERKILL

*This story, like the Sidra and Leech stories and 'A Token for Celandine,' is set in the world of* Nightseer. *The main character is an assassin, and like Edward in the Anita books, Jessa found that killing ordinary humans was too easy. She kills only wizards. This story shows some of her origins, and that you really can't go home again.*

JESSAMINE SWORDWITCH STOOD among the ruins of Threllkill village. The forest had moved in to reclaim the small clearing. Twenty houses it had been at its largest, a tiny inconsequential place, but it had been home.

One of her mother's roses had gone wild. It climbed over the broken chimney, pale pink flowers clustered against the sun. The air was thick with its scent, cloying sweet. The black-limbed cherry still stood against the shattered pile that had once been the garden wall.

Jessamine felt her mother's magic pulse through the wild growth. An earth-witch's touches stayed with the plot of land. Mother would not have minded that an orange-flowered trumpet vine strangled her garden or that wild grass grew where she had tended her strawberries.

The thought that her mother's body could still be there, hidden in the green growth, came suddenly. She caught her breath, eyes darting for a glimpse of white bone amidst the wilding strawberries. But there was nothing left of her mother save the roses and the cherry tree. Scavengers had long since picked apart the bones. Twelve years was a long time this close to the forest.

'What happened here, Jessa?'

She jumped, startled, and turned. Gregoor leaned against a soft green mound that had once been a part of the kitchen. 'I'm sorry, my thoughts were elsewhere.'

He snorted. 'I could see that.' He gestured, arms wide. 'What destroyed this place?'

'Old age, an act of the gods.'

He frowned and crossed arms tight over his chest. 'Are you going to tell me the story behind this place or not? You drag me out to the wilderness. Tell me nothing. You accept a job without consulting me and then tell me I don't have to come along.' He pushed a hand through his short brown hair. 'Jessa, we've been swordmates for a year. Don't I deserve some type of explanation?'

She smiled at that and walked over to stand against the leaf-covered wall, beside him. Her hazel eyes looked at a place somewhere over his head, while her strong, small hands stroked his hair. 'In Zairde there are no peasants, only the poor. We were poor, but I didn't know that as a child. We had food, shelter, toys, love. I did not think we were poor, but we were not rich. My mother was the village earth-witch. She never used her magic for personal gain or to harm, unless attacked. Even then she was squeamish of the kill. She wouldn't understand my entombing people in living rock.'

'You've only done so twice, and both times it saved our lives.'

She smiled down at him. 'Yes, there is that. But I stand here with my mother's magic still strong in the earth and I shield myself.'

'Why?'

'I'm afraid, Gregoor.' The summer wind stirred her dark hair. 'I promised my mother I would never use my power for evil. I have broken that promise many times.'

'You're afraid her disapproving ghost will haunt you.'

'Yes.'

'Jessa.' He hugged her to him. 'Please tell me what happened here.'

'One day an old sorcerer and his son came to spend the night. I had never seen a truly old sorcerer, for they can live a thousand years. But this one was old. His son was young and strong and handsome; the village girls watched him out the corners of their eyes. During the night the old sorcerer died.' Jessamine's hands stopped moving. She stood absolutely still. 'The son accused us of poisoning his father. He destroyed our village with fire and lightning, storm and earthquake. My father and my brothers were all killed. When it was over, only my mother and I crawled away.'

Jessa took a deep, shaky breath. 'My mother, as the village earth-witch, took our grievance to the Zairdian courts. They did nothing. Two days after they declared the sorcerer's son innocent of wrong-doing, an assassin killed my mother.' She looked down at him, meeting his eyes.

His brown eyes were wide, astonished, pain-filled. 'Jessa.'

She placed fingertips over his lips. 'It was a very long time ago, Gregoor. A very long time ago.'

He gripped her hand. 'What happened to the sorcerer who destroyed this village?'

'He died.' She smiled down at him. It was a smile he had seen before – a slow, tight spreading of lips that filled her eyes with a dark light. He called it her killing smile. 'He was the first wizard I ever killed.'

'And that is why we specialize in assassinating wizards?'

'That is why I do. I do not know why you do it.'

He stood eye to eye, no taller, no shorter than she. 'I do it because you do it.'

'Ah,' she said and gave him what no one else had received from her in twelve years – a smile full of love.

'You took this job so you could come home, then?'

'I took this job because the sorcerer I slew had a mother, as I had a mother. It seems she has gone mad. The entire province wants her dead. The sorceress is Cytherea of Cheladon.'

'You have sent us to kill Cytherea the Mad, Jessa . . .'

She stopped him with a gesture. 'She seeks her son's killer, Gregoor, and has killed hundreds seeking me. I think it is time she found me.'

They came to the first town at dusk. A gibbet had been erected in front of the town gates. Three corpses dangled from it, moving gently in the summer wind. They had been hung up by their wrists, and there was no mark of ordinary violence upon them. No hangman's knot, no knife, no axe had killed the three.

Gregoor hissed, 'Mother Peace preserve us. I have never seen anything like that.'

Jessa could only nod. The corpses, one man and two women, had been drained of life, magic of the blackest sort. The flesh was a leathered brown, like dried apples. Their eyes had shriveled in their heads. They were brown skeletons. The women's hair floated around their faces that were cracked with horror, mouths agape in one last silent scream.

Jessa shook her head: that was nonsense. The dead did not retain the last look of horror. The jaws had simply broken and gaped open, nothing more.

'Come, Gregoor, let us get inside.'

He was still gazing at the dead. 'This is Cytherea's work?'

'Yes.'

'And you have set us the task of killing her?'

'It would seem so.'

Gregoor pushed his horse against hers and grabbed her arm. 'Jessa, I am not a coward, but this . . . Cytherea drained their lives like you or I would squeeze an orange dry.'

Jessa stared at him until he loosened her arm. 'We have killed sorceresses before.'

'None that could do this.'

Jessa nodded. 'She took their lives when she took their magic, Gregoor.'

He caught his breath. 'I am only an herb-witch. I can't tell. Did she steal their souls?'

Jessa shivered. Though she shielded her magic, protected herself, she could still feel the answer. She understood now why she had thought the corpses were screaming silently. 'No. Their souls are still there, trapped in their bodies.'

'Verm take that pale bitch.'

Jessa nodded. 'That is the plan, Gregoor, that is the plan.'

They were challenged at the town gates. A woman called down, 'What do you want here, soldiers?'

Jessa answered. 'A room for the night, food if you have it to spare, and stabling for the horses.'

'Don't you know that you ride into a town that is cursed?'

Jessa kept the surprise from her face. 'Cursed? What do you mean?'

The woman gave a rude snort of bitter laughter. 'Did you not see the gibbet and its burden?'

'I saw three corpses.'

'They are the mark of our curse. You would do better to ride on, soldiers.'

Jessa licked her lips and eased back to speak with Gregoor. 'I don't feel a curse, except on the corpses, but I am shielding myself.'

He looked surprised. 'You've been wasting energy shielding yourself, for how long?'

'Since we entered the edge of Cytherea's blight.'

'Blight. What are you talking about?'

It was her turn to be surprised. 'Look around you. Look at the plants.'

The summer trees hung with limp black leaves. The grass was winter dead at the side of the road, crumbling and brown. It was utterly silent.

'Where are the little birds, the brownkins? There are always brownkins.'

'Not here, not anymore.' Jessa wanted to ask him how he had not noticed, but she knew the answer. He was an herb-witch, a maker of potions; his magic was a thing of incantations and ritual. Her magic was tied to the earth and what sprang from it. This desolation wounded her in a very private way. This was blasphemy. And Gregoor had seen nothing in the summer twilight.

'If you will distract the guard, I will spy out the curse, and see if it is safe to enter.'

He nodded. 'They might not be happy to see more spell casters after Cytherea.'

'Yes, I would rather not be advertised as an earth-witch.'

He rode over to the gate. 'What has happened to your land?'

Jessa turned inward and did not hear the rest. She listened to the rhythm of her own body, blood flowing, heart pumping, breathing, pulsing. She came to the silence deep in her own body where everything was still. Jessa released her shield and swayed in her saddle. It took all she had not to cry out. The land wailed around her. Death. The land was wounded, dying. It was not just the witches on their scaffold that Cytherea had drained, but the earth itself. She had taken some of the life-force of the summer land. It would not recover. The town was doomed. It could not survive where no crops would grow. There were no brownkins because the birds had fled this place; everything that could had fled this place. Everything but the people. And they would leave soon enough. When autumn came and there were no crops, they would leave.

The destruction was so complete that it masked everything else. Jessa was forced to turn the horse so she could look at the town, concentrate on it, and see if it was indeed cursed. Her eyes passed the corpses and three sparks of life fluttered in the corpses, bright and clean. The souls wavered and struggled. Jessa turned away and stared at the walled town.

She stretched her magic outward, no longer flinching from the earth-death around her. The town was just a town. There was no curse. A curse would be redundant after what Cytherea had done to the land.

Jessa rode up beside Gregoor. She whispered, 'There is no curse on the town. We can enter safely.'

The guardswoman called down, 'What was your lady friend doing so long?'

Jessa answered, 'I was praying.'

The woman was silent a moment. 'Prayers are a good thing. Enter, strangers, and be welcome to what is left of Titos.'

There was one small tavern in the town, and they were the only strangers. The windows were shuttered, though the summer night was mild. An elderly woman muttered in her sleep, dreaming before an unnecessary fire. Jessa wondered if they thought fire and light would keep out the evil, like a child crying in the night. The place stank of stale beer and the sweat of fear. The tavernkeeper himself came to take their orders. He was a large beefy man, but his eyes were red-rimmed as if from tears.

The tavern sign had said simply, 'Esteban's Tavern.' Jessa took a chance. 'You are Esteban?'

He looked at her, eyes not quite focused, as if he were only half-listening. 'Yes, I am he. Do you wish to eat?'

'Yes. But more than food we would like information.'

She had his attention now. His dark eyes stared at her, full of anger, and a fine and burning hatred, like the sun burning through glass. 'What kind of information?'

Gregoor brushed her hand, a warning not to press this man. But Jessa felt a magic in the room, untapped but there. It was not coming from the tavernkeeper. 'A gibbet stands outside your town gates. How did it come to be there?'

Large hands knotted the rag he had stuck in his belt. His voice was a dark whisper. 'Get out.'

'Excuse me, tavernkeep, I meant no offense, but such a sight is uncommon.'

'Get . . . out.' He looked up at her as he spoke and there was death in his eyes, death born of grief.

Jessa knew about such grief and how it ate you from the inside out until there was nothing left until you died or satisfied your vengeance. She spoke, low and clear, 'Where is your wife, tavern-keep?'

He threw back his head and screamed, then flung their table to the side and advanced on Jessa. She kept out of his reach, a knife in her hand, but she did not want to harm him. The magic she had felt flared and crept along her skin: sorcery.

The old woman by the fire was standing now, leaning on her walking stick. One hand was clawlike in the air before her. 'Enough of this.' Power rode her voice, a lash of obedience. The big man stood unsure, arms drooping at his sides, tears sliding down his cheeks.

Jessa sheathed her knife, unable to do anything else. Very few people could have forced an obedience spell upon Jessa.

The old woman turned angry eyes on her. 'Did you have to hurt him?'

'You would not show yourself.'

'Well, I am here now, girl. What do you want? And I warn you, if it is not something worthy of the pain you have caused, you will be punished for your rudeness.'

Jessa bowed, never taking her eyes from the woman. She felt Gregoor close at her side and caught the glint of steel in his hand. So the obedience spell had affected only Jessa and the man. That was something to remember. 'I seek the death of Cytherea the Mad.'

The woman stared at Jessa for the space of heartbeats. Jessa knew she was being weighed and measured, tested. The old woman laughed then, an unexpectedly young sound, but the body remained old. 'An assassin. Two assassins.'

Jessa and Gregoor shifted uncomfortably, for there was nothing that should have given them away. 'We are not . . .'

The old woman said, 'Do not lie, whoever you are. I have the gift of trueseeing.'

Jessa swallowed. It was a rare talent, and one that was proof against all lies, magical or mundane. 'We did not enter this town under false pretenses. If you are a truthseer, then you know I mean what I say. I am here to kill Cytherea.'

The woman's face was solemn as she studied them. 'You believe what you say, that much is true. But saying you will kill her and doing so are not the same thing.'

'That is true. We seek information to aid us in our task.'

Esteban said, 'Can you kill her?'

Jessa looked at him. His eyes were grief-filled wounds. 'Yes. I am Wizardsbane, and this will not be the first, or even the tenth, wizard I have slain.'

The old woman said, 'And you, who follow her like a shadow, who are you?'

Gregoor sheathed his blade. 'I am Gregoor Steelsinger, also known as Deathbringer.'

'Such auspicious names, young ones. But can you live up to them?'

Jessa said, 'We are willing to risk our lives to prove worthy of our names. Are you willing to help us destroy the madwoman who has raped your village?'

'I will tell you what I can, Jessamine Wizardsbane, but it is precious little. I am Teodora Truthseer.'

Esteban brought food out to them, then sat to listen. Jessa would have protested, but Teodora said, 'His wife and daughter hang on the gibbet outside our town. Surely he deserves a seat at this table.'

Jessa nodded.

'The first we knew of trouble was a snowstorm from a clear summer sky. It was a storm driven by an ice elemental, cold as the netherhells. Cytherea came out of that storm, an ice demon at her side. She told us her terms for saving our town.' Teodora paused and took a drink. 'I fought Cytherea when she arrived at our gates. I challenged her to win safety for my town.' Teodora smiled and looked at her age-gnarled hands. 'I lost. But I did not lose through sorcery. There I could have matched her. She wore a ring on her left hand, an enchanted ring. I walked out the town gates a woman of thirty and was carried back in a woman of sixty.'

Jessa and Gregoor exchanged glances. 'What sort of ring could age a woman like that?' Gregoor asked.

'Cytherea did not age me, so much as curse me with old age. She wears a ring of curses.'

Gregoor gave a low whistle. 'That is an expensive item.'

Jessa said, 'Is that how she bound . . .'

Teodora interrupted her. 'Esteban, could you please refill my glass?'

The man looked suspicious, but got up to do as the sorceress asked.

Teodora spoke low to them. 'You were asking if the ring is how Cytherea bound the souls to the bodies.'

'Yes.'

'Esteban does not know his wife and daughter are still in torment. I think it would be unwise to mention it in front of him.'

Gregoor asked, 'Is it what she used?'

'Yes.'

Esteban set the mug down and Teodora said, 'Thank you, Esteban.'

Jessa asked, 'How did she take the earth-witches' magic and the land's magic as well?'

Teodora stared at her full mug, brown-spotted hands tight gripped. 'She wears a necklace, a square-cut emerald set in gold. It is a unique enchantment. It is attuned to earth-magic and steals only that.'

'So this necklace contains all the earth-magic she has stolen?'

Teodora nodded.

'You are a truthseer. Is there a way to release the magics or to destroy the enchantments?'

'The ring of curses is not unlimited in power. It has so many curses in it just like a human curse-maker. If the ring is used up, empty before being re-enchanted, then all the curses the ring caused this time will be undone.'

'You would be young again?'

'Yes.' Teodora studied the food on her plate and talked without looking at anyone. 'The necklace is different. It has perhaps an unlimited ability to absorb power. The only way to release the magic is to destroy it.'

Gregoor asked, 'And how do we do that?'

'You might give it back to the earth from which it came.'

'The exact earth,' Jessa asked, 'or metaphysically speaking, so any earth would do?'

'Any earth will do.'

Jessa smiled.

Gregoor said, 'You've thought of a plan, haven't you?'

'I've thought of a possibility.'

Teodora asked, 'How can we help?'

'Gregoor will need some herbs to make a potion. And I was wondering if your town can boast a curse-maker.'

Esteban and Teodora exchanged glances. 'Why, yes, but he is old and not powerful enough to curse Cytherea.'

'I don't want him to curse Cytherea, I want him to curse me.'

Two days later they rode out of Titos, a new potion at their belts and a curse for each of them.

Gregoor grunted and twisted in his saddle, trying to scratch the middle of his back.

'It will only be worse if you claw at it.'

He looked at Jessa through red, inflamed eyes, nearly swollen shut. 'You said pick a curse, so I did. How was I to know the Verm-cursed rash would get this bad?'

Jessa sighed. 'I suggested a curse that would have been serious enough, but would not have hampered your fighting skills.'

He clawed at his hand. 'You wanted me rendered impotent. No, thank you.'

She almost laughed. 'I am childless until my curse is removed.'

'But that's different. You were taking a potion to prevent children anyway. I have a use for my manhood.'

Jessa smiled, but she felt a heaviness in her stomach, an empty heaviness. She felt the loss. 'If this rash grows any worse, you will be all but useless by the time we face Cytherea.'

He rode up beside her. 'I am sorry, Jessa. I did not understand. If I had known, I might even have let him unman me.' He shivered in the sunlight, skin twitching. 'I would not have you be killed because I was distracted by this infernal itching.' He clawed at his arms, raising welts.

'You're going to bleed if you keep scratching. Don't you have an ointment to help yourself?'

'Yes, but I was hoping to save it until we were nearer our destination.'

'I think we are close enough. Use the ointment before you flay yourself alive.'

Gregoor rummaged in his saddlebags and came up with a sealed pot. 'This will take some time.'

'We have time. I have a spell to do myself.'

He nodded and dismounted. The grass was shoulder high to him and brushed the horse's bellies. Wild bellis flowers filled the air with their delicate scent. A swift, quarreling flock of brownkins flew overhead. Jessa breathed in the summer bounty. Her magic pulsed and swelled with the ripening grass, the swift flight of birds, the tiny hidden creatures. Everything was magic for the taking, for an earth-witch.

Gregoor came to stand at her stirrup. His face was coated with an oily lotion. 'You sparkle like pale flame.'

She grinned at him, stretching arms skyward. 'I feel like I should burst into flame, swollen with power.'

He frowned.

Jessa laughed. 'There's no danger of that, Gregoor. Don't frown so; it will make you itch.' She touched his shoulder.

He jumped as if burned. 'Your power poured over my arm. It was . . . unexpected.'

'Surely making your herb potions fills you with magic?'

He shook his head. 'Nothing like that. I'm an herb-witch, Jessa. Our magic is a quieter thing. You could pass for a sorceress, now.'

'It's always like that in spring and summer, but winter,' she shivered, 'winter is a poor time for earth-witches.'

'Then what will you do behind Cytherea's spell line?'

'I have absorbed enough power to do a few spells, if I am careful.'

'Then what?'

'Then I won't be able to pretend I am a sorceress anymore. Cytherea will know me for an earth-witch, and our plan had better work.'

Gregoor looked up at her, the swelling and redness already leaving his eyes.

'You look much better. How do you feel?'

'The best I've felt in three days of travel. I'll be able to watch your back.'

'I never thought you wouldn't.'

Gregoor remounted and they pushed through a stand of pine trees. Bushtails chattered and scolded overhead, showering them with pine needles. Jessa felt the first cool tendril of power, someone else's power. She slammed down her shields, cutting herself off from the land, but protecting herself from what lay ahead.

The horses pawed nervously at the top of the ridge. Up through the trees, mist was oozing. Sunlight cut through the mist, sparkling on a line of ice-covered trees. The summer leaves were crumbled, blackened, ice coated. Frost and snow lay in glittering drifts at the foot of the ridge.

Jessa glanced up at the waving greenery overhead. Yellow snake lilies nodded on the forest floor. 'Definitely the work of elementals and demons.'

'Do you think we can bargain with the demon?'

'Our plan depends on it.'

'What if it doesn't agree?'

She smiled at him. 'Then, Gregoor, we will see if the god Magnus truly does cry tears of blood.'

'I did not plan on meeting Him so soon.'

'Nor I. Let's get out the winter gear.'

Sweat trickled down Jessa's spine. The fur hood was oppressive. Gregoor waited beside her, sweat-carved runnels melting the ointment on his face.

Cool mist swirled around the horses' legs, but the summer sun beat down on them. Winter was a slash of brilliant diamond ice. Snow lay inches deep. The green belt of summer had been sliced cleanly and completely.

Jessa urged her horse forward. The hooves crunched in the snow's edge. The chill breath of winter cooled the sweat on her face instantly. Her breath fogged and began to crystallize on the fur trim of her hood. Something large moved in the trees. Jessa signaled Gregoor to wait.

She could see nothing and yet she knew something had moved. The winter-ruined trees were utterly still. Snow stretched smooth and untouched. But . . . there was a spot near a large straight elm tree that Jessa could not look at. No matter how hard she tried to stare at it, her vision kept slipping by it. *Don't look at me*, it seemed to say, *I am not here*, but of course that meant something was there. The question was, what?

She signaled Gregoor to come up beside her, slowly.

They had ridden only a few strides when the air wavered and a demon was leaning against the elm. Both sets of arms were crossed over his chest. He was about ten feet tall, only a little less white than the snow. His scales shimmered like mother-of-pearl. Two slender horns grew from his head. His tail twitched in the snow. Jessa was reminded of a cat about to pounce.

The demon's bat-ribbed ears curled and uncurled. 'I am the

guardian of this spell line. If you cross even one step farther, you will be trapped until the spell is complete.'

'When will that be?' Jessa asked.

He blinked large purple eyes. 'When Cytherea the Mad wills it, and not before.' A forked tongue licked his lips, exposing teeth like ice daggers. 'So turn back while you may. You have been warned.'

'Thank you for the warning. If we ride farther, what will happen to us?'

He shrugged one pair of shoulders. 'Cytherea will decide.'

'What will you do if we ride farther in?'

'I,' he said, placing a claw on his chest, 'nothing, yet. You will have to huddle in the town while Cytherea does her business.'

'How long will that take?'

The demon looked up at the ice trees. He smiled, flashing fangs. 'Not long, I think.'

Jessa said, 'Then we will cross and wait if we must.'

'Come across, then.' The demon made a sweeping bow, motioning with his many arms.

They rode forward, skirting out of the demon's reach, though distance alone would not save them if the demon chose to be nasty.

The demon called, 'Herb-witch.'

Jessa looked back at Gregoor. He was staring at the ground, very determinedly.

'Look at me, herb-witch, look at me,' the demon hissed.

'Stop it,' Jessa said. 'He does not have the magic to resist you.'

'And you do?' He turned his gaze upon her, perfect violet, like the eyes of the blind. Jessa would not meet his gaze. The demon laughed.

'You said you would not harm us if we passed.'

'I lied.'

She looked at him without meeting his eyes. 'Will you stand in our way?'

'Not now. But when Cytherea is done with her little . . . chore, then she will let me choose my reward.' The demon was suddenly standing before them. Jessa's horse screamed and reared, hooves lashing the air.

The demon grinned as Jessa fought to control the animal. 'Perhaps I will ask for you, sorceress.'

Jessa glared at him. 'Will you beg for a treat like a well-trained dog?'

The demon's ears curled into tight rolls, his claws flexing the air. 'I am no dog, woman. I am ice demon and I will show you what that means.'

'You will harm me before Cytherea sees me? Is that wise?'

The demon roared, clawing at the trees, raking ice and wood into splinters. The horses went wild. When Jessa and Gregoor slowed the trembling animals, Jessa found a splinter of ice in her cheek. She pulled it out and found it bloody. She would have thrown it on the ground, but the demon was watching her, eyes intent, a strange eagerness in his scaled face. She held the bloody crystal, unsure what to do with it.

Gregoor whispered, 'Jessa, try not to make it more angry than you have to.'

'Cytherea is your enemy, not us. She has bound you into her service. What if we could free you?'

The demon stared at her. 'How?'

'If she is dead, then you are free.'

He snorted. 'You cannot kill her with sorcery.'

'We will not kill her with sorcery.'

'Why tell me, when now I can warn her?'

'You want your freedom. We want her death.'

'What do you want of me, sorceress?'

'An oath that you will not help Cytherea against us.'

The demon flashed fangs. 'Of course, I promise, I will not hurt either of you.'

'No, demon, an oath to Verm and Loth.'

His ears furled in surprise. 'A vow to the dark ones will sever Cytherea's control over me. Will allow me to stand and watch.' He grinned. 'One of the few things that will. You are not just a sorceress, are you?'

'No,' she said.

'And what do you vow, mortal?'

'We vow to free you.'

'I simply watch while you kill Cytherea. Then I am free.'

Jessa nodded.

'The exchange is fair, and because of that I cannot take it.'

Gregoor started to protest, but Jessa silenced him. 'I understand, demon; you must come out the better in the bargain.'

He nodded. 'You have dealt with demons before.'

'Perhaps.' She caught Gregoor's shocked look and ignored it.

'What do you offer to sweeten the bargain?' the demon asked.

She held up the bloody splinter. 'Blood.'

The demon licked his lips. 'And from the man?'

Gregoor said, 'No.'

Jessa frowned at him. 'Will you bargain with just my blood?'

'If I cannot harm either of you, then I must have blood from both of you, or we fight here and now.'

'Gregoor, just a few drops . . .'

'Look at its face.'

The demon's face was lined with hunger; he seemed almost to have grown thinner. He shimmered with a horrible eagerness. 'I see him,' Jessa said softly.

'Then how can you offer him our blood? I am an herb-witch, and I could kill with a single drop of it. What could a demon do with blood?'

'I will taste your soul,' the demon whispered.

Gregoor said, 'I will not give that thing my blood.'

'Then we will fight it here and now. It is your choice, Gregoor. I understand your uneasiness and I will abide by your decision.'

He shifted in his saddle, hand stroking his sword hilt.

'Fight me, wizard. I will have your blood one way or another.'

'No,' Gregoor suddenly said. 'I will give what is asked.'

Jessa held out the bloody shard. The demon reached for it, and she covered it with her hand. 'Swear, demon. Swear by Verm and Loth.'

'Let the wizard draw blood first.'

Gregoor took off his gloves and drew his dagger. He nicked one finger, letting three drops of blood fall into the snow. 'There is your blood.' He wiped his dagger clean and applied pressure to the small wound.

Jessa said, 'Make oath, demon.'

'I swear by the birds of Loth and the hounds of Verm that I will not harm you by direct actions.'

The demon grimaced, claws clicking like ice breaking, but he repeated it word perfect. Jessa handed over the ice shard with its cold blood. The demon took it delicately in his claws and licked it, daintily as a cat with cream. He licked it clean, but the ice did not melt. He chewed up the ice, crunching it with his teeth.

Then the demon knelt in the snow, all glittering in a shaft of light. He rolled his eyes at Gregoor and scooped up the bloody snow. Sucking sounds filled the forest, obscene and joyous. The snow did not melt at his touch, and he swallowed. He grinned and stood, stretching arms wide. 'I will see you in your dreams.' He vanished.

Gregoor said, 'What does that mean?'

'We will relive this in our nightmares, with certain changes.'

'Jessa, what have we done?'

'We have bargained with a demon. Did you think to come out of it untouched?'

He stared down at his gloved hands. 'I don't know what I thought.' He drew a deep shuddering breath and looked at her. 'Let's go kill this bitch and get out of here.'

Jessa smiled, her eyes full of a strange dark light. 'Let us go

STRANGE CANDY          331

hunting. May Magnus guide our strokes and strengthen our spells.'

The village of Bardou lay in a small hollow, trusting to be hidden rather than protected by a stout wall. Perhaps a dozen houses huddled in the snow. There was activity near one end, people moving. A scream carried through the cold air. Two figures were left isolated in the snow as the rest backed away into the houses. A tall figure in red, fur-cloaked, stood alone before the two who had been cast out.

Gregoor said, 'It would be better to wait until she is in the middle of her spell. We could catch her by surprise.'

Jessa shook her head. 'Enough have died in my place already. I cannot let these two die while I watch.' She met Gregoor's eyes. The killing light had faded from her face, replaced by something he could not decipher. 'By saving these people our plan falls apart.'

'I know, but this is your choice, Jessa. I will abide by your decision.'

Jessa smiled. 'Perhaps I have been playing the mercenary too long.' She kicked her horse into a gallop and Gregoor followed. The red-cloaked figure was chanting strange twisted words that slid along Jessa's mind and left a stain. Jessa called, 'Hold, Cytherea, mother of Soldon.'

The woman looked up, startled. Jessa glimpsed a pale face. As she rode closer, the woman stared at her with eyes the cold gray of good steel. There was no expression on Cytherea's face, only a blank waiting. Thin yellow hair blew in strands around a fox-lined hood. The reddish-brown fur made the face paler.

'You seek the earth-witch who killed your only son. Is that not true?'

There was no change in the pale eyes, but she nodded.

Gregoor had a potion open in his hand, waiting.

'Let these poor fools go; I am here.'

Cytherea shook her head, slowly. Her voice was as flat and unemotional as her face. 'You are a sorceress. Do not stand in my way, or I will destroy you.'

Jessa rode her horse between the two huddled earth-witches and Cytherea. The first flicker of emotion passed those gray eyes: anger. Gregoor dismounted, staying off to one side.

'Do you remember the village of Threllkill?'

Cytherea frowned. 'They killed my husband, and my son destroyed them for it.'

'Your husband died of old age. Even sorcerers die, Cytherea.'

'No,' she said.

'Your son destroyed innocent people, but I survived. When I was grown, I hunted him down and I killed him.'

Anger flared and turned the eyes a darker color, the color of storm clouds. 'Get out of my way, little sorceress, or I will kill you as I slew the earth creatures that killed my son.'

Jessa dismounted and pushed back her hood. Gregoor poured the potion upon the ground.

Suddenly, the world was cold; the cold that numbs bones and steals air from lungs. A glittering figure of ice appeared beside Cytherea; vague eyes and mouth appeared, but nothing more. The ice elemental whispered to the sorceress, 'The man spilled a potion on the ground.'

Cytherea blinked as if trying to focus on what was happening. 'Demon, where are you? Jecktor?'

The demon appeared and bowed before her. 'Kill them, Jecktor, get them from my sight.'

The demon said, 'I fear I cannot.'

She turned on him, anger flashing sorcery like embers on the wind. 'What?'

Jessa reached out to the earth where Gregoor's potion lay, pooling and still warm in the snow. She touched it with her earth-magic. There was the scent of green growing earth, strong and clean.

Cytherea turned back from the cowering demon. 'What are you?'

Jessa said, 'I am earth-witch.'

The earth exploded upward, showering down dirt and rock. A

figure stood full-grown from the ground. It was ten feet tall, roughly man-shaped, formed of rich black earth and the redness of clay. One eye was a diamond, the other an emerald. It took a heavy step forward, and the ground moved.

The ice elemental grew like an ice fire and rushed over the earth elemental, shrieking like a banshee wind.

Cytherea screamed, 'Then die, earth-witch!' She pointed her left hand and its ring at Jessa. A shriveling, killing magic flashed outward. Jessa staggered from its touch, but it washed past her as if she were a rock in a stream.

Cytherea stared at her. 'No!' Again she raised the ring. The ground began to smoke and pop to either side of Jessa.

Cytherea turned to Gregoor. 'Die!' He stood unmoved and unharmed. 'What is happening here?'

'We are both already cursed. You cannot curse someone twice,' Jessa said.

The sorceress shrieked and tore her cloak away. She stood, hair streaming in the wind, the emerald necklace sparkling in the cold light. She put a hand over the emerald and began to chant.

Encased in ice, the ice elemental moved forward, its movements stiff. Ice froze the earth, until the earth-giant moved in agony. The ice wind shrieked in triumph.

Jessa felt the power growing. She felt the pull of the enchantment. It called to her magic; it beckoned, a poisoned seduction. Her magic answered it, flaring and shredding on the winter wind. It drew off the magic she had absorbed. Jessa drew her sword and started forward, but she could not move against the necklace. It was sucking her dry.

A throwing knife blossomed in Cytherea's side. She shrieked and staggered.

Jessa saw Gregoor coming forward, another knife in his hand. She fell slowly to her knees in the snow.

Gregoor screamed, 'Jessa!'

Cytherea had regained her control. She gestured and sorcery flared in her hands. Blue flame enveloped Gregoor.

There was a crackling thunder and the earth elemental burst free of the ice. Then it was suddenly running, shaking the ground as it came. Cytherea was forced to turn her attention to the earth-giant.

Gregoor fell face down into the snow, unmoving.

Blue light and ice crawled over the earth elemental. Jessa felt it scream through the frozen ground. She began to crawl toward Cytherea, naked sword dragging over the snow.

Cytherea was bathed in blue flame; she crackled and seemed to glow. Jessa was almost close enough to touch her skirts. Stray bits of power crawled along Jessa's skin, burning with cold fire. She staggered to her feet, sword held two-handed for an upward thrust.

The ice elemental hissed, 'Behind you, mistress.'

It was too late. The steel bit into Cytherea's back; the blue fire shredded and vanished. Jessa shoved the blade upward, seeking her heart. Cytherea shrieked, but she would not die. She put a hand on the emerald necklace and Jessa felt the power begin to grow.

Jessa screamed, 'Die, damn you, die!'

The earth elemental leaned over them, one massive hand reaching. Cytherea yelled, 'No, the necklace is mine! You can't have it!' The earth elemental stood, the broken chain dangling from his massive fingers. Earth-magic poured out of the broken enchantment, free at last. Magic that swelled and flowed and carried Jessa with it until she thought she would explode with the power. It rushed over and through her, a magically visible green fire.

Jessa drew her sword free. Bloody, but still alive, Cytherea turned and began another spell. Jessa's blade crawled with emerald fire. The silver-green blade sliced outward. The sorceress's head spun off into the snow. The body toppled into the crimson-washed snow.

Jessa dropped to the ground, unsure of how to cope with so much power. Gregoor was huddled against the earth, staring wide-eyed. Green grass showed in the snow. Summer warmth beat down. Earth-magic pulsed and spread from the earth elemental as it grasped the emerald necklace in one massive hand.

The ice elemental had fled. The demon bowed to Jessa. 'Earth-witch, I am most impressed.' As he faded from sight, he said, 'Perhaps we will meet again, some winter's night.'

Gregoor crawled to her. 'I can't stand up. The earth pulses like a great heartbeat.'

Jessa could not speak past the magic. She could feel it racing over the ravaged land, healing, awakening, reviving.

Finally, she said, 'Begone, earthling, back to the depths from which you came. Thank you for aid.' The elemental melted into the earth, taking the necklace with it. Cytherea's body lay in a circle of black fresh-turned earth.

Jessa crawled to the dead sorceress and looked down on her. The face was blank as any dead man's. 'Peace at last, mother, peace at last.'

Gregoor was scratching his face. 'You did it.'

'We did it, Gregoor.'

He grinned, then grimaced as he tore his coat to get to new itches. Jessa smiled. 'Perhaps the village of Bardou boasts a curse-maker.'

He looked at her, a hopeful light in his eyes. 'Oh, that would be a blessing indeed.'

'Come, they should be grateful enough to remove a couple of curses.' Jessa paused, staring at a pale hand; the ring of curses was still on the left hand. It was a slim band of iron, empty now, but wait-ing. Jessa slipped the ring from Cytherea's finger.

'It's expensive to get something like that re-enchanted,' Gregoor said.

She slipped the ring into her pouch. 'But well worth it, don't you think?'

'I can think of a few uses for it.'

Jessa reached out and touched him and green fire flowed from her across his skin. He gasped, then forced a grin.

'Extraordinary,' he whispered.

They helped each other to stand and began to limp toward the village.

There was a strong scent of roses on the air, almost choking in its sweetness. Jessa turned.

There in the earth was a fresh rosebush, blossoms flared to the new sun. The roses were yellow, the color of Cytherea's hair.

Jessa called softly, 'Mother.' A breeze began to blow gently against them. The earth-fire began to melt into the ground. Jessa found herself crying. She walked alone to the roses, on unsteady legs. The flowers moved, stretching toward her hands, without aid of wind. One small blossom rubbed against her hand.

Gregoor asked, 'What is it?'

'I think I am being forgiven.'

'Forgiven for what?'

Jessa did not answer; for some things there were no words. And some things were not meant to be shared.

# STEALING SOULS

*This is the first story I ever sold. It's the one I sent to Marion Zimmer Bradley after she rejected 'A Token for Celandine.' This story is also the one I edited after going through my one and only writing workshop. The writers who taught it were Emma Bull, Will Shetterly, and Stephan Gould. All working, selling writers, which is what you should look for in a workshop. They didn't teach me how to be a better writer, but they did teach me how to be a better editor of my own work. I also met the beginnings of my writing group, The Alternate Historians, there. Only two of the original members are still left, me and Deborah Millitello. But we've existed as a group for over ten years now. The seven of us have over forty books, and untold short stories, published. All but one of us had never sold a thing before joining the group. Not a bad track record. This story is the first appearance of Sidra and Leech, who would later appear in 'The Curse-Maker.'*

STEALING SOULS WAS hard; stealing them back was harder. Sebastiane had spent fifteen years learning just how hard.

The Red Goat Tavern was full of people. They swirled, laughing, round Sebastiane's table but did not touch her. For she was the mercenary Sidra Ironfist. And she had passed through many lands as Sidra until she had more stories told about her under that name than her own. She towered over most of the people in the room. The two swords at her waist, one long and one short, looked well cared for and much used. Scars decorated her arms and hands like spider tracings. Her cool gray eyes had a way of staring through a person, as if nothing was hidden.

She had been Sidra so long that sometimes she wondered where Sebastiane had gone. But fighting was not her true occupation. It was more an avocation that allowed her entrance to places her occupation would have closed to her. Most people did not welcome a thief. Especially a thief who had no intention of sharing her prize with the local thieves' guild. Sidra had traveled half a continent and bartered a piece of her soul to be here. She would share with no one.

But then the local thieves' guild did not traffic in souls. And that was the goal this time. There would be jewels and magic items to bring out, but like every good thief, she did not allow baubles to distract her from the main goal.

The herb-witch had said that the bones she sought would be in two earthenware pots. They would be bound with black and green braided cord and suspended from a thin branch made up of some white wood. They would be hung high up in the room where the wizard performed his magic.

The souls in question belonged to Sebastiane's older sisters. They had vanished when she was ten. No one knew what had happened to them, but there were rumors. Rumors of a wizard that had needed twin girls for a forbidden spell done only twice before in all history. A spell to bring great power to a mere herb-witch. Enough power to allow the wizard to taste other magics.

The spell was forbidden because not only did the girls have to die but their souls were imprisoned. Imprisoning souls was a very serious offense if you never intended to let them go.

Sebastiane, the child, had been an apprentice thief and had little hope of confronting such a powerful wizard. But Sidra Ironfist, mercenary and master thief, had a chance.

The little girl of long ago had vowed to Magnus of the Red Hand, god of assassins and god of vengeance. The vow had held firm for fifteen years until she sat only an hour's ride from the wizard who had murdered her sisters.

The hatred of him was gone, killed in the years of surviving. Her sisters' faces were distant things that she couldn't always see clearly. But the vow remained. Sebastiane had come for the bones of her sisters.

The wizard's death would be an added sweetness, but she was no true warrior to go seeking blood vengeance. She was a thief at heart, which is a more patient and practical creature. Her goal was to rescue her sisters' souls from the spell. The wizard's death was secondary.

She had left Sidra's friends behind, all save one, Milon Songsmith. The minstrel leaned back in his chair, a grin on his face. He drained his fourth tankard of ale and grinned wider. He was her bard and had been so for eight years. He had made Sidra Ironfist a legend, and his own talents were in great demand.

He would follow her until she died, and then perhaps he would find another hero to follow.

Sidra had not denied him the right to come on this adventure. If she died here, then Milon would sing of it. There were worse things to leave behind than songs.

But somehow she was not the perfect vengeance seeker she had wanted to be. Her life seemed more precious now than it had fifteen years ago. She wanted to live to see her mercenary band again. Black Abe was all right for a temporary command, but he let his emotions carry him away at awkward times. Sidra had welded them into a fighting force that any king in the civilized lands would welcome. Gannon the Sorcerer, Brant the Ax, Emil Swordmaster, Jayme the Quick, and Thetis the Archer. She would have Black Abe's heart if he let one of them die without just cause.

Sidra waved the barmaid away when Milon called her over for the fifth time. 'You've had enough, Songsmith.'

He flashed a crooked smile. 'You can never have enough ale or enough adventure.' His rich tenor voice was precise, no slurring. His voice never betrayed him no matter how much he drank.

'Any more ale and there won't be any adventuring tomorrow, at least not for you. I am not going to wait all morning while you sleep it off.'

He looked pained. 'I would not do that to you.'

'You've done it before,' Sidra pointed out.

He laughed. 'Well, maybe once. To bed then, my dear Sidra, before I embarrass you any further.'

Morning found them the first ones up. They were served cold meat and cheese by a hollow-eyed barmaid. She clasped a shawl around her nightdress, obviously intending to go back to sleep after they had gone. But she brought out some fresh, though cold, bread and dried fruit. And she did not grumble while she did it.

They walked out into a world locked in the fragile darkness just before dawn. The air seemed to shimmer as the dark purple sky faded to blue and the stars were snuffed out like candles in a wind.

Milon drew his cloak about him and said, 'It is a chilly morning.'

She did not answer but went for the horses. The stable boy stood patiently holding the reins. Sidra had paid extra for such treatment, but it was worth it to be off before curious eyes could see.

Sidra led the way and Milon clucked to his horse. He and the horse were accustomed to following Sidra without knowing where they were going, or why. The forest trail they followed turned stubbornly away from their destination. Not even a deer path led to where they wanted to go. Then, abruptly, the trees ended. It was a clearing at least fifty feet across. The ground was gray as if covered in ash. Nothing grew in it. Grass and wildflowers chased round the edges but did not enter. In the middle of the ash circle was a tower. It rose arrow straight toward the brightening sky. The first rays of sun glimmered along it as if it were made of black mirrors.

The tower was all of one shining ebony piece. There were no marks of stone or mortar; it seemed to have been drawn from the earth whole and complete. Nothing broke its black perfection. There was no door or window.

But Sebastiane the thief knew that there was always a way in. It was only a matter of finding it. She led the way onto the ash ground and Milon followed. The horses were left loosely tied to the trees some distance away. If neither one of them came back, the horses could eventually break loose and find new homes.

The ground crunched underfoot as if it were formed of ground rock. And yet it couldn't be stone; stone did not crumble to ash. Milon whispered to her, 'Demon work.' She nodded, for she felt it, too. Evil clung to the black tower like a smothering shroud.

Sidra stood beside the tower. She laid her shield on the ground and knelt beside it. She ran hands down the scars of her arms. The scars were far too minor to be battle wounds.

She unlocked the sword guard that held the short sword in place. Rising of its own accord, it sprang to her hand. And the sword laughed, a tinny sound without lungs to hold it.

Milon shifted and moved far away from the naked blade.

Sidra noticed it and politely moved so he would not see the entire ritual. This was one thing that her bard did not like to sing about.

The sword crooned, 'Free, bare steel, feel the wind, ahhh.'

Sidra said, 'Our greatest task is before us, blood blade.'

The sword hissed, 'Name me.'

'You who were Blood-Letter when the world was new. You who were Wound-Maker in the hands of a king. You who were Soul-Piercer and took the life of a hero. You who were Blood-Hunger and ate your way through an army. I name thee blade mine, I name thee Leech.'

It chortled, 'Leech, Leech, I am Leech, I live on blood, I crave its crimson flow, I am Leech. So named, power given.'

Sidra had risked her soul five years ago to name the sword. But it had seemed inordinately pleased from the very first at such a name as Leech.

Milon had complained that it wasn't poetic enough. But she left the poetry to the minstrel. Her job was to survive.

The blade whispered, 'Feed me.'

Sidra held the blade out before her, naked steel at face level. She pressed the flat of the blade between the palms of her hands. She spoke the words of invocation. 'Feed gently, Leech, for we have much work to do.'

There was always that moment of waiting when Sidra wondered if this time the sword would take too much and kill her. But it bobbed gently between her hands. The razor-sharp blade brought blood in a sharp, painful wash down her hands. But the cut was narrow, slicing just below the skin. The blade said, 'Sacrifice made, contract assured.'

Sidra ignored the wound. It would heal in a moment or two to become another scar. She did not bother to clean the blade, as all blood was absorbed cleanly. For it truly did feed.

She resheathed the blade, and it hummed tunelessly to itself, echoing up through the leather sheath. Sidra set to searching the black stone with her fingers. But she found nothing. It was like touching well-made glass without even a bubble to spoil its smoothness.

There was nothing there, but if illusion hid the door, then Leech could find it. She bared the humming sword and said, 'Find me a door, Leech.'

The humming picked up a note to a more cheerful tune. She recognized the tune as the new ballad of Cullen Tunemaster. Leech seemed very fond of Cullen's tunes.

They paced the tower three times before the sword could make the door visible to her. It looked ordinary enough – just a brown wooden door with metal studding. It was man height.

'Can you see the door now, Milon?'

'I see nothing but blackness.'

Sidra reached her hand out toward him, and he moved to take it. Leech fought her left-handed grip and slashed at the man. Sidra jerked the sword sharply. 'Behave, Leech.'

'I hunger. You did not feed me.'

'You did not ask.'

It pouted. 'I'm asking now.' By the rules she could have refused it, for it had done its task. But keeping the sword happy assured that she could wield it and live; doing both was not always easy. An unhappy blood blade was an untrustworthy blood blade. She held the blade against her left forearm and let it slice its own way into the skin. It was a mere nick of crimson. She offered her hand once more to Milon.

A drop of sweat beaded at Milon's hairline, and he took her hand tentatively, as far from the sword as possible. 'I can see the door.' He released her hand and backed away from the sword once more.

Sidra knelt before the door, but before she could touch the lock, she noticed that the door moved. It wasn't much of a movement, just a twitch like a horsehide when a fly settles on it. She asked the sword, 'What is it?'

'It is an ancient enchantment not much used now.'

'What is the quickest and quietest way to win past it? The wizard will notice us setting his door on fire.'

'True, but would you rather chop through that much meat? Even I cannot kill it, only damage it. Oh, it would be a glorious outpouring of Mood. But it would not be quick.' It sounded disappointed.

Sidra hated to use the day's only fireball so early on.

She hoped she would not need it later. She faced the door and pointed the sword's tip toward it. A fireball the size of her fist shot from it. It expanded in a whirling dance of heat. The wildfire exploded against the door. A high keening wail sounded. When the fire died away, the door was a blackened hull encircling the doorway. The ruined door was screaming.

The sword said, 'Such work deserves a hearty meal.'

Sidra did not argue but let the blade slice over her left wrist. The vein was slashed and blood welled dark and eager over the hungry blade. It stayed near, lapping at the wound until it closed.

'Follow close, Milon, but be wary. Not everything in a demon-made tower will be civilized enough to know you for a bard.'

He nodded. 'I have followed you into many adventures. I would not miss this one out of fear.'

She said, 'Then come, my brave bard, but watch your back.'

She stepped over the blackened door rim of the door creature. It whimpered as she and the sword passed through it. They stood in a circular chamber made of the same black rock. But a staircase made of good gray stone curved downward in the center of the room.

'Light the lantern here, Milon, and carry it high.'

The lantern's flickering yellow light soon danced in the small room.

Sidra led the way and tripped the first trap. Three darts clanged against her shield and fell to the steps. She knelt carefully, shield up and alert. The dart's tips were blackened with a thick tarry substance. She did not touch it.

She spoke for Milon's benefit. 'Poisoned. Don't touch anything unless you have to. Watch where you step.'

Sidra found the next trap and tripped it with the sword. A spear shot out and buried itself into the stone of the far wall. It would have taken her through the chest. And still the stone stairs wound deeper into the earth. There was nothing for a long time save the lantern's golden shadows and their footsteps echoing on the stairs. Then the stairs ended at a small landing in front of a door. But there was one last trap. And Sidra was not at all sure she could trip it without being harmed.

She studied it for a time, directing Milon to point the lantern here and there. There were six separate pressure points on the stairs that she had found. They were set in a pattern that would make it difficult if not impossible to walk the last five steps. They could jump, but Sidra didn't trust the landing either. And they were too far away for her to find traps on it yet.

She could not pass the stairs, but the sword could. If it would do it. Moving without human aid was something Leech did not prefer to do. Only twice before had she asked it to and each time the blood price had been high.

'Leech, I want you to set off the traps on the stairs and then come gently back to my hand.'

'Payment,' it whispered.

'Blood, as always.'

'Fresh blood,' it asked.

She offered the blade her naked arm, but it remained unmoving against her skin. 'What do you want, Leech?'

'Fresh blood.'

'I'm offering it to you.'

'Fresher blood, new blood.'

Milon said, 'Oh, no, no.'

Sidra said, 'I agree. You are my weapon. You taste my blood, no one else's.'

'When we kill, I taste blood.'

'I will not sacrifice Milon to feed you.'

She could almost feel it thinking, weighing its options. 'A taste, a fresh taste, just a nick, just a bite.'

Milon said, 'No, absolutely not. That steel monster is not going to taste my blood.'

Sidra sighed and said, 'Then I will attempt to remove the traps.'

He gripped her arm. 'You said you couldn't do it.'

'I said that I didn't see how I could do it without getting killed.'

'It's the same thing.'

'No, it isn't.'

'I can't let you be killed.'

She just looked at him, waiting for him to make up his mind.

He shuddered and held out his arm. She unlaced the sleeve and pushed it back to bare the pale skin. The sword chuckled. 'Just a taste, just a bite, just a nibble.' She held the sword firmly two-handed, for she didn't trust it, and placed it against Milon's arm. The sword bit deep and quick like a serpent's strike. Milon cried out, and opened his eyes to stare in horror as the blade lapped up his blood. The wound quickly closed and the sword sighed, 'New blood, fresh, good, yum.'

Sidra felt that the last was added for Milon's benefit. Milon took it very seriously. He yanked down his sleeve and said, 'Yum or not, that is the last of my blood you ever get, you bloodsucking tooth-pick.'

The sword laughed.

Sidra pulled Milon back up the stairs and then released the blade. It settled onto the first pressure point. A rain of poisoned darts filled the hall like black snow.

Leech floated back to her, obediently. 'I have cleared the way, O master.' Sidra ignored the sarcasm and led Milon to the landing. It was not trapped. But the door was.

The poisoned darts were soon removed. And the well-oiled lock clicked under her pick. The door opened into a short straight hall-way. Doors dotted the walls in geometric lines to right and left.

Torches were set at regular intervals along the walls. In the still air there was the sound of chanting.

Milon started to blow out the lantern, but Sidra stopped him. She spoke close to his ear so the sound wouldn't carry. 'We may need light if we have to leave quickly.'

The sword started to hum in time to the chanting and she hushed it.

Sidra stared at the floor and said, 'Place your feet exactly where I place mine.'

He nodded to show he had understood and then concentrated on following her over a five-foot-wide area of floor. She let out a breath of air as if she had been holding it. He relaxed as well, stepping back just a half step. The floor fell out from under him and he was tumbling backward helplessly. Sidra caught his arm, but his weight pulled them both downward. He was left dangling over a pit, and she on her stomach, holding him by one arm. The torches glimmered off silvered spikes set into the floor of the pit.

She hissed, 'I told you to walk where I walked.'

'Let us argue this later. Pull me up.'

She did, rubbing her shoulder. 'You're lucky you didn't dislocate my arm.'

He shrugged an apology and picked up the fallen lantern.

The chanting seemed to be coming from the last door on the right-hand side. They were only three doors away from it when Sidra stopped the bard with a hand movement and knelt to study the floor. She shook her head, sending light bursts from her helmet to the walls. She said, 'When I say jump, leap forward as fast as you can.'

'Why?'

She stared at him a moment and then looked upward.

He would have missed it, but with her gaze to direct him, he saw the portcullis spikes ready to come crashing down. He swallowed and said, 'When do we jump?'

She stood beside him and said, 'Now.' They stepped forward and flung themselves across the stones. Sidra rolled easily, coming to her feet before the spikes had bitten into the floor. They were trapped.

There was a swimming in the air near the torches in one corner. Sidra pointed Leech at it and concentrated. Illusions bled near fire. A demon stood at the end of the hallway.

He was perhaps eight feet tall, fairly short for an ice demon. His scales were the color of new frost and winked in the light like diamond glints on snow. His teeth were ivory daggers. His four arms were crossed over his chest and his tail rustled over the floor. He grinned and said, 'Welcome.'

His bat-ribbed ears rolled into tubes and then unrolled. 'I would speak with you before we fight.'

Sidra found herself staring into his smooth blue eyes, no pupil, just empty blue like a frozen lake. Peaceful.

Milon gripped her arm and pulled her back. 'Sidra.'

She shook her head roughly and faced the demon in a fighting crouch, shield close, sword ready.

He said, 'Perhaps you are right. Enough talk, let us fight.' He strode forward and said, 'And you, bard, I know the rules; by touching her, you gave up your safe conduct.'

'I do not regret what I did, ice demon. You cannot harm me if you are dead.'

He chuckled, then, low in his chest.

Sidra whispered to the sword, 'I want you to burn for me and aid me in slaying this ice demon.'

It said, 'Price will be high.'

She had expected nothing less. 'When is the last time you tasted demon blood?'

The sword paused and said, 'Demon blood.'

'If we kill it, then all its blood is yours to consume.'

It gave a nervous expectant giggle. 'All that demon blood, all of it. You won't remove me until I have drunk my fill?'

'I won't remove you.'

It snickered. 'Payment is more than generous. I will do as you ask.'

The ice demon strode forward, still laughing to himself. His claws clicked together with a sound like breaking ice. Sidra kept Leech half hidden behind her shield as if she meant to only cower before the demon. Leech burst into flame with its blade like a wick in the center of the good orange fire.

The first threads of cold oozed round her shield and she knew, magic weapon or not, the first blow must be a good one. Milon simply stared up at the creature with his back pressed against the fallen portcullis. The demon stood almost directly in front of Sidra, and she kept her head down as if she could not bear the sight of him. He spoke to the bard. 'Your protector is not doing much protecting, but be patient. When I have finished with her, you will have my undivided attention.'

Sidra forced Leech up while the demon was looking at Milon. The sword took him through the chest, burning brightly as the demon blood gushed over it. The blade bit through a clawed hand and sent fingers spinning. The demon screamed.

A casual swipe of the tail knocked her to the ground, and a claw raked along the shield. The nails left grooves in the metal. A hand caught her helmet and sent her head ringing back against the floor. Leech moved of its own accord, bringing her hand with it. The blade shot through the demon's throat, and blood poured out acrid and stinking. Sidra struggled to her knees, gagging from the stench. She fought upward with the blade and shield. A claw slipped past the edge of the shield, and she felt claws sink into her thigh. Leech bit into the demon's arm, half-severing it. And he began to fade. He was running as a proper demon does when it is hurt badly enough and has the choice of leaving.

Leech screamed after the fading creature, 'No, no!'

It flamed in her hand a while longer and then faded back to normal. 'Cheated.'

Sidra leaned against the wall, favoring her wounded leg. 'It was not my doing that the demon left. I kept my part of the bargain.'

The sword was dangerously silent. Sidra was almost relieved that all its magic was spent for the day. It was never reliable when it was pouting.

The last door was not locked. It opened easily to reveal the wizard in the middle of a spell. A protective code chased the edges of a pentagram, and the wizard stood in the center of it all. He was short, balding, and did not look like a demon master or an evil man. But standing outside his magic circle was no mere demon but a devil.

It was why the wizard had not aided his ice demon. It was death to abort the spell. He was trapped as if in a cage until he released the devil to its home plane. Now their only danger was the devil.

It was still only half formed, with the bottom half of its body consumed in a strange black smoke. Its upper half was vaguely manlike, with shoulders and arms. It resembled the demon they had banished, with its bat-ribbed ears and teeth, but it was covered in black skin, the color of nothing above ground. High above it all, suspended from the ceiling, were the two earthenware jars on the end of a white pole.

A rope held the pole in place and the rope was tied off near the door around a peg. Sidra smiled. She raised the sword and chopped the rope. The wizard seemed to notice what she did. But he could not stop to plead with her. If he stopped, then the devil would be freed and it would kill him. Devils were very reliable that way, or unreliable, depending on the point of view.

The pole came crashing to the ground, but the jars did not break. They were spelled against such mundane accidents. Sidra stepped toward them carefully, one eye on the devil. She sheathed Leech, for fighting devils was not a matter of swords.

She untied the two jars from the pole and passed one out to Milon. The other she balanced under her sword arm. Just before she passed out of the room with his precious power, the wizard broke and shrieked, 'No.'

The devil laughed. 'Take your pots and go, warrior-thief. Your business is finished here.'

The floor quivered. Sidra turned to Milon and said, 'Run.'

They ran only as far as the fallen gate. It blocked their way completely, and the floor shivered once more. 'There must be a hidden lever that will raise this. Search.' They felt along the walls to either side, and Milon found something that he pressed. Slowly the gate rose upward. The walls lurched as if someone had caught the tower and twisted it.

They ran full out. There would be no more fighting, no more trap finding. It was a race to the surface.

Milon said, 'The pit, what about the pit?'

'Jump it.'

'Jump it?'

'Jump it or die.'

He ran harder to keep up with her longer legs and he tried not to picture the spikes on the floor of the pit. It was there suddenly and they were leaping over it. Sidra went down, betrayed by her wounded leg, but was up and running with the blood pumping down her leg. The floor twisted under their feet and cracks began to form on the walls.

The stairs were treacherous. The lantern was a bouncing glow that showed widening cracks and falling rock. They came up into the tower room.

The door had healed itself shut. The tower gave a shudder as its foundations began to crumble. Sidra drew Leech from its sheath and pointed it at the door. She decided to bluff. 'Open, door, or I'll burn you again.' The door whimpered uncertainly and then it swung outward. They raced through the door and kept running across the ash circle and into the trees. With a final groan the tower thundered to its death. The world was full of rock and dust.

They lay gasping on the ground and grinning at each other. Milon said, 'Let me look at your leg.'

She lay back in the grass, allowing him to probe the stab wound. 'Deep but not bad. It will heal. Now will you tell your minstrel what was so important about two earthenware jars?'

Sidra smiled and said, 'I have a story for you, Milon. A story of a little girl and a vow she made to a god.'

# THE GIRL WHO WAS
# INFATUATED WITH DEATH

*Well here we are, at the last story. This is Anita very solidly in her world, as it appears in the books. We have Jean-Claude on stage, and a distraught mother, a missing teenage girl, and a vampire who's about to get himself killed, but doesn't know it yet. This story is set before the novel* Narcissus in Chains. *This is back when Anita is fighting the good fight to try not to give in every time she gets too close to her vampire boyfriend. Ah, how the mighty have fallen.*

IT WAS FIVE days before Christmas, a quarter till midnight. I should have been asnooze in my bed, dreaming of sugarplums, whatever the hell they were, but I wasn't. I was sitting across my desk sipping coffee and offering a box of Kleenexes to my client, Ms Rhonda Mackenzie. She'd been crying for nearly the entire meeting, so that she'd wiped most of her careful eye makeup away, leaving her eyes pale and unfinished, younger, like what she must have looked like when she was in high school. The dark, perfect lipstick made the eyes look emptier, more vulnerable.

'I'm not usually like this, Ms Blake. I am a very strong woman.' Her voice took on a tone that said she believed this, and it might even be true. She raised those naked brown eyes to me, and there was fierceness in them that might have made a weaker person flinch. Even I, tough-as-nails vampire-hunter that I am, had trouble meeting the rage in those eyes.

'It's all right, Ms Mackenzie, you're not the first client that's cried. It's hard when you've lost someone.'

She looked up, startled. 'I haven't lost anyone, not yet.'

I sat my coffee cup back down without drinking from it and stared at her. 'I'm an animator, Ms Mackenzie. I raise the dead if the reason is good enough. I assumed this amount of grief was because you'd come to ask me to raise someone close to you.'

She shook her head, her deep brown curls in disarray around her face as if she'd been running her hands through what was once a perfect perm. 'My daughter, Amy, is very much alive and I want her to stay that way.'

Now I was just plain confused. 'I raise the dead and am a legal vampire executioner, Ms Mackenzie. How do either of those jobs help you keep your daughter alive?'

'I want you to help me find her before she commits suicide.'

I just stared at her, my face professionally blank, but inwardly, I was cursing my boss. He and I had had discussions about exactly what my job description was, and suicidal daughters weren't part of that description.

'Have you gone to the police?' I asked.

'They won't do anything for twenty-four hours, but by then it will be too late.'

'I have a friend who is a private detective. This sounds much more up her alley than mine, Ms Mackenzie.' I was already reaching for the phone. 'I'll call her at home for you.'

'No,' she said, 'only you can help me.'

I sighed and clasped my hands across the clean top of my desk. Most of my work wasn't indoor office work, so the desk didn't really see much use. 'Your daughter is alive, Ms Mackenzie, so you don't need me to raise her. She's not a rogue vampire, so you don't need an executioner. How can I be of any help to you?'

She leaned forward, the Kleenex wadded in her hands, her eyes fierce again. 'If you don't help me by morning, she will be a vampire.'

'What do you mean?' I asked.

'She's determined to become one of them tonight.'

'It takes three bites to become a vampire, Ms Mackenzie, and they all have to be from the same vampire. You can't become one in a single night, and you can't become one if you're just being casual with more than one.'

'She has two bites on her thighs. I accidentally walked in on her when she was getting out of the shower and I saw them.'

'Are you sure they were vampire bites?' I asked.

She nodded. 'I made a scene. I grabbed her, wrestled with her so I could see them clearly. They are vampire bites, just like the pictures they passed around at the last PTA meeting so we could recognize it. You know one of those people lecturing on how to know if your kids are involved with the monsters.'

I nodded. I knew the kind of person she meant. Some of it was valuable information, some of it was just scare tactics, and some of it was racist, if that was the term. Prejudiced at least.

'How old is your daughter?'

'She's seventeen.'

'That's only a year away from being legal, Ms Mackenzie. Once she turns eighteen, if she wants to become a vampire, you can't stop her legally.'

'You say that so calmly. Do you approve?'

I took in a deep breath and let it out, slow. 'I'd be willing to talk to your daughter, try to talk her out of it. But how do you know that tonight is the night? It has to be three bites within a very short space of time or the body fights off the infection, or whatever the hell it is.' Scientists were still arguing about exactly what made someone become a vampire. There were biological differences before and after, but there was also a certain level of mysticism involved, and science has always been bad at deciphering that kind of thing.

'The bites were fresh, Ms Blake. I called the man who gave the lecture at our school, and he said to come to you.'

'Who was he?'

'Jeremy Ruebens.'

I frowned now. 'I didn't know he'd gotten out of prison,' I said.

Her eyes went wide. 'Prison?'

'He didn't mention in his talk that he was jailed for conspiracy to commit murder — over a dozen counts, maybe hundreds. He was head of Humans First when they tried to wipe out all the vampires and some of the shape-shifters in St Louis.'

'He talked about that,' she said. 'He said he would never have condoned such violence and that it was done without his knowledge.'

I smiled and knew from the feel of it that it was unpleasant.

'Jeremy Ruebens once sat in the chair you're in now and told me that Humans First's goal was to destroy every vampire in the United States.'

She just looked at me, and I let it go. She would believe what she wanted to believe; most people did.

'Ms Mackenzie, whether you, or I, or Jeremy Ruebens approve or not, vampires are legal citizens with legal rights in this country. That's just the way it is.'

'Amy is seventeen; if that thing brings her over underage, it's murder, and I will prosecute him for murder. If he kills my Amy, I will see him dead.'

'You know for certain that it is a he?'

'The bites were very, very high up on her thigh —' she looked down at her lap — 'her inner thigh.'

I would have liked to have let the female vamp angle go, but I couldn't because I was finally beginning to see what Ms Mackenzie wanted me to do, and why Jeremy Ruebens had sent her to me. 'You want me to find your daughter before she's got that third bite, right?'

She nodded. 'Mr Ruebens seemed to think if anyone could find her in time, it would be you.'

Since Humans First had also tried to kill me during their great cleansing of the city, Ruebens's faith in me was a little odd. Accurate probably, but odd. 'How long has she been missing?'

'Since nine, a little after. She was taking a shower to get ready to go out with friends tonight. We had an awful fight, and she stormed up to her room. I grounded her until she got over this crazy idea about becoming a vampire.'

'Then you went up to check on her and she was gone?' I made it a question.

'Yes.' She sat back in her chair, smoothing her skirt. It looked like a nervous habit. 'I called the friends she was supposed to be going out with, and they wouldn't talk to me on the phone, so I went to her best friend's house in person, and she talked to me.' She smoothed the skirt down again, hands touching her knees as if the hose needed attention; everything looked in place to me. 'They've got fake ID that says they're both over twenty-one. They've been going to the vampire clubs for weeks.'

Ms Mackenzie looked down at her lap, hands clasped tight. 'My daughter has bone cancer. To save her life they're going to take her left leg from the knee down, next week. But this week she started having pains in her other leg just like the pains that started all this.' She looked up then, and I expected tears, but her eyes were empty, not just of tears, but of everything. It was as if the horror of it all, the enormity of it, had drained her.

'I am sorry, Ms Mackenzie, for both of you.'

She shook her head. 'Don't be sorry for me. She's seventeen, beautiful, intelligent, honor society, and, at the very least, she's going to lose a leg next week. She has to use a cane now. Her friends chipped in and got her this amazing Goth cane, black wood and a silver skull on top. She loves it, but you can't use a cane if you don't have any legs at all.'

There was a time when I thought being a vampire was worse than death, but now, I just wasn't sure. I just didn't have enough room to cast stones. 'She won't lose the leg if she's a vampire.'

'But she'll lose her soul.'

I didn't even try to argue that one. I wasn't sure if vampires had souls, or not, I just didn't know. I'd known good ones and bad ones, just like good and bad people, but one thing was true . . . Vampires had to feed off humans to survive; no matter what you see in the movies, animal blood will not do the job. We are their food, no getting around that. Out loud, I said, 'She's seventeen, Ms Mackenzie. I think she probably believes in her leg more than her soul.'

The woman nodded, too rapidly, head bobbing. 'And that's my fault.'

I sighed. I so did not want to get involved in this, but I believed Ms Mackenzie would do exactly what she said she would do. It wasn't the girl I was worried about so much as the vampire that would be bringing her over. She was underage, and that meant if he turned her, it was an automatic death sentence. Death sentences for humans usually mean life imprisonment, but for a vamp, it means death within days, weeks at the most. Some of the civil rights groups were complaining that the vampire trials were too quick to be fair. And maybe someday the Supreme Court will reverse some of the decisions, but that won't make the vampire 'alive' again. Once a vamp is staked, beheaded, and the heart cut out, all the parts are burned and scattered on running water. There is no coming back from the grave if you are itty bits of ashy fish food.

'Does the friend know what the vampire looks like, maybe a name?'

She shook her head. 'Barbara says that it's Amy's choice.' Ms Mackenzie shook her head again. 'It isn't, not until she's eighteen.'

I sort of agreed with Barbara, but I wasn't a mother, so maybe my sympathies would have been elsewhere if I were. 'So you don't know if the vampire is male or female.'

'Male,' she said, very firm, too firm.

'Amy's friend told you it was a guy vampire?'

Ms Mackenzie shook her head, but too rapid, too jerky. 'Amy would never let another girl do that to her, not . . . down there.'

I was beginning not to like Ms Mackenzie. There's something about someone who is so against all that is different that sets my teeth on edge. 'If I knew for sure it was a guy, then that would narrow down the search.'

'It was a male vampire, I'm sure of that.' She was working too hard at this, which meant she wasn't sure at all.

I let it go; she wasn't going to budge. 'I need to talk to Barbara, Amy's friend, without you or her parents present, and we need to start searching the clubs for Amy. Do you have a picture of her?'

She did, hallelujah, she'd come prepared. It was one of those standard yearbook shots. Amy had long straight hair in a rather nondescript brown color, neither dark enough to be rich, or pale enough to be anything else. She was smiling, face open, eyes sparkling; the picture of health and bright promise.

'The picture was taken last year,' her mother said, as if she needed to explain why the picture looked the way it did.

'Nothing more recent?'

She drew another picture out of her purse. It was of two women in black with kohl eyeliner and full, pouting lips, one with purple lipstick and the other with black. It took me a second to recognize the girl on the right as Amy. The nondescript hair was piled on top of her head in a casual mass of loose curls that left the clean, high bone structure of her face like an unadorned painting, something to be admired. The dramatic makeup suited her coloring. Her friend was blond and it didn't match her skin tone as well. The picture seemed more poised than the other one had, as if they were playing dress-up and knew it, but they both looked older, dramatic, seductive, lovely but almost indistinguishable from a thousand other teenage Goths.

I put the two pictures beside each other and looked from one to the other. 'Which picture did she go out looking like?'

'I don't know. She's got so much Goth clothing, I can't tell what's missing.' She looked uncomfortable with that last remark, as if she should have known.

'You did good bringing both pictures, Ms Mackenzie; most people wouldn't have thought of it.'

She looked up at that, almost managed a smile. 'She looks so different depending on what she wears.'

'Most of us do,' I said.

She nodded, not like she was agreeing, but as if it were polite.

'How old is Barbara, her friend?'

'Eighteen, why?'

'I'll send my friend the private investigator over to talk to her, maybe meet me at the clubs.'

'Barbara won't tell us who it is that's been . . .' She couldn't bring herself to finish the sentence.

'My friend can be very persuasive, but if you think Barbara will be a problem, I might know someone who could help us out.'

'She's very stubborn, just like my Amy.'

I nodded and reached for the phone. I called Veronica (Ronnie) Sims, private detective and good friend, first. Ms Mackenzie gave me Barbara's address, which I gave to Ronnie over the phone. Ronnie said she'd page me when she had any news, or when she arrived at the club district.

I dialed Zerbrowski next. He was a police detective and really had no reason to get involved, but he had two kids, and he didn't like the monsters, and he was my friend. He was actually at work, since he belonged to the Regional Preternatural Investigation Team and worked a lot of nights.

I explained the situation and that I needed a little official muscle to flex. He said it was a slow night, and he'd be there.

'Thanks, Zerbrowski.'

'You owe me.'

'On this one, yeah.'

'Hmm,' he said. 'I know how you could pay me back.' His voice had dropped low and mock seductive. It had been a game with us since we met.

'Be careful what you say next, Zerbrowski, or I'll tell Katie on you.'

'My darling wife knows I'm a letch.'

'Don't we all. Thanks again, Zerbrowski.'

'I've got kids, don't mention it,' he said, and he hung up.

I left Ms Mackenzie in the capable hands of our nighttime secretary, Craig, and I went out to see if I could save her daughter's life, and the 'life' of the vampire who was a close enough personal friend to have bitten Amy twice on the very upper thigh.

\* \* \*

The vampire district in St Louis was one of the hottest tourist areas in the country. Some people credit the undead with the boom we've experienced in the last five years since vampires were declared living citizens with all the rights and privileges that entailed, except voting. There was a bill floating around Washington that would give them the vote, and another bill floating around that would take away their new status and make it legal to kill them on sight again, just because they were vampires. To say that the United States was not exactly united in its attitude toward the undead was an understatement.

Danse Macabre was one of the newest of the vampire-run clubs. It was the hottest dance spot in St Louis. We'd had actors fly from the West Coast to grace the club with their presence. It had become chic to hobknob with vampires, especially the beautiful ones, and St Louis did have more than its fair share of gorgeous corpses.

The most gorgeous corpse of them all was dancing on the main floor of his newest club. The floor was so crowded there was barely room to dance, but somehow my gaze found Jean-Claude, picked him out of the crowd.

When I first spotted him, his long pale hands were above his head, the graceful movement of those hands brought my gaze down to the whirl of his black curls as they slid over his shoulders. From the back, with all that long hair, the shirt was just scarlet, eye-catching but nothing too special; then he turned, and I caught a glimpse of the front.

The red satin scooped over his bare shoulders as if someone had cut out the shoulders with scissors; the sleeves were long, tight to his wrists. The high red collar framed his face, made his skin, his hair, his dark eyes look brighter, more alive.

The music turned him away from me, and I got to watch him dance. He was always graceful, but the pounding beat of the music demanded movements that were not graceful but powerful, provocative.

I finally realized, as he took the woman into his arms, as she plastered herself against the front of him, that he had a partner. I was instantly jealous and hated it.

I'd worn the clothes I'd had on at the office, and I was glad that it was a fashionably short black skirt with a royal-blue button-up shirt. A long black leather coat that was way too hot for the inside of the club and sensible black pumps completed the outfit – oh, and the shoulder holster with the Browning Hi-Power 9mm, which was why I was still wearing the coat. People tended to get nervous if you flashed a gun, and it would show up very nicely against the deep blue of the blouse.

To other people it must have seemed like I was trying to look cool, wearing all that leather. Nope, just trying not to scare the tourists. But nothing I was wearing compared to the sparkling, skintight dress and spike heels the woman had on; nope, I was woefully underdressed.

It had been my choice to stay away from Jean-Claude for these last few months. I'd let him mark me as his human servant to save his life and the life of the other boyfriend I wasn't seeing, Richard Zeeman, Ulfric, wolf king of the local pack. I'd done it to save them both, but it had bound me closer to them, and every sexual act made that mystical tie tighter. We could think each other's thoughts, visit each other's dreams. I'd fallen into Richard's dreams where he was in wolf form chasing human prey. I'd tasted blood underneath a woman's skin because Jean-Claude had been sitting beside me when he thought of it. It had been too much for me, so I'd fled to a friendly psychic who was teaching me how to shield myself metaphysically from the boys. I did okay, as long as I stayed the hell away from both of them.

Watching Jean-Claude move like he was wed to the music, to the room, to the energy, anticipating not just the music but the movements of the woman who was in his arms, made me want to run screaming, because what I really wanted to do was march over there and grab her by her long hair and punch her out. I didn't have that right; besides, they were only dancing. Sure.

But if anyone would be able to tell me who was about to bring

Amy Mackenzie over to be the undead, it would be Jean-Claude. I needed to be here. I needed the information, but it was dangerous, dangerous in so many ways.

The music stopped for a few seconds, then a new song came on, just as fast, just as demanding. Jean-Claude kissed the woman's hand and tried to leave the dance floor.

She took his arm, obviously trying to persuade him to have another dance. He shook his head, kissed her cheek, and managed to extract himself, leaving her smiling. But as she watched him walk toward me, the look was not friendly. There was something familiar about her, as if I should have known her, but I was almost certain I didn't know her. It took me a second or two to realize she was an actress, and if I ever went to movies I would have known her name. A photographer knelt in front of her, and she instantly went from unpleasant to a perfect smile, posing, choosing another partner. A second photographer followed after Jean-Claude, not taking pictures, but alert for a photo opportunity. Shit.

I had two choices. I could either stand there and let him take pictures of Jean-Claude and me, or I could flee to the back office and privacy. I wasn't news, but Jean-Claude was the vampire cover boy. The press had been amused that the woman the other vamps called the Executioner, because she had more vamp kills than any other vampire hunter in the country, had been dating the Master of the City. Even I could admit it was nicely ironic, but being followed around by paparazzi had gotten old very fast. Especially when they tried to take pictures of me while I was working on preternatural murders for the police. For the American media, if you stood next to the gruesome remains, they wouldn't air the pictures or print them, but European papers would. Some of the European media make American media look downright polite.

When I stopped dating Jean-Claude, they drifted away. I was not nearly as photogenic, or as friendly. I didn't have to worry about winning the press over; there wasn't a bill in Washington that was trying to get me killed. The vamps needed the good press, and Jean-Claude was tagged as the one to get it for them.

I decided not to watch Jean-Claude walk toward me because I'd seen what my face looked like when I did – in color on the front of the tabloids. I'd looked like some small prey animal, watching the tiger stalk toward it; that explained the fear, but the fearful fascination, the open . . . lust, that had been harder to see in print. So I kept my eyes on the circling photographer and tried not to watch Jean-Claude glide toward me, as I leaned against the far wall, right next to the door that would lead into the hallway that led to his office.

I could have fled and avoided the press, but it would have meant I would be alone with Jean-Claude, and I didn't want that. All right, truth, I did want that, and that was the problem. It wasn't Jean-Claude I didn't trust, it was me.

I'd been concentrating so hard on not watching him come toward me that it was almost a surprise when I realized I was staring into the red satin of his shirt. I looked up to meet his eyes. Most people couldn't meet the gaze of a vampire, let alone a master one, but I could. I was a necromancer and that gave me partial immunity to vampire powers, and I was Jean-Claude's human servant whether I wanted to be, or whether I didn't, and that gave me even more immunity. I wasn't vampire-proof by any means, but I was shut up pretty tight to most of their tricks.

It wasn't vampire powers that made it hard to meet those midnight-blue eyes. No, nothing that . . . simple.

He said something, and I couldn't hear him over the beat of the music. I shook my head, and he stepped closer, close enough that the red of his shirt filled my vision, but it was better than meeting that swimming blue gaze. He leaned over me, and I felt him like a line of heat, close enough to kiss, close enough for so many things. I was already flat against the wall; there was nowhere else to go.

He had to lean his mouth next to my face, a fall of his long hair moving against my mouth, as he said, '*Ma petite*, it has been too long.'

His voice, even over the noise, caressed down my skin as if he'd touched me. He could do things with his voice that most men could-n't do with their hands.

I could smell his cologne, spicy, exotic, a hint of musk. I could almost taste his skin on my tongue. It took me two tries to say, 'Not nearly long enough.'

He laid his cheek against my hair, very lightly. 'You are happy to see me, *ma petite*, I can feel your heart trembling.'

'I'm here on business,' I said, but my voice was breathy. I was usually better than this around him, but three months of celibacy, three months of nothing, and being around him was worse. Damn it, why did it have to be worse?

'Of course you are.'

I'd had enough. I put a hand on that satin-covered chest and pushed. Vampires can bench-press small trucks, so he didn't have to let me shove him, but he did. He gave me some room, then his mouth moved, as if he were saying something, but I couldn't hear him over the music and crowd noise.

I shook my head and sighed. We were going to have to go back into the office so I could hear him. Being alone with him was not the best idea, but I wanted to find Amy Mackenzie and the vampire she was going to get executed. I opened the door without looking at him. The photographer took pictures as we went through the door. He had to have been taking pictures when Jean-Claude had me practically pinned to the wall, I just hadn't noticed.

Jean-Claude shut the door behind us. The hallway was white, with harsher lighting than anywhere else in the club. He'd told me once that he had made the hallway plain, ordinary, so if a customer opened the door they'd know instantly that it wasn't part of the entertainment.

A group of waiters, vampires all, came out of the left-hand door, wearing vinyl short-shorts and no shirts. They'd spilled out of the door in a cloud of excited talk; it stopped abruptly when they saw us. One of them started to say something, and Jean-Claude said, 'Go.'

They fled out the door without a backward glance, almost as if they were scared. I'd have liked to think it was Jean-Claude that they were afraid of, but I was the Executioner, their version of the electric chair, so it might have been me.

'Shall we retire to my office, *ma petite*?'

I sighed, and in the silence of the hallway, with the music only a distant thrum, my sigh sounded loud. 'Sure.'

He led the way down the hallway, gliding ahead of me. The pants were black satin and looked as if they'd been sewn on his body, tight as a second skin. A pair of black boots graced his legs. The boots laced up the back from ankle to upper thigh. I'd seen the boots before; they were really nice boots. Nice enough that I watched the way his legs moved in them rather than the way the satin fit across his butt. Very nice boots, indeed.

He started to hold the door for me, then smiled, almost laughed, and just walked through. It had taken me a while to break him of opening doors for me, but I'd finally managed to teach a very old dog a new trick.

The office was done in an Oriental motif complete with framed fans around a framed kimono. The colors in all three ran high to reds and blues. A red lacquer screen had a black castle sitting atop a black mountain. The desk was carved wood that looked like ebony and probably was. He leaned against that desk, long legs out in front of him, ankles crossed, hands in his lap, his eyes watching me as I shut the door.

'Please, be seated, *ma petite*.' He motioned to a black and silver chair sitting in front of the desk.

'I'm fine where I am.' I leaned against the wall, my arms crossed under my breasts, which put my hand comfortably close to the gun under my arm. I wouldn't really shoot Jean-Claude, but the gun being close made me feel better. It was like a small, lumpy security blanket. Besides, I never went anywhere after dark unarmed.

His smile was amused and condescending. 'I do not think the wall will fall down if you cease to lean against it.'

'We need to figure out who the vamp is that's been doing Amy Mackenzie.'

'You said you had pictures of the girl. May I see them?' The smile had faded round the edges, but his eyes still held that amusement, faint and condescending, which he used as a mask to hide things.

I sighed and reached into the pocket of my leather coat. I held the two pictures out toward him. He held his hand out for them but made no move to come to me.

'I won't bite, *ma petite*.'

'Only because I won't let you,' I said.

He gave that graceful shrug that meant everything and nothing. 'True, but still I will not ravish you because you stand a few feet in front of me.'

He was right. I was being silly, but I could taste my pulse in my throat as I walked toward him, the new leather coat sighing around me, the way new leather always does. It was a replacement coat for one that a vampire had ripped off me. I held the pictures out to him, and he had to lean forward to take them from me. I even sat down in the chair in front of the desk while he looked at them. We could be civilized about this. Of course we could. But I couldn't stop looking at the way his bare shoulders gleamed against the scarlet cloth, the way the high collar made his hair a pure blackness almost as dark as mine. His lips looked redder than I remembered them, as if he were wearing a light lipstick, and I wouldn't have put it past him. But he didn't need makeup to be beautiful, he just simply was.

He spoke without looking up from the pictures. 'I do not recognize her, but then she could come here occasionally and I would have no reason to.' He looked up, meeting my eyes, catching me staring at his bare shoulders. The look in those eyes said he knew exactly what I'd been looking at. The look was enough to make me blush, and I hated that.

My voice came out angry, and I was pleased. Anger is better than embarrassment any day. 'You said on the phone that you could help.'

He laid the pictures on his desk and clasped his hands back in his lap. The placement of his hands was utterly polite, but they also framed a certain area of anatomy, and the satin was very tight, and I could tell that other things were tight as well.

It made me blush again, and it made me angrier, just like old times. I'd have liked to be a smart alec and say something like, *That looked uncomfortable*, but I didn't want to admit that I'd noticed, so out of options that were polite, I stood up and turned away.

'None of my vampires would dare bring over anyone without my permission,' he said.

That made me turn around. 'What do you mean?'

'I have ordered a . . . how will you say . . . hiring freeze, until that nasty bill in Washington is defeated.'

'*Hiring freeze*,' I said. 'You mean none of your vamps can make more of you until Senator Brewster's law goes down in flames?'

'*Exactement*.'

'So you're sure that none of your vamps is doing this?' I said.

'They would not risk the punishment.'

'So you can't help me. Damn it, Jean-Claude, you could have told me that over the phone.'

'I called Malcolm while you were en route,' he said.

Malcolm was the head of the Church of Eternal Life, the vampire church. It was the only church I'd ever been in that had no holy objects displayed whatsoever; even the stained glass was abstract art. 'Because if it's not one of your vamps, then it's one of his,' I said.

'*Oui*.'

Truthfully, I had just assumed it was one of Jean-Claude's vampires because the church was very strict on when you brought your human followers over to the dead side, and the church also checked backgrounds thoroughly. 'The girl's friend said she'd met the vampire at a club.'

'Can you not go to church and go to a club on the weekends?'

I nodded. 'Okay, you've made your point. What did Malcolm say?'

'That he would contact all his followers and give strict orders that this vampire and the girl are to be found.'

'They'll need the picture,' I said. My beeper went off, and I jumped. Shit. I checked the number and it was Ronnie's cell phone.

'Can I use your phone?'

'Whatever I have is yours, *ma petite*.' He looked at the black phone sitting on the black desk and stood to one side so I could walk around the desk without him leaning over me. Considerate of him, which probably meant he was going to do something else even more irritating.

Ronnie answered on the first ring. 'Anita?'

'It's me, what's up?'

She lowered her voice to a whisper. 'Your detective friend convinced Barbara that if Amy got herself killed, she'd be charged with conspiracy to commit murder.'

'I don't think Zerbrowski could make that stick.'

'Barbara thinks he can.'

'What did she tell you?'

'The vampire's name is Bill Stucker.' She spelled the last name for me.

'A vamp with a last name. He has to be really new,' I said. The only other vamp I'd ever met with a last name had been dead less than a month.

'Don't know if he's old or new, just his name.'

'She have an address for him?'

'No, and Zerbrowski pushed her pretty hard. She says she's never been there, and I believe her.'

'Okay, tell Zerbrowski thanks. I'll see you Saturday at the gym.'

'Wouldn't miss it,' she said.

'Oh, and thanks to you, too, Ronnie.'

'Always happy to save someone from the monsters, which reminds me, are you with you-know-who?'

'If you mean Jean-Claude, yes, I am.'

'Get out of there as soon as you can,' she said.

'You're not my mother, Ronnie.'

'No, just your friend.'

'Good night, Ronnie.'

'Don't stay,' she said.

I hung up. Ronnie was one of my very bestest friends, but her attitude toward Jean-Claude was beginning to get on my nerves, mainly because I agreed with her. I always hated being in the wrong.

'The name Bill Stucker mean anything to you?' I asked Jean-Claude.

'No, but I will call Malcolm and see if it means something to him.'

I handed him the phone receiver and stepped back out of the way, i.e., out of touching distance. His side of the conversation consisted mainly of giving the name and saying 'Of course' and 'Yes.' He handed the phone to me. 'Malcolm wishes to speak to you.'

I took the phone, and Jean-Claude actually moved away and gave me some room. 'Ms Blake, I am sorry for anything my church brethren may have done. He is in our computer with his address. I will have a deacon at his doorstep within minutes.'

'Give me the address and I'll go down and check on the girl.'

'That will not be necessary. The church sister that is attending to this was a nurse before she came over.'

'I'm not sure what Amy Mackenzie needs is another vampire, no matter how well-meaning. Let me have the address.'

'And I don't believe that my vampire needs the Executioner shooting down his door.'

'I can give the name to the police. They'll find his address, and they'll knock on his door, and they may not be as polite as I would be.'

'Now that last is hard to imagine.'

I think he was making fun of me. 'Give me the address, Malcolm.' Anger was tightening across my shoulders, making me want to rotate my neck and try to clear it.

'Wait a moment.' He put me on hold.

I looked at Jean-Claude and let the anger into my voice. 'He put me on hold.'

Jean-Claude had sat down in the chair that I'd vacated; he smiled, shrugged, trying to stay neutral. Probably wise of him. When I'm angry I have a tendency to spread it around, even over people who don't deserve it. I'm trying to cut down on my bad habits, but some habits are easier to break than others. My temper was one of the hard ones.

'Ms Blake, that was the emergency line. The girl is alive, but barely; they are rushing her to the hospital. We are not sure if she will make it. We will turn Bill over to the police if she dies, I give you my word on that.'

I had to take his word, because he was a centuries-old vampire and if you could ever get them to give their oath, they'd keep it.

'What hospital, so I can call her mom?'

He told me. I hung up and called Amy's mother. One hysterical phone call later I got to hang up and now it was my turn to sit on the edge of the desk and look down at him.

My feet didn't touch the ground and that made it hard to look graceful. But then I'd never tried to compete with Jean-Claude on gracefulness; some battles are made to be lost.

'There was a time, *ma petite*, that you would have insisted on riding to the rescue yourself, questioning the girl's friend, and refusing to bring in the police at all.'

'If I thought threatening Barbara with violence or shooting her would have made her talk, I'd be perfect for the job. But I'm not going to shoot, or hurt, an eighteen-year-old girl who's trying to help her best friend save her leg, if not her life. Zerbrowski could threaten her with the law, jail time; I can't do that.'

'And you never threaten anything that you cannot or will not do,' he said, softly.

'No, I don't.'

We looked at each other. He at ease in the straight-backed chair, his ankle propped on the opposite knee, fingers steepled in front of his face so that what I mostly saw of him were those extraordinary eyes, huge, a blue so dark it treaded the edge of being black, but you never doubted his eyes were pure, unadulterated blue, like ocean water where it runs achingly deep and cold.

Ronnie was right, I should leave, but I didn't want to leave. I wanted to stay. I wanted to run my hands over his shirt, to caress the naked surprise of those shoulders. And because I wanted it so badly, I hopped off the desk, and said, 'Thanks for your help.'

'I am always willing to be of assistance, *ma petite*.'

I could have walked wide past his chair, but that would be insulting to both of us. I just had to walk by the chair and out the door. Simple. I was almost past the chair, almost behind him, when he spoke. 'Would you have ever called me if you hadn't needed to save some human?' His voice was as ordinary as it ever got. He wasn't trying to use vampire tricks to make the words more than they were and that stopped me. An honest question was harder to turn my back on than a seductive trick.

I sighed and turned back to find him staring straight at me. Looking full into his face from less than two feet away made me have to catch my breath. 'You know why I'm staying away.'

He twisted in the chair, putting one arm on the back of it, showing that flash of bare shoulder again. 'I know that you find it difficult to control the powers of the vampire marks when we are together. It was something that should have bound us closer, not thrust us farther apart.' Again his voice was as carefully neutral as he could make it.

I shook my head. 'I've got to go.'

He turned in the chair so that he leaned both arms on the back, his chin resting on his hands, his hair framing all that red cloth, that pale flesh, those drowning eyes. Less than two feet apart, almost close enough that if I reached a hand out I could have touched him. I swallowed so hard it almost hurt. I balled my hands into fists, because I could feel the memory of his skin against my hands. All I had to do was close that distance, but I knew if I did, that I wouldn't be leaving, not for a while anyway.

My voice came out breathy. 'I should go.'

'So you said.'

I should have turned and walked out, but I couldn't quite bring myself to do it. Didn't want to do it. I wanted to stay. My body was tight with need; wet with it, just at the sight of him fully clothed, leaning on a chair. Damn it, why wasn't I walking away? But I wasn't reaching for him either; I got points for that. Sometimes you get points for just standing your ground.

Jean-Claude stood, very slowly, as if afraid I'd bolt, but I didn't. I stood there, my heart in my throat, my eyes a little wide, afraid, eager, wanting.

He stood inches away from me, staring down, but still not touching, hands at his sides, face neutral. He raised one hand, very slowly upward, and even that small movement sent his fingertips gliding along my leather coat. When I didn't pull away, he held the edge of the leather in his fingertips inside the open edge of the coat at the level of my waist. He began to slide his hand upward, above my waist, my stomach, then the back of his fingers brushed over my breasts, not hesitating, moving upward to the collar of the coat, but that one quick brush had tightened my body, stopped my breath in my throat.

His hand moved from my collar to my neck, fingers gliding underneath my hair until he cupped the back of my neck, his thumb resting on top of the big pulse in my neck. The weight of his hand on my skin was almost more than I could take, as if I could sink into him through that one hand.

'I have missed you, *ma petite*.' His voice was low and caressing this time, gliding over my skin, bringing my breath in a shaking line.

I'd missed him, but I couldn't bring myself to say it out loud. What I could do was raise up on tiptoe, steadying myself with a hand on his chest, feeling his heart beat against the palm of my hand. He'd fed on someone, or he wouldn't have had a heartbeat, some willing donor, and even that thought wasn't enough to stop me from leaning my face back, offering my lips to him.

His lips brushed mine, the softest of caresses. I drew back from the kiss, my hands sliding over the satin of his shirt, feeling the firmness of him underneath. I did what I'd wanted to do since I saw him tonight. I passed my fingers over the bare skin of his shoulders, so smooth, so soft, so firm. I rolled my hands behind his shoulders, and the movement let our bodies fall together, lightly.

His hands found my waist, slid behind my back, pressed me against him, not lightly, hard, hard enough that I could feel him even through the satin of his pants, the cloth of my skirt, the lace of my panties. I could feel him pressed so tight and ready that I had to close my eyes, hide my face against his chest. I tried to keep my feet flat to the floor, to move away from him, just a little, just enough to think again, but his hands kept me pinned to his body. I opened my eyes then, ready to tell him to let me the hell go, but I looked up and his face was so close, his lips half parted, that no words came.

I kissed those half-parted lips almost as gently as he'd kissed me. His hands tightened at my back, my waist, pressing us tighter against each other, so tight, so close. My breath came out in a long sigh, and he kissed me. His mouth closing over mine, my body sinking against his, my mouth opening for his lips, his tongue, everything. I ran my tongue between the delicate tips of his fangs. There was an art to French-kissing a vampire, and I hadn't lost it; I didn't pierce myself on those dainty points.

Without breaking the kiss, he bent and wrapped his arms around my upper thighs, lifted me, carried me effortlessly to the desk. He didn't lay me on it, which is what I half-expected. He turned and sat down on the desk, sliding my legs to either side, so that he was suddenly pressed between my legs with only two pieces of cloth between us. He lay back on the desk, and I rode him, rubbing our bodies together through the satin of his pants and my panties.

His hands rubbed up my leg, tracing my thigh, until his fingers found the top lace of the thigh-high hose. I pressed myself into him hard enough for his body to arch, spasming our bodies together. And there was a knock on the door. We both froze, then Jean-Claude said, 'We are not to be disturbed!'

A voice I didn't recognize said, 'I am sorry, master, but Malcolm is here. He insists that it is urgent.'

Evidently Jean-Claude did know the voice, because he closed his eyes and cursed softly under his breath in French. 'What does he want?'

I slid off Jean-Claude, leaving him lying on his desk, with his legs dangling over the end.

Malcolm's smooth voice came next. 'I have a present for Ms Blake.'

I checked my clothing to make sure it was presentable; strangely it was. Jean-Claude sat up, but stayed on the edge of his desk. 'Enter.'

The door opened and the tall, blond, dark-suited figure of Malcolm walked through. He always dressed like he was a television preacher, conservative, immaculate, expensive. Compared to Jean-Claude he always looked ordinary, but then so did most everyone. Still, there was a presence to Malcolm, a calm, soothing power that filled every room around him. He was a master vampire and his power was a thrumming weight against my skin. He tried to pass for human, and I'd always wondered if the level of power he gave off was his version of toned down, and if this was the toned-down version, then what must his power truly be like?

'Ms Blake, Jean-Claude.' He gave a small bow of his head, then moved from the door and two vampires in the dark suits and white shirts of his deacons came through carrying a chained vampire between them. He had short blond hair and blood drying on his mouth, as if they'd chained him before he'd had time to clean himself.

'This is Bill Stucker; the girl, I am sorry to say, passed over.'

'She's one of you, then,' I said.

Malcolm nodded. 'This one tried to run, but I gave you my word that he would be punished by your law if she died.'

'You could have just dropped him off at the police station,' I said.

His eyes flicked to Jean-Claude, to me, to my leather coat forgotten on the floor. 'I am sorry to interrupt your evening, but I thought it would come better if the Executioner delivered the vampire to the police rather than us. I think the reporters will listen to you when you say we did not condone this, and you are honorable enough to tell the truth.'

'Are you saying the rest of the police aren't?'

'I am saying that many of our law enforcement are distrustful of us and would be only too happy to see us lose our status as citizens.'

I'd have liked to argue, but I couldn't. 'I'll drop him off for you and I'll make sure the press knows you delivered him.'

'Thank you, Ms Blake.' He looked at Jean Claude. 'Again, my apologies. I was told that the two of you were no longer dating.'

'We aren't dating,' I said, a little too quickly.

He shrugged. 'Of course.' He looked back at Jean-Claude and gave a smile that said more than anything that they didn't quite like each other. He liked interrupting Jean-Claude's evening. They were two very different kinds of vampire, and neither really approved completely of the other.

Malcolm stepped over the struggling, gagged form of the other vampire and went out the door with his deacons. None of them even looked back at the vampire chained on the floor.

There were a flock of waiters and waitresses in their skimpy uniforms huddled in the doorway. 'Take this vampire and load him in *ma petite*'s car.'

He looked at me, and I got my keys out of the leather coat and tossed it to one of the vampires. One of the women picked the chained vamp off the floor and tossed him over her shoulder like he weighed nothing. They closed the door behind them without being told.

I picked my coat off the floor. 'I have to go.'

'Of course you do.' His voice held just a little bit of anger. 'You have let your desire for me out and now you must cage it again, hide it away, be ashamed of it.'

I started to be angry, but I looked at him sitting there, head down, hands limp in his lap, as dejected as I'd seen him in a while, and I wasn't angry. He was right, that was exactly how I treated him. I stayed where I was, the coat over one arm.

'I have to take him down to the police station and make sure the press gets the truth, not something that will make the vampires look worse than they already do in all this.'

He nodded without looking up.

If he'd been his usual arrogant self, I could have left him like that, but he was letting his pain show, and that I couldn't just walk away from. 'Let's try an olive branch,' I said.

He looked up at that, frowning. 'Olive branch?'

'White flag?' I said.

He smiled then. 'A truce.' He laughed, and it danced over my skin. 'I did not know we were at war.'

That hit a little too close to home. 'Are you going to let me say something nice, or not?'

'By all means, *ma petite*, far be it from me to interrupt your gentler urges.'

'I am trying to ask you out on a date.'

The smile widened, his eyes filling with such instant pleasure that it made me look away, because it made me want to smile back at him. 'It must have been a very long time since you asked a man out; you seem to be out of practice.'

I put on my coat. 'Fine, be a smart alec. See where it gets you.'

I was almost to the door when he said, 'Not a war, *ma petite*, but a siege, and this poor soldier is feeling very left out in the cold.'

I stopped and turned around. He was still sitting on the desk trying to look harmless, I think. He was many things: handsome, seductive, intelligent, cruel, but not harmless, not to body, mind, or soul.

'Tomorrow night, pick a restaurant.' One of the side effects of being his human servant was that he could taste food through me. It was the first time he'd been able to taste food in centuries. It was a minor power to share, but he adored it, and I adored watching him enjoying his first bite of steak in four hundred years.

'I will make reservations,' he said, voice careful again, as if he were afraid I'd change my mind.

Looking at him, sitting on his desk all in red and black and satin and leather, I didn't want to change my mind. I wanted to sit across the table from him. I wanted to drive him home and go inside and see what color of sheets he had on that big bed of his.

It wasn't just the sex; I wanted someone to hold me. I wanted someplace safe, someplace to be myself. And like it or hate it, in Jean-Claude's arms I could be perfectly who and what I was. I could have called Richard up and he'd have been just as glad to hear from me, and there would have been as much heat, but Richard and I had some philosophical differences that went beyond his being a were-wolf. Richard tried to be a good person, and he thought I killed too easily to be a good person. Jean-Claude had helped teach me the ultimate practicality that had kept me alive, helped me keep others alive. But the thought that Jean-Claude's arms were the closest thing I had to a refuge in this world was a sobering thought. Almost a depressing one.

He slid off the desk in one graceful movement as if his body were pulled by strings. He started to glide toward me, moving like some great cat. Just watching him walk toward me made my chest tight. He grabbed each side of the leather coat and drew me into the circle of his arms. 'Would it be pushing the bounds of our truce too far to say that it is hours until dawn?'

My voice came out breathy. 'I have to take him to the police and deal with reporters; that will take hours.'

'This time of year dawn comes very late.' He whispered it as he bent to lay his lips against mine.

We kissed, and I drew back enough to whisper, 'I'll try to be back before dawn.'

It was four days before Christmas, an hour before dawn, when I knocked on Jean-Claude's bedroom door underneath the Circus of the Damned, one of his other clubs. His voice called, 'Come in, *ma petite.*'

An hour. It wasn't much time, but time is what you make it. I had stopped by the grocery store on the way and picked up some ready-made chocolate icing in one of those flip-top canisters. He could taste the chocolate while I ate it, and if it just happened to be on him while I was eating it, well . . . The silk sheets on his bed were white, and we laughed while we covered him in chocolate and stained the sheets. But when every inch of him that I wanted was covered in thick, sweet chocolate, the laughter stopped, and other noises began, noises even more precious to me than his laughter. Dawn caught us before he could take a bath and clean himself of the sticky sweetness. I left him in a pile of chocolate-smeared white silk sheets, his body still warm to the touch, but his heart no longer beating. Dawn had found him and stolen his life away, and lifeless he would remain for hours; then he would wake, and he would be 'alive' again. He truly was a corpse. I knew that. But he had the sweetest skin I'd ever tasted, candy-covered or plain. He had no pulse, no breath, no movement, dead. It should have made a difference, and it did. I think the siege, as he called it, would have been over long ago if he'd been alive, or maybe not. Being a vampire was too large a part of who Jean-Claude was for me to separate them out. It did make a difference, but I laid one last icing-coated kiss on his forehead, and went home. We had a date tonight, and with the feel of his body still clinging to mine, I could hardly wait.

# COPYRIGHT INFORMATION

'A Token for Celandine' copyright © 1989 by Laurell K. Hamilton. Originally published in *Memories and Visions*, ed. Susanna J. Sturgis. Freedom, CA: Crossing Press, 1989.

'A Clean Sweep' copyright © 1995 by Laurell K. Hamilton. Originally published in *Superheroes*, ed. John Varley and Ricia Mainhardt. New York: Ace, 1995.

'The Curse-Maker' copyright © 1991 by Laurell K. Hamilton. Originally published in *Dragon Magazine* #165, January 1991.

'Geese' copyright © 1995 by Laurell K. Hamilton. Originally published in *Sword and Sorceress* #8, ed. Marion Zimmer Bradley. New York: DAW, 1991.

'House of Wizards' copyright © 1989 by Laurell K. Hamilton. Originally published in *Marion Zimmer Bradley Fantasy Magazine*, Spring 1989.

'Winterkill' copyright © 1990 by Laurell K. Hamilton. Originally published in *Sword and Sorceress* #7, ed. Marion Zimmer Bradley. New York: DAW, 1990.

'Stealing Souls' copyright © 1989 by Laurell K. Hamilton. Originally published in *Spells of Wonder*, ed. Marion Zimmer Bradley. New York: DAW, 1989.

'The Girl Who was Infatuated with Death' copyright © 2005 by Laurell K. Hamilton. Originally published in *Bite*. New York: Jove, 2005.

It's time to satisfy your bloodlust . . .

Turn the page for a preview of the next sensational novel featuring Anita Blake.

# LAURELL K. HAMILTON

# DANSE MACABRE

An Anita Blake,
Vampire Hunter, Novel

headline

# I

IT WAS THE middle of November. I was supposed to be out jogging, but instead I was sitting at my breakfast table talking about men, sex, werewolves, vampires, and that thing that most unmarried but sexually active women fear most of all – a missed period.

Veronica (Ronnie) Sims, best friend and private detective, sat across from me at my little four-seater breakfast table. The table sat on a little raised alcove in a bay window. I did breakfast most mornings looking at the view out onto the deck and the trees beyond. Today, the view wasn't pretty, because the inside of my head was too ugly to see it. Panic will do that to you.

'You're sure you missed October? You didn't just count wrong?' Ronnie asked.

I shook my head and stared into my coffee cup. 'I'm two weeks overdue.'

She reached across the table and patted my hand. 'Two weeks – you had me scared. Two weeks could be anything, Anita. Stress will throw you off that much, and God knows you've had enough stress.' She squeezed my hand. 'That last serial killer case was only about two weeks ago.' She squeezed my hand harder. 'What I read in the paper and saw on the news was bad.'

I'd stopped telling Ronnie all my bad stuff years ago, when my cases as a legal vampire executioner had gotten so much bloodier than her cases as a private eye. Now I was a federal marshal, along with most of the other legal vamp hunters in the United States. It meant that I had even more access to even more awful shit. Things that Ronnie, or any of my female friends, didn't want to know about. I didn't fault them. I'd rather not have had that many nightmares in my own head. No, I didn't fault Ronnie, but it meant that I couldn't share some of the most awful stuff with her. I was just glad we'd made up a long-standing grumpiness in time to have her here for this particular disaster. I was able to talk about the bad parts of my cases with some of the men in my life, but I couldn't have shared the missed period with any of them. It concerned one of them entirely too much.

She squeezed my hand hard and leaned back. Her gray eyes were all sympathy, and apology. She was still feeling guilty that she'd let her issues about commitment and men rain all over our friendship. She'd had a brief, disastrous marriage years before I met her. She'd come here today to cry on my shoulder about the fact that she was moving in with her boyfriend, Louie Fane – *Dr* Louis Fane, thank you very much. He had his doctorate in biology and taught at Washington University. He also turned furry once a month, and was a lieutenant of the local wererat rodere – their word for pack.

'If Louie wasn't hiding what he was from his colleagues, we'd be going to the big party afterward,' she said.

'He teaches people's kids, Ronnie; he can't afford to find out what they'd do if they found out he had lycanthropy.'

'College isn't kids, it's definitely grown-up.'

'Parents won't see it that way,' I said. I looked at her, and finally said, 'Are you changing the subject?'

'It's only *two weeks*, Anita, after one of the most violent cases you've ever had. I wouldn't even lose sleep over it.'

'Yeah, but your period is erratic, mine's not. I've never been two weeks late before.'

She pushed a strand of blond hair back behind her ear. The new haircut framed her face nicely, but it didn't stay out of her eyes, and she was always pushing it back. 'Never?'

I shook my head, and sipped coffee. It was cold. I got up and went to dump it in the sink.

'What's the latest you've ever been?' she asked.

'Two days, I think five once, but I wasn't having sex with anyone, so it wasn't scary. I mean, unless there was a star in the east I was safe, just late.' I poured coffee from the French press, which emptied it. I was so going to need more coffee.

Ronnie came to stand next to me while I put more hot water on the stove. She leaned her butt against the cabinets and drank her coffee, but she was watching me. 'Let me run this back at you. You've never been two weeks late, ever, and you've never missed a whole month before?'

'Not since this whole mess started when I was fourteen, no.'

'I always envied you the regular-as-clockwork schedule,' she said.

I started dismantling the French press, taking out the lid with its filter on a stick. 'Well, the clock is broken right now.'

'Shit,' she said, softly.

'You can say that again.'

'You need a pregnancy test,' she said.

'No shit.' I dumped the grounds into the trash can, and shook my head. 'I can't go shopping for one tonight.'

'Can't you make a quick stop on the way to Jean-Claude's little tête-à-tête tonight? It's not like this is the main event.'

Jean-Claude, Master Vampire of the City of St Louis, and my sweetie, was throwing one of the biggest bashes of the year to welcome to town the first ever mostly-vampire dance company. He was one of their patrons, and when you spend that much money, you apparently get to spend more to throw a party to celebrate that the money was helping the dance troupe earn rave reviews in their cross-country tour. There was going to be national and international media there tomorrow. It was like a Big Deal, and I, as his main squeeze, had to be on his arm, smiling and dressed up. But that was tomorrow. Tonight's little get-together was sort of a prelim to the main event. Without letting the media know, a couple of the visiting Masters of the City had snuck in early. Jean-Claude had called them friends. Master vampires did not call other master vampires friends. Allies, partners – but not friends.

'Yeah, Ronnie, I'm riding in with Micah and Nathaniel. Even if I stop, Nathaniel will insist on going in whatever store with me, or wondering why I don't let him go. I don't want any of them to know until I've got the test and it's yes or no. Maybe it's just nerves, stress, and the test will say no. Then I won't have to tell anybody.'

'Where are your two handsome housemates?'

'Jogging. I was supposed to go with them, but I told them you'd called and needed me to hold your hand about moving in with Louie.'

'I did,' she said, and sipped her coffee. 'But suddenly me being nervous about sharing space with a man for the second time in my life doesn't seem like such a big deal. Louie is nothing like the asshole I married when I was young and stupid.'

'Louie sees the real you, Ronnie. He's not looking for some trophy wife. He wants a partner.'

'I hope you're right.'

'I don't know much today, but I'm sure Louie wants a partner, not a Barbie doll.'

She gave me a weak smile, then frowned. 'Thanks, but I'm supposed to be comforting you. Are you going to tell them?'

I leaned my hands against the sink, and looked at her through a curtain of my long dark hair. It had gotten too long for my tastes, but Micah had made me a deal: If I cut my hair, he'd cut his, because he preferred his hair shorter, too. So my hair was fast approaching my waist for the first time since junior high, and it was really beginning to get on my nerves. Of course, today everything was getting on my nerves.

'Until I know for sure, I don't want them to know.'

'Even if it's yes, Anita, you don't have to tell them. I'll close up my agency for a few days. We'll go away on a girls' retreat, and you can come back without a problem.'

I pushed my hair back so I could see her clearly. I think my face showed what I was thinking, because she said, 'What?'

'Are you honestly saying that I don't tell any of them? That I just go away for a while and make sure that there's no baby to worry about?'

'It's your body,' she said.

'Yeah, and I took my chances by having sex with this many men on a regular basis.'

'You're on the pill,' she said.

'Yeah, and if I'd wanted to be a hundred percent safe I'd have still used condoms, but I didn't. If I'm . . . pregnant, then I'll deal, but not like that.'

'You can't mean you'd keep it.'

I shook my head. 'I'm not even sure I'm pregnant, but if I was, I couldn't not tell the father. I'm in a committed relationship with several of them. I'm not married, but we live together. We share a life. I couldn't just make this kind of choice without talking to them first.'

She shook her head. 'No man ever wants you to get an abortion if you're in a relationship. They always want you barefoot and pregnant.'

'That's your mother's issues talking, not yours. Or at least not mine.'

She looked away, wouldn't meet my eyes. 'I can tell you what I'd do, and it wouldn't involve telling Louie.'

I sighed and stared out the little window above the sink. A lot of things to say went through my head, none of them helpful. I finally settled for, 'Well, it isn't you and Louie having this particular problem. It's me, and . . .'

'And who?' she said. 'Who got you knocked up?'

'Thanks for putting it that way.'

'I could ask, who's the father, but that's just creepy. If you are, then it's this little tiny, microscopic lump of cells. It's not a baby. It's not a person, not yet.'

I shook my head. 'We'll agree to disagree on that one.'

'You're pro-choice,' she said.

I nodded. 'Yep, I am, but I also believe that abortion is taking a life. I agree women have the right to choose, but I also think that it's still taking a life.'

'That's like saying you're pro-choice *and* pro-life. You can't be both.'

'I'm pro-choice because I've never been a fourteen-year-old incest victim pregnant by her father, or a woman who's going to die if the pregnancy continues, or a rape victim, or even a teenager who made a mistake. I want women to have choices, but I also believe that it's a life, especially once it's big enough to live outside the womb.'

'Once a Catholic, always a Catholic,' she said.

'Maybe, but you'd think being excommunicated would've cured me.' The Pope had declared that all animators – zombie raisers – were excommunicated until they repented their evil ways and stopped doing it. What His Holiness didn't seem to grasp is that raising the dead was a psychic ability, and if we didn't raise zombies for money on a regular basis, we'd eventually raise the dead by accident. I had accidentally raised a deceased pet as a child, and a suicidal teacher in college. I'd always wondered if there had been others that never found me. Maybe some of the accidental zombies that occasionally show up are the result of someone's psychic abilities gone wrong, or untrained. All I knew was that if the Pope had ever woken up as a child with his dead dog curled up in bed with him, he'd want the power controlled. Or maybe he wouldn't. Maybe he'd believe that it was evil and he'd pray it into submission. My prayers just didn't have that kind of punch to them.

'You can't mean you'd actually have this . . . thing, baby, whatever.'

I sighed. 'I don't know, but I do know that I could never just go away, get an abortion, and never tell my boyfriends. Never tell them that one of them might have made a child with me. I just couldn't do it.'

She was shaking her head so hard that her hair fell around her face, covered the upper half of it. She ran her hands through it sharply, like she was pulling on it. 'I've tried to understand that you're happy living with not one, but two men. I've tried to understand that you love that vampire son of a bitch, somehow. I've tried, but if you actually breed . . . actually have a baby, I just don't get that. I won't be able to understand that.'

'Then don't, then go. If you can't deal, then go.'

'I didn't mean that. I just meant that I can't understand why you would complicate your life this way.'

'Complicate, yeah, I guess that's one way of putting it.'

She crossed her arms tight over her chest. She was tall, slender and leggy, and blond. Everything I'd wanted to be as a child. She was small-chested enough that she could fold her arms over her breasts instead of under them, something I couldn't have done. But her legs went on forever in a skirt, and mine did not. Oh, well.

'Okay, then if you're going to tell them, tell Micah and Nathaniel and get a test and test yourself.'

'I told you, I don't want anyone to know until I know for sure.'

She looked up at the ceiling, closed her eyes, and sighed. 'Anita, you live with two of them. You sleep over with two more of them. You are never alone. When are you going to have time to run in and get a test, let alone have the privacy to use it?'

'I can pick one up at work on Monday.'

She stared at me. 'Monday! It's Thursday. I'd go fucking crazy if I had to wait that long. You'll go crazy. You can't wait nearly four days.'

'Maybe my period will start. Maybe by Monday I won't need it.'

'Anita, you wouldn't have told me if you weren't pretty sure you needed a pregnancy test.'

'When Nathaniel and Micah get back, they'll jump in the shower, we'll get dressed up, and go straight to Jean-Claude's. There won't be time tonight.'

'Friday, promise me that Friday you'll get one.'

'I'll try, but . . .'

'Besides, when you start asking your lovers to use condoms, won't they figure something out?'

'Jesus,' I said.

'Yeah, I heard you say if you'd used condoms you'd be safe. Don't tell me that you're not going to want to use them for a while. Could you really have unprotected sex right now, and enjoy it?'

I shook my head. 'No.'

'Then what are you going to tell the boys about this sudden need for condoms? Hell, Micah had a vasectomy before you even met him. He's like super-safe.'

I sighed again. 'You're right, damn it, but you are.'

'So pick up the test on the way to the thing tonight.'

'No. I'm not going to rain all over Jean-Claude's meeting. He's planned this for months.'

'You didn't mention it to me.'

'I didn't plan it, he did. The ballet isn't really my thing.' Truthfully, he hadn't mentioned it to me until they were coming to St Louis, but I kept that part to myself. It would just give Ronnie another reason to say that Jean-Claude was keeping secrets from me. He'd finally admitted that the Masters of the City all coming here had been something he hadn't planned, at least not from the beginning. He'd just negotiated it so the vampire dancers could cross many different vamp territories without problems. Jean-Claude agreed the meet was a good idea, but he was also nervous about it. It would be the largest gathering of Masters of the City in American history. And you don't bring that many big fish together without worrying about shark attacks.

'And how will Mr Fang-Face feel about being a father?'

'Don't call him that.'

'Sorry, how will Jean-Claude feel about being a daddy?'

'It's probably not his.'

She looked at me. 'You're having sex with him, a lot. Why isn't it his?'

'Because he's more than four hundred years old and when vampires get that old, they aren't very fertile. That goes for Asher and Damian, too.'

'Oh, God,' she said. 'I'd forgotten that you had sex with Damian.'

'Yeah,' I said.

She covered her eyes with her hands. 'I'm sorry, Anita. I'm sorry that it's weirding me out that my uptight monogamous friend is suddenly sleeping with not one, but three vampires.'

'I didn't plan it that way.'

'I know that.' She hugged me, and I stayed stiff against her. She wasn't being comforting enough for me to relax in her arms. She hugged me tighter. 'I'm sorry, I'm sorry, I'm being a jerk. But if it's not the vampires then who else but your houseboys.'

I pulled away from her. 'Don't call them my houseboys. They have names, and just because I like living with someone, and you don't, don't make that my problem.'

'Fine, that leaves Micah and Nathaniel.'

'Micah is fixed, remember? So it can't be him.'

Her eyes went wide. 'That leaves Nathaniel. Jesus, Anita, *Nathaniel* as the father-to-be.'

A moment ago I might have agreed with her, but now it pissed me off. It wasn't her place to disparage my boyfriends. 'What's wrong with Nathaniel?' I said, and my voice was not entirely happy.

She put her hands on her hips and gave me a look. 'He's twenty and a stripper. Twenty-year-old strippers are the entertainment at your bachelorette party. You don't have babies with them.'

I let the anger seep into my eyes. 'Nathaniel told me you didn't see him as real, as a person. I told him he was wrong. I told him you were my friend, and you wouldn't disrespect him like that. I guess *I* was wrong.'

She didn't back down or apologize. She was angry and staying that way. 'Last time I checked, Nathaniel was supposed to be food, just food, not the love of your life.'

'I didn't say he was the love of my life, and yeah, he started out as my *pomme de sang*, but that doesn't . . .'

But she interrupted me. 'Your apple of blood, right, that's what *pomme de sang* means?'

I nodded.

'If you were a vampire you'd be taking blood from your little stripper, but thanks to that bloodsucking son of a bitch you have to feed off sex. *Sex*, for God's sake! First that bastard made you his blood whore, and now you're just a—' She stopped abruptly, a startled, almost-frightened look on her face, as if she knew she'd gone too far.

I gave her a flat, cold look. The look that says my anger has moved from hot to cold. It's never a good sign. 'Go on, Ronnie, say it.'

'I didn't mean it,' she whispered.

'Yeah,' I said, 'you did. Now I'm just a whore.' My voice sounded as cold as my eyes felt. Too angry and too hurt to be anything but cold. Hot anger can feel good, but the cold will protect you better.

She started to cry. I just stared at her, speechless. What the hell was going on? We were fighting – she wasn't allowed to cry in the middle of it. Especially not when she was the one being a cruel bastard. I could count on one hand the times I'd seen Ronnie cry and still have fingers left over.

I was still angry, but I was puzzled, too, and that took a little of the edge off. 'Shouldn't I be the one in tears here?' I asked, because I couldn't think of what else to say. I was mad at her and I'd be damned if I would comfort her right now.

She spoke in that breathless, hiccuping voice that serious crying can give you. 'I'm sorry, oh, God, Anita, I'm sorry. I'm just so jealous.'

I raised my eyebrows at her. 'What are you talking about? Jealous of what?'

'The men,' she said in that shivering, uncertain voice. It was like she was someone else for a moment, or maybe this was just part of Ronnie that she didn't let people see. 'All the damned men. I'm about to give up everybody. Everybody but Louie, and he's great, but damn it I've had lovers. I hit triple digits.'

I wasn't sure that being able to number your lovers at over a hundred was a good thing, but it was something that Ronnie and I had agreed to disagree over a long time ago. I did not say, *Look who's the whore*, or other hurtful remarks I could have made. I let all the cheap shots I could have made go. She was the one crying.

'And now I'm giving it all up, all of it, for just one man.' She leaned her hands against the cabinet as if she needed the support.

'You said sex with Louie was great. I think you've used words like *fantastic* and *mind-blowing*.'

She nodded, her hair spilling around her face so that I couldn't see her eyes for a moment. 'It is, he is, but he's just one man. What if I get bored, or he gets bored with me? How can just one be enough? The last time we were both cheating a month after the wedding.' She looked up at that last remark, her gray eyes wide and frightened.

I made a small helpless gesture, and said, 'You're asking the wrong person, Ronnie. I'd planned on monogamy. It seemed like a good idea to me.'

'That's exactly what I mean.' She wiped at the tears on her face in harsh, angry motions, as if the touch of them made her even more upset. 'How is it that you, my girlfriend who had only three men in her entire life, ends up dating and fucking five men?'

I didn't know what to say to that, so I tried to concentrate on the hard facts. 'Six men,' I said.

She frowned at me, her eyes taking on that look that meant she was counting in her head. 'I only count five.'

'You're leaving someone out, Ronnie.'

'No –' and she started counting on her fingers – 'Jean-Claude, Asher, Damian, Nathaniel, and Micah. That's it.'

I shook my head, again. 'I had unprotected sex with one more man last month.' I could have said it differently, but maybe if we got back to my personal disaster, we could stop talking about Ronnie's penis envy. She needed more therapy than I knew how to give lately.

She frowned harder, then she got it. 'Oh, no, no,' she said.

I nodded. Happy to see from her expression that she got the full awfulness of it.

'You just had sex with him once, right?'

I shook my head no, over and over again. 'Not just once.'

She was looking at me so hard that I couldn't hold her gaze. Even with the tear tracks drying on her face, she was suddenly Ronnie again. Ronnie had a good hard stare. I couldn't meet it, and was left looking at the cabinets. 'How much more than "not just once"?' she asked.

I started to blush and couldn't stop it. Damn it.

'You're blushing – that's not a good sign,' she said.

I stared down at the countertop, using my long hair to hide my face.

Her voice was gentler when she said, 'How many times, Anita? How many times in the month you've been back together?'

'Seven,' I said, still not looking up. I hated admitting it, because the number alone said louder than any words just how much I enjoyed being in Richard's bed.

'Seven times in a month,' she said. 'Wow, that's . . .'

I looked up, and the look was enough.

'Sorry, sorry, just . . .' She looked as if she wasn't sure whether she was going to laugh, or be sad about it. She controlled herself, and finally sounded sad when she said, 'Oh, my God, Richard.'

I nodded again.

'Richard.' She whispered his name, and looked suitably horrified. It was worth a little horror.

Richard Zeeman and I had been off-again, on-again, for years. Mostly off. We'd been engaged briefly until I saw him eat someone. Richard was the leader – Ulfric – of the local werewolf pack. He was also a junior high science teacher, and an all-around Boy Scout. If Boy Scouts were six foot one, muscled, amazingly handsome, and had an amazing ability to be self-destructive. He hated being a monster, and he hated me for being more comfortable with the monsters than he was. He hated a lot of things, but we'd made up just enough to have fallen into bed in the last few weeks. But as my Grandma Blake told me, once was enough.

Of all the men in my life, the worst possible choice to be the father would be Richard, because he of all of them would try for the white picket fence and a normal life. Normal wasn't possible for me, or him, but I knew that and he didn't, not really, not yet. Even if I was pregnant, even if I kept being pregnant, I wasn't going to marry anyone. I wasn't going to change my living arrangements. My life worked the way it was, and Richard's idea of domestic bliss was not mine.

Ronnie gave an abrupt laugh, then swallowed it. I was glaring at her. 'Come on, Anita, I'm allowed to be impressed that you've managed to have sex with him seven times in the space of a month. I mean, you don't even live together, and you're having more sex than some of our married friends.'

I kept giving her the look that makes bad guys run for cover, but Ronnie was my friend, and it's harder to impress your friends with the scary look. They know you won't really hurt them. The fight was dying under the weight of friendship, and of my problem being more immediate than her years of issues unresolved.

Ronnie touched my arm. 'Oh, it wouldn't be Richard's. You're having sex with Nathaniel at least every other day.'

'Sometimes twice a day,' I said.

She smiled. 'Well, my, my . . .' Then waved her hand as if to keep from distracting herself. 'But the odds are that it's Nathaniel's, right?'

I smiled at her. 'You sound happy about that now.'

She shrugged. 'Well, a choice of evils, ya know.'

'Thanks a lot, Ronnie.'

'You know what I meant,' she said.

'No, I don't think I do.' I think I was ready to be angry about her thinking the men in my life were a choice of evils, but I didn't get a chance to be angry, because two of the men in my life were coming through the front door.

I heard them unlocking the door before it opened, and their voices came raised and a little breathless from the run. They'd been able to run faster, and farther, without me along. I was, after all, still human, and they were not.

Standing between the island and the cabinets we couldn't see the door, but only heard them laughing as they came toward the doorway to the kitchen.

'How can you do that?' Ronnie asked, voice soft.

'What?' I asked, frowning.

'You were smiling.'

I looked at her.

'You smiled just at the sound of their voices, even with everything . . .'

I stopped her with a hand on her arm. One way I knew I didn't want them to find out about the maybe-baby was by overhearing a conversation. Their hearing was a little too keen to risk it. And here they came, my two live-in sweeties.

Micah was in front, looking back over his shoulder, still laughing, talking. He was my height, short, slender, and muscular in that swimmer sort of way. He had to have his suits tailored because he needed an extra-small athletic cut. You didn't get that off the rack. He'd come to me tanned, and stayed that way from jogging outside, mostly shirtless, all summer and autumn. He'd added a T-shirt to the short-shorts today. His hair was that deep, rich brown that some people get after starting life as very blond. His dark hair was tied back in a low ponytail that couldn't hide how curly it was, almost as curly as mine. He'd taken off his sunglasses, so when I moved into his arms I could look up into his chartreuse eyes. Yellow-green leopard eyes in his delicate face. A very bad man had once forced him to stay in leopard form until, when he came back to human, he couldn't come all the way back.

We kissed and our arms just seemed to automatically glide around each other, to press our bodies as close together as we could with clothes on. He'd affected me this way almost from the moment we had seen each other. Lust at first sight. They say it doesn't last, but we were six months and counting.

I melted against his body and kissed him fiercely, deeply. Partly it was what I always wanted to do when I saw him. Partly I was scared, and touching and being touched made me feel better. Not long ago I'd have been more discreet in front of company, but my nerves just weren't good enough to pretend today.

He didn't get embarrassed, or tell me, 'Not in front of Ronnie,' the way Richard would have done. He kissed me back with the same drowning intensity. His hands holding me like he'd never let me go. We drew back, breathless and laughing.

'Was that for my benefit?' Ronnie asked, and her voice was not happy.

I turned around, still half in Micah's arms. I looked at her angry eyes and suddenly was ready to be angry back. 'Not everything is about you, Ronnie.'

'Are you telling me you kiss him like that every time he comes home?' The anger was back, and she used it. 'He's been gone, what, an hour? I've seen you greet him after a day's work, and it was never like that.'

'Like what?' I asked, voice sliding down. If she wanted to fight, we could fight.

'Like he was air and you couldn't breathe him in fast enough.'

Micah's voice was mild, placating, trying to talk us both down. 'Did we interrupt something?'

I turned to face Ronnie, squarely. 'I'm allowed to kiss my boyfriend the way I want to kiss him without getting your permission, Ronnie.'

'Don't try and tell me you weren't rubbing my face in it, just now, with the show.'

'Go get some therapy, Ronnie, because I am fucking tired of your issues raining all over me.'

'I confided in you,' she said, voice strangled with some emotion I didn't understand, 'and you put on a show like that in front of me. How could you?'

'Oh, that wasn't a show,' Nathaniel said from just inside the doorway, 'but if it's a show you want, we can do that, too.' He glided into the kitchen on the balls of his feet, showing both the grace of his dance training and that otherworldly grace of the wereleopard. He pulled his tank top off in one smooth gesture and let it fall to the floor. I actually backed up a step before I caught myself. I hadn't realized until that moment that he was angry with Ronnie. What little cutting remarks had she been making to him, that I hadn't heard? When he told me she didn't see him as real, he'd been trying to tell me more than I had heard. That I'd missed something big was there in his angry eyes.

He tore the tie from his ponytail and let his ankle-length auburn hair fall around his nearly naked body. The jogging short-shorts just didn't cover that much.

I had time to say, 'Nathaniel—' and he was in front of me. That otherworldly energy that all lycanthropes could give off shivered off his skin and along my body. He was five-six, just tall enough for me to have to look up to meet his eyes. His anger had turned them from lavender to the deeper color of lilacs, if flowers could burn with anger and force of personality. Nathaniel was in those eyes and with that one look he dared me, challenged me, to turn him down.

I didn't want to turn him down. I wanted to wrap his body and that skin-crawling energy around me like a coat. Lately almost any stress seemed to feed into sex. Scared? Sex would make me feel better. Angry? Sex would calm me. Sad? Sex would make me happy. Was I addicted to sex? Maybe. But Nathaniel wasn't offering actual sex. He just wanted as much attention as I'd given Micah. Seemed fair to me.

I closed the distance between us with my hands, my mouth, my body. The energy of his beast spilled around us like being plunged into a warm bath that had a mild electric charge. He'd been one of the least of my leopards until a metaphysical accident had taken him from *pomme de sang* to my animal to call. I was the first human servant to a vampire to gain the vampire ability to call an animal. All leopards were mine to call, but Nathaniel was my special pet. We'd both gained from the magical bonding, but he'd gained more.

He lifted me up, using just his hands on my thighs. Even through my jeans he made sure I knew he was happy to be pressed against my body. So happy that it forced a small sound from me.

Ronnie's voice came harsh, ugly, like she was choking on her anger. 'And when the baby comes, are you going to fuck in front of it, too?'

Nathaniel froze against me. Micah's voice came from behind us. 'Baby?'

Now you can buy any of these bestselling
books by **Laurell K. Hamilton** from your bookshop
or *direct from her publisher*.

FREE P&P AND UK DELIVERY
(Overseas and Ireland £3.50 per book)

| | |
|---|---|
| Guilty Pleasures | £7.99 |
| The Laughing Corpse | £7.99 |
| Circus of the Damned | £7.99 |
| The Lunatic Cafe | £7.99 |
| Bloody Bones | £7.99 |
| The Killing Dance | £7.99 |
| Burnt Offerings | £7.99 |
| Blue Moon | £7.99 |
| Obsidian Butterfly | £7.99 |
| Narcissus in Chains | £7.99 |
| Cerulean Sins | £7.99 |
| Incubus Dreams | £7.99 |
| Micah and Strange Candy | £7.99 |
| Danse Macabre | £7.99 |
| The Harlequin | £7.99 |
| Skin Trade | £7.99 |

TO ORDER SIMPLY CALL THIS NUMBER

**01235 400 414**

or visit our website: www.headline.co.uk
Prices and availability subject to change without notice.